DARING TO
DATE HER BOSS

BY
JOANNA NEIL

MILLS &
BOON

Published in Great Britain 2014
by Mills & Boon, an imprint of Harlequin (UK) Limited,
Eton House, 18-24 Paradise Road, Richmond, Surrey, TW9 1SR

© 2014 Joanna Neil

ISBN: 978-0-263-90785-8

Printed and bound in Spain
by Blackprint CPI, Barcelona

Dear Reader

Islands hold a special place in most people's hearts, I would imagine. The idea of love blossoming on a palm-fringed paradise is wonderfully romantic, and conjures up all kinds of possibilities.

But things may not always be what they seem. Living and working on an island comes with its own set of problems—as my heroine soon begins to find out.

I had a great time seeing how Saskia managed to contend with all her difficulties—Tyler being first and foremost among them. Falling for the boss was never going to be a good idea as far as she was concerned, and the fact that they were total opposites added a whole other dimension to her troubles.

I hope you, too, enjoy the journey as Tyler and Saskia work together to find a solution to their problems.

Love

Joanna

**These books are also available in eBook format
from www.millsandboon.co.uk**

CHAPTER ONE

'Drop it, Boomer. Right now. Drop it and give it back.'

Saskia turned over in bed and pulled the duvet more closely around her. What was going on? Why was there so much noise? Dimly, her sleep-befuddled brain made out eight-year-old Becky's voice, growing shrill with urgency. Saskia blinked, and drowsily stretched her limbs before opening her eyes a fraction. She peered groggily around the unfamiliar room.

Soft sunlight filtered through the chenille curtains, highlighting the glazed, Georgian-style wardrobe doors and the wide dressing table with its plush upholstered stool. It was a lovely room, but for a moment or two Saskia stared at it, perplexed. What was she was doing here? And what on earth was all the shouting about? She was used to peaceful mornings, to gradually waking to the low sound of the radio on her bedside table. There was no such luck today.

A loud wail shocked her into sitting upright. Groaning softly, she swung her legs out from under the cosy duvet and rested her bare feet on the carpeted floor. What time was it?

She reached for the short silk robe that was draped over a nearby chair. Pulling it on over her thigh-length nightshirt, it was all starting to come back to her. Her circumstances had changed pretty dramatically over the past few days. She was here to look after the children. A small wave of panic engulfed her. In that case, what was she doing in bed while they were up and about?

'You're a bad dog, Boomer. I don't like you any more. Go away.'

There was a sharp tap on the bedroom door and Saskia must have muttered acknowledgement because two seconds later the door was flung open and an irate Becky stood in front of her, angry tears staining her flushed cheeks.

'Boomer's chewed Milly's bottle and now it's ruined—look.' The child thrust the offending object towards her, and Saskia gazed blearily at what had once been a doll's feeding bottle. Becky was right. It was ruined, that was for sure.

Saskia put a comforting arm around her niece's shoulders and laid her head against the child's golden curls. 'I'm sure we'll manage to get another one for you next time we go to the shops. You have to keep these things out of Boomer's way, you know. He might be two years old, but he still acts like a pup a lot of the time.'

'Well, he's a bad dog.'

'Yes.' Straightening, she glanced at the watch on her bedside table. It was ten o'clock already? Another quiver of alarm washed through her until she remembered that she didn't have a job to go to and, anyway, it was Saturday. So…no worries there, were there? Hah. As if.

The doorbell rang a couple of minutes later as she wandered into the living room to check that all was well with Becky's brother and sister. Boomer, the family's exuberant springer spaniel, set up a frantic barking in response to the door chimes, and Saskia frowned. Her head was beginning to ache.

Who could that be? She really wasn't in the mood for visitors. Besides, the place was a mess, with packing crates everywhere and half-opened boxes taking up every available surface.

Six-year-old Charlie was trailing his cars over the play mat in a corner of the room and acknowledged her with an absent 'Hiya' as she greeted him with a smile.

Seeing her, Boomer stopped barking and raced up to her, wagging his tail and almost knocking her over in his excitement. She patted his silky, chocolate-coloured fur as she glanced around. Caitlin was nowhere to be seen. Most likely she was still tucked up in bed, like teenagers everywhere. The thought filled her with envy.

'Perhaps you should come in,' she heard Becky saying cautiously. 'My mummy isn't here, but you can talk to my auntie if you like.'

Saskia immediately tensed and hurried out of the room and into the hallway, ready to avert disaster. She wasn't dressed properly—how could she possibly meet up with anyone while she was in this state?

But she was already too late…a man carrying a large package, a box of some sort, was following Becky down the hallway towards the living room.

For a second or two, as she studied him, Saskia's breath caught in her throat. He was in his mid-thirties, she guessed, and he was absolutely stunning…long, lean and incredibly fit looking, dressed in smart casuals, a dark, open-neck shirt and cream-coloured trousers. She closed her eyes briefly to savour the moment. Wow! So this was what the Isles of Scilly had to offer.

His jet-black hair was cut in a short, crisp style that

perfectly suited his angular features. As to his eyes—
well, his stunning blue gaze was mesmerising, except
that right now it was directed at her, bringing warm colour flooding to her cheeks as she realised she'd been
caught staring at him.

But he, too, seemed to have been knocked off balance by their unexpected meeting. She heard the sharp
intake of his breath and saw his eyes widen as his glance
moved over her in turn, taking in every softly feminine curve. He was suddenly rooted to the spot, his
gaze sweeping like a lick of flame over the smooth expanse of legs that were lightly bronzed from a summer
of sunshine.

A sudden arc of electric tension sparked between
them, an intense, sensual intimacy that brought with it
a wave of heat that raced through her body. She couldn't
move, didn't know how to go on.

Then the stranger made a rough-edged, broken kind
of sound, as though he meant to say something but instead the words seemed to choke in his throat.

Coming to her senses, Saskia tugged awkwardly at
the hem of her robe, trying to cover a bit more thigh, an
action that only resulted in drawing the edges of the gar-
ment further apart. Taking a deep breath, she wrapped
the silk more firmly around herself and tied the belt in
what she hoped was a secure knot.

'I—uh…' He hesitated, drawing his gaze back to
her face. Like her, he seemed to be struggling to get
himself back together. 'I um…I gather you're not Mrs
Reynolds…'

'Er, no, I'm her sister-in-law…Saskia.'

'Ah, I see.' He nodded acknowledgment, then pulled
in a deep breath and straightened his shoulders. 'I'm

Tyler, Tyler Beckett. I have a parcel for Mrs Reynolds.' He indicated the large box he was carrying, marked '*Glass, Handle with Care*'. 'I've been hanging onto it for a couple of days, ever since the courier dropped it off next door.'

'Oh…thanks.' Her breathing had settled down at last to a heavy thud and now her brow furrowed. 'My brother said something about Megan ordering a new light fitting…I guess this must be it. He said she'd checked with the landlord to make sure it would be okay to change things.'

'Yes, I told her I'm okay with it, as long as she runs things by me first.'

He was the landlord? That came as a bit of a surprise. She went to take the box from him but he hesitated, saying, 'Actually, this is quite heavy. Maybe it would be better if I put it down for you, somewhere safe?'

'Oh…yes, of course.' She studied him surreptitiously. This could be difficult. If he owned the place, how was he going to react to seeing what had happened to his once pristine property now that three children and a dog had cut a swathe through it? There was already a scuff mark on the wall where Charlie had run amok.

He was watching her expectantly and she galvanised herself into action. Fighting back a nervous quiver of apprehension, she showed him into the L-shaped living room, padding barefoot across the smooth oak floorboards to the dining area. 'You could put it down here, if you like.'

To her shame, there were four dirty soup bowls on the table, the remnants of last night's hastily prepared supper. She'd been too tired to clear away after the meal and, besides, she'd figured it was more important to try to sort out the childcare arrangements, or at least find out what her options were. She still had to see if there was anyone around who would be prepared to walk the dog—if she managed to find a job it would be unfair to leave Boomer cooped up at home all day.

She quickly moved the crockery out of the way, along with a jumble of household ornaments, and waved a hand towards the clear space on the large, solid wood table.

Her brother had rented the house partly furnished and she was impressed—from what she'd seen so far, his new landlord certainly had an eye for quality.

At the moment, though, he was looking around, a bewildered expression on his face as he took in the chaos. Charlie had spread his toys generously around the room—his was the first box that had been opened as he'd been desperate to be reunited with his belongings, and Saskia had been anxious to keep him occupied. Next in line had been Boomer's collection of chew toys—a couple of facsimile bones, a rubber ring, a pull toy made of knotted strings and his favourite, a plastic, squashy ball. They, too, were strewn across the floor.

Tyler frowned, absorbing everything in that one glance, and Saskia winced. She wondered if he was familiar with the mayhem of family life. The slight bracing of his shoulders seemed a dead giveaway.

Still, he didn't comment. 'I was busy at work the last couple of days,' he said, as he set down the parcel, 'and I could see you were dealing with the removal van until late in the evening yesterday, so I didn't like to disturb you.'

'That was thoughtful of you,' she murmured, leaning forward to help with the positioning of the parcel and faltering a little when she realised he was running his gaze over her once more. Heat flickered in his smoke-dark eyes as he took in the cloud of coppery curls that framed her oval face and brushed against the creamy slope of her shoulders.

Belatedly, she realised that her shoulder was indeed bare, and she quickly tugged her robe back in place. The wide neckline of her nightshirt had somehow managed to slide partway down over her arms.

'I…um…I should apologise for being dressed like this…only you caught me unawares. I overslept. It's not something I do regularly,' she added hastily, 'it's just that…uh…' It was just that she'd been up half the night, using her laptop to sort out the route to school and trying to find suitable day care for the children after school and a whole host of other things he didn't need to know about. Doing it when the children were tucked up in bed had seemed like the best opportunity. 'We did a lot of travelling on Thursday to get here. Then there were two and a half hours on the ferry and the journey from where we docked to here. And we don't seem to have stopped since. I haven't caught up with myself yet.'

'It's all right. You don't have to explain yourself.' His expression was wry, and she could guess what he was thinking. She'd already burned her boats on that one.

She started to move away from the table and his glance slid down to her bare feet, lingering there as though he'd only just noticed her toenails were painted a shimmering, luscious pink. He seemed intrigued, curious even, and he certainly didn't seem to be in any hurry to leave, leading her to wonder uncomfortably if she ought to offer him coffee. It would be the neighbourly thing to do, wouldn't it?

'Um…can I offer you—?' She broke off as Boomer, abandoning his knotted pull toy, bounded up to her once more and joyfully nudged her hip, tipping her off balance.

Reacting swiftly, Tyler put out his arms to steady her. 'You were saying…?'

'Oh, yes…um…' It was totally distracting, having him stand so close to her, and for some reason it took a real effort to unscramble her brain. His hands lightly circled her arms, sending small eddies of warmth throughout her body. While he was holding her like this she simply couldn't think straight.

'Coffee,' she said at last. 'I was going to offer you coffee.'

'Thanks, I'd like that.' He released her and she let out a long, silent breath of relief. 'You can perhaps fill me in on one or two things,' he added, 'like what's happening with your brother and his wife.'

She nodded, but a quiver of anguish rippled through her. That wasn't going to be easy to recount, was it, with Sam and Megan both in hospital and neither of them likely to recover very soon? As their landlord, she supposed he had a right to know, but it was hard for her to talk about it. Coming out of the blue on a busy road, the accident had shocked all of them.

Boomer followed them into the kitchen, still nudging her gently, as though anxious that she should head in the right direction, and it dawned on her that he must be eager for his breakfast. 'Okay, Boomer,' she told him. 'I'll feed you. Just give me a minute.'

Caitlin had finally put in an appearance and was sitting at the round table in one corner of the room, her mid-brown hair falling across her cheek like a curtain as she hunched over her mobile phone. 'He's used to being fed at eight o'clock,' the teenager remarked, a faint note of censure in her voice as Saskia emptied kibble into Boomer's food bowl. The girl tossed her hair out of the way with a shake of her head. 'You were late with his meals yesterday as well, and the day before that.'

'Well, we've had a lot going on over the last few days,' Saskia defended herself, uneasily conscious of Tyler showing an interest in the conversation. 'I'll be much more organised once I get the hang of things.'

'Yeah, right. It'll probably be better if I take over feeding him.' Caitlin sighed and pushed a half-eaten bowl of dry cereal towards Saskia. 'I can't eat that. Mum always buys the proper branded version.' She pressed her lips into a flat, disgruntled line. 'And Charlie's finished off all the milk again.'

'Oh, dear.' Saskia frowned. As well as being upset about what had happened to her parents, Caitlin, at fourteen, was going through a definite grumpy phase.

Tyler intervened. 'Don't worry about coffee. It doesn't matter.'

She shook her head. 'I have some sachets somewhere. We even have a choice—latte or cappuccino. I think you'll like them.' Her gaze travelled around the room, searching for the box where they were packed, and after a moment or two she realised that he was looking with her.

'There are quite a few boxes to choose from, aren't there?' His gaze settled on a collection of crockery and cookery books that were spread out over the worktop and slowly his eyes half closed as he though he was trying to shut out this alien world he'd stumbled into.

'No, it's okay, they're in the cupboard,' Saskia said

in triumph. 'I remember I put them where they would be near to the kettle. Yay!' She hurried forward to retrieve them at the same time that Boomer came and dropped his ball in front of her and then gazed at her in panting anticipation.

'Ow, ow, ow...' She yelped in pain as she stepped on one of his plastic chew toys and began to hop around the tiled floor, clutching her foot.

'What's wrong?' Caitlin asked, getting up from her seat to come and look. Then, 'Oh...that's blood,' she said in an anxious voice. 'You're bleeding, Sass.' She inspected the hard nylon, bone-shaped toy. 'It's really rough around the edges where he's been having a go at it. Are you going to be all right?'

Saskia pulled in a deep breath. 'Of course I am.' She stopped hopping and gingerly put her foot to the floor. 'I'll be fine. Don't worry.' The last thing she needed was for the children to be concerned about her. They had enough on their plates right now. Instead, she flicked the switch on the kettle and tried to ignore the stinging in her foot, busying herself adding coffee powder to a couple of mugs.

'I don't suppose you have a first-aid kit to hand, do you?' Tyler asked, and Saskia thought about it then shook her head.

'I recall seeing it somewhere.' She frowned.

'I'll go and fetch mine.'

'There's no need, really. I'll be fine.'

He gave her an assessing look. 'You won't be if you go on the way you're doing now. Sit down and stop spreading blood over the floor. You don't want to get an infection, do you?'

'N-no, of course not.'

'Good. Then sit down and wait there until I get back.'

After he'd gone, Caitlin finished making the coffees and then studied the chew toy once more. 'I'm going to put this in the bin,' she said. 'Maybe Boomer should go out in the garden and get some fresh air. He has way too much energy.'

'That's a good idea. Perhaps Charlie would like to play with him out there? Anyway, he and Becky need to go and feed their rabbit.'

'Yeah, I'll tell them as soon as I've cleaned up the floor.'

Saskia smiled at her. 'Thanks, Caitlin. You're a treasure.'

Tyler was back within a couple of minutes. Noticing that Boomer was nowhere to be seen, he glanced out of the kitchen window and saw that the dog was racing around outside, having a whale of a time with the two younger children.

Hearing their laughter, Saskia guessed Becky must have forgiven Boomer for his earlier misdemeanour.

Tyler placed a fresh carton of milk in the fridge and then set out a fully equipped medical pack on the kitchen table.

'I guess that's the flower border done for,' he murmured on a rueful note, glancing out of the window once more as he went over to the sink and poured warm water into a bowl.

'I'm really sorry about all this,' Saskia said. She waved a hand towards his coffee mug. 'Please, help yourself.' Perhaps a reviving drink would help him to feel better.

'Thanks.' He went on setting out his equipment.

Saskia bit her lip. 'Maybe I could put some sort of

decorative fencing up to keep him away from the plants.'
She frowned. 'You've caught us at a bad time, but we
planned on getting to grips with everything today—
well, over the weekend, at least. Caitlin's just gone to
start unpacking clothes and to put things right upstairs.'

He nodded, drawing up a chair in front of her and
laying a towel over the seat. 'Rest your leg on there. I'm
going to bathe your foot first to make sure there are no
bits of debris in the wound.'

'Okay…thanks.' She watched him as he hunkered
down and began to work. He was very thorough, clean-
ing her foot with meticulous care and then gently dry-
ing it.

'There are several small puncture wounds,' he commented. 'I'll press some gauze against it for a while
until the bleeding stops.'

'You look as though you've done this sort of thing
before,' she murmured, looking over his medical pack
with interest.

'I have, although I usually have to deal with rather
more serious injuries than this,' he answered soberly.
'I'm a doctor. I work at the hospital on the island, in
the emergency department, and I'm on the rota as a
first attender where the paramedics need a doctor to
go along and help out.'

'Ah, that explains it,' she said, speaking half to herself.

'I beg your pardon?' He glanced at her, absently resting his hand lightly on her leg before pausing to check
under the gauze to see if the bleeding had stopped.

She cleared her throat. His touch was doing very
strange things to her nervous system. Things she'd
thought she'd long forgotten. 'It's just that you have

that kind of air about you,' she explained, 'as though you're very capable, well organised, and know exactly what has to be done. I expect seeing the state we're in here has been a bit of a shock for you.'

He didn't answer, but his mouth moved in a faint curve. He applied a topical antiseptic and then bound up her foot, securing the neat bandage with tape.

'That should be a bit more comfortable for you,' he said. Finally, he stood up, reaching for his coffee and taking a long swallow. He paused for a moment, staring at his cup in puzzlement, and she guessed he was faintly surprised to discover that he quite liked the taste. 'So how do you fit into the picture here?' he asked. 'Did you decide to move over here with your brother and his family, or were you already living on the island?'

'Uh, I came over here when my brother and his wife were…delayed.' She still didn't want to talk about what had happened and hoped he wouldn't persist. 'I have to get the children into school for the new term, and of course the removal had been planned and booked a few weeks ahead. It was important that things went smoothly.'

He nodded. 'What do you think of our island? Have you been here before?'

She shook her head, making the silky, copper curls quiver and dance. 'I saw it for the first time on Thursday. It's so beautiful, it took my breath away—the lovely beaches and the clear blue water, the palm trees… It's like a subtropical paradise.'

His mouth curved. 'Yes, it is.' He stood up and started to clear away his equipment just as the kitchen door burst open and Charlie came rushing in.

'Boomer's been sick all over the flowers,' he an-

nounced. 'It's yucky. He's brought up all of his breakfast and there's lots of grass in it, too.'

Saskia groaned. 'Did you let him out into the garden
first thing this morning?'

'Becky did.'

She sighed. 'That must have been when he did it.
We'll have to stop him eating grass somehow.' She
looked at Charlie. 'Okay, I'll come and hose it down in
a bit. Try to stop him from running around, will you,
but keep him out there for a bit longer if you can until
his stomach settles down?'

'Okay.' Charlie went outside once more and Tyler
sent her a brief, sympathetic glance.

'I'd better leave you to get on. It looks as though you
have your hands full.'

She nodded, giving him a regretful look. 'Like I said,
it should all be sorted out over the weekend.'

She stood up, testing her foot against the hard floor.
'That feels good,' she said. 'It must be all the padding
you put in there. Thank you so much for helping me out.
And thanks for the milk—I appreciate it. You'll have
earned yourself a thousand brownie points with Caitlin.'

He smiled. 'You're welcome.' He left by the kitchen
door, and she heard him saying goodbye to the children
as he left. As she glanced out of the window, she saw
him briefly pat Boomer on the head.

She looked disconsolately at the mess around her.
There couldn't have been a worse time for the landlord
to pay them a visit, but that wasn't the worst of it, was
it? They shared the same profession. She was a doctor,
too. How would it be if he heard about her application
for a job at the hospital where he worked? She couldn't
see that going down too well.

For all that he'd been pleasant to her and he had helped her out, she suspected that he didn't think very much of her lackadaisical ways. There was no point suggesting that she would put everything right…she had a strong feeling that, left to him, he would have organised things properly from the start, and everyone, probably even the dog, would have been given a job to do to help out.

Still, she couldn't help wishing things had been different. After all, he was the kind of man women dreamed of, and she was by no means immune…even though she'd sworn off men. He'd made her body tingle just by being near… And when he'd rested his hand on her bare leg…phew.

She sighed. Maybe it was just as well she'd made a bad impression on him. It would nip things in the bud from the outset…because she really ought to have learned her lesson by now. After all, it was only when you got to know men that things started to go wrong.

CHAPTER TWO

'CHARLIE, WILL YOU hurry up, please? We need to get a move on or we'll be late.'

Saskia looked around the kitchen, mentally ticking off a list in her head. 'Becky, don't forget your PE kit—you need to take that with you as well as your backpack.'

'Yeah, okay.'

'Do you have everything you need, Caitlin?' She peered into the hallway to look at the teenager, who was frowning at her hair in the mirror and trying to brush loose strands into place, something she'd been doing for the last several minutes. 'What about your geometry set—did you remember to put it in your bag? Perhaps I should have a quick look, just to make sure.'

Caitlin whipped the backpack away from her before Saskia had a chance to investigate. 'I can sort my own things out,' she said, turning away and pressing a hand against her forehead as though her head was aching. 'I don't need anyone checking up on me.'

Saskia winced. So far, nothing was going to plan. Her vision of a smooth, hassle-free morning getting ready for this first day of the school term was dissolving with every minute that passed. Caitlin had been tetchy ever since she'd dragged herself out of bed, and when you added in Becky's insistence on taking time to go outside to pet her lop-eared rabbit, and Charlie's complete oblivion to everything going on around him, getting them all organised and ready was rapidly turning into a stressful situation.

'Charlie, can you switch off that computer game? We're leaving right now.'

It must be great for Tyler next door to simply ease himself into his sleek, shining BMW and head off for the hospital without a care in the world. She'd seen him leave his house about half an hour ago, perfectly groomed, dressed in an immaculate dark suit, his hair crisply styled. She'd caught the glint of a cufflink as he'd reached to open the car door. His whole life was probably streamlined.

She shepherded everyone towards the front door, but as they were about to leave Becky said urgently, 'Saskia—wait. I think Boomer's being sick in the kitchen. I can hear him.' The little girl went back in there to take a closer look. 'Yeuw! It's got lots of bits of tissue in it.'

Saskia sighed. Tyler certainly never had to deal with anything like this, did he? She looked at Charlie. 'Have you been feeding Boomer paper towels again?'

He shook his head vigorously, but she noticed he couldn't quite meet her eyes.

'It's bad for him,' she said firmly. 'And it's not helping us either, because now I have to stop and clean up after him when we're already pushed for time. Perhaps you'd better come and give me a hand. Go and let him outside in case he needs to be sick some more.'

A few minutes later she settled Boomer down in his

bed in the kitchen and they finally started out on the walk to school. It was a good thing the primary and secondary schools were on the same site, Saskia reflected. At least it made things a little easier.

Of all the mornings to be delayed, this was the worst, because as soon as she had dropped off the children she was supposed to go for her interview at the hospital. She really needed that job, and she was more than a little anxious about it. In fact, she was beginning to feel quite apprehensive. There was money coming in from her brother's bank account to pay the rent, but now she had three extra mouths to feed and the bills were mounting up. Her savings would only take her so far.

Arriving at the school a few minutes later, she gave Becky and Charlie a hug and told a still fractious Caitlin she hoped she'd have a good day. She would have hugged her, too, but the teenager made it clear she didn't want any demonstration of affection, especially not in front of the other students.

She was about to leave when someone said, 'Ah, Miss Reynolds—or should I call you Dr Reynolds? I saw you helping Charlie to find his peg in the cloakroom a little while ago and realised you must be the newcomers to our school.'

Saskia glanced at the woman who had approached her. She was tall, with medium-length dark hair cut in a stylish bob, and there was an undeniable look of authority about her. 'Hello. Yes, that's right. I'm Dr Reynolds.'

The woman smiled. 'I'm Elizabeth Hunter, the headmistress—I'm so glad I managed to meet up with you.' She was keen to talk to Saskia about the children's parents and how their accident might have affected the youngsters. 'We want to be as supportive as possible,' she said.

'Thank you. I appreciate that. It has been a difficult time for them, but I'm hoping that if we let the children talk about their worries it might help.' Saskia spoke to the headmistress for a few minutes, wanting to ease the children's transition into their new school as best she could but conscious all the while that the clock was ticking and she needed to get away to the hospital.

At last, though, she was free to rush away to keep her appointment. Glancing at her watch, she realised with growing alarm that there was no way she was going to make it to the interview on time.

Perhaps it had been a mistake to walk to school. It had taken a lot longer than she'd anticipated, with Charlie dawdling and Becky stopping to search for wild flowers in the hedgerows, but this was a small island and she'd hoped she might get away without buying a car. Walking, she'd reasoned, would at least give them the opportunity to enjoy the green hills and valleys along the way and let them take in the view of the bay and the bustling harbour in the distance. Now, though, she still had a further ten minutes' walk ahead of her.

The hospital, she discovered, was relatively small, a pleasing, white-painted building, with a deep, low-slung roof. Alongside it was a health centre and a pharmacy. She hurried through the automated glass doors at the entrance.

The receptionist was talking to a young woman, a slender girl with chestnut hair arranged into an attractive braid at the back of her head. She was a doctor, Saskia guessed, judging by the stethoscope draped around her neck.

'Hello. Can I help you?' The receptionist broke off their conversation so that she could attend to the new arrival.

'Oh, hello. Yes, thanks,' Saskia said, a little out of breath from her exertions. 'I'm Dr Reynolds. I'm here to see Dr Gregson.'

'Oh, yes,' the woman answered with a smile, ticking her name off a list on her desk, 'you're the nine-fifteen appointment. They're waiting for you. If you'd like to come with me, I'll take you along to the office.'

The woman doctor glanced down at her watch and made a face. Noting her reaction, Saskia almost did the same. She could guess what she was thinking. She wasn't making a very good start.

'Just tell Dr Beckett that I'd appreciate his involvement in the new cardiovascular clinic, would you?' the doctor murmured. 'Perhaps he might be able to spare me a few minutes later today?'

'I'm sure he'll make the time,' the receptionist answered.

She walked with Saskia along the corridor. 'Here we are,' she said, knocking lightly on a door marked in bold, black lettering 'Dr James Gregson'.

A gravelly voice responded, 'Come,' and Saskia pulled in a deep breath before going into the room. She took in her surroundings in one vague sweep.

A large, mahogany desk dominated the room, and behind it sat a well-dressed, distinguished-looking man who studied her with interest over rimless reading glasses that sat low down on his nose. There were two other, younger, men on either side of him, some small distance away, seated at an angle to the table.

One of them had his head down, immersed in studying papers in a manila file, and for a dreadful moment, as she stared at the top of his dark head, Saskia felt a wash of stomach-lurching familiarity run through her. Her heart began to thump, increasing in tempo as though she'd been running. Could this really be her new neighbour?

'Dr Reynolds, it's good to see you. Please, come in and take a seat.' Dr Gregson stood up and waved her to a leather chair in front of the desk. He was a man of medium build, with square-cut features and dark hair, greying a little at the temples. Above the glasses his brown eyes were keen, missing nothing.

'Let me introduce you to my colleagues,' he said. 'This is Dr Matheson—Noah Matheson. He's our man in charge of the minor injuries unit.'

Dr Matheson stood up to shake hands with her. He was young, handsome, in his early thirties, tall, lithe, and it was obvious right away that he was most definitely taken with Saskia. Interest sparked in his hazel eyes as he drank in the cloud of her Titian hair and his gaze skimmed her slender, curvaceous figure. She was wearing a cream-coloured suit with a pencil-line skirt and a jacket that nipped in at the waist. It was a feminine outfit yet at the same time businesslike, and it gave her a fair amount of confidence to know that she looked her best.

'It's a pleasure to meet you,' Noah said, holding onto her hand for a second or two longer than was strictly necessary.

'And this is Dr Beckett—Tyler Beckett. He's in charge of Accident and Emergency.'

Her spirits plummeted, her worst fears confirmed.

Tyler stood up and clasped her hand firmly in his.

His glance moved over her, clearly appreciative. His
smile was warm, welcoming, and she relaxed a little. Maybe this wasn't going to be so bad after all. He
looked terrific, lean and flat-stomached, every bit as
good as the first day she'd seen him. The jacket of his
suit was open, revealing a deep blue shirt teamed with
a silver-grey tie. His cufflinks were of the same silver-
grey pattern.

'Dr Reynolds and I have already met,' he said, ad-
dressing his colleagues. 'It turns out that she's a neighbour of mine.' He looked into her green eyes, adding in
a low voice, 'I didn't know the name of our applicant
until this morning, and even then I wasn't sure it would
turn out to be you.' His well-shaped mouth made a faint
curve. 'Perhaps I should have guessed as time went on.
It sort of fitted somehow.' He didn't look at his watch,
but she caught his drift all the same.

He released her and she sat down carefully. She
cleared her throat. 'I must apologise for being so late,'
she said, looking from one to another. How much should
she tell them? 'I had a few unavoidable domestic issues
to contend with this morning—and then the dog was
sick just as I was leaving the house. Um…on top of that,
I didn't realise quite how long it would take me to walk
to the hospital.' She winced inwardly. She was babbling,
wasn't she, saying too much? They didn't need to know
all that. 'It was my mistake, but I'll be certain to make
better arrangements from now on.'

'I'm sure you will.' Dr Gregson picked up a folder
and leafed through it, saying after a while, 'Would you
like to tell us a bit about your last post? You worked at
a hospital in Cornwall, I believe?'

'That's right.' She was on much safer ground with

this. 'I started off there as a senior house officer in the A and E department. I had to deal with all kinds of emergencies, both traumatic and general. A good percentage of my patients were youngsters.'

'That's valuable experience. Good…good…' Dr Gregson riffled through his papers. 'Your references are all in order from what I can see, and your qualifications are impeccable. You've specialised in emergency medicine and paediatrics, as well as spending some time in general practice—that's excellent, exactly what we're looking for.' He glanced at her. 'It's a little unusual, though, to mix hospital work with general practice, isn't it?'

She faltered briefly, caught on the back foot. 'Ah… that's true, of course…but…initially I wasn't sure which specialty appealed to me the most.' She squirmed a little. Tyler Beckett would never be unsure of himself, would he? 'I enjoyed working in a GP's surgery for a year, but after attending several emergency cases during that time I realised that's what I wanted to do more than anything.'

Dr Gregson nodded. 'I see.' He turned to his colleagues. 'Do you have any questions you'd like to put to Dr Reynolds?'

Tyler nodded. 'I do have one query,' he said, his tone sober. 'Ah…about these references…' He was sifting through his copy of the paperwork, and she glanced at him, sitting stiffly upright, suddenly on alert.

'Is there a problem?'

'Not a problem as such… I'm just a little concerned about one aspect of your work that hasn't been mentioned here…'

She frowned. 'I can't think of anything I might have left out.'

He gave her a direct look. 'No, except—there was an occasion when you lost a patient, I believe. Would you like to tell us about that incident…about what happened?'

Saskia sucked in a sharp breath. 'But how did you…? I thought—' She broke off, uncertain where this line of questioning was coming from.

Noah frowned, sending Tyler a questioning, disbelieving look, as though he couldn't fathom why his colleague would want to upturn the apple cart this way.

'It's just something your previous consultant mentioned.' Tyler used a soothing voice, as though he wanted to put her at ease. 'I didn't fully understand the implications and I thought you might be able to clear it up for us.'

'M-my consultant?' She gazed at him in consternation, her green eyes troubled.

'Yes. It just happened that I rang the hospital in Truro this morning,' explained, 'to enquire about a patient of mine who was recently admitted, and I was put on to Michael Drew. He was your consultant, wasn't he?'

Michael. The breath left her body in a soft gasp and her stomach began to churn. She might have known this would come up to bite her. She'd made a mistake, getting involved with Michael. In the end he'd been more than just her consultant, and that's when things had started to go downhill, hadn't they?

It had been fine at first. They'd dated for a time, and she'd enjoyed his company, but eventually, when she'd realised he was becoming too controlling, she'd called a halt to things between them. Michael hadn't taken it well, and eventually the situation between them had deteriorated to a point where life at work had become intolerable. That was partly why she'd made up her mind it was time to look around for another job.

And now this… It looked as though Michael had thrown a spanner into the works at the worst possible time. She hadn't been able to avoid giving his name for a reference, and he'd assured her that she had nothing to worry about. But now—what could he have said to Tyler? Clearly their break-up still rankled with him, and although she'd hoped he would be adult about things, she really wouldn't put it past him to try to make life difficult for her.

Tyler watched the variety of expressions flit across her face. He said quietly, 'When I realised who he was, that you and he had worked together, we got to chatting, and that's when he mentioned your patient. He only brought it up as a humorous anecdote.'

Her mouth made a wry twist at that and he paused momentarily. 'He said you'd lost her and there was a big hue and cry until she was found again. But by then she needed treatment for another condition.'

He rested his hands on top of the file, lacing his fingers together. 'It might have seemed slightly amusing afterwards, when the worry was over, but I'm sure you can see why this has to be cleared up, can't you? We need to be reassured that our patients are going to be in the best possible hands.'

'Yes, of course, I understand perfectly.' Saskia moistened her lips, unhappily aware that Noah and Dr Gregson had both straightened and were paying her close attention. 'The truth is I didn't find anything at all humorous about the situation at any time, when it was going on or afterwards. And I didn't lose her—not exactly.'

'So, what happened?'

'She was a woman in her sixties suffering from what appeared to be dementia. A passer-by had brought her into the hospital because she'd had a fall and hurt her arm.'

She was silent for a moment, remembering the hectic activity in the emergency unit that day. 'We were very busy in A and E that morning, and we were short-staffed. Some of the nurses were off sick with a bug that was going around. I didn't have anyone to assist me, but I was keen to do further tests on my patient—alongside my concerns over her arm I wasn't absolutely convinced she had dementia. Anyway, I asked her to stay in the treatment cubicle while I went to find a porter to take the blood samples over to Pathology. But when I came back to see her a couple of minutes later, she'd gone walkabout.'

'That was tough luck,' Noah sympathised.

She nodded. 'It was worrying. We couldn't find her anywhere nearby. Then it occurred to me that she might have wandered outside into the hospital grounds so I followed the stairs to the exit. I found her sitting on the bottom step, nursing a swollen ankle. Apparently she'd missed her footing.'

Tyler's mouth made a wry shape. 'It just wasn't her day, was it?'

'No, unfortunately, it wasn't.'

'So, what was the final diagnosis?' he asked. His expression was thoughtful, his blue gaze skimming her features as though he was trying to weigh her up.

'She had a thyroid problem—her body was producing too little of the hormone, causing symptoms that mimicked dementia. And to add to her troubles she had a cracked bone in her forearm from the earlier fall, along with a sprained ankle from taking the stairs.'

Dr Gregson gave her a reassuring smile. 'Well, I think you've cleared that up for us nicely, Dr Reynolds. Thank you for that.' He looked at her over his glasses. 'And it's good to know that you weren't prepared to accept things at face value.'

She inclined her head briefly and tried to breathe slowly and steadily. That had been a deeply uncomfortable few moments. Tyler was clearly a stickler for getting things right, but she might have hoped he'd be less thorough in following up every detail arising from her application. Did he have to dot every i and cross every t? Michael could very easily have ruined things for her.

'You'll certainly need to be on the ball in this job,' Dr Gregson remarked. 'It isn't quite the same as being on the mainland where you have all manner of resources to hand. Those patients who are too ill to be managed in our small hospital have to be flown over to Cornwall for treatment.'

'I'm sure I'll be able to handle whatever's asked of me, Dr Gregson. I've had to cope with a huge change of circumstances recently but I think I'm dealing with it.'

Noah was clearly interested in this. 'Do you want to tell us more about that?'

She closed her eyes fleetingly, wishing she could take back the words and steeling herself against the pain. 'My brother and his wife were involved in a nasty road accident.' She took a deep breath. 'They're both in hospital in Truro at the moment—and it's beginning to look as though they'll be there for some time.'

Tyler frowned, leaning forward in his seat. 'You didn't mention this to me before, at the house.'

'No—perhaps I should have, but it was painful for me to talk about it. I was still getting over the shock. I still am.' She hesitated, then went on, 'They were preparing to move over here for Sam's job—he works for the wildlife trust and they wanted him as part of their team in the Isles of Scilly. Sam was bringing his family over that day so that they could see the house—they were going to rent before they decided where to make a permanent home. They wanted to spend some time looking around the island, but before they could get here they were in collision with a lorry that took a bend too wide. Luckily, the children escaped relatively unhurt, though they were traumatised, of course.'

'I'm sorry.' Tyler was genuinely concerned. 'That must have been devastating for you. And I suppose you've taken over caring for the children in the meantime?'

'That's right. That's why I came over here, and it's the reason I'm looking for work.'

'Is there no one else who can care for them?' Noah was full of compassion and understanding, although at the same time it seemed he sensed there was an opportunity to be explored here. 'Is there no one to support you—you've no ties?'

Tyler sent him a sharp look and Noah checked himself, drawing back.

Saskia shook her head. 'Not right now…at least, not close by.' She guessed Noah was never one to let the grass grow under his feet. With his looks and easygoing manner he'd probably left behind a string of female conquests who'd fallen for his charms.

'I admire your sense of loyalty,' Tyler said, frowning as he glanced through the paperwork once more, 'and I can see why finding work here must be important to you…but hadn't you handed in your notice before your brother's accident?'

Saskia's shoulders lifted awkwardly. Didn't he ever miss anything? 'I'd already decided I wanted a change.'

'Wasn't that a little irresponsible—to leave your job on a whim?'

She flattened her lips briefly. She wasn't about to go into detail about her failed relationship. 'Perhaps it was,' she conceded, 'but the way I saw it there's pretty much always a need for emergency doctors in the UK.'

He nodded. 'On the mainland, maybe. I think you'll find there's not quite the same demand out here, though.'

'Yes, I'm starting to realise that.' Her heart sank. This wasn't going at all the way she'd hoped. From the doubts he was expressing it looked very much as though he didn't want her for this job, and she could hardly blame him.

For someone as thorough and organised as Tyler Beckett it would go against the grain to take on a young woman who appeared to work on impulse and followed wherever her heart led.

She didn't know how many people they had interviewed for this post, but she guessed she wasn't the only candidate. There had been at least three names on the receptionist's tick sheet.

'I did have another job in mind in Cornwall at the time,' she ventured, 'and I was about to be interviewed for it, but all my plans had to change after the accident.'

Dr Gregson decided it was time to intervene. 'With regard to the post you're applying for here, you should understand that our work isn't just centred on the hospital. We often travel to the islands to visit patients in emergency situations. In those circumstances, we use the ambulance boat to reach them.'

'Oh, I see.' She swallowed carefully. She'd said she'd be able to cope with the demands of the job, but going by boat wasn't something she had bargained for. And yet it should have been fairly obvious to her that travelling between the islands was a necessity. Perhaps she'd simply tried not to think about it.

The trouble was, ever since she was a child she'd been plagued by seasickness—how could she possibly tell them that? If she owned up, there was absolutely no way she'd get the job.

'Does that bother you?' Tyler was watching her, a small frown indenting his brow. 'You seem distracted somehow.'

She tried what she hoped was a convincing smile. 'No, not at all. I'd be quite all right with that.'

Dr Gregson appeared satisfied. 'Well, then, Dr Reynolds, my colleagues and I have one more person to interview before we get together to talk things through. We should be able to let you know our decision before the end of the morning, though. In the meantime, perhaps you'd like to look around our hospital—Janine, my secretary, will be happy to give you the grand tour. You might want to spend some time in the minor injuries unit to see how we do things there, and then familiarise yourself with the A and E department.'

She nodded. 'Yes, thank you. I would. That's a good idea.' At least she could stay around until they were ready to announce their decision.

His secretary showed her around the different areas

of the hospital, pointing out the new cardiovascular wing and the obstetrics department. They made light conversation along the way, but Saskia felt weighed down inside with defeat. In her imaginings things would have gone very differently.

'We have a few inpatient beds here,' Janine told her, 'but we're probably not at all like the hospitals you've been used to. Everything here is on a much smaller scale.'

Saskia nodded. 'I've been impressed with what I've seen so far. It's all exceptionally clean and efficient-looking.'

Finally, they arrived at the A and E department. There were a couple of resuscitation rooms, several treatment bays and an area where doctors could go to type up their notes or access computers.

'I love the way this small area has been set apart for the younger patients,' Saskia commented. 'That mural must help to take their minds off their troubles, for a start.'

Janine smiled. 'It's great, isn't it? Dr Beckett commissioned it from a relative of one of his patients. The children love trying to find the chicks hiding in the farmyard. And, of course, the ceiling mural helps distract them when they have to lie down.'

'Yes, I imagine it does.' It had been made to look like a vivid blue sky, with cotton-wool clouds, a mixed assembly of birds and colourful box kites to keep the children amused.

If only she could be so easily distracted. She sighed inwardly, thinking about the members of the interview panel who were most likely deciding her fate at that very moment. Her stomach gave an uncomfortable lurch.

A nurse came over to them as they walked towards the nurses' station. 'Janine, I've been paging Dr Beckett—do you know if he's in the hospital today? I haven't seen him all morning and we've had a patient come in with an injury to his wrist. We need him to come and take a look at it.'

'He's definitely here. He's been doing interviews since first thing, but they should be finished by now. I expect he'll along in a minute or two.'

'Okay, thanks.'

Janine glanced at Saskia. 'You might want to be in on this—see how we do things here.'

'Are you sure?' Saskia frowned. 'I don't want to get in the way.'

Janine shook her head. 'I'm sure it won't be a problem. We're all very friendly and informal around here.'

'You have a patient for me?' Dr Beckett strode into the A and E unit, his manner brisk and ready for action. Saskia stiffened. Had the interview panel finished their discussion and come to a conclusion?

'He's in here,' the triage nurse told him, pointing out one of the treatment rooms. 'We've done X-rays and given him painkillers.' She handed him the patient's file.

'Thanks.' He glanced at the notes in the file, and then went over to the computer and studied the films. Frowning, he said, 'I'll need someone to assist. Who's free?'

The nurse shook her head. 'No one right now. I'm needed in several places at once, and as for the rest—we're busy with an influx of patients just now. There was a minor explosion at a building site and we've had a number of casualties…something to do with a propane gas cylinder. Nothing dreadfully serious regarding casualties, thankfully, but some quite nasty burns.'

He inclined his head in acknowledgement. 'Okay, I suppose I'll just have to wait until you can spare someone.'

Saskia said quickly, 'I could help, if you want.'

He glanced at her. 'Are you sure?'

'Of course. If there's anything at all I can do…' She frowned. 'I understand this man has a broken wrist. Was that something to do with the explosion?'

He shook his head. 'Totally different, apparently. He came off his motorcycle while taking a bend too sharply.'

'Oh, dear.'

They went into the treatment room, where they found a young man in his early twenties nursing a badly deformed wrist.

'Well, Mason,' Tyler said, pulling up a chair and carefully examining the man's injury, 'I could have told you even without looking at the X-rays that you've broken your wrist.' He glanced at Saskia. 'Have you seen this kind of fracture before?'

She nodded. 'It's a Smith's fracture,' she murmured, 'and that's a typical garden-spade deformity.' She looked at Mason. 'I expect you fell awkwardly off your bike and landed on the back of your hand. I suppose you can count yourself lucky you don't have any other injuries—apart from cuts and grazes, that is.'

The young man gave her a rueful smile. 'I guess I can. Though this feels bad enough.'

'I'm sure it does.'

'We'll get you sorted out in no time,' Tyler said. 'I'll give you a local anaesthetic and a sedative, and then we'll realign the bones for you and get you fixed up with a splint.' He looked at Saskia. 'I'll need you to hold his elbow steady while I reduce the fracture—are you okay with that?'

'Yes, of course.'

A few minutes later, when their patient's wrist had been fully anaesthetised, they worked together to manipulate the bones back into position. 'Okay,' Tyler said, checking the shape of the wrist and testing the pulses there. 'That seems to have done the trick. We'll get that splinted up and then do further X-rays to make sure everything's as it should be.'

Mason was clearly relieved some time later when the procedure was finished and had been pronounced a success.

'Okay, we'll see you back here in a couple of days to check how things are going,' Tyler told him. 'And in the meantime I'll write up a prescription for some painkillers for you to take home with you.'

'Thanks.'

At Tyler's signal, a nurse came to take Mason along to the nurses' station so that she could go through the discharge process with him and give him his medication.

Tyler turned to Saskia. 'Thanks for your help with that. I'm sure he was relieved to get it over and done with.' His glance moved over her fleetingly. 'You've been very patient. You must be anxious to know the result of your interview?'

She nodded. 'Has it been decided?'

He shook his head. 'Not yet. I gave the others my input before I left the meeting, so I expect they'll let us know shortly. Shall we go along to my office while we wait? I expect you could do with a cup of coffee.'

'That would be good, thanks,' she said, although all she really wanted to do now was get out of there and start working out what she was going to do for the best. She didn't hold out much hope for a successful outcome.

His office was everything she might have expected. It was a beautifully turned out room with satisfying neutral colours in soft greys and blues and an overall sense of calm. A good deal of light came in through deep, wide windows that looked out onto a paved terrace beyond, where stone planters were filled with bright chrysanthemums, adding a splash of colour.

The furniture was made of pale golden beechwood. A desk with a pigeonholed upstand stood to one side of the room, and against another wall neat cupboards were interspersed with glass-fronted bookcases. There were even a couple of plants, billowy ferns that provided a pleasing touch of green.

'Please, sit down,' he said, waving her towards a chair. He switched on the filter machine, and soon the delicious aroma of coffee filled the room.

'I'm sorry if I seemed a bit hard on you this morning,' he said, placing a cup on the desk beside her. 'I know it must have been difficult for you.'

She took a sip of the hot liquid. 'I had the feeling you weren't at all keen on having me as part of your team,' she murmured, 'though I don't really know what you have against me.'

'It's not that I don't want you,' he demurred. He went to stand with his back to the window. 'I have one or two reservations, that's all. I have the feeling that you're inclined to be impulsive—which is not a bad thing at all unless it intrudes on your work, but it wouldn't do to be making impulsive decisions in A and E.'

'Unless they were based on instinctive knowledge, maybe.'

He shrugged. 'Possibly. The other thing is that I can't help feeling you're holding something back. I'm not sure yet what that might be.'

He studied her once more, but she didn't offer any explanation. Instead, she lowered her head and swallowed her coffee as though it was a lifesaver.

He appeared to be deep in thought for a while, but then he said, 'I suppose the biggest hurdle for me was that I had a particular type of candidate in mind—someone who was on the ball, alert and ready to face up to the challenges of the job.'

He smiled, gentle humour reflected in his eyes and in the curve of his mouth. 'But instead you came along—and from what I saw back at the house you strike me as being…distracted, disorganised and probably stressed out with the strain of looking after your family. Medicine's a difficult profession, even for the hardiest of people, and I can't help feeling that this is probably not the best time for you to be taking on a responsible position.'

Dismayed, she stared at him. 'You can't judge me on one meeting. You must realise that you came to the house at a particularly difficult time.'

'Yes…but that one time made a big impression on me.' He made a wry face. 'The problem is I'm finding it difficult to be detached when it comes to making this decision. Try as I may to keep a clear mind, the fact is whenever I look at you, in my mind's eye I keep seeing a beautiful, half-naked young woman surrounded by chaos. It's kind of hard to shake off that image.'

Her cheeks flushed with hot colour. 'I… You caught me unawares. I wasn't ready to receive visitors.'

He chuckled. 'No, I realised that, and I should have left right away, but I must admit, the temptation to stay was just too great.'

She sucked in a sharp breath. 'Tyler, I need this job.'

He nodded. 'I know,' he said, becoming serious once more. 'And the truth is we need a woman on the team to balance things up. I might be a bit concerned that you're not exactly what I had in mind, but I suppose, since we would be working together initially, I'd be able to keep an eye on you.'

Her eyes widened. 'Are you saying that you voted in my favour?'

'I am, albeit with reservations.' The phone rang just then and he came over to the desk to half sit, half lean on the edge as he reached for the receiver. She was conscious of him being close to her, the fabric of his trousers stretched taut against his thigh, and she felt a sudden, unbidden, rush of heat race through her veins. 'Okay, thanks,' he said to whoever was on the other end of the line. 'Will do.'

He replaced the receiver and looked at her. 'That was Dr Gregson. He said to tell you the job's yours if you want it.'

She gave a small gasp. 'Really? Oh, I do. Definitely, I do.'

His mouth curved, giving his features an irresistible sex appeal. 'Good. That's settled, then.' His expression sobered. 'Though there is one proviso I should add.'

'And that is…?' She frowned, on edge all over again.

'We feel there should be a three-month trial period to give us all time to decide whether we think things will work out. It'll be a mutual arrangement. After all, you may decide you don't care for the way we do things here, and once your brother and his wife are out of hospital, you may want to go back to the mainland.'

She mulled it over. Right now, she couldn't see that happening, because she would always want to be close to her family, but it was true she had friends back in Cornwall, people she would miss.

'I can see how a three-month trial might work both ways.' She was troubled, though. This result was a positive one for the time being, but it wasn't quite what she'd hoped for, not with this inevitable sense of insecurity hanging over her. Tyler was the one who would have pushed for that condition, she was sure. How could she convince him that she wouldn't let him down?

She said carefully, 'Look, I know you have your doubts about me, but I'm sure I can show you that I'm as sensible and methodical as you or anyone else.'

She thought about it for a moment or two and then added hastily, 'In fact, why don't you come over for supper one evening…Saturday, perhaps? Then I can show you that I don't always live surrounded by chaos and upheaval. You'll see, I can be every bit as efficient and on the ball as you are.'

'You don't have to do that—'

'I know. I want to.'

He inclined his head a fraction. 'Then, yes, thank you. I'd like that—that is, provided I'm not called out to any sudden emergencies.' He frowned. 'I believe I'm on call over the weekend. I wouldn't want to put you to any trouble unnecessarily.'

'Don't worry about that. I always cook too much, anyway. I haven't managed to work out everyone's appetites yet. But if you can make it, that would be good. I'll look forward to it.' She hesitated. 'Um—do you have any particular likes or dislikes about food? I mean, I'd hate to come up with something hot and spicy, for instance, if you couldn't abide that kind of thing.'

'I like hot and spicy, and I'm willing to try anything,' he said. 'But please don't go to a lot of bother. I know you have enough to cope with already.'

'I'll be fine,' she answered with as much confidence as she could muster, but her smile was strained as she left his office a few minutes later. What was she doing, acting as though she was so self-assured? How on earth did she know that she could carry it off? Life was anything but routine for her these days and heaven alone knew what she was letting herself in for.

CHAPTER THREE

'YOU MADE IT, then—there were no callouts to drag you away, after all.' Saskia did her best to put on a cheerful front as she opened the door to her neighbour and soon-to-be boss. Everything had to go well today. She mentally crossed her fingers, smiling at Tyler as she stood to one side to let him into the house.

'Not one,' he agreed, stepping into the hallway and handing her a bottle of chilled wine. 'I hope this is all right. I thought it might go down well with supper and it would help us to celebrate your new job.'

'Thanks. That was thoughtful of you.'

'It was the least I could do, to make some small contribution.' He smiled, a faint curve to his mouth that had the unexpected effect of making her go weak at the knees, so that she had to inwardly shake herself to pull herself together. He was her boss—she had to keep remembering that. She wasn't going to even think about him any other way. She'd been down that road before, and look where it had led her.

It didn't help, though, that he looked fantastic. His appearance was flawless as usual, with black chinos moulding his long, muscled legs and a deep blue, open-necked shirt resting easily against the smooth, flat line of his stomach. It was very unsettling.

'Actually, I wasn't sure whether you would still be up for it,' he murmured. 'Supper, I mean. I noticed you've been out for most of the day. I saw you all leave early this morning, and I knew when you'd come back because I heard the children.' He looked concerned. 'I can't help thinking this must all have been a bit of a rush for you.'

'Uh…yes, it has been a bit hectic, but it's okay.' She frowned, thinking about the trip they'd made to Cornwall, and a shiver of unhappiness snaked down her spine. 'We went to visit my brother and his wife in hospital on the mainland.'

She led the way to the kitchen and placed the bottle of wine in the fridge before turning to look at him once more. 'It was a bit of a last-minute, spur-of-the-moment decision. The children have been desperate to go and see their parents, but neither Sam nor Megan has been well enough to receive visitors up to now. Then, when I phoned the hospital this morning, the nurse said they might be able to cope with a brief visit and I thought maybe we should make the trip over there.'

She flicked the switch on the coffee filter machine and waved him to a chair.

'It sounds as though they were involved in a really bad accident,' he commented, frowning as he sat down by the pale oak table. 'What exactly happened to them? Do you mind talking about it?'

She shook her head. 'No, it's all right. I think I'm over the worst now. It was just such a shock before.' She set out cups, a sugar bowl, and filled a small jug with cream. 'Sam had a really bad chest injury—they had to open up his chest to give him heart massage. Megan's was a blunt abdominal trauma, with a pelvic fracture.' Just thinking about it gave her chills.

He sucked in his breath. 'That must have been horrendous. It sounds as though they're lucky to be alive.'

'Yes, it was touch and go for both of them.' She slid a cup of coffee towards him and took a sip of hers to soothe her nerves. 'It was a relief to be able to see them today.'

'I'm sure it was,' he agreed, 'and I dare say it was good for them to see the children, too.'

'Yes, I think it cheered them up a bit. It's not easy for any of them, with the family being split up like this.'

He nodded. 'It's bound to be difficult.' He frowned, pausing momentarily before saying in a cautious tone, 'Was everything all right when you arrived back home? Only I couldn't help hearing a lot of shouting. Were the children upset by the visit?'

'Oh…' It was disturbing that he was so aware of everything that was going on in her life. 'Um…they were all a bit unsettled, but I suppose that was to be expected. Charlie, especially, was shocked to see his mum and dad looking so ill.' She pulled a face. 'But I think the shouting was over something different. That was because of Boomer.'

'Oh?' He gave a wry smile. 'More trouble?'

'Oh, yes.' She grimaced, remembering the havoc that had greeted her on their arrival home. 'I think he objected to being cooped up on his own for so long. He'd taken out his frustration on the rug in the living room— we found it in bits all over the floor.' She saw his frown and said quickly, 'I'll pay for a replacement, of course.'

As the landlord, he must be wondering just how much damage this family could inflict on his property.

She hurried on. 'Not content with that, he'd sunk his teeth into Caitlin's electronic photo album and Charlie's steering-wheel—you know, those things they use with computer games? Then Caitlin had a set-to with Charlie over him rummaging through things in her room, and Charlie started arguing with Becky over tidying up his toys so well that he couldn't find something he wanted.' She shrugged awkwardly. 'Things blew up out of proportion. I think it was probably something to do with the aftermath of the visit—they were all a bit strung out. So everything escalated and it was as though all hell was let loose in here for a while.'

He seemed perplexed by the sheer chaos she described. 'I'd no idea family life could be so fraught. I'm much more used to an orderly way of going on. I'm not sure I could deal with what you're having to put up with of late.'

He finished off his coffee and said briskly, 'But that was bad luck with the dog—don't worry about the rug. Hopefully, it was a one-off and we can mark it down to experience.' He was thoughtful for a moment and then asked on a reflective note, 'Isn't it going to be a problem for you when you start work? I mean, Boomer's not going to take kindly to being left at home, from the sound of things. That could prove to be something of a problem.'

She winced inwardly. She might have known he would pick up on that. 'Yes, that's true, and I've been giving it some thought.' She pulled in a deep breath. 'I've arranged for someone to come in and walk him a couple of times a day. She's the wife of someone who knows my brother, Sam, through his work, so I know she's trustworthy and I'm pretty sure she'll be dependable. She likes dogs and offered to help when she heard I'd be going out to work. She even said she'd lend a hand with the children if ever I was stuck, so she's a good friend to have.'

'It certainly looks that way.' He glanced at Boomer, who was sleeping in a corner of the room, worn out after his rampage, and said with a faint smile, 'It's a shame she wasn't around earlier today.'

'Yes. Unfortunately, when I made the phone call I made up my mind to go there and then and I didn't think too much about what would happen while we were out.' She frowned. She'd been far too busy making arrangements for them to get to the ferry on time and trying to work out how she would fit in all the preparations for supper once they got home. She'd only just remembered in time to take her travel sickness pills.

Of all the days for Boomer to decide to create havoc, this was one of the worst. Five hours there and back on the ferry hadn't done much to help anybody's temper and her stress level had been rising steadily since they'd arrived back.

Still, she wasn't doing too badly. She'd found time to shower and change into a little black dress that clung to her in all the right places and that at least helped to boost her confidence. She'd seen Tyler's glance skim her figure more than once since he'd arrived, so perhaps it was having the desired effect. Things might not be so bad after all.

As for supper, she'd chosen a Mexican theme—it was a favourite with the children and she hoped Tyler would like it, too.

The enchiladas, filled with tender chicken and vegetables then topped with sauce and a generous coating of
grated cheese, were baking in the oven—a quick fifteen
minutes was all that was needed to melt the cheese—
and the rice was steaming gently on the hob. She went
over there now and lifted the lid on the pan so that she
could peer inside.

Tyler sniffed the air appreciatively. 'Something
smells good.'

'Oh, thanks. I thought I'd go for something spicy…
chicken enchiladas and Mexican rice.' A sudden qualm
hit her. 'Would that be okay for you? I mean, if not I
could—'

'That sounds absolutely fine,' he said quickly, and
she tried to relax a little.

'Oh, good. I've made some dips to go along with it,
and I have some cheesecake for dessert.' She was an
idiot. What would she have done if he'd said no—started
again with something simple, like cheese on toast? She
was far too jumpy. She must calm down.

'It should be ready any time now.' So far, despite her
anxieties, everything was going according to plan. She
even allowed herself a quiet moment of satisfaction but
that small oasis of peace was brutally shattered when,
all of a sudden, shrill voices erupted from the living
room and spilled over into the kitchen. The smile froze
on her lips. What now?

'I'm keeping it. I found it.' It was Charlie's voice.

'No, you didn't. You stole it. It's mine. Saskia gave it
to me.' Becky marched into the room, righteous indig-
nation bringing hot colour to her cheeks as she glared
furiously at her brother.

'What are you two arguing about?' Saskia threaded

her fingers through her hair, trying to push back her unruly curls. It was hot in the kitchen, and she was overly conscious of anything that threatened to disrupt her timetable. A ripple of alarm ran through her at this latest intrusion. Everything had to run smoothly if she was to make a good impression on Tyler—she needed to finish setting the table, add a squeeze of lime juice to the salsa, stir cheese into the rice, and take the enchiladas from the oven. What else was there to do? Her mind had suddenly gone blank.

'He's got my buzzy bee pencil,' Becky complained, stormclouds brewing in her eyes.

'It was on the floor, so now it's mine,' Charlie retorted. 'If I hadn't picked it up, Boomer would have had it.'

'That doesn't count. It's mine. Give it back.' Becky gave him a push.

Charlie shoved back hard in return and Becky's flailing arms sent a potted plant flying through the air like a guided missile. It landed on the floor, breaking into a mess of shattered china, soil and broken fronds.

Through all this, Saskia was ultra-conscious of Tyler, who had sprung to his feet to steady Becky and was now standing by the worktop, watching everything with an air of bemused expectation.

She braced herself. 'Enough,' she said. 'All this fuss is about a pencil?' She couldn't believe this was happening to ruin her careful preparations. What would he think of them, and of her ability to cope? 'Where is it? Let me see.' She held out a hand, and Charlie reluctantly passed it to her.

'Well, if it's going to cause all this fuss, perhaps no one should have it—for now, at any rate.' She put it away in a cupboard, high up where neither of them could reach.

'That's not fair!'

'Give it back!'

'You can have it back after supper, Becky. For now, why don't both of you go and see if you can fill in some more pieces to the jigsaw puzzle? You like doing that.'

Both children were scowling at her now, and she said quietly, 'Out of the kitchen now, both of you. I'm trying to cook here.' She felt as though she'd been parachuted into the middle of a menagerie.

She glanced at Tyler. 'I'm sorry about all the noise,' she said. 'I thought I'd settled them down with colouring books and word puzzles, but it looks as though their interest has worn thin. And Charlie's been out of sorts ever since we went over to the hospital.'

'It looks that way, doesn't it?' He seemed distracted, then added in a vaguely warning tone, 'You know, I don't want to tell you your business, but I think I can smell something burning.'

Saskia looked at him, her whole body stiffening. In all the confusion had she missed the alert of the kitchen timer? With every minute that passed she could see her well-laid plans turning to rubble all around her.

She gave a small gasp. 'The enchiladas…the rice.'

Becky and Charlie hadn't moved from the spot and now they were looking on, wide-eyed as she skirted the broken plant pot to turn off the heat under the pan of rice. Then with growing trepidation she reached into the oven to slide out the hot baking trays.

It was scary how fast things could fall apart. 'They're burnt,' Charlie pronounced in his usual blunt fashion, and her shoulders slumped a little.

'Um…I don't think they're too bad,' she said, a dubious note creeping into her voice.

Tyler glanced at the once perfect tortilla wraps. 'Actually, I think it's only the edges that are a little overdone,' he murmured, 'just where the sauce has stuck a bit. Shall I ease them out for you? Do you have a spatula?'

'Uh…yes, I'll get it for you. Thanks.'

She handed him the spatula and fetched the serving trays from the warming oven. It was bad enough that he'd been here to witness all the shouting that had been going on, but now…what must he think of her? He probably thought that if she couldn't handle things in the kitchen, she would be hopeless in the emergency room—but it wasn't true, that was totally different. She was good at her job and she could handle A and E as though she had been born to it…even though Michael had made life difficult for her and tried to undermine her and trip her up at every opportunity after their split.

Swiftly, she pulled herself together. 'Charlie, go and fetch the dustpan and brush, please, and sweep up that plant. Becky, we need the guacamole and salsa to be put out on the table, and then perhaps you could go and tell Caitlin that supper's ready.'

What had possessed her to invite Tyler here? How could he ever see her at her best in these circumstances? She wasn't used to having children around. In her normal, everyday life she was organised, capable, efficient. Wasn't she…most of the time?

She sagged against the cupboard, wiping her forehead with the back of her hand, and gazed for a moment into space, gathering her wits.

'How about a glass of wine?' Tyler popped the cork

on the bottle he had brought with him and hunted for glasses in the cupboards. 'That might make you feel a bit better.'

She managed a smile. 'Thanks. That's a good idea.'

She swallowed the smooth, chilled wine gratefully, and then put down her glass and set to work to serve up the meal. Tyler found dinner plates warming in the oven and put them out on the table, along with a jug of orange juice for the children. Between them, they set out platters of enchiladas and tortilla chips along with a dish of hot Mexican rice and a salad bowl that she'd prepared earlier.

'It doesn't look bad at all,' Tyler commented charitably, and Saskia winced.

'Caitlin says she doesn't want anything to eat.' Becky came and sat down at the table, surveying all the food on display. 'I'm starving,' she said.

Saskia frowned. Caitlin wasn't coming downstairs? Something was definitely not right with her. She'd not been herself for days now and she really needed to get to the root of what was wrong.

'Are you worried about her?' Tyler asked, watching her expression. 'If you want to go up and have a chat with her, we'll be fine here.'

'Are you sure? I really feel I ought to…' She threw him an apologetic look. 'But, please, make a start on the food before it gets cold.'

'Don't worry about it. We'll be fine.' He looked at Becky and Charlie for agreement and they both nodded vigorously, pushing their plates forward slightly as he started to serve out the food.

Saskia hesitated, waiting as Charlie cut the singed ends from his enchilada and tentatively bit into it. He savoured it for a second or two, and then said, 'Yeah, that's good.'

Relieved, she hurried away to find Caitlin. It would be something of an achievement if she could persuade her to come down and try just a morsel of food, but she'd have to tread carefully. The teenager had been very touchy of late.

'I feel a bit sick,' Caitlin said. 'I just want to lie down for a bit.'

'Are you worrying about anything?' Saskia asked, sitting down on the bed beside her, but Caitlin gave a slight, negative shake of her head and didn't answer. 'Did it upset you, seeing your mum and dad today?'

'Yeah, it did a bit.' Caitlin bit her lip. 'They're really ill, aren't they? Mum looked as if she was in a lot of pain, and Dad was white as a sheet.'

'That's true, but they're in the right place,' Saskia said carefully. 'I had a word with the nurse, and she's going to ask the doctor to prescribe a different pain-killer for your mother. They're both being well looked after and they should start to get better from now on.'

She talked to her niece for a while, gently stroking the girl's silky hair. 'Are you sure you won't come down and try some food—just a little?'

'I'm not hungry.'

'Okay. I'll save some for you in case you change your mind later on.'

She went to join the others in the kitchen and found the three of them talking animatedly about the latest game that Charlie was playing on his Xbox. 'The dragons breathe fire and you can cast spells on people,' Charlie was saying.

Tyler smiled. 'Wow, that sounds great.' He looked

up as Saskia came into the room and said softly, 'How is she?'

'Worrying about her mum and dad, I think. It's been a difficult day for her…for us all.'

'I miss them,' Becky said, her eyes suddenly bright with unshed tears. 'They looked really poorly.'

Charlie stopped eating and looked at Saskia. 'When will they come home?' There was a wobble in his voice. 'I don't like them being so far away.'

'I know, sweetheart. I understand how you both feel.' She looked at the children, saddened by the distress she saw written on their faces. 'I'm not sure yet when they'll be home, but they're getting stronger every day, and that's good, isn't it? I know you miss them. It's hard, having to get used to what's happened, but we'll look after each other, and together we'll get through this the best way we can.'

They were still clearly upset, and Saskia searched for some way to steer them away from this downhill path.

'Perhaps you could make them a card or take them something that will cheer them up next time you visit?' Tyler suggested.

Becky nodded, while Charlie looked thoughtful. 'Like a box with sweets in it? Dad likes mints and toffees. I could make a box out of card…'

'That sounds like a good idea.' Tyler gave him an encouraging smile. 'Maybe you and Becky could make one each?'

'Yeah.' Becky's mind had ticked into craft mode. 'I want to make one for Mummy…one with shiny love hearts on it.' The children looked at one another and returned to their food with renewed vigour. They obviously wanted to get started on their project straight away.

Saskia sent Tyler a quick, grateful look. 'Thanks,' she said softly. 'That could have been difficult.'

'It's an awkward situation.'

They ate their meal, chatting about this and that. 'Are your parents able to help out while all this is going on?' Tyler asked after a while.

'My parents divorced some years ago,' she told him as she spooned more rice on to her plate. 'Now my father lives in Spain, and we don't really get to see him all that often. My mother eventually married again and moved to Somerset. She runs her own company so it's difficult for her to get away for long periods of time, but she's very worried about what's happening. She visits Sam as often as she's able to.' She glanced at him. 'What about you? Do you have any family close by?'

He nodded. 'My mother lives not too far away from here, and I have a younger sister who's working as an office manager in Tresco. I keep in touch with them on a regular basis. We've always been very close.'

She frowned. 'And your father?'

'He died a few years back—a heart attack.'

'Oh, I'm sorry. That must have been very difficult for you.'

'It was unexpected; it came out of the blue so, yes, it was painful at the time.'

She tried to imagine him with his mother and sister. He'd probably be very protective of them, especially of his sister, taking the place of the father they had lost.

They finished the main course, and he helped her to clear away the dishes. 'That was good,' he told her. 'Very tasty.'

'I suppose it wasn't too bad, once we'd rescued it from the inferno,' she said with a bleak smile. 'It's kind of you to say so, anyway.' She took the cheesecake from the fridge and placed it in the centre of the table. 'Perhaps this will make up for any failings in the first course.'

It did look good, a crumbly biscuit base, topped with cream cheese and generously covered with luscious strawberries. Charlie's eyes widened. 'Yum!'

'Definitely yum,' Tyler said with a grin, as they tucked in. He freshened Saskia's glass of wine and proposed a toast. 'Here's to your new job. Let's drink to it working out well.'

She clinked glasses with him, wondering if she would manage to convince him that she was the right person for the job. He seemed to be on her side, for the moment at least, so maybe things would work out all right after all.

Then again, a three-month trial might throw up all manner of pitfalls along the way. What if Tyler were to speak to Michael again? That could easily happen if he transferred patients over there—he'd already shown that he liked to check up on their progress to reassure himself that all was well.

Would Michael try to discredit her all over again? Maybe he couldn't do it professionally, but it wouldn't be beyond him to tell lies about her private life. He'd done that once before when she'd refused to take him back after their break-up. He'd hinted that she'd slept around and cheated on him, both outright lies. She'd been fortunate in that her friends knew she wasn't like that. They knew that she'd always behaved with honesty and integrity, but people who didn't know her so well might have harboured doubts.

'Is something wrong?'

She looked up, startled out of her reverie by Tyler's gentle probing. How did he manage to read her so easily?

'No, nothing at all,' she said. 'I was just thinking about what lies ahead. If you'd told me two months ago that I would up sticks and move to the Isles of Scilly to look after three children, a dog and a pet rabbit, I'd have said you were way out. And yet here I am.' She frowned.

'My life has changed so much lately. Instead of being footloose and fancy-free, I'm doing laundry for four, and most mornings I end up doing some last-minute ironing because there's something they've forgotten to tell me they need. And then there are school bags and gym kit to be found and lunch money that needs to be handed out.'

Charlie's ears pricked up at that. 'I need some money for Tuesday for swimming lessons. We're going on the bus. And I need some new swimming trunks.'

She gave him a puzzled look. 'Did I get a letter about this?'

He thought about it. 'Yeah.'

'I don't remember it. Where is it?'

He frowned. 'In my school bag.'

Saskia glanced at Tyler. 'I guess that's another job for the end of the school day—checking the school bags for scraps of paper.'

His mouth quirked at the corners. 'I'm sure you're doing the best you can.'

They finished dessert, and while Saskia started to make coffee Becky and Charlie shot off upstairs to rummage through their craft boxes.

'Thanks for inviting me here today,' Tyler said a few minutes later as he drank coffee, standing by the worktop. 'It's been…' he hesitated '…an experience. I have to admit I'm not used to the ups and downs of family life…not like this, anyway.'

'Me neither. I always got on well with my brother.'

'It was the same for me with my sister. I suppose I looked out for her. Still do, to a certain extent. Things at home were…complicated. But I like my life how it is now. I like the challenge of work in the emergency department, and I look forward to the contrast of peace and quiet when I get home.'

Saskia bit her lip. It had definitely been a mistake to invite him over here.

She glanced out of the window. Darkness was falling outside, filling the garden with inky-black shadows. 'I know things didn't go quite to plan this evening, but I'm glad you came. I thought it might be a good way for us to get to know one another—since we're neighbours and it looks as though we'll be working together quite closely.'

He nodded. 'It was a good idea.'

Her brow furrowed. 'Actually, I'm not sure exactly what that involves—working together, I mean.'

At the interview it had sounded as though he expected her to slip up at some point and he wanted to be there to prevent any mistakes from happening. 'I'm assuming we'll both be in A and E, dealing with our own patients, and I'll refer to you as the head of the team.'

'That's right. But initially we'll go out on call together, so that you'll get the lie of the land more easily. The same applies to going over to the hospital in Cornwall, should the need arise—at least until you find your feet.'

'Oh, I see. Well, that will certainly help.' He was

being casual about it, but the truth remained that he would be keeping an eye on her. She'd have to earn his trust.

'In fact,' he said, 'I could give you a lift in to work every day, if you like. There's no point in us both going separately, is there?'

'No, that's true…' She was startled by his unexpected offer. 'That would be great…it's really thoughtful of you…but I have to take the children to school…'

'That's okay. We'll drop them off on the way.'

'That's very good of you. I appreciate it.'

He was being helpful, co-operative, and she could only hope she would live up to his expectations. Perhaps the situation with Michael had shaken her confidence and filled her with self-doubt. He'd made her question every action she'd taken, every drug she'd prescribed. Towards the end he'd made her life at work seem like hell on earth.

Troubled by these unsettling thoughts, she moved over to the sink unit, where Tyler was standing. She needed something to do to keep herself active and shake off the negativity of the past. It was dark outside now, an inky blackness, and she reached over to close the blind just as Tyler decided to set down his coffee cup on the draining board. Their bodies met in a soft collision. His hand lightly brushed the swell of her hip and an instant shock wave of heat pulsed through her body.

'Uh, I'm sorry.' He drew back as though he'd been stung.

'It's all right,' she managed, struggling to calm the pounding beat of her heart. 'It was an accident.'

'Yes.' He was watching her, seemingly mesmerised by her. His blue gaze drifted down over the gentle curves of her body, outlined by the soft material of the black dress. She could feel the warmth of his gaze searing her skin, almost as though he'd touched her, and her heart skipped a beat. A pulse began to throb at the base of her throat, an erratic, fluttery sensation that made her catch her breath.

Neither of them moved. It was as though they were imprisoned in some kind of force field where all her senses were heightened. He felt it too, she was sure.

Slowly, the magnetic tension that held them began to dissipate. In the background she could hear the thud of children's footsteps clattering down the stairs. The spell was broken and Tyler glanced towards the kitchen door as the sound drew nearer.

'I—uh… Perhaps I should be going now,' he said huskily. 'It sounds as though you're going to be needed soon.' He drew in a quick breath. 'Thanks again for supper. I—uh—I must return the favour some time.'

'That's okay, you're welcome.' She managed to find her voice, even though her throat was suddenly bone dry. 'I'll see you out.'

He left by the back door, looking back briefly before setting off down the moonlit path at the side of the house. She acknowledged him with a wave.

After he'd gone, she stood for some time, slowly breathing in the night air, trying to get her thoughts back together.

He had an extraordinary effect on her, and it seemed that he wasn't immune to her either. That could be tricky. She wasn't looking for a relationship, didn't want to get involved with any man after her experience with Michael. She hadn't bargained for any of this when she'd come here, or when she'd applied for the job at the hospital.

But now it looked as though they might both be treading on dangerous ground, and if this evening's events were anything to go by, she'd have to be on her guard.

She was just getting over one bad experience, and she wasn't about to let herself in for another.

CHAPTER FOUR

'HEY, IT'S GOOD to see you, Saskia.' Noah Matheson caught up with Saskia and Tyler at the entrance to A and E. 'Are you all set for your first day with us?'

'I think so.' She returned his smile. 'Thanks for asking.'

'You'll do fine, I'm sure, but if you have any problems, just holler. I'll be right next door.' He waved a hand in the direction of the minor injuries unit.

'I'll remember that. Thanks. Though I'm hoping Tyler will be here to help me out, for the next few weeks at least.' She looked at Tyler and he inclined his head in acknowledgement.

Noah shot him a quick glance. 'Hmm…luck of the devil, that one.' He leaned closer to Saskia, saying in a stage whisper, 'Just remember, if you need anything at all, I'm your man.'

'Of course you are.' She laughed at his teasing. Noah was never going to be serious, was he? He was one of life's charmers, a cheerful, buoyant soul who couldn't resist trying his luck.

Tyler gave him a steely-eyed look. 'We'll see you later, Noah,' he said firmly. He rested a hand lightly in the small of Saskia's back and shepherded her away from their colleague and through the doors of the A and E unit.

Saskia was all too aware of Tyler's gentle but determined guidance. His touch was warm and supportive, sending ripples of heat eddying along her spine in a way that was profoundly unsettling. It flustered her, and she could only hope he wouldn't notice the flush of colour that swept along her cheekbones.

He was oblivious to the effect he was having on her, though, wasn't he? There wasn't anything to read into his innocent action. All Tyler wanted was to put some distance between her and Noah, because they both knew his colleague had the potential to be way too much of a distraction.

Once in the emergency department he was completely businesslike, introducing her to the staff on duty and showing her the areas she might have missed on her brief tour on the day of the interview.

'We keep lab request forms in here,' he told her, opening up a cupboard that housed myriad specialist documents, blank charts and so on. 'You'll find swabs, dressings, et cetera, in the cabinet over there, and tubing, surgical gloves and specimen bottles are stored in the cupboard right next to it.'

'Okay, I'll remember that.'

'It'll probably take a while for you to get to know where everything is, but the nurses are always willing to help out if you're unsure of anything.' His mouth made a crooked line. 'Most important place of all, of course, is the staff lounge. That's our main port of call for coffee, tea, biscuits and offloading all the frustrations of the day. It's along here.'

He led the way down a wide corridor to a room

marked 'Staff only' and gave her a quick look inside. A couple of people were sitting in there, and she recognised one of them as the young woman doctor she had seen a few days ago, talking to the receptionist.

'Dr Imogen Lancaster,' he said, 'and our Registrar, Dr Jason Samuels. This is our new A and E doctor, Saskia Reynolds.' They acknowledged one another with murmured comments and smiles, and then she headed back with Tyler to the main body of the emergency unit.

'Officially, I'm on call this week,' Tyler murmured, 'so it could be a baptism of fire for you. We'll only go out to those cases that the paramedics can't handle, but you'll need to be prepared for that. In the meantime, we'll work through the list of people who've turned up in A and E.' He glanced at the white board that showed the status of patients being seen that morning. 'It looks as though we have someone here who might fit in with your paediatric specialty,' he remarked. 'Tom Carter, in treatment room two, eleven years old. Abdominal pain. Do you want to go and see him while I take a look at the man in the next bay?'

'Okay.' She left Tyler and headed towards the room he had pointed out.

A young boy was lying on the treatment couch, looking feverish and ill, while his mother sat in a chair beside his bed. She was extremely anxious, clasping her hands tightly in her lap, the strain showing in her creased brow and the taut line of her mouth.

A nurse was with them, noting down temperature and blood-pressure measurements on the boy's chart.

Saskia greeted them with a smile and then glanced through the chart the nurse handed to her.

'I hear you're not feeling too good, Tom?' she said,

going over to the couch. 'Can you tell me what the matter is?'

'My tummy hurts—and my back—and I keep feeling sick,' he told her. His eyes were puffy, she noticed, and there was some other facial swelling. From the readings the nurse was taking, she saw that his blood pressure was abnormally high.

'I'll just do a quick examination of your tummy,' she said, 'if that's all right?'

He nodded, and she proceeded to carefully check him over, asking his mother various questions as she did so to try to find out what might be causing his symptoms.

'He's not eating properly,' his mother said, 'and he told me his urine's a dark colour. Do you think there's something wrong with his waterworks?'

'Possibly,' Saskia murmured. 'I'm seeing quite a bit of swelling, which is due to salt and water retention, and that means his kidneys aren't working as well as they should. There could be some inflammation there.' The nurse had done a urine test that showed there was blood in the boy's urine and leakage of protein. They were not good signs.

She listened to the boy's chest and then examined the glands in his neck and asked him to open his mouth so that she could look at his throat. 'We need to do some tests to find out what's causing the problem,' she said, looking over at his mother. 'Some simple blood tests and another urine test. Has he been poorly in the weeks leading up to this?'

'He had a sore throat,' the woman answered. 'We thought it was just a cold and that it would clear up on its own but it seemed to hang on for quite a while.'

'It hurt me to swallow,' Tom put in.

'Yes, your glands are still a bit swollen,' Saskia said. 'I think I'll take a throat swab to see whether you have an infection there that we need to treat.' Tom looked anxious at that and she said hurriedly, 'It's nothing to worry about—I'll use a small cotton wool swab and just gently stroke inside your throat. It won't hurt.'

He relaxed, and she excused herself while she went to find the testing kit. Tyler was standing outside the nearby treatment room, talking to a nurse about his patient, but he broke off when he saw Saskia. 'How's it going? Is everything okay?'

Saskia nodded. 'It's looking as though the boy has a problem with his kidneys and I'm a bit worried about him. There's some swelling to his face and abdomen and he's quite poorly. I'm just going to do a throat swab to see if it's the result of a streptococcal infection.'

He winced. 'That sounds nasty. Okay. Let me know how you go on.'

'I will.'

She went back to her young patient a few minutes later and took a swab from his throat.

'When will we know the results?' his mother asked.

'In a few minutes,' Saskia answered. 'I'll check the swab here and now, but in the meantime I'll organise some medication to help bring down the swelling and get his blood pressure back down to a reasonable level. I think we're going to have to admit him to hospital for a few days so that we can limit his fluids and put him on a special diet to reduce his protein and salt intake.' She wrote out a prescription for the nurse and then went to set up the testing kit to determine the results of the swab.

A short time later she went back to the bedside. 'The

swab was positive for a streptococcal infection,' she told the boy's mother, 'so we need to treat that with antibiotics. Does Tom have any problems with taking penicillin? Any allergies at all?'

His mother gave it some thought and then shook her head. 'No, I don't think so.'

'Okay, then. We'll start him on the tablets right away.' She smiled reassuringly at the boy and his mother. 'I know this might be very confusing for you, but if you have any questions at all, we're here to help.'

'Thank you.' The woman clasped Tom's hand in a comforting gesture. 'I'll stay with you, sweetie,' she told him. 'You're going to be all right.'

Saskia left them a few minutes later and went to the nurses' station to make arrangements to admit Tom to one of the wards. Passing by one of the treatment rooms, she saw Tyler deep in conversation with Dr Lancaster. The woman was smiling up at him, her long, chestnut-coloured hair falling in a silky swathe about her shoulders and swishing gently as she moved her arms to illustrate a point. Tyler grinned at something she said, and a moment or two later he lightly touched her shoulder in a farewell gesture as he made to leave the room.

Saskia hurriedly dragged her gaze away from them, not wanting to be caught staring. All the same, she frowned. Was there something going on between the two of them? Imogen seemed completely at ease with Tyler and he was relaxed and animated in her company.

But why wouldn't he be? she admonished herself a moment later. They must have worked together for some time, and they were obviously friendly with one another. Wasn't that how things should be?

She went to see her next patient, a toddler who was

suffering from a respiratory infection, and when she was satisfied that he was comfortable and responding to oxygen treatment and nebulised salbutamol, she headed over to the computer area to type up her notes.

'Hi, there.' Tyler came to stand beside the desk, watching as she entered the details of the medication into the file on screen. 'I hear you've decided to admit the boy with the kidney problem. Is there no way he can be treated at home?'

She shook her head. 'No, or I wouldn't have taken that decision. Why, is there a problem?'

'Not at all. It's just that we only have a few inpatient beds here, so we have to be careful about admissions.'

'I understand that, but I think this child is suffering from acute glomerulonephritis and I don't want to take any risks. He follows all the criteria for admission.'

Perhaps her words came out with more of a sharp edge than she intended, because he said calmly, 'That's okay. You don't need to defend yourself. I was only—'

He broke off as the nurse who had been assisting Saskia earlier hurried towards them. She seemed worried and her tone was urgent. 'I need you to come and take a look at Tom Carter,' she said, looking at Saskia.

'What's wrong, Katie? What's happened?' Tyler was immediately on the alert, already starting towards the treatment room.

'I don't know. He suddenly collapsed. He started to complain of dizziness and feeling faint and his blood pressure has dropped far too quickly. Now he can't get his breath and he's losing consciousness. We're giving him oxygen.'

'All right. That was good thinking.'

Saskia hurried alongside him. What could have gone

wrong? She'd made all the necessary checks and was confident in her diagnosis, but there had been nothing in the child's condition that might have led them to expect this sudden deterioration.

Once in the treatment room, though, she could see straight away that Tom was in trouble. White faced, she checked him over, noting that his pulse was weak and his skin was turning a bluish colour. Understandably, his mother was frantic with worry. 'What's wrong with him?' she asked. 'Why is this happening?'

Tyler shot a glance at Saskia and she said huskily, 'He must be reacting to the medication—to the penicillin.'

Tyler nodded agreement. 'He's gone into anaphylactic shock. We need to give him an adrenaline shot, fast.'

Saskia was already preparing the injection, while Tyler pulled up the boy's trouser leg to expose his thigh in readiness.

They waited anxiously for the injection to take effect, and as time went on, Saskia realised that she was holding her breath. This had to work. This had to bring him round.

After what seemed like an age Tom gasped and began to breathe erratically, sucking air wheezily into his lungs.

'He's coming out of it,' Tyler said, beginning to relax a little, 'but I think we should give him a dose of antihistamine and corticosteroids.'

Saskia nodded agreement. She couldn't speak just then. She wanted to, but the words just wouldn't come out. This was her first patient on the first day of her new job and he'd collapsed from something she'd prescribed for him. It was awful to see the boy in this state, and even worse to know that she had unwittingly been the cause of his troubles.

She set up an intravenous line so that Tom could be given the medication he needed. She stayed with him as the drugs began to take effect, and all the time she could hear Tyler talking to the mother, asking about the boy's previous medical history and experience with penicillin.

'Well, he had a chest infection about a year ago,' the woman told him. 'The doctor prescribed penicillin for it. He took the tablets, as he was supposed to, but afterwards he was wheezing more than ever and he said he didn't feel right. We didn't think the antibiotics were working, so we took him back to the GP and he gave him something else to take.'

Tyler nodded, and carefully explained that Tom should never be given penicillin after this reaction. 'He'll need to wear a medic-alert bracelet,' he said, 'and we need to make sure everyone who treats him in the future knows about his sensitivity to the drug. In the meantime, we'll treat him with a different antibiotic.'

By now, Tom was breathing more easily, but was still feeling too unwell to say very much, and when the orderlies came to take him along to his new ward Saskia could do nothing but watch, heart in mouth, as they wheeled him away.

It was a dreadful start to her first day in her new job.

'Shall we go to my office?'

She realised with a jolt that Tyler was waiting for her to go with him. 'Yes, of course.' Things looked bad. The nurse, Katie, was frowning, concerned for the boy, obviously, but could it be that she was wondering if Saskia knew what she was doing?

Saskia followed Tyler to his office. Perhaps she

should be grateful that he was considerate enough to talk to her in private about what happened.

'So, tell me about it,' he said, coming straight to the point as they stood and faced each other across the room. He had his back to the window, making a tall, dark silhouette that was framed against the grey, rain-soaked backcloth of the sky. For Saskia, it felt as though the weather was accurately following the course of her mood. 'How did you come to prescribe penicillin if the boy had already had one bad reaction to it?'

'I didn't know about it. His mother didn't mention what happened before.'

'She talked about it just now.'

'Yes, but she must have thought it was his illness that caused him to wheeze and feel unwell, not the tablets, and perhaps the GP didn't pick up on it. I asked her if he was allergic to anything and she said she didn't think so.'

'Okay. Make sure it's written up in his notes, and send a letter to his GP.' He paused briefly. 'Perhaps you'd better let me see your prescription charts for the time being.'

She stiffened. 'You don't trust me to do my job properly?'

He shook his head. 'It's not that. It's just a precaution. I need to have your back—you're new here and people will be looking at everything you do. This is a relatively small community. It's for your own protection.'

'Why would you think I need protecting?' She stared at him fixedly for a moment or two, and saw the darkness come into his eyes. He wasn't doing this because of a one-off adverse reaction, was he? There was more to it than that. He'd had misgivings about her all along, and this was just one more black mark to substantiate his fears. Why was he so cautious about letting her do her job?

'This is Michael's doing, isn't it? That's why you don't trust me.' She saw the faint widening of his eyes and knew she'd hit the mark. 'What has he said about me now...that I might make mistakes?' She pressed her lips together in a flat line. 'I'm surprised you even let me set foot in this hospital.'

'This latest information came to me after we'd given you the job,' he admitted. 'I spoke to Michael Drew this morning about a patient I transferred over there— a woman who had a bleeding ulcer. It prompted him to mention that you prescribed anti-inflammatories for a patient who subsequently was ill through taking too high a dosage.'

'And I suppose you took that to mean that I'd inadvertently prescribed the wrong dose?' She gritted her teeth. 'It isn't true. I don't suppose he told you that the patient had been buying over-the-counter anti-inflammatories and continued to take them alongside the prescription drug—even though I'd warned him against doing that?'

He shook his head. 'No, he didn't mention that.'

'I'm sure he didn't. Michael's working to his own agenda. The patient thought he was doing himself some good by doubling up on the tablets—that it didn't matter because they were different sorts of anti-inflammatories. He very nearly ended up with a gastric ulcer.'

Tyler went to sit on the edge of the desk. 'So what agenda is your ex-boss following? Why would he want to put obstacles in the way of you keeping this job?'

She gripped the back of a chair, pressing her fingers

into the soft leather until her knuckles whitened. 'Who knows what goes on in his mind? Perhaps he's hoping I'll go back to Cornwall and beg for my job back. He didn't want me to leave.'

'That's a very peculiar way for him to behave.' He gave her an assessing look. 'Did you two have some kind of relationship going on?'

'We did…for a while. But it ended when I found out what he was really like. I knew things wouldn't work out for us…but I think I'm only just beginning to see the true extent of his capabilities.'

He sucked in a deep breath. 'I'm sorry this has been going on and that it's causing problems for you. I can see why you might feel the need to be on the defensive…but that's probably all the more reason for me to double-check everything for the time being. It's for your own safety.'

'I don't need protecting,' she said, her green eyes flinty. 'I'm not a junior doctor.'

'All the same, I have overall responsibility for the patients as well as the people on my team, and I think it's important to put controls in place.'

'Then there's nothing more to be said, is there?' She lifted her chin. 'Is that all? Are we done here?'

'Yes, we're done.'

She left his office, angry and upset at the way things had turned out. It didn't matter that he wasn't blaming her…he was acknowledging that other people might. As for Michael, she would have to give him a call and ask him why he was doing this.

'Are you okay?' Katie gave her a concerned look as Saskia went to look in on her next patient. 'You've had a bit of a rough morning, but it could have happened to anyone, you know.'

'I'm fine, thanks, Katie. Or, at least, I will be. Do you know if young Tom is all right?'

Katie nodded. 'I rang the ward to see how he's settling in. I thought you'd want to know. He's responding to treatment—his blood pressure's gone back up towards a more normal level, and he's breathing more easily now.'

'That's good to hear. Thanks for checking up.'

Saskia made a conscious effort to calm down and concentrate on the problems of her next patient, a child who had taken a nasty tumble in the school playground. 'I'm going to have to put a few stitches in this cut,' she told the nurse. 'Would you prepare the suture kit for me?'

'Of course.'

Noah caught up with Saskia around lunchtime as she was leaving one of the treatment rooms.

'Hi, there,' he said with a smile. 'I was hoping you might be about ready for some lunch. Would you let me take you to our restaurant and treat you to something tempting and nutritious? From what I've heard, you might need a bit of pampering.'

'Oh, dear.' Her stomach gave a peculiar lurch. 'Does everyone around here know what's been going on?'

He nodded. 'I'm afraid news travels fast, especially in this place. That's why I bought you these.' With a flourish he produced a posy of flowers from behind his back. 'I thought you might need cheering up.'

Tears stung her eyes. 'That's so thoughtful of you, Noah. Thank you.' She held the beautifully wrapped freesias and breathed in the delicate scent. 'They're lovely—my favourites.'

'Really? I didn't know that. I'm glad you like them.' He crooked his arm and held it out to her. 'Shall we go? They're doing casseroled beef and vegetables as the special today. You're not vegetarian, are you?'

She shook her head. 'No. Just let me put these in water, and I'll be with you.'

'Okay.'

She went to find a vase from near the nurses' station and set the flowers down on the desk where they could be enjoyed by everyone who passed by. Tyler was there, slotting a file in a drawer, and he turned to cast a thoughtful glance in Saskia's direction.

'I wouldn't like you to misconstrue what I'm saying,' he murmured, 'but I think you need to tread carefully. Noah's a good man and a great doctor, but he does have something of a reputation when it comes to women. I'd hate you to jump from the frying pan into the fire.'

'I'll bear it in mind,' she said. Then she walked away from the desk to where Noah was waiting patiently for her, and all the time she was conscious of Tyler's smoke-dark gaze boring into her back.

CHAPTER FIVE

'How did your lunch with Noah go yesterday? Did he manage to make you feel better?' Tyler flicked a sideways glance at Saskia as they drove along the main road towards the coastal town. There was a small frown around his eyes, though whether that was from him needing to concentrate on the road or something to do with her and Noah she couldn't guess. 'I meant to ask you in the afternoon,' he said, 'but things were a bit hectic in the department and on the way home we were too busy discussing other things—it being your first day.'

'And an eventful one at that,' she acknowledged soberly. 'But, yes, it was thoughtful of Noah to try to cheer me up.' She smiled, remembering how Noah had persuaded her to taste a luscious fruit tart and whipped cream and teased her out of her melancholy with tales of his exploits as a junior doctor. 'He can be very entertaining. He made me see that these things happen, things go wrong and I shouldn't take it all personally. I think maybe I've tended to be a bit uptight lately with everything that's happened.'

'That's hardly surprising in the circumstances. You've had to come to grips with an awful lot just lately.'

'Yes.' She looked out of the window, watching the

scenery pass by. It was a murky, cold day, with a brisk wind blowing, but nothing could detract from the beauty of the bay with its clear, emerald waters and long stretch of white sand. 'Perhaps I should take more time to appreciate this lovely island.'

'You should. That's a good idea.' Tyler turned the car off the main road and negotiated a maze of streets. 'I often go for a walk by the harbour when I want to clear my head.'

She couldn't imagine him needing to do that. He always seemed so very much in control of everything. 'I'll try to find time to do that,' she said. They were nearing their destination and that prompted her to ask, 'Who is it that we're going to see today? You mentioned the paramedics were having some difficulty treating a patient.'

'That's right. They were called out to a man who has a heart problem, but he didn't respond to the medication they gave him. We're quite close by so I said I'd come out to look at him.'

He drove along a wide avenue and drew the car to a halt behind an ambulance that was parked by the roadside. Quickly, they gathered up their medical kit and hurried into a small semi-detached house.

'Okay, can you fill me in on what's happening here?' Tyler asked as they approached a paramedic who was frowning at the readout on the defibrillator. Another medic was giving their patient oxygen through a mask.

'This is Simon Jenkins,' the paramedic told him. 'He was complaining of chest pain, headache and dizziness, as well as feeling sick.'

'Has he actually been sick?'

The paramedic nodded. He frowned, pressing a hand to his temple as though to relieve a throbbing pain.

It seemed he, too, wasn't feeling too good. 'He's also short of breath and complaining of difficulty breathing. We've checked out his heart rhythm and it's showing atrial fibrillation, but he's not responding to calcium channel blockers.'

'Okay, thanks.' Tyler knelt down and spoke quietly to Simon, who was fading in and out of consciousness. 'How are you doing, Simon? Can you hear me?' Worryingly, there was only a mumbled response and Tyler began to swiftly check him over.

Saskia went down on her knees beside the man, hastily setting up an intravenous line. Atrial fibrillation meant that the electrical impulses from the heart were disorganised, causing the muscles in the heart to quiver. In turn, this meant the circulation of blood around the body became inadequate, and if this went on for too long there was a strong possibility he could suffer a stroke.

Out of the blue, Simon's limbs started to twitch and Tyler said urgently, 'We need to give him diazepam. He's having a seizure.'

Saskia nodded, but even as she prepared the injection she was thinking about why the drugs he had already been given had not done their job. Something was wrong somewhere. She frowned. Even the paramedics seemed to be out of kilter, as though they were both feeling under the weather. Perhaps it was the heat in the room that was causing the trouble.

She looked around. They were in the living room and because of the chilly morning Simon had lit the wood-burning stove. It burned softly, filling the room with suffocating warmth so that she, too, was beginning to feel lethargic. The room was neat, clean, but near the stove the wall was grubby, with dark, sooty marks spoiling the paintwork. Seeing this, all the connections suddenly came together in her brain.

'Someone needs to switch off the fire,' she said in a brisk, insistent tone. 'I think it could be unsafe, giving off carbon monoxide, and that might be why he didn't respond to the drug he was given earlier.' It was a worrying situation. Once convulsions had started, the man's chances of recovery were dire unless they could counteract the poison—they had to get him out of there, fast.

Tyler was administering the diazepam, but he looked around, suddenly on the alert, and said, 'You're probably right. Let's get him outside into the fresh air—and we need to open the windows in here.'

The paramedics wheeled the man outside, where they went on giving him lifesaving treatment, but after a while Tyler shook his head and said, 'I'm going to call for the air ambulance. At least the seizure's stopped, but his blood pressure's still way too low and his circulation's totally inadequate. The carbon monoxide could have exacerbated the atrial fibrillation, but going on his medical history he's going to need catheter ablation to deal with this heart problem once and for all.' He frowned. 'We'll go with him in the helicopter to try to stabilise him on the journey.'

Saskia nodded, but at the same time her heart gave a small jump. They would be taking Simon to the hospital where her brother and his wife were patients. Might there be a chance she could look in on them while she was over there?

She tried to put those thoughts from her mind while she concentrated on setting up a fluid line to help improve Simon's blood pressure. Tyler was right. None of the measures they were taking would deal with the basic condition that was causing his heart rhythm to go awry. That would only be successfully managed by eliminating the abnormal tissues within his heart, a procedure that had to be done in the electrophysiology suite at the main hospital in Cornwall.

To her relief, the air ambulance touched down close by a few minutes later and they were able to transfer their patient to the well-equipped aircraft.

'You did well back there, picking up on the carbon monoxide,' Tyler said quietly once they were airborne. He checked Simon's vital signs. 'His colour seems to be improving a bit now with the oxygen, but if he'd stayed in that room for just a little longer I think it would have been the end for him. In fact, we might all have been in trouble if you hadn't pointed it out.'

She nodded cautiously, a small shudder going through her at the thought of what might have happened. 'I think it was the heat from the fire that alerted me. I was beginning to feel drowsy, and I couldn't work out why that was happening. Perhaps, being a woman, I'm more susceptible than you and the paramedics.'

'It's possible, though you were closer to the stove than any of us.' He pulled his mobile phone from his pocket. 'I'd better give the police a ring and ask them to sort out some action to make the fire safe or at least stop anyone from using it.'

'Yes, I was thinking of doing that myself—though until today I hadn't realised you could get carbon monoxide poisoning from those kinds of stoves.'

'It can happen if the stove's badly fitted. The gas is formed when wood or any other kind of fossil fuel burns without a good supply of air.'

'I'll bear that in mind if I ever get around to buying one. They're really popular these days.' She looked at Simon and checked the monitor. 'His blood pressure's improving. Hopefully, by the time we get him to the hospital he'll be stable enough to cope with the preparations for the ablation. I expect he'll need to be on blood thinners for a few days before they can do it.'

Tyler nodded. 'You know, since we're going to be at the hospital, you might want to take the opportunity to pay a visit to your brother and his wife.'

Relieved, she smiled at him. 'Thanks for suggesting that. I was wondering if it would be possible for me to go and see them.' It had been thoughtful of him to make the offer. 'I've been feeling quite anxious over the last couple of days,' she admitted. 'Apparently my brother has some kind of infection that's pulling him down, and when I rang yesterday the doctors were quite worried about Megan as well. She's developed some unexpected bruising and swelling to her abdomen. I'd really like to find out what's happening.' She shook her head, as though that would help to rid her of these anxieties. 'I just don't know how I would tell the children if anything were to happen…'

He reached out to her and gently squeezed her hand. The simple gesture melted her heart and made her feel incredibly sorry for herself. Sometimes, over these last few weeks, she'd felt intensely alone, as though her life was one long runaway roller-coaster ride and she was powerless to stop its relentless course. If only she had someone to lean on, someone who might take away some of the burden… It was a foolish, impossible dream, and she was ashamed of herself for succumbing to that moment of weakness.

'It's amazing you've been able to concentrate on any-thing at all lately,' he said. 'If you need anything at any time, Saskia, or if you just want to talk, I want you to know that I'm here for you. Don't suffer in silence.'

'Thank you.' She was grateful for his consideration, and the warmth and compassion in his touch and in his voice helped to lift her spirits a little. Tyler might not actually be able to do anything to help but she did ap-preciate his offer.

She stared out of the window and tried to divert her thoughts by gazing down at the craggy Cornish coast-line. Soon they were flying over green fields, broken up by wooded valleys, isolated hamlets and the occasional white-painted farmstead. Gradually, as they moved in-land, the nature of the landscape changed, with the ham-lets giving way to towns, until at last she saw ahead of her the sprawling city of Truro. Any time now they would set down at the hospital where they would offload their passenger.

'Are we all set?' Tyler asked.

'Yes.'

The helicopter landed and they quickly climbed down onto firm ground, handing over their patient to the waiting medical team.

Tyler walked with them to the emergency unit, tell-ing the doctor in charge everything he needed to know about Simon's condition. Saskia followed in his wake. Then they stood back and watched as their patient was wheeled away to the resuscitation room.

'Shall we go and get coffee?' Tyler asked after a while. 'You might want to give yourself a few minutes to compose yourself before you go and see your brother and Megan.'

'That sounds like a good idea.' She looked around the emergency room, a little anxious now that they were in Michael's territory. She certainly didn't want to hang around here any longer than necessary, because every minute meant there was more danger of running into him. Her head felt muzzy and she wasn't in a fit state to deal with him right now.

She'd spoken to him on the phone, wanting to know why he was trying to jeopardise her career, but the answer had been simple. 'I want you back here,' he'd said.

That was never going to happen. It had been bad enough after the accident when Sam and Megan had been brought here. She'd had to liaise with Michael, and that had brought all kinds of tensions to the fore. He hadn't been responsible for saving their lives, but he had been the man in charge and she'd not been able to avoid him initially. She was beginning to bitterly regret ever getting involved with him.

'Are you okay?'

Startled out of her reverie, she looked at Tyler. 'Yes, I'm fine. Coffee would be great. It might help to clear my head—perhaps I'm still suffering some of the effects of the carbon monoxide.'

'Fresh air will help. We'll find a table by an open window.'

They went to the restaurant and Tyler picked out sticky buns to go along with their coffee. 'That should give you a bit of a boost,' he said, smiling as he slid a plate towards her. He stirred brown sugar crystals into his coffee and said cautiously, 'You seemed distracted back in A and E. Were you worried you might come across Michael Drew?'

'Yes, I suppose I was.' She was surprised by his per-

ception. 'Not worried, exactly, but I really don't want
to have to deal with him just now.'

He gave her a thoughtful look. 'Had you been dat-
ing for some time?'

'About a year. He seemed like a good man, caring
and attentive, and at one time I thought we had a good
chance of being happy together.' She frowned. 'But he
started to become possessive, wanting to know who
I was with and where I was going. That was just the
beginning of it. Later he tried to tell me what kind of
clothes I should wear and how much make-up I should
use. He said we needed to spend more time together and
tried to stop me from seeing my friends.'

Tyler pulled a face. 'That sounds pretty awful. I'm
not surprised you wanted to break free.' He tested his
coffee for heat and then took a careful swallow. 'Have
you dated anyone since?'

'No. He was the last. After the way things were,
I'm not sure I want to get heavily involved with anyone again. It seems to me that relationships are fraught
with problems and none of them turn out really well.'
She grimaced. 'I should have learned a lesson from my
parents' example. Somehow they managed to make a
complete mess of things.'

'Oh?' His expression was quizzical. 'What went
wrong with them?'

She wriggled her shoulders, as though that would rid
her of the disturbing memories. 'I suppose, basically, it
was that my father couldn't settle for one woman. His
head was easily turned.' Her lips flattened. 'He always
made promises, said he was going to change, but he
never did, and in the end my mother decided enough
was enough.'

'I'm sorry.' His blue gaze was sympathetic. 'That must have been difficult for all of you, not just for your mother.'

'Yes, it was. Sam and I were still young, and we saw my father fairly often at first after he left. But that changed. He couldn't stick to arrangements that had been made. Instead, he'd come up with all sorts of reasons why he hadn't been able to come to a birthday celebration or why at the last minute he couldn't come with us on a trip to the zoo, or whatever.'

'There were a lot of disappointments, then?'

'Yeah.' She took a sip of her coffee. 'Don't get me wrong, I love my father—I just don't have any respect for him. And I think it's taught me to be cautious around men. The experience with Michael just intensified that feeling. I can't say that I hold out any hope for a relationship with long-term stability.'

He frowned. 'But your mother married again, you said. Doesn't that do anything to make you feel better about things?'

She made a wry smile. 'A bit, I suppose, but I can't help seeing her weaknesses—the way she let my father ride roughshod all over her—and I don't want to go down that same route. She's not good at sorting her life out. She used to look on me as a kind of agony aunt, someone who could help her to work through her problems. I did what I could, but for myself I couldn't bear to be tossed this way and that on a wave of emotional upheaval every time my love life went wrong. My mother went to pieces when my father strayed, and I'm not going to let that happen to me. I know the pain she went through.'

She bit into the glazed bun, relishing the sweet, sugar

rush of energy that it promised. She hadn't realised how much she'd needed to get that outburst off her chest, and now, surprisingly, she felt much better.

She looked up, suddenly very conscious of Tyler watching her, his gaze lingering on the moist curve of her lip, and for a moment or two she floundered uncertainly, licking away any stray sugar crystals with the tip of her tongue.

He seemed to give himself a mental shake. 'So you have everything under control now, do you? You more or less know where you go from here, how you're going to deal with situations?'

She gave a short laugh. 'Heavens, no. I wish I did. I just get on and deal with stuff and hope I'm doing the right thing. I found out a long time ago that there's no point in making plans if they're going to be constantly overturned.' She put down the bun and licked the stickiness from her fingers. 'All I've ever wanted, really, is to make sure that my brother is okay. We're quite close in age and we turned to one another when we were small and our mother was too busy with her own problems to notice when we needed comforting or cosseting. So we're very close. I need to know that he's going to be all right.'

Tyler studied her briefly. 'It seems to me he's lucky to have a sister like you.'

'Yeah?' She smiled. 'Maybe.' She picked up her bun once more. 'It'll be good to see him today, anyway. I'll try not to keep you waiting for too long.'

'That's okay. I want to check up on Simon and one or two other patients I've transferred recently, just to see how they're doing. And then I'll have to organise the transport back home.'

'Oh...yes, of course. I hadn't thought about that.' She stared at him, a horrible thought creeping into her mind. They wouldn't be flying back, would they? And that left just one way of crossing from the mainland to the island—a way that didn't bode well for her, because her travel sickness pills were in the medicine cupboard back home. It hadn't occurred to her that she might need them at some point today. 'Um...how will we be getting back?'

'I'll book us a couple of seats on a motor launch. They run fairly frequently from the mainland to the islands.'

She was quiet for a while, absorbing that. How on earth was she going to cope with the journey by sea? Car travel she could manage to a point, and the helicopter ride hadn't been too bad, but a sea crossing...no way. She'd always had trouble with boats of any kind.

'Something's on your mind.' Tyler was watching her and his blue gaze missed nothing. 'Out with it. What is it that's bothering you?'

'Um...I get...uh...I have...' She sighed and decided to come right out with it. 'I have a bit of a problem with seasickness. Usually, it wouldn't matter, but unfortunately I...uh...didn't bring my tablets with me today. I wasn't expecting that we'd be going anywhere but locally.'

His eyes narrowed on her thoughtfully. 'I knew there was something you were keeping back at the interview when James mentioned travelling to the off islands. You suddenly went very quiet.'

'I'm sorry.' She sought for a way around the situation. 'It's not usually a problem—I mean, the tablets work well for me...as long as I take them in good time...

if I have some warning that I'll be needing to travel, that is. It doesn't mean I can't cope with sea trips.' She frowned. 'Except…maybe today.' She didn't relish the idea of spending two hours or so leaning over the side of the boat with her stomach heaving. It would be unpleasant at best and undignified to say the least. 'I…uh…perhaps I'll be able to sort something out with the pharmacy here.'

'A bit of a problem, you said. How badly do you suffer from it?'

She winced. 'It's pretty bad.'

'Hmm.' He was quiet for a moment or two, thinking things through. 'As you know, most of the travel sickness medications take a while to work, but I could give you an injection. It just means you'll be quite drowsy for a while, and you might even want to sleep, but we can cope with that, I expect.'

The idea of falling asleep while she was with Tyler and supposedly at work didn't appeal at all. She said carefully, 'I think I'd prefer to stick with my usual prescription if you don't mind. Maybe I could take the tablets before I go to see Sam and Megan, and then by the time we go on board the launch I'll be better able to cope.'

'Okay.' He nodded. 'I'll sort it out for you—if I go and get the tablets for you now, you can take them with your coffee.'

'Thanks.' Troubled, she glanced at him. 'Will this make a difference to my keeping this job?'

He made a face. 'It all depends whether we can work out some way of managing the unexpected. Perhaps you could take the tablets as a matter of course when you

know we're going to be on call? That way you'll be covered, even if we don't need to use the medical launch.'

'Yes, I could do that.'

'Or you could use a hyoscine skin patch, which will
last for up to seventy-two hours. Either way, we'll have
to see how the medication affects you. If it makes you
too drowsy and unable to think clearly, we might have
a problem. We'll just have to wait and see how things
work out.'

It wasn't the most encouraging answer but at least he
was being honest with her and it was all out in the open
at last. She had no idea how things would turn out, but
given the start she'd had in this job it was beginning to
look as though it would take a miracle for her to keep it.

Tyler left her in order to go over to the pharmacy,
but he was back shortly with the tablets and she swallowed them gratefully. 'Thanks,' she said. 'I'm sure I'll
be fine now for the journey back.'

He nodded and glanced at his watch. 'You'd better
go and see your brother and his wife. I hope things are
going better for them by now.'

'So do I.' She hurried away, anxious to know what
was happening.

The breath caught in Saskia's throat at the sight of her
brother. He was propped up in bed when she went into
the intensive care unit, his dark hair spiky against the
white pillow. He looked gaunt and his skin was pallid.
His eyes were closed and there were rasping sounds
coming from his chest.

'He's very breathless,' the nurse told her. 'There's
a lot of fluid on his lungs and the doctor's had to put
in another chest tube to drain the infection. He's on

very strong antibiotics and we're all hoping they'll do the trick, but I'm afraid the doctor is very concerned about him.'

'Thank you for being honest with me. I know you're looking after him really well.'

She went over to her brother and gently squeezed his hand. 'I need you to get better, Sam,' she whispered. 'We're all counting on you to fight this.' He didn't answer, and she guessed he was too exhausted to acknowledge her. He'd been through such a lot of late—a terrible chest injury that had left him fighting for his life, with only the skill of a watchful surgeon to keep him from slipping away. And now this.

She stayed with him for a while, distressed by the sight of all the tubes and wires that were attached to him. As a doctor, she knew why they were there, what they were for, but it was heart-breaking to see someone she loved in such a vulnerable state.

'The children are always asking about you and they send you their love,' she told him. 'They've made some cards and presents to bring with them next time they come here. Please try to get better. We need you.'

After a few minutes, when the doctor came to administer medication via the catheter in Sam's hand, Saskia left his bedside and went to find Megan.

Her sister-in-law was in an equally poor condition and Saskia was more worried than ever when she saw the monitor readings.

'What's caused her to go downhill like this?' she asked the nurse. 'Has she been bleeding internally?' The bruising and swelling both pointed to that as a reason for Megan's problems.

'I'm afraid so,' the nurse answered. 'The tests we

took yesterday revealed a leak from one of the pelvic blood vessels. She's had surgery to put it right, but it looks as though there's another problem to worry about—an abscess has formed.'

Saskia grimaced. That was very bad news, coming on top of all her injuries, and the chances of Megan making a good recovery were lessening by the hour. 'But they've put in a drainage tube?'

'Yes.' The nurse nodded. 'And she's receiving antibiotics to try to stop the infection.'

'Okay. That's good… Thank you.'

None of it was good, though, and Saskia left the unit feeling deeply unhappy. Megan was a lovely, sweet-natured young woman, who made everyone around her feel better. To see her suffering like this was soul-destroying.

Her eyes were bright with unshed tears. By now she'd hoped and prayed that both Sam and Megan would be starting to heal and would be showing signs of recovery, but that prospect seemed further away than ever. It was heart-breaking to see them this way.

'You've no colour in your face at all,' Tyler commented when she met up with him by the main entrance to the hospital a few minutes later. He looked concerned as he studied her bleak expression. 'Was it bad—worse than you expected?'

She nodded, unable to find her voice just then.

'Perhaps you should sit down for a while,' he said. 'There's a bench seat over there, where we can be private.' He led her to a quiet, landscaped corner of the hospital grounds, set back in a green, wooded area to one side of the car park.

She sat down and as he came to sit beside her he

searched her face closely once more. 'Are you warm enough? You're looking really peaky.'

Her shoulders lifted almost imperceptibly. She didn't know what she felt just then. She felt numb inside.

'They're both fighting for their lives,' she whispered. Tears began to slowly spill down her cheeks. 'Right now, I don't even know if they're going to make it.'

'I'm sorry,' he said. He put his arms around her and drew her to him, cradling her head against his chest. She felt the warmth of his body seep into her, and the firmness of his embrace was deeply comforting, shoring her up and giving her the strength that she needed to go on.

'I couldn't bear it if anything were to happen to Sam,' she whispered. 'He's everything to me. And Megan—we're like sisters… How would I cope without them?'

'Don't think like that,' he said softly. 'You need to be strong, for yourself and for the children. They mustn't see that you have any doubts. You're all they have.'

'But what if I can't do it?' The anguish showed in her face and he lifted a hand to gently caress her cheek.

'Of course you can do it. I've seen the way you are with those children, and you won't let them down. You'll do whatever's necessary.'

'You seem so certain of that.' Her mouth trembled and she looked at him through tear-drenched eyes. 'I w-wish I could b-be so sure.'

He moved closer, and it was clear her distress had had a profound effect on him. 'You're not on your own in this,' he said huskily. 'I'm here for you. I promise you, Saskia, I'll help you through it, any way I can.' His gaze lingered on the soft, vulnerable curve of her mouth and slowly, as though he simply couldn't help himself, he bent his head and gently claimed her lips.

The kiss was tender and sweetly seductive, easing her troubled soul like an exquisite soothing balm. He gave a soft, shuddery sigh, as though he'd fought a battle within himself and lost, and now he was like a man drowning in need.

She, too, lost herself in that kiss, in his comforting arms, in the hands that caressed her and invited a response. She was safe here, nothing bad could happen because he was holding her and he would keep the world at bay. It was like an unspoken promise that hung on the air between them.

He stroked her hair, his fingers sliding into the silky curls at the nape of her neck. 'You'll get through this,' he said, his voice threaded with emotion. 'Please, don't cry. You'll be all right.' He held her as though he would take all of her pain away. 'I hate to see you hurting like this…but you will overcome all these hurdles. I know you will—somehow we'll get through it, together.'

He couldn't know that things would turn out all right, could he? But she nodded faintly, accepting his reassurances, wiping the dampness from her cheeks with the tips of her fingers.

He cared about her enough to want to protect her, to help her to feel better, and for a few moments he had succeeded. She had been able to cast it all aside and think of nothing but him.

She carefully eased herself away from him and he watched her slowly straighten up. He moved towards her, edging closer, as though some inner compulsion was urging him to take her in his arms once more, but at the last moment he stopped himself. He seemed wary all at once, guarded, and locked in conflict with himself. She didn't know what to make of him. Was he already regretting his actions?

He hesitated before saying what needed to be said. 'I shouldn't have kissed you,' he said quietly. 'I should have known better, should have had more self-control. I'm your boss, your mentor, so to speak, and I overstepped the mark. I'm sorry, really sorry.'

'It's all right,' she murmured. 'I shouldn't have let my feelings show…we were both caught off guard. I was a bit off balance for a while, but I'm all right now.'

She wasn't all right, of course. Her lips still tingled from his kiss. Those few blissful moments in his arms had been wonderful, and for just a little while he had managed to blot everything from her mind.

But it should never have happened. He was right about that. That kiss had been extra-special, incredibly moving, tender and full of promise, but it wasn't right for them to have explored their feelings for one another that way.

It would be a mistake to get involved with anyone from her place of work, and especially with him, wouldn't it? He'd already said he was finding it difficult to reconcile his professional obligations with his feelings towards her.

It wouldn't be fair to either of them to let their emotions get out of hand, would it?

But wasn't it already too late?

CHAPTER SIX

'IS EVERYTHING ALL right between you and Tyler?' Noah came into the staffroom and saw Saskia standing by the coffee maker.

'Um…' Saskia thought about that for a moment or two. 'Yes, I think so,' she answered cautiously. She frowned. How had Noah managed to pick up on their difficulties? Hadn't she and Tyler been ultra-careful around one another ever since the day he'd kissed her? In fact, Tyler seemed to be going about his work in a perfectly normal fashion—she was the one who was finding things difficult.

'Why?' she asked Noah. 'What makes you think there's a problem?'

He shrugged lightly and helped himself to biscuits from the cookie jar. 'He's been quite tense these last few days, and that isn't like him at all.' He frowned. 'I suppose it could be that his plans for the house aren't going too well.'

'Plans? What plans?'

'Oh, you haven't heard about them? He wants to re-model the interior of his house to make it more light and open, but he isn't too sure yet how to go about it. I think he feels everywhere's too cluttered at the moment.' He

smiled. 'It isn't, of course, not by normal people's stan-
dards, but Tyler likes everything to be streamlined, very
neat and everything in its place. It's a thing with him.
He's the same with the garden.'

He propped himself up against the worktop, facing
her. 'You must know what he's like by now. Everything has to be faultless...a bowling-green lawn and
manicured flower borders. Even the trees and the shrub
garden are pruned to conform to his idea of perfect
symmetry. And have you seen his small patch of kitchen
garden? It looks as though it's been planted out along
regimental lines.'

'Oh, dear.' Saskia paused, holding the coffee jug motionless in mid-air. 'Yes, I'd noticed his beautiful garden. These things are important to him, aren't they?'
Absently, she poured coffee into her cup. 'I'm afraid I'm
probably to blame if he's not himself of late. I might
have upset the apple cart.'

He looked at her askance. 'How? Why? What could
you have done? It's certainly not your work—people
speak very highly of you.'

'Well, that's a relief.' She pulled a face. 'Although I
still think Tyler's waiting for me to trip up somehow.
But actually it's nothing to do with work.' She placed
the coffee jug back on its stand. 'The thing is, the children and I took Boomer for a walk the other day, and
I let him off the lead as we came back towards the
house—as I always do. Usually there's not a problem,
he'll wait for me by the front door...but not this time.
He must have picked up a scent of some sort because he
took off at top speed and before I could stop him he'd
dashed into Tyler's back garden.'

'That doesn't sound good.'

'No.' Her mouth turned down at the corners. 'There were a couple of loose slats in one of the fence panels—well, to be honest, I think Boomer was responsible for those in the first place. Whenever the postman calls Boomer tries to head butt his way out of the garden and onto the side path.'

She frowned. 'Anyway, he managed to get through the other day. Of course, I went after him—through the gate, not the fence,' she added hastily, and Noah's mouth curved. 'I'd no idea what was going on, or what he was after. But then the children admitted that some-one—probably Charlie, though he wouldn't own up to it—had left the rabbit's cage undone and Bugsy had es-caped about an hour earlier. They'd looked everywhere apparently, but couldn't find him.'

'Uh-oh…this is getting worse by the second.' Noah grinned as he took a cup down from the shelf. 'I sup-pose the rabbit had managed to find his way into Tyler's garden as well?'

She nodded. 'Oh, yes. By the time I caught up with him he'd had a whale of a time, eating his way through the carrots and peas, and when Boomer started chas-ing him the pair of them ran amok in the flower beds. The chrysanthemums and the dahlias were trampled into the ground. I felt awful.'

Noah tried unsuccessfully to suppress a smile. 'Oh, dear. What did Tyler have to say about that? I'd love to have seen the look on his face.'

Saskia's mouth twitched a fraction. 'He didn't say very much at all, to be honest. When Boomer started barking Tyler came out of the house and asked what was going on, but once he'd taken in what was happening I don't think he could trust himself to speak. He grabbed

Bugsy and put him back in his cage and then he just glared at the dog. I've a feeling he wanted to grab him by the scruff of the neck and shake him, but he managed to hold back. I'd been trying to catch Boomer all this time, but he thought it was a game and kept running off. Tyler was too quick for him, though. He just grabbed him by his collar and marched him over to me.'

'He must have said *something* to you.' Noah pushed his cup towards her on the worktop and she filled it with hot coffee.

She made a wry smile. 'Yes…well, he did say a few choice words between gritted teeth. The gist of it was along the lines of "How long was this tenancy supposed to last?" and then he muttered something under his breath. I didn't catch it all, but I think the end product might have been "There has to be some way the agreement can be broken."' She rolled her eyes. 'I'm hoping he didn't mean it. I did say that we would go over to his place and try to put the damage right as far as possible, but he looked horrified at the thought. I'm sure he expected us to make matters worse.'

Noah laughed. 'I wouldn't take it to heart. I've never known Tyler to lose his self-control or stay annoyed for too long. This will all blow over soon enough.'

'Hmm, maybe, but I wish there was something I could do to put things right. I'm wondering if I should offer to help him out with his plans for the house. If he's having trouble visualising them, I might be able to come up with a solution.'

'It could be worth a try.' Noah sipped his coffee. 'I know Imogen spends quite a bit of time at his place, but she obviously hasn't been able to come up with anything. She's pretty much like him—she's very organised. I think she suggested taking out some of the furniture and removing a bookshelf here and there, but he didn't seem too keen on that idea.'

Saskia's brow furrowed. Imogen—Dr Lancaster—seemed to be the one person Tyler trusted. He was always pleasant to her and seemed to be in a good mood whenever she was around. But, then, Imogen probably never put a foot wrong. She was always perfectly groomed, her hair was sleek and smooth, and she ran her cardiovascular clinic with flawless efficiency. She was probably Tyler's ideal woman. A wave of depression rolled over her.

'Does that bother you—about Imogen seeing Tyler outside work?' Noah's voice cut into her thoughts and she came back to earth with a bump.

'I…I'm not sure,' she hedged, aware that he was watching her carefully. 'Maybe. A bit.' She didn't want to own up to her true feelings, but Noah seemed to see quite easily through her subterfuge.

'You've fallen for him, haven't you?' His mouth made a rueful shape. 'Perhaps I should have guessed before this.'

'I don't know what I feel,' she murmured. 'I'm not looking to get involved with anyone.'

'No, maybe not.' He gave her a wry smile. 'I had the feeling I wouldn't get anywhere with you…but I'm here for you, you know, any time you need a friend.'

'Thanks, Noah.' She stroked his arm lightly. 'And I do appreciate you listening to me. You've been a great help.' She hesitated. 'I'm sorry if you had any other expectations.'

'Don't worry about it.'

She went to rinse out her cup at the sink. 'I'd better

get back to work,' she said. No doubt he would work his charm on some other young woman. It was his nature not to be downhearted for too long.

And at least he'd given her an idea as to how she could make things up to Tyler. She left him to his coffee and went back to A and E.

'Would you come and take a look at the woman in room four?' Katie asked as soon as she saw Saskia. 'I'm worried about her. She's complaining of nasty chest pain and aching in her jaw, but according to the ECG readout there's no sign of a heart attack. She has a history of high blood pressure and she keeps feeling faint.'

'Okay, I'll come right away.'

Saskia followed Katie into the treatment room and could see at once that the woman was in a great deal of pain, too restless even to sit comfortably on the bed. She was in her late forties, with dark hair that clung damply around her face. Katie was encouraging her to breathe oxygen through a face mask but she put that briefly to one side to answer Saskia's questions.

'Can you tell me what happened?'

'I've been feeling ill for a few days.' She was clearly breathless. 'I thought it might be flu, but then I started to get this pain in my jaw. It's a horrible, throbbing pain. But the pain in my chest is the worst.'

Saskia nodded. 'Can you describe it?'

'It's unbearable. It was like a ripping, tearing sensation, and now…now it's really awful, the worst ever.' She paused to get her breath, and Saskia quickly ran the stethoscope over her chest.

'All right, Mrs Miller—Jenny…' She smiled at her. 'I'll give you something stronger for the pain, and I'm going to arrange for you to have X-rays and a CT scan.'

Jenny's blood pressure was dropping, and while that would be a good sign in someone who was usually hypertensive, in this case Saskia felt it was something else entirely.

'It's bad, isn't it?' Jenny slumped against her pillows. Her features were grey and drawn with anxiety and beads of perspiration had broken out on her brow. 'Am I going to die?'

Saskia laid a hand on her shoulder. 'You're very poorly, but nothing bad is going to happen to you while I'm looking after you.' She was almost tempted to cross her fingers behind her back as she said that. If what she suspected was true, this woman was in real, life-threatening danger. Above all, she had to keep her from becoming severely stressed. 'In the meantime, I just want you to rest and not worry about anything.'

Jenny nodded wearily and went back to gulping oxygen through the breathing mask.

As soon as she had arranged for a porter to take Jenny along to Radiology, Saskia went in search of Tyler. Katie was right to be concerned about this patient—something dire was going on here and if her tentative diagnosis was correct they would have to act super-fast. Jenny's life could be at stake.

She found Tyler in one of the other treatment rooms and as she entered he looked up, sending her an oblique glance. 'Is something wrong?' he asked, and she nodded.

'Okay, give me a minute.' He finished checking his patient's reflexes and then asked the nurse to admit the man to the observation ward.

Stepping out of the treatment room, he gave Saskia a narrowed look, and she guessed he thought it unusual that she should come in search of him. So far, whenever possible, she had tried to sort out any problems for herself without involving him. She'd wanted to show him that she didn't need to be constantly monitored, that she was perfectly capable of acting independently.

Now, though, she was afraid this was something she couldn't deal with on her own. Jenny would need expert surgical intervention.

'What's the problem?' he asked. His manner was brisk and professional, and she found herself missing his former friendly approach.

'My patient is very seriously ill, and I don't believe we can treat her here, in this hospital. I think we need to call out the air ambulance.'

'Uh-huh. Tell me more.'

Quickly, she outlined Mrs Miller's condition. 'She isn't showing the symptoms of a heart attack, but I'm afraid it could be far worse.'

He frowned. 'There are several things it could be—an ulcer, gallstones. They can cause severe pain. We wouldn't need to call out the helicopter for those.'

'But she does have a heart murmur. What if it's a tear in the aorta? That's a possibility, too, isn't it? She described a tearing pain.' The aorta was the heart's major blood vessel and anything going wrong with that could have dreadful consequences.

'Hmm…do you think you might be making too much of this? People's descriptions of pain aren't necessarily accurate. It's all subjective.'

She stood her ground. 'Either way, it will show up on the CAT scan. I think you need to come and look for yourself.'

'You've had the results already?' He started to walk with her to the radiology unit.

'Not yet, but I'm fairly certain they'll show a problem with the artery. If we're lucky it has only just started leaking—that could be why her blood pressure is dropping. If not, she might only have a few hours left.'

He frowned. 'You seem very sure about this.'

'I've seen it before. That's how I've learned to be on the lookout for it.'

They went into the CAT scan booth and after studying the films on the monitors for a few minutes Tyler made a whistling sound through his teeth. 'There's an aneurysm—here, do you see? The artery's blown at a weak spot—probably due to the persistently high blood pressure.'

He moved away from the screens and spoke briskly. 'Okay, let's put in a couple of large-bore IV lines and get her started on beta blockers to reduce the forces on the arterial wall. We'll keep her on morphine for the pain.'

'I'll see to it.'

'Good. I'll alert the hospital in Truro that they need to have a team standing by.'

She nodded and hurried away, immensely relieved that he had listened to her. Her priority now was to prevent the tear in the artery from getting any worse.

By the time Tyler came back to her a few minutes later, she had done everything she could to stabilise their patient. 'Will we be going with her in the helicopter?' she asked, but he shook his head.

'They're sending over one of their cardiac specialists to stay with her on the journey. She'll go for surgery to repair the damage as soon as they arrive back at the hospital.' He studied her with renewed respect. 'That was well spotted. You might just have saved her life.'

'I hope so.'

Tyler spoke to Jenny for a while, reassuring both her and her husband, who had arrived at her bedside in a state of great anxiety. He promised them both that she would be well looked after. He answered all their questions and Saskia could see that they felt comforted by his compassionate, capable bedside manner. Then, when he judged they needed some time to talk things through, he excused himself and left them in the care of the nurse.

He walked with Saskia to the nurses' station. 'How are things with you? Have you heard anything more from the hospital about your brother and his wife?'

'There's been no real change,' she told him. 'The doctors have identified the specific bacterium causing Sam's infection and they're trying him on a different antibiotic. They've put him on diuretics to try to reduce his fluid load, but so far it's still an uphill struggle. It's much the same with Megan, too. The abscess doesn't seem to be responding to treatment, so they're having to try other drugs.'

'I expect it will take some time before you see any real results. At least things are no worse. Perhaps that's something to bear in mind.'

'Yes, I suppose so.'

He gave her a quick, cautious glance. 'If you need any help with getting over there to see them, I could arrange things for you with a friend who has a motor launch. I know how expensive it can be on the ferry. He'll just need to know when exactly you plan to travel.'

'Thanks, I appreciate that.' Grateful, she laid a hand

fleetingly on his arm, needing that brief moment of intimacy. He gave her shoulder a light squeeze in return.

'Any time. I'll do whatever I can.'

Despite the tension between them, he was keeping his word about helping her, and she appreciated that. He was a thoughtful, considerate man, and she didn't want to put up barriers between them. Even in the short space of time she'd known him she'd found herself looking for him, at home and at work, wanting to be near him.

She couldn't forget that kiss, the way he'd held her. It had been something special, deliciously tender, and even now she went hot all over at the thought of it.

It wouldn't do, of course. She was tormented by the knowledge that falling for someone like him could only ultimately lead her to pain and heartbreak. If they started a relationship and things went wrong between them she would be the one to pay the price. Her working life would become a nightmare.

If she didn't want to go through the problems she'd had with Michael all over again, she had no choice but to put up a wall of sorts between them.

The air ambulance arrived within a few minutes and she went with Tyler to hand over their patient to the specialist doctor. 'We have a team waiting, ready to operate,' the doctor said. 'We'll keep you informed, but judging by the scans you sent us she'll be in surgery for several hours.'

'Okay, thanks.' Tyler waited near to the helipad, watching as the aircraft took off. 'We should know one way or another by this evening,' he said, giving Saskia a quick, sidelong glance.

'Yes. I hope she makes it.'

Back at home later that day Saskia was on edge, waiting for news. Spotting Tyler out in the garden, doing what he could to tidy up the flowerbeds, she decided to go over to the fence to talk to him. Maybe he'd heard something.

'I haven't, not yet.' He finished staking and tying up the chrysanthemums and then straightened, looking around as he heard laughter and shouts coming from behind her. Becky and Charlie were playing cricket in the garden.

'They seem to be enjoying the fresh air.'

'Yes, I've been trying to encourage them to play outside more.' She'd pushed some cricket stumps into the lawn, hammering them into place, and the children were having great fun taking it in turns with the bat and ball. It only occurred to her now, as she watched them running about, that the once unspoiled grass was becoming worn down by the steady tramp of children's feet. What would Tyler think of that?

Swallowing down on her guilt, she tried to push those thoughts to the back of her mind and said, 'Actually, they're going off in about half an hour on a camping weekend. Some teachers from the school are taking quite a few of the children to explore the wildlife and natural vegetation of the island. It's part of a school project.'

'Are they looking forward to it?'

'I think so. I'm the one who's not so sure. I'll miss them.'

He smiled. 'Yes, I suppose you were bound to get attached.' His expression sobered as his glance moved over the house and garden and she wondered if he was imagining a different set of people living there...a couple without small children and pets perhaps?

'Do you still regret letting out your property?' she asked. 'I'm sorry about what happened the other day with the fence and the plants—but I suppose if you have tenants there are always going to be problems of some sort.'

'That's probably true,' he acknowledged. 'No, on the whole, I don't have any regrets.'

That was a bit of a relief, at least. 'How did you get into the property business?'

'By accident, I suppose. I inherited my house from my grandparents—my father's parents. I didn't need to live in it to begin with because I was working in another town, so that's when I first thought of renting it out. And then later I bought the property next door when it came on the market.'

She frowned. 'How is it that the house didn't go to your father?'

'He'd already died of a heart attack. So the property went to me and my sister—I offered to buy out Suzie's half and she was happy to go along with that.'

She looked at the mellow stone building with its Georgian-style windows. 'It's a beautiful old house.'

'Yes, it is. It needs work, some modernising, but it's solid, and I'm happy with it.'

She said curiously, 'It must have been difficult for your mother when your father died—for all of you. I would imagine you were fairly young at the time.'

'It's always upsetting when someone dies.' He pulled in a sharp breath. 'But, to be honest, life was never easy when he was around. He spent his time chasing dreams, starting up one failed business venture after another. For us, it meant that there was never enough money, and we were always moving from one place to another, following his schemes. We were never able to put down roots.'

'I'm sorry.' She was shocked. She'd always imagined that everything in his life had gone smoothly for him. 'I'd no idea. It must have been so hard for you.'

He shrugged. 'It was unsettling more than anything. You never knew what was around the corner, how long you'd be able to stay at the same school, whether you'd have to say goodbye to your friends and try to make new ones. But children do tend to adapt to circumstances fairly easily—I think it was much harder for my mother. She constantly had to start afresh, and after he died she was lost and vulnerable. I felt it was up to me to look after her and Suzie.'

Saskia absorbed all that, studying the varying emotions that crossed his face as he spoke. What part had his troubled childhood played in his continuing search for order in his life? It all seemed to make sense now.

'Saskia—' Caitlin burst in on her train of thought, coming over to where she was standing by the fence. She was rubbing her neck as though it ached, and at the same time she wriggled her shoulders as if that might ease discomfort of some sort.

'Are you all right?' Saskia asked. 'Do you have a neck ache?'

'It's just a muscle pain. I've got a bit of a headache—but I'll be fine. Perhaps I'll take a couple of painkillers...'

'Yes, okay. That sounds like a good idea.'

Caitlin came closer, saying quietly, 'I just thought that if Becky and Charlie are going away this weekend, would it be all right if I go and have a sleepover with a friend from school? You've met her—it's Gemma, the one who lives on a farm.'

Saskia lifted a doubtful brow. 'Are you sure you're up to it if you're not feeling well?'

'I'm fine. I really want to do this.'

Perhaps it would do her good to get away from the house for a while. 'Well, all right, then, if you're sure. Are your friend's parents okay with it?' Caitlin nodded, and Saskia added, 'Make sure you ring me if you change your mind and want to come home again. And you'd better give me Gemma's home phone number just in case.'

Caitlin bridled at that. 'So you don't trust me?'

Saskia put an arm around her, trying to calm her down. She sensed Tyler watching the exchange with interest…why was it she had so much difficulty dealing with Caitlin? She wanted to do the right thing, but somehow she always managed to strike sparks. 'Of course I trust you. It's just a precaution, in case I need to get in touch with them for any reason. I want to know you're safe.'

'Hmmph. Okay, I suppose. I'll go and get ready.' Caitlin turned away and walked quickly back to the house.

'She's not too happy, is she?' Tyler murmured. 'Is this the typical moody teenager syndrome?'

'I'm not sure.' Saskia stared thoughtfully after her. 'She's anxious about her parents, of course, and I think she's missing her friends from back home. She was settled in Cornwall and it's taking her a while to adjust to the move. I suggested they talk to one another via video chat. I'm pleased she's found new friends over here, though. It's a good start.'

'It is.' He studied her briefly. 'If you're going to be on your own this evening, perhaps you'd like to come over to my place for supper? I can't promise anything special—I don't do a lot of cooking—but I was planning on making pizza. It's simple enough that even I can do it. There's no point in both of us cooking, is there?'

Her heart gave a small lurch of anticipation at the prospect of spending time with him, but at the same time she was at war within herself. Should she accept his offer? Oughtn't she to steer clear of invitations like this one? The instinct of self-preservation kicked in and was nudging her, telling her that she should turn him down...but a wilful, tempestuous streak fought back. Did she really want to spend an evening by herself when he was just next door?

'I'd like that,' she said.

'Good.' He smiled. 'Give me half an hour or so to get freshened up?'

'Okay.'

She made sure Becky and Charlie had everything they needed for their weekend away, and then waved them goodbye when their driver came to pick them up. 'Have a good time,' she told them.

Caitlin had packed an overnight bag with hair straighteners, pyjamas and a change of underwear, and as soon as she had set off for the bus stop Saskia went to get changed.

She pulled on blue skinny jeans and a pretty beaded top, and spent a few minutes applying a light touch of make-up. She was looking forward to being with Tyler. In spite of all her misgivings and inner warnings, she wanted to be with him.

'Hi,' she said, when he opened the front door to her a short time later. 'Am I too early?'

'Of course not.' His gaze swept over her, his blue eyes appreciative. 'You look lovely,' he said.

Inside, she fizzed with elation at the compliment. 'Thanks.' He looked pretty good himself, in dark, beautifully cut trousers and a short-sleeved designer top.

He took a step back. 'Come in.' The hallway opened up to a closed-in staircase on one side, and further along the hallway a door led into a large lounge/dining room. 'This is the main room of the house,' he said, 'the one where I spend most of my leisure time—except for the kitchen, of course.'

She looked around. It was a high-ceilinged room, with tall Georgian windows and a beautiful feature fireplace. 'This is lovely,' she said. 'You've kept all the original features in here.' She daren't even think about what would happen if the children were let loose in this house. And as for Boomer...

'Yes, I wanted to keep the character of the place. It feels a bit oppressive to me, though, and I'd like to do something to modernise it and add some light.'

She nodded. 'Noah told me...he said you weren't sure what to do. I think it's really elegant.' The furniture was simple, minimal, even, but what there was had a classic, timeless feel to it.

He sent her a quick glance. 'You and Noah seem to be getting on pretty well...'

'Yes, he's easy to talk to.'

His mobile phone warbled just then and he said quickly, 'Excuse me. It might be the hospital.' He checked the display. 'Yes, it is.' He connected the call and listened carefully for a minute or two. 'All right, thanks for letting me know.'

'Is it Jenny Miller?' Saskia asked when he'd slipped his phone back into his pocket. 'Did she come through the operation okay?'

'Yes, she did. Obviously, she's still in Intensive Care, and they're concerned about her blood pressure and respiration, but at least she came through the surgery.' He sent her a long, assessing look. 'If it hadn't been for you noticing the signs, it's quite likely she might not even have reached that far.'

She breathed a sigh of relief. 'I'm really glad for her.' A high percentage of people didn't survive when they suffered a tear in the main artery, so the fact that Jenny had been able to undergo surgery was a huge blessing—and a great weight off her mind. 'That's wonderful news.'

'It is.' He reached for her and gave her arms a gentle squeeze. They stood there for a while, not moving, simply basking in the moment, until at last Tyler pulled himself together and said, 'Come on, let me show you the rest of the house. The kitchen's through here. The food should just about be ready.'

Still glowing inside from his thoughtful, tender embrace, she followed him out of the room.

The kitchen was warm, filled with the appetising smell of the pizza that was baking in the classical white-painted Aga. There was a large free-standing island unit in the middle of the room, painted a gentle cream colour, with drawers and cupboards in slatted wood, and around the walls were various bespoke pieces in a pleasing mixture of white and cream. To one side of the room, facing the wide window, there was a deep porcelain sink, and further along, near the glass doors that opened out on to a patio, there was a hand-crafted table and chairs.

'This is perfect,' she said, gazing around in awe. 'Why would you want to change anything in here?'

He looked surprised. 'I don't, particularly. I had this room renovated a couple of years ago, so it's probably the best room in the house. It's the rest I'm concerned about. I don't know how best to make changes without spoiling the original features of the house.'

'Perhaps you don't need to do much.' She helped him to set the table, putting out plates and cutlery, a bowl of salad and bread sticks. There was a warm intimacy to sharing the simple domestic tasks, and more than once she had to pull her attention back to their conversation. 'The curtains in the living room are quite heavy look-ing,' she murmured. 'You might want to change them for something much lighter in texture and colour, and maybe change the wall colour to something pale with just a hint of warmth.'

He waved her to a chair. 'You think that would make much of a difference?' He sounded doubtful as he drew the pizza from the oven and transferred it to a circular board. Next to that, he set down a plate of hot barbe-cued chicken wings.

'I do. I think you'll be surprised at the result. It might also lighten things up if you add two or three cush-ions—perhaps a pale green and cream silk would look good.'

'I might try that. Like you say, it wouldn't take much, but it could change the whole atmosphere of the room.' He gestured towards the food spread out on the table. 'Help yourself,' he said, coming to sit opposite her, 'but be careful—it's hot.' He started to cut the pizza into triangular wedges, then wiped his hands on a serviette and began to pour wine into two crystal wine glasses.

She watched his deft, supple movements, and then took a quick sip of wine to cover her uncertainty. There was something about his long, lithe body that made her senses quiver in anticipation.

'Thanks,' she murmured. 'It smells delicious. I didn't realise how hungry I was.' She bit into the pizza, savouring the melted cheese and luscious peppers. It was mouth-wateringly good and as she lifted her little finger to wipe a faint line of moisture from her lower lip, she looked up to see that Tyler was watching her with rapt attention.

'Pizza makes a tasty meal,' she said awkwardly, feeling self-conscious, 'but it's not always easy to eat it with any kind of elegance.'

'Oh, I don't know about that,' he murmured. 'It looks pretty good from where I'm sitting.'

Warm colour flowed along her cheekbones. 'Um… about the house,' she said huskily, searching for a way back to safe ground, 'perhaps you could open up the staircase in the hall—take off the wooden boards that have been used to enclose it and expose the spindles. It would give a completely different feel to that part of the house.'

He thought about that. 'You're very good,' he said, giving her a shrewd look. 'How do you know these things?'

She smiled. 'Well, I have to confess my mother has her own interior design business—she's always trying out new ideas, and I think over the years some of her knowledge must have rubbed off on me.'

'Ah…that explains it.' He picked up a chicken wing and bit into it. 'I expect it's in your blood.'

'Maybe.' It was fascinating to watch him eat, to see those strong, capable fingers curled with such finesse around a morsel of food. He licked the sauce from his thumb and forefinger, and then paused to study her thoughtfully once more. 'Are you okay?'

'Uh…yes, I'm fine.' She bent her head to add a helping of salad to her plate.

'I think you said you don't see too much of your parents—have they been to visit your brother and Megan? You haven't mentioned it.'

'Yes, they've been to see them a few times. My mother commutes—she has to leave someone else in charge of the business while she's away, but she always has her laptop with her so that she can keep an eye on things. And my father has flown over from Spain a couple of times.' She wiped her fingers on a serviette and then rested her hand by her wine glass. 'They're very worried.'

'I'm sure they must be.' He laid his hand on hers and gave her a long, thoughtful look. 'It's hard on all of you, but you seem to be managing to keep it all together. I think you're doing an amazing job with the children. It can't have been easy to take them on.'

'Thanks.' She smiled, comforted by the warm reassurance of his gentle touch. It took away all the loneliness of her situation. 'I've always been involved with them from the day they were born. They're the next best thing to having a family of my own.' She studied him in return. 'What about you? Do you ever think about having a family of your own one day?'

He was silent for a moment, reluctantly releasing her

hand and frowning as he turned his attention back to
his meal. 'I haven't given it a lot of thought,' he said at
last. 'I suppose I'm used to the solitude of this house.'
He smiled. 'Or at least I *was*. It's something else to think
of a horde of youngsters running around the place. I'm
not averse to it, but it would take some getting used
to, I think.'

'Perhaps it's different if they're your own.'

'Maybe.'

Deep down she might have been hoping for a different kind of answer, but she really ought to have known
better. Tyler was used to perfection in everything. He'd
moulded his life to the pattern he wanted, and he wasn't
likely to change that any time soon, was he? Why did
that bother her so much?

'I think I ought to give Caitlin a call and see if she
arrived safely at her friend's house,' she said, anxious
to shift the conversation to less controversial ground.
'She should be there by now.'

He nodded. 'I'll get the dessert.'

'Oh, I'm sorry.' She looked at him in dismay. 'I'll
phone her later. I didn't realise you'd made a dessert
as well.'

'No, no. Go ahead and make the call. It's important.' He gave her a quick smile before going over to
the fridge and taking out two glass dishes. 'I must confess the dessert is the simplest I could think of—fruit
salad with cream.'

'Mmm…my favourite, next to blackberry and apple
crumble.' She smiled as he speared a pineapple chunk
with a fork and let it float in the air irresistibly close
to her mouth. 'Oh, bliss.' She bit off the sweet fruit

and let the juice trickle down her throat. 'Mmm…
mmm…mmm.'

She laughed as he gave her a gleaming, wickedly
seductive look, and then she gave in to temptation and
finished off the delicious fruit. It was a delightful med-
ley of white and black grapes, orange, pineapple, pear
and apple. 'That was exquisite,' she said.

'I'm glad you liked it.' His mouth curved. 'It was
worth it, just to see the expression on your face.'

He started to clear away the dishes and murmured,
'Call Caitlin. I'll make coffee.'

She did as he suggested, keying in Caitlin's number,
but even though she let it ring for a while, there was
no answer. Frowning, she rang the house where Caitlin
was supposed to be staying and waited for a response.

'I was just about to ring you,' Gemma's mother answered. 'We've been expecting her for the last half-hour
or so, but she still hasn't arrived.'

They spoke for a minute or two more before Saskia
finally cut the call.

'What is it?' Tyler asked. He looked concerned.

'She hasn't arrived at her friend's house,' she told
him, fear rising in her throat. 'I must go and look for
her. I can't think what might have happened. It was only
a ten-minute ride by bus.' She stood up and started to
look around for her bag. 'I have to go.'

'Wait for a moment. There's no need to panic.' Tyler
came over to her and held her, wrapping his arms
around her when she would have run from the house.
'Let's take a minute or two to think this through.'

'But she… Anything could have happened. She
might have had an accident. She could have been ab-
ducted…' Her voice became frantic with worry.

'That's not likely in this small community. Calm down and we'll decide what we need to do.'

He'd said 'we'll decide' and that was what eventually made her stop wanting to rush out into the street. That and the warm pressure of his arms encircling her, soothing her and letting her know she wasn't alone.

'I must go after her.'

'We will. Let's assume she caught the bus, shall we? I'll drive us to the stop where she would have got off the bus, and we'll retrace her footsteps from there.'

'Yes, okay.'

He held her for a second or two longer and she laid her hand on his chest, reassured by the strong, steady beating of his heart. 'Thanks,' she said. 'Thanks for being here for me.'

He brushed her forehead with a gentle kiss. 'We'll find her.'

She nodded. 'Yes.' It was just intended as a comforting gesture, that kiss, wasn't it? But she could still feel the warm imprint of it on her skin and, whether it meant anything or not, she had already taken it into her heart.

CHAPTER SEVEN

TYLER DROVE TOWARDS the east side of the island, following the route that the bus would have taken. Darkness had fallen some time ago, making it difficult to see anything very clearly, but Saskia looked out of the car windows anyway, desperately searching for any sign of Caitlin.

Soon they left the town behind them and began to cross wild heathland as they approached the coastal area. Some half a mile further on, when the road petered out at the bus terminus where Caitlin would have been set down, Tyler drew the car to a halt. They set off to walk the rest of the way to Gemma's house.

'How far is it from here to the farmhouse?' Tyler asked. 'I'm assuming she would have followed the footpath.'

'It's about a ten-minute walk, I think. I feel so awful now for letting her come out here alone, but she's been here before and never had any problems and I felt sure it would be all right.' Her voice shook as she thought about what might have happened and she took a deep breath to calm herself. 'We need to follow the path towards the coast.'

From here they could already see the craggy outline of the cove up ahead. Moonlight shimmered on the water and silhouetted the sand dunes where marram grass blew this way and that in the wind that came in off the sea.

Saskia shivered a little. She had put on a thin jacket but it wasn't too effective against the evening breeze that had sprung up. 'Here, let me keep you warm,' Tyler said, putting an arm around her and drawing her against the warmth of his body.

His thoughtfulness cheered her. Having him hold her like this helped to take some of the chill from around her heart. He was warm and supportive and everything she needed just then. It was hard to believe that such a pleasurable evening could change so fast and turn into this awful nightmare.

They walked slowly, taking care to look all around them, searching for Caitlin in the bracken and among the hedgerows and all the while calling out her name.

'She wouldn't have run away, would she?' All kinds of dreadful scenarios were running through Saskia's head. 'I know she was unhappy, but I put it down to teenage angst, on top of everything else.' She couldn't conceal her anguish. 'I should have spent more time with her, tried to get her to talk to me a bit more.'

'Stop beating yourself up about it,' Tyler said. 'You did your best. And if she *was* trying to run away, where would she go? There's no ferry to get her to the mainland at this time of night.'

'No, I suppose you're right.'

They walked on, stopping every now and again to examine the hedgerows on either side, calling for Caitlin as they went. Saskia strained to distinguish the night sounds—the occasional hoot of an owl, the rustle of a shrew or a hedgehog scuffling through the undergrowth. But then, a few minutes later, there was another sound, a faint rasp, a murmuring of some sort.

'Wait…what was that?' She stood still, suddenly on alert. 'I think I heard something.'

There was only silence, though, and she called again. 'Caitlin, where are you?'

'Saskia…' It was very faint, a whisper almost, but she felt her heart begin to thud heavily.

'Did you hear that?'

Tyler nodded. 'I did. I think it came from over there, by the verge.' He pointed to where a hawthorn spread its branches, dipping low to the ground. There was a ditch covered in brushwood, filled with tangled undergrowth.

The low moaning sound came again. 'Sass…'

Through the darkness Saskia could barely make out a shadowy figure curled up on a bed of grass and leaves. The buckle of a belt shone dimly in the light of the moon, and elsewhere there was the faint gleam of a jewelled hair slide.

'Caitlin—thank heaven we've found you…' She moved forward to get closer to her, but her foot caught in the spreading roots of a gnarled tree and she gave a small moan of frustration as she struggled to release herself. 'Tyler, can you get to her?'

'Yes, it's all right, I have her.' Tyler clambered into the ditch and knelt down beside Caitlin. He carefully slid his hand under her head. 'Are you hurt?' he asked quietly. 'Can you tell us what happened?'

'I felt a bit dizzy…' Her voice was barely audible and she seemed to be having trouble thinking clearly. 'I must have fallen.' She closed her eyes, exhausted by the effort, and mumbled, 'My head hurts…and my ankle.'

'It's okay, Caitlin. You'll be all right now. I'll just quickly check you over and then we'll get you out of here.'

'Gemma—she'll be... I need to...'

By now Saskia had freed herself from the undergrowth and came to crouch down beside her niece. She held the girl's hand in hers, shocked by how cold it felt, as she soothed her and tried to ease her fears. 'I'll phone Gemma and let her know what happened. You don't need to worry about anything. We'll take care of whatever needs to be done.'

Tyler finished his examination. 'I don't think anything's broken,' he said, 'but I can't be sure about the ankle until we get her to the hospital. There has to be a reason for the dizziness, so we'd better be extra careful how we move her.'

Saskia nodded. 'Can we make a collar from my jacket? It's thin enough to fold.'

'Yes, we can try that.'

Saskia shrugged out of her jacket and rolled it into the shape of a neck collar. 'It's very makeshift, but it'll do for now,' she said. 'We'll have to tie the ends as best we can.'

When they were satisfied the collar was in place, it was at long last time to get Caitlin out of the ditch. 'I'll hold her head still while you lift her,' Saskia said.

'Okay, here we go.'

He carried Caitlin to the car and when Saskia opened the car doors he gently lifted the girl into the back seat and made sure she was safely secured.

Shivering a little, Saskia slid into the seat beside her. 'She's so cold from lying out there. It's been chilly today and the ground was damp.'

'Yes. She's suffering from hypothermia, I expect, but it's all right, I'll get a blanket from the boot. We'll keep her as warm as we can. In the meantime...' He took off his jacket and laid it over the ghostly-pale child, before going to rummage in the boot of the car.

He came back shortly and replaced his jacket with a new-looking fleecy blanket that he tucked around Caitlin. Then he draped his jacket around Saskia. 'Here, wear this. We can't have you collapsing from the cold as well.'

'Thanks.' Gratefully, she snuggled into it. It was still warm from his body and smelled faintly of his subtle cologne. It was the next best thing to being up close to him and for a little while she gave in to the guilty pleasure of imagining herself in his arms. She was beginning to realise that was what she wanted more and more, to be with him. She needed to have him near.

At the hospital, Tyler made sure that they were able to stay with Caitlin while she was being assessed. The makeshift collar was carefully exchanged for a proper one that would keep her neck stable, and then the team concentrated on trying to get her temperature back to normal. They gave her a warmed, humidified air/oxygen mix to inhale and wrapped her in special heat-retaining blankets. It was probably going to be a slow process, but Caitlin had been lying in the cold, damp ditch for some time and she was chilled to the bone.

Jason Samuels, the registrar on duty, took charge of Caitlin's care. He was quiet at first, making sure they were keeping tabs on her vital signs, but as time passed he recognised that she was a little more able to understand what was going on.

'I'll give you something for the pain in your ankle,'

he told her, 'and as soon as you've warmed up a bit we'll take you over to X-Ray. I don't think anything's broken, but it's as well to be sure.'

A nurse handed her a mug of drinking chocolate. 'This should warm you from the inside,' she said, and handed her some tablets to take along with it.

'Have you had trouble with dizziness before this?' Jason asked.

Caitlin hesitated before answering. She was still having some trouble getting her thoughts together. 'It's been happening for a while,' she admitted. 'On and off, ever since Mum and Dad's accident.'

Startled, Jason glanced at Saskia. 'It sounds as though there might be a connection.'

Saskia frowned. 'I thought it was just the once—I'd no idea you'd been having problems ever since then. Why didn't you tell me?'

Caitlin wriggled her shoulders. 'It wasn't too bad and I didn't want to make a fuss, not after what happened to Mum and Dad.' She huddled into her blankets. 'They've been so ill, and the dizziness was nothing really.'

'But you were in the car with them when it happened, weren't you?' Saskia was swamped with feelings of guilt for not investigating further. 'Did you feel a nasty jolt at the time?'

'Yes, but I was okay.' She looked thoroughly miserable. 'It was just…my head's been feeling a bit muzzy ever since then and I've been getting a ringing in my ears.' She sighed wearily. 'I thought it would go away. I've been feeling really irritable—I'm sorry I've been so bad-tempered, Sass. I didn't know what was wrong with me.'

'Sweetheart, I wish you'd told me.' Saskia gave her a gentle hug.

'I'm sorry. I didn't want to complain when Mum and Dad were so ill. I thought this is nothing compared to what they've been through.'

'I think we need to get an X-ray and maybe a CT scan, to try to find out what's going on,' Jason said. 'It does sound as if you might be suffering from whiplash, but we'll have a look at the films to be sure.' He turned to Saskia. 'I'm thinking it might be a good idea to keep her here overnight for observation, as she collapsed—just as a precaution, really, as her blood pressure's quite low. And, of course, we need to get her temperature back up.'

'Yes, I think you're right.' Saskia glanced at Caitlin. 'I'll pop home and pick up a few bits for you—everything you had with you is wet from being in the ditch. I could do that while you go down to Radiology—would you be okay with that? I'll be as quick as I can.'

'Yes, that's all right,' Caitlin agreed, adding anxiously, 'But you'll stay with me when you come back, won't you?'

'Yes, of course I will.' Saskia smiled at her. 'Don't worry about anything. I want you to try and get some rest.'

Tyler waited with her while Caitlin was wheeled away to X-Ray, and then they walked together back to the car park.

'I think she'll be all right,' Tyler murmured as he started the car. 'She's still a bit shivery, but I think we found her in time, before deep hypothermia set in. And if there'd been a lot of damage from the whiplash we would probably have seen more specific symptoms before this.'

'Yes, I expect you're right.' She sent him a quick look. 'I'm really glad you were with me when we went to look for her. It made me feel so much better, having you there.'

His gaze flickered over her. 'I wouldn't have let you go alone. I wanted to be with you.'

They arrived back at the house a few minutes later and Saskia slid out of the car, in a hurry to get into the house to sort out a few bits.

'I'll go and change into some clean clothes while you put a few things in a bag,' Tyler said as he walked her to her door. He made a rueful smile. 'After scrabbling around in a ditch and being caught up on thorns, I'm afraid these trousers are only fit for the dustbin.'

She made a face. 'I'm sorry about that. You looked great in them, too.'

He laughed. 'Really?' One dark brow quirked upwards. 'Well, that's good to know.' Instinctively, he moved closer to her, his hand moving as though he was going to slide it around her waist in a warm, intimate embrace...but at the last second he stopped, perhaps thinking better of it, and contented himself instead with sliding a hand down her arm in a light caress. 'I'm glad we managed to get some time together earlier,' he murmured. 'We should do it more often—but maybe without the drama next time.'

'I think you're right.' On impulse, she reached up and kissed him fleetingly on the mouth, her palms flattening on his chest. 'I don't know what I'd have done without you.'

She heard the breath catch in his throat. He seemed

stunned by that kiss, momentarily pinned to the spot, motionless. But when he would have responded and tugged her into his arms she swiftly evaded him.

'I should get these things for Caitlin.' She didn't know what had come over her, what had possessed her to kiss him, and she was awkwardly conscious that she'd stepped over the invisible line he'd drawn. But she wanted him, needed him—and all her thoughts of steering clear of men and being afraid for the future had flown out of the window since she'd got to know Tyler. Was this love? It had to be—it was all-encompassing, it filled her up, took over her being, and she'd never felt this way before, never cared for any man so much.

'I won't be long,' she said. 'I promised Caitlin we'd be back at the hospital before she knew it. Let yourself in if you're ready before me—I don't always hear the doorbell if I'm upstairs.'

'Uh…yeah…okay.'

As landlord, he had his own key to the house, though he'd never presumed to use it. Was this yet another line she was crossing? Somehow, after the events of the evening, it didn't seem to matter any more.

She went into the house and dashed upstairs. Caitlin was usually fussy about what she wore, but Saskia gathered up a fresh outfit of skirt, leggings and a warm top for the morning, in the hope that the teenager would be well enough to come home by then. Of course, she would need pyjamas and set of underwear along with a toothbrush and comb, and Saskia quickly added these to an overnight bag.

Then she went into the bathroom and freshened up, changing into a clean pair of jeans and a different pair of shoes. She added a light touch of make-up and after looking around to make sure she'd not forgotten anything she went back down the stairs.

The doorbell rang and she smiled faintly. Did this mean Tyler didn't feel right about letting himself in? Perhaps she'd been presuming too much.

She opened the door, ready to greet him and show him that she had everything in hand. They could leave right away.

Only it wasn't Tyler who was standing there, and the smile faded from her lips, her heart tripping in an uncomfortable, jerky beat.

'Hi,' Michael said. 'I've been waiting around for ages, hoping you would come home.'

She stared at him, nonplussed. 'Michael, what are you doing here? How did you find out where I was living?'

'You phoned me, remember? It was fairly easy to find you after that.' He studied her, a slight smile playing around his mouth. 'Aren't you going to ask me in?'

'I can't,' she said. 'I have to go out—to the hospital. I can't stay here.'

'Just for a minute or two? I won't keep you. I just wanted to say I'm sorry if I've been making life difficult for you. At first, when you were still working with me, it's true, I wanted to punish you, but after you left… well, I suppose I thought if you had nowhere else to go you would come back to me…back to your old job.'

Reluctantly, she stepped back to let him in. As soon as Tyler arrived they would leave, and maybe this would be her one last chance to show Michael that things were well and truly over between them.

'I only phoned you to find out why you were implying that I'd made mistakes with my patients,' she said. 'I didn't mean to give you the impression that I wanted us to get together again. I'm sorry if you got the wrong idea.'

'I know. I do understand.' He walked with her to the kitchen. 'I don't blame you for breaking things off—I was difficult to get along with, I know. But I hated it when you left. I always hoped—'

'I'm not coming back, Michael,' she said. 'I thought I made that clear to you.'

'Yes, you did.' He ran a hand through his dark hair. 'But I want you to know that I can change. I could be everything you want…' He came towards her and she kept moving backwards until she came up against the hard rim of the worktop.

'No,' she told him. 'It isn't going to happen.'

'But if you would just let me show you…' By now he was so close that he was almost touching her and she felt stifled. She didn't want to make a scene, but things might easily get out of hand.

'She said it isn't going to happen.' Tyler's voice cut in, breaking through the tension in the room. 'I'm afraid you've had a wasted journey, Michael. You should go back to wherever it is that you're staying tonight and then head out on the ferry in the morning. There's no point in you hanging around here any longer.' Instinctively, Saskia edged sideways, trying to get closer to him.

Michael's eyes widened as he looked from Tyler to Saskia and back again. 'You and she—? Are you…?' He couldn't bring himself to say the words.

'That's right.' Tyler looked him straight in the eye and, watching him, Saskia felt her jaw drop. He'd implied they were together, a couple. Conscious of Michael's scrutiny, she quickly tried to pull herself together. 'So, you see,' Tyler went on, 'you need to believe what Saskia's been telling you. It's over between you two. It's finished.'

Michael crumpled as though he'd received a blow to the stomach, and much as she wanted him to get the message Saskia hated to see him suffering like this.

'I'm sorry, Michael,' she said. 'It's just that you and I were never really suited, and this was bound to happen some time.' She studied him thoughtfully, with some sympathy. 'You know, there are lots of women out there who would love to be with you. You're a good-looking man, you do a great job—you're a caring, wonderful doctor. You have everything going for you. All you need to do is put this behind you and move on.'

'I didn't know,' he said. He turned away and began to walk a little unsteadily back along the hallway. Saskia followed him. 'I never dreamt…' He looked as though he was in a state of shock.

Tyler came to stand by the door. 'Are you safe to drive? Where are you staying?'

'I'm booked in at The Schooner.' He sent Saskia a piercing glance. 'I'll be there until after breakfast tomorrow morning if you want to talk to me again.'

'I don't think so,' she said. 'I'm sorry, Michael. Goodbye.'

They watched him drive away and then she turned to Tyler. 'You let him believe we were a couple,' she said. Her green eyes were clear and bright as she looked at him. She wanted so much for it to be true. But had he made it up to persuade Michael to leave, or could it be there was a germ of truth hidden behind the statement? She longed for him to say he wanted them to be together.

Instead, he hesitated, turning away from her so that his features were shadowed. He shrugged.

'It was a white lie. There didn't seem to be any other way he would get the message.' He gave her a quick, searching glance as she struggled to hide her disappointment. 'Why, does it bother you?'

She shook her head. 'Not really.' She desperately searched for a way out of the situation, to come up with a reason for her reaction. 'If he starts to tell people that we're an item, sooner or later it will get back to everyone at the hospital. How will you feel then?'

His mouth made a crooked shape. 'I doubt anyone will believe it. They all have me hooked up with Imogen.'

She stared at him. 'Imogen?' Pain lanced through her. She'd vaguely suspected something like this, that he and Imogen had something going between them, but was he really admitting it?

But if that was the case, why had he kissed her the other day? Had it only been meant as a comforting gesture after all, something that had quickly got out of hand?

She'd been growing more and more close to Tyler, but it looked as though the feelings and emotions were all on her side, not his.

'It's natural enough, don't you think? Imogen and I are very much alike, and we work well together. Why wouldn't we be a couple?'

'But…' She was staggered by what he was saying, struggling to take it in. 'You work with her—doesn't that go against your principles? After you kissed me you told me it wasn't right because you were my boss.'

He made a wry smile, but his head went back a fraction and she sensed his hesitation. 'I don't pretend to be perfect. Maybe I was caught unawares and my self-control slipped. After all, I'm as vulnerable as the next man when it comes to being with a beautiful, sexy woman who needs help. But…' his mouth flattened '…when all's said and done, I meant what I said. It wouldn't be right to take advantage of you when you're here on a three-month trial.'

'And nothing could come of it anyway…isn't that right?' She shot him a bleak, challenging glance. 'We're opposites, aren't we? My life's pretty much a shambles, and I'm living from day to day, hoping to get by, whereas you have everything mapped out. You're at the peak of your career, you have a lovely house where everything has its place, and all you need is the ideal woman to share it with you…someone who would keep it in immaculate condition.'

She frowned. 'I suppose Imogen fits the bill perfectly.' It was a sour comment, and she regretted it as soon as she'd made it.

'We should go to the hospital,' she said, exasperated with herself. 'Forget what I said. It's been a long day and I guess I'm out of sorts.'

He sent her a long, brooding look, but he didn't say anything. Instead, he picked up Caitlin's bag and led the way out of the house.

CHAPTER EIGHT

'How is she? What do the scans show?' Saskia hurried into A and E with Tyler, anxious to hear any news of Caitlin.

For now she had no choice but to put any problems she had with Tyler to one side. She couldn't help how she felt about him…she loved him and couldn't bear to think of him not being in her life…but was it possible that he didn't return those feelings? Had she been misreading the signals he'd been giving out? She was convinced he wanted her, and at the same time he had struggled to draw back from her—was it really so important to him that he didn't confuse his role as mentor with his feelings for her? Or was it really Imogen who lay at the root of him holding back?

Jason put the films up on screen for her and Tyler to see. 'It looks as though the muscles and ligaments in Caitlin's neck have been strained, which, of course, makes them inflamed, painful and obviously tender. It'll probably take a couple of months or so before they're back to normal.' He glanced at Saskia. 'She's lucky in that the facet joints and the discs seem to be okay.'

Saskia gave a sigh of relief. 'And the dizziness…do we know what's causing that?'

He shook his head. 'It's possible that there was some sort of minor injury to the inner ear—to the balance centre. That, too, should eventually right itself.'

'So what's the procedure now—anti-inflammatories?'

'Yes, I've started her on them and we'll prescribe them for when she leaves hospital. We can fix her up with a soft collar, too, if she'd like to wear one. If she finds it helps, that's all well and good. If she still has problems after a week or two I could try her with muscle relaxants.'

'Massage therapy might help,' Tyler put in. 'It would increase the blood flow to the region and help with healing.'

Jason nodded. 'It's worth a try.'

'Thanks for everything you've done,' Saskia said. 'I'll go and sit with her, though I expect what she needs most of all is sleep.'

Tyler shot her a quick glance. 'Would you like me to stay with you?'

She hesitated. More than anything, she wanted to say yes, but he'd already done enough and it wouldn't be fair to keep him waiting around any longer, would it? None of this was his problem. She shook her head. 'No, that's all right. We'll be fine. But thanks for bringing me back here. I really appreciate it.'

'That's okay. Give me a call tomorrow when you're ready to leave and I'll come and pick you up.'

'Uh…thanks.' She doubted that she would call him. It was one thing to accept his help when she thought he cared for her, but quite another if he was just along for the ride. She'd try to get home by any other means if possible.

He gave her an oddly puzzled look and she wondered if there was something in her tone or her expression that had given her thoughts away.

He turned, though, and she watched him walk away before going over to the observation ward to sit by Caitlin's bedside. She felt totally alone and empty inside.

A glance at the monitor showed her that Caitlin's blood pressure was still low and her pulse was slow. 'How are you feeling?' she asked her. 'Are you a bit warmer now?'

'Yes, thanks. As soon as my temperature was up enough I persuaded them to let me have a warm bath—they made the room all hot and steamy—and all I want now are my own pyjamas. I hate this cotton, backless thing they've given me to wear and this stripy hospital dressing gown.'

'Oh, well, that's soon remedied.' Saskia smiled and unzipped the holdall she'd brought with her. 'I brought your favourite pjs and your bathrobe. Do you want some help to put them on?'

'Yes, please. My neck and shoulders are a bit stiff. In fact, I'm achy all over.'

'I expect it'll take a while before you're back to your usual self,' Saskia said, as she helped Caitlin put on her pyjamas. 'Have you had any more dizziness?'

'Just a bit, but I'm okay.'

'Hmm. I expect a good night's sleep will help. Close your eyes if you want, and try to get some rest. I'll be here right next to you.'

Caitlin looked relieved. 'I think I will, if you don't mind.'

Saskia gave her a hug and settled back in her chair. At some point in the night she, too, dozed off, but she woke up in the morning when the nurse came along to check Caitlin's blood pressure.

'Oh, that's a lot better,' the nurse said with a smile. 'We'll see if she can manage to eat some breakfast and then Dr Samuels will be along to see at her.'

Caitlin sat up in bed and rubbed her eyes. 'Do you think I'll be able to go home today?' she asked Saskia.

'Perhaps a bit later on, if you're feeling all right.' She looked at her niece carefully. There was certainly more colour in her cheeks now.

It was a couple of hours into the afternoon, though, before Jason decided she was well enough to be discharged. They had to wait for the hospital pharmacy to dispense Caitlin's medication before they could leave, but it gave Saskia an opportunity to pack the teenager's belongings into the holdall and make sure she didn't leave anything behind.

'Hi, there. Are you girls ready to go home?'

Saskia's heart skipped a beat as she looked up and saw Tyler walking into the observation ward. He was dressed in casual clothes, dark trousers and an open-necked shirt, and he looked terrific.

'What are you doing here?' she asked, looking at him in surprise. 'I wasn't expecting you.'

'I asked Jason to keep me informed of what was going on,' he said. 'I had the feeling you might be foolish enough to pay for a taxi—I was pretty sure you wouldn't decide to walk home with Caitlin just out of hospital.'

A flush of pink stole across her cheeks. 'Well, you've done so much for us already. I didn't want to put you to any more trouble.'

'If I didn't want to do it, I'd tell you.' He picked

up the holdall. 'The medication's ready for you at the nurses' station,' he told Caitlin, 'so we can leave as soon as you're ready.'

Caitlin glanced at him. She didn't say anything, but she smiled and dropped into step beside him, accepting the help of a supporting arm from Saskia.

It was only later, when they were back home and Tyler had gone back to his own house to catch up on some research he was doing, that she looked at Saskia and said, 'I think he has a thing for you.'

Saskia shook her head. 'No, I don't think so. There's someone at work who's much more his type.'

Caitlin frowned. 'He can't be that serious about her. He's always looking at you—he can't take his eyes off you. He just doesn't want you to know it, for some reason.'

Saskia smiled and tried to make light of it, but Caitlin had certainly given her something to think about. Why would he not want her to know how he felt about her? Was it really the three-month trial that was making him keep her at arm's length? And how had she managed to get herself so hot and bothered about him when she knew she should have been doing her best to stay away from him? It was all very confusing.

Deep down, though, she knew the answer. It was impossible for her *not* to care for him. Somehow he'd worked his way into her heart and now she couldn't contemplate life without him. Was she being irrational? Would it all end in tears and recriminations, the way it had with Michael?

Tyler was different, though, she felt sure. He would never be mean or deliberately hurtful, or react in the way that Michael had done, would he?

* * *

At the hospital, over the next week, they both tried to keep things between them on a professional footing. They managed to forge a reasonable, if somewhat tense way of going on together. It was as though neither of them dared relax their guard.

'I need to go and see a patient on the way home from work,' he told her a short time before their shift was due to end on Friday. 'It's as a favour for a friend who's a bit worried about her son.'

'Okay.' They'd both had a difficult, busy day, so she guessed this must be important to him.

'She lives in the opposite direction from us, but I could drop you off at home and then double back, if it's going to be a problem for you.'

She shook her head. 'No, it's all right. You don't want to have to do that.' He'd had a particularly fraught day, dealing with one emergency after another, so he could probably do without the extra burden. 'The children will be at Rosie's house after school. I can ring her and tell her I'll be a little late picking them up. I'm sure she won't mind.'

'Good. Thanks. That will save me some time—I've quite a lot on this weekend with this hospital administrators' meeting coming up, so time's precious.'

'Oh… I heard about that—it's scheduled for tomorrow afternoon, isn't it? Aren't you going to be one of the speakers—at the hospital in Truro? Noah said you'd been working on it with Imogen this last day or so—something to do with reorganising cardiovascular facilities for the region.' She didn't want to think about how unsettling that had been, knowing that he and Imogen were closeted together in his office for long stretches of time. 'He said something about a presentation.'

'That's right. I was called in at the last minute when someone had to drop out, so I have to spend the next few hours working on my speech. I need things to run as smoothly as possible if I'm to get it finished in time.'

She nodded. 'You could have done without this call-out, I expect. Have you any idea what's wrong with your friend's son?'

He frowned. 'I don't think it's anything too serious—at least, I hope it isn't. He's been having some headaches these last few months. Apparently he's suffering a particularly bad one today and she's concerned about him.'

'Hmm.' She thought about it. 'I know it sounds odd, but perhaps it's something to do with the weather—it's been quite hot and humid these last few days and some forecasters are predicting a storm. It's surprising, but a lot of people get headaches in those conditions. It's all due to hot air sweeping across the Atlantic from the Azores, or something along those lines.'

'That's your candid opinion?' Amusement glinted in his blue eyes. 'I can't see that going down too well if I start basing my diagnoses on the vagaries of the weather, can you? We'd probably do better if we stick to looking at actual symptoms and work our way back from there, don't you think?'

'Yeah, well…I was just saying…' She broke off, seeing his shoulders moving with suppressed laughter, and she aimed a mock thump at his arm. 'Stop making fun of me. I'm right, I know I am—I've read about it.'

'Yeah…yeah…if you say so.'

A short time later they drove along the main highway to his friend's house. 'I know Nicole and her husband through my sister,' he explained. 'We've known each other since we were teenagers.'

As soon as they arrived at Nicole's address Tyler introduced Saskia and they were shown into the sitting room where a boy aged around ten was lying curled up in a foetal position on the sofa. He was covering his eyes with his hands.

'Thanks for coming,' his mother said quietly. 'He's been like this for the last couple of hours. He's been sick quite a bit and complaining of the light, and any kind of noise upsets him and seems to make things worse.'

Tyler went to sit on the edge of the settee. 'Hi, Lewis. Would it be all right if I take a look at you? Perhaps we'll be able to do something about this headache of yours.'

Lewis slowly drew himself up into a sitting position. It was plain to see that he was completely incapacitated by the headache. He looked drowsy, utterly exhausted, and there were dark circles under his eyes. Beads of sweat had broken out on his forehead. 'Can you make it go away?' he pleaded.

'I'm sure we can. Do you want to tell me about it? When did it start?'

'This afternoon, at school. I kept seeing all these sparkly lights in my eyes and one of the teachers had to bring me home.'

Gently, Tyler examined him, checking his reflexes and paying particular attention to his ears, throat and glands.

'First of all,' he said when he had finished, 'you need to know that nothing dangerous is going on here. It's just a very nasty headache that can be treated.'

Nicole relaxed her shoulders and gave a soft sigh

of relief. 'It's not like an ordinary headache, though, is it?' she said.

'No, that's right…it's a migraine. They're usually brought on by some kind of trigger—fluorescent light, flickering lights, certain foods or smells, stress, tiredness…even changes in the weather can do it in some circumstances.' He sent Saskia a quick glance and she gave him a superior, *I told you so* look in return. 'What you need to do,' he added, 'is find Lewis's particular trigger and get him to avoid it as best he can. It will help if you keep a diary to note down the circumstances around when the headaches start.'

He opened his medical case and drew out a packet of tablets. 'He should take one of these now—if he doesn't manage to keep it down I can give him an injection, but this should help with the sickness and the headache. I'll write you out a prescription for some more tablets, and he'll need to take one of them at the first sign of a migraine. The sooner he takes it, the better it will work.'

'Thanks, Tyler. I know I shouldn't have bothered you, but I couldn't get an urgent appointment with the family doctor and I was so worried. I knew you wouldn't let me down.'

'That's all right. I'll send a letter to his GP and he'll follow up on his treatment from here on.'

They waited with Lewis for a while to make sure he kept the medication down, and it was only when the boy finally fell asleep that Tyler made a move to leave. 'I'm sure he'll be okay now,' he said, 'but if you're worried at all, give me a call.'

They said goodbye and left the house. It was getting dark outside and around them the trees were billowing, their branches bending in the wind.

Saskia slid into the passenger seat of the car. 'The sky looks heavy with cloud,' she said, adding, tongue in cheek, 'You know, I might already have mentioned it, but I think we've been through a low-pressure system lately and we're definitely in for one of those storms that builds up over the Atlantic.'

Tyler grinned and turned the car off the main road, heading for home. 'Okay, okay…I get the point.'

They picked up the children from Rosie and then Saskia shepherded them into their house as thunder grumbled overhead and the first rain began to fall. Tyler parked the car in the garage and cast a quick glance at the sky before hurrying next door.

The storm continued to rumble for the next hour or so while Saskia went about her chores, and she was baking Cornish pasties when the lights suddenly went out. She stood in darkness for a while, trying to work out what to do for the best. There was a lantern somewhere around and a couple of torches in one of the kitchen drawers, but it was difficult to find her way about until her eyes grew accustomed to the dark.

'What's happened?' Becky asked.

'The electricity's gone off,' Caitlin answered.

'It's because of the storm, isn't it?'

'Yes,' Saskia agreed, as she felt her way around the kitchen to the drawer she needed. 'I expect the power lines are down. We'll just have to do the best we can for now. Try to stay where you are,' she told the children. 'We don't want you bumping into things.'

A flash of lightning lit the room and everyone stared, caught like rabbits in headlights. Charlie's bottom lip quivered and Boomer looked up from his bed in the corner of the room briefly, before going back to sleep.

'It's all right, Charlie,' Saskia murmured, pulling open the drawer and feeling inside it for one of the torches. 'There's nothing to worry about. It just means we don't have any lights or any means of cooking until the engineers get the power back on.' The Aga was powered totally by electricity and, of course, they would have no means of heating.

'Won't we get any dinner?' Charlie asked fretfully in the darkness. 'I'm hungry.'

'Um—I think the pasties are just about cooked. I'll leave them in the hot oven for a while to finish off.' She found the torch and switched it on. 'Becky, you can hold the other one. Caitlin, you need to sit down. We don't want you getting dizzy in the dark.'

The doorbell rang some fifteen minutes later and she went to answer it, guided by the beam of the torch.

'I wondered how you're managing with the power cut?' Tyler was holding a lantern that burned brightly in the darkness. Rain lashed at him, and she quickly drew him inside the house. 'Do you have enough candles or lamps?' he asked.

She shook her head. 'It didn't occur to me to get any in,' she said, biting her lip at her lack of foresight. 'We're all in the kitchen, sitting round the table by torchlight.' She made a wry smile. 'The children are bored to tears already because they can't get Wi-Fi.'

His mouth curved briefly. 'Well, luckily I have plenty of battery-powered lamps and a duel-fuel Aga, so at least I can boil a pan of water for hot drinks and one of the ovens is working.' His brow creased. 'Why don't you all come round to my house while the power's out? If the lines are down it could take quite a while to get the lights back on—last time this happened it was several hours before things were back to normal.'

'Okay…if you're sure?' It sounded as though they might be in this for the long haul, and although she was certain she would be able to cope, she doubted the children would manage for long. 'Would it be all right if the children bring some toys with them? And what about Boomer?'

'Yes, that's fine…and, of course, Boomer must come.' He moved restlessly. 'Get them to bring whatever they need. The only thing is, I'm afraid you'll have to excuse me while I get on with my presentation—I printed out what I'd done of the speech because I was worried the power might go off, but I still have to make alterations to it and sort out the slide presentation while the battery power lasts on the laptop.'

'Of course. I understand.' She glanced at him. He'd taken the time to think about how they were getting along, but he seemed tense, in a hurry to get on, and she was concerned for him. He'd missed lunch at work today because of an emergency that had come in, and she suspected he was driving himself way too hard.

He handed her the lantern. 'Take this with you while you find what they need. I'll manage with the torch.'

'Thanks, Tyler.'

They quickly gathered together whatever they thought they might need, and finally Saskia took the pasties from the oven and put them all in a large oven-proof dish with a lid to keep the heat in. At least they wouldn't go hungry.

A few minutes later they all hurried over to Tyler's house, keeping their heads down because of the driving rain and clutching their coats around them to keep out the fierce wind. Another flash of lightning cracked across the sky, and a few seconds later thunder rumbled ominously overhead.

'I don't like it,' Charlie said, pinned to the spot, his face crumpling, and Tyler swooped him up into his arms and carried him into the house.

'It's fine. It's nothing to worry about,' he told him. 'If you count how many seconds pass between the lightning flash and the thunder, you can tell how far away the lightning is. Try it next time. Every five seconds is about one mile, so I reckon the lightning's about two miles away.' He looked at Charlie, but the boy had his head buried in his jacket. 'Anyway, it's not going to hurt you.'

Once they were all inside the house, Tyler made sure they were comfortable and settled in the living room before he excused himself to go back to work in his study. 'Do you think you have enough light in here?' he asked Saskia. 'I can bring in some more lamps if you need them.'

'No, we're fine,' she said. She looked around. 'They've already sorted themselves out…see?' Becky and Charlie had tipped a tub of small plastic building blocks over the large Oriental rug and were busy building a castle of some sort, and Caitlin was cosy in an armchair, listening to music through her earphones.

'And you—what will you do? Will you be all right? I hate to leave you like this, but I need to get this presentation sorted. I have to be on my way to the mainland by ten in the morning.'

'I've brought a book with me,' she said. 'I should be able to read it well enough with the light from the lamp.' He'd placed an oil-burning lamp on the table by the sofa. 'Don't worry about us. We'll be okay.'

'All right, then. Make yourselves hot drinks and snacks whenever you want them. You'll find everything you need in the cupboards in the kitchen.'

'Thanks.' She sent him a quick glance. 'Have you eaten yet? I know you didn't have time for lunch.'

'I grabbed something from the snack bar this afternoon,' he said. 'I'm fine.'

'Hmm. What was that—a sticky bun?' She knew she'd guessed right from the crooked slant of his mouth. She didn't think he was fine at all. It wasn't like him to appear pressured in any way, but his features were taut and from the way his silky black hair peaked in small spikes she guessed he'd been running his hand through it.

He escaped to the study, leaving Saskia to make her way to the kitchen, where she set about serving up the hot pasties. The appetising smell soon wafted on the air. The combination of beef, onion and potato in a thick pastry crust should make for a warming, filling meal, and would keep everyone happy for a while.

When the children were settled around the table, tucking in, she made a pot of tea and slid a couple of pasties on a plate for Tyler.

She knocked on the door of his study and went in. 'I thought you might like something to eat,' she said.

He looked up at her, frowning. 'I can't take food from you,' he protested. 'You'll have made enough for yourself and the children. I'll get something later when I've finished working.'

She shook her head. 'We've all eaten—I made plenty

because I never know who's going to want more. Please, eat up. I made you some tea as well.'

He made as though to prevaricate and she said firmly, 'You have to get some food inside you or you won't be in any fit state to do anything. You're a doctor—I shouldn't have to tell you that.'

He smiled and gave in, pushing away his paperwork and accepting the plate she offered. 'Mmm…these are good,' he said, biting into a golden pasty and savouring the moment. 'Perfect.'

'I'm glad you think so.' She glanced at the piles of paper on his desk and the colourful diagram that was displayed on the laptop screen. 'How's it going?'

'All right, I think. I'm trying to get as much done as I can while the battery lasts. I have to change the order of some of the points in the speech and edit some of the slides, but I'm getting there.' He took another bite from his pasty.

'Good, I'm glad. But perhaps the power will come back on soon and you won't need to worry.'

'Actually, this is going to last for quite a while,' he said. 'I rang the electricity company and they say the lines are down and it could take several hours before the problem's fixed. It might even be as late as tomorrow morning.'

He gave it some thought. 'Perhaps you should sort out some nightwear for yourself and the children if you're going to stay here overnight. Caitlin and Becky can have the large guest bedroom, and Charlie should be okay in the room next to them.' He glanced at her. 'There's a second en suite room that you could use.'

'Oh…' She was startled. 'I hadn't expected it would come to that. It's thoughtful of you to offer. Thank you.'

'You're welcome.' He swallowed some of the hot tea and then gave her a searching glance. 'So, how are things going with you lately? Is there any more news about your brother and his wife?'

'Megan seems to be feeling much better now, but Sam…' she sent him a troubled look '…Sam is having some problems with his breathing. They're not sure what's causing it. It's not the infection any longer because that cleared up.'

'I'm sorry. It's a worry for you.'

'Yes.'

'You've had a lot to deal with. And what about that business last weekend? Have you heard any more from Michael? I take it he went back to Cornwall without giving you any more trouble?'

'He did.' She sat down on the edge of his desk and his gaze followed her movements, gliding over the neat fit of her skinny jeans and lingering on the floaty, scoop-necked top that she was wearing. 'Uh…he rang me a couple of days ago to say that he was sorry for the way he'd behaved over the last few months. He said he'd come to his senses and that I could have my old job back any time I wanted. He said he wouldn't give me any trouble.'

His eyes narrowed a fraction. 'How do you feel about that?'

She hesitated. 'I'm not sure. I think I trust him not to cause problems for me any more—he said he acted the way he did because he'd become obsessed with me and he wanted me back. He thought if I didn't have a job here I would end up going back to him. It's a sort of twisted logic—but he seems to be aware of his behaviour and wants to change.'

She sighed. 'I suppose talking things through with him made me take stock of my situation. If things don't work out for me here, getting my old job back might seriously be an option after all.'

His brows shot up in astonishment. 'You wouldn't really consider going back there, would you?'

She gave a small shrug. 'I might not have any choice—after all, I don't have any guarantee of a job here, do I? I'd have to look for work—not necessarily at my old hospital but somewhere on the mainland.'

Guardedly, he stood up. 'I wouldn't have thought there was going to be a problem over you working here. After all, you only have to get through the next few weeks—'

'Maybe, but how do I know that at the end of it you won't decide I'm not up to the job? What if another patient decides to go walkabout or someone's medication doesn't do what it's supposed to do? Or if my seasickness becomes a problem?'

She looked at him, her green eyes troubled. 'After all, you're the one who had doubts about me in the first place—you're the one who set up the three-month trial condition, aren't you? Under any other circumstances, with a different employer, I would have been given the job outright. It was only because Michael planted the seed of doubt in your mind that you thought I might one day let you down.'

She frowned. 'I've been on edge ever since I started work here. I'm not sure I want to go on feeling that I'm somehow not up to scratch and have to go on proving myself.'

'You don't have to prove yourself and you shouldn't feel that way. You're a good doctor, Saskia. I'm sorry if I made you feel otherwise.' He ran his hand lightly down her arm. 'You're right, I was concerned in the beginning, but I was wrong. I realise that now. But I can't change the contract terms—James Gregson is a stickler for following procedure. It isn't too long to wait, is it? I don't want you to leave…you must know that.'

He was thoroughly shaken by what she'd said, that was plain to see, but the truth was she didn't feel secure, and she didn't know how he truly felt about her. 'Perhaps. I'm not really sure. I don't always understand where you're coming from. I think I'm getting mixed signals from you, Tyler. It's confusing. I don't know where I am.'

'I think you're a great doctor and a wonderful, caring woman…' His blue gaze searched her face. 'I hate to think of you leaving. All I know is I can't bear the thought of you going back to him. I need you to stay here, Saskia…with me.' His hand slid around her waist and came to rest, palm flat, against the small of her back. 'I need you. I can't stop thinking about you. You're beautiful, irresistible…you take my breath away.'

He drew her up against him, pressuring her against his long, hard body, and before she knew what was happening his head bent towards her and he was kissing her, an urgent, passionate kiss full of pent-up emotion. She felt the taut strength of his body next to hers, his powerful thighs compelling her into the rounded edge of the mahogany desk, and all the while his arms enclosed her, his hands stroking her soft curves.

'I've tried to hold back all this time,' he said huskily, 'but it's been nothing but torment.' His hands swept along the length of her and came to linger on the firm swell of her hips. 'You can't really be thinking of going back to him, can you?'

'Not to him…I never said that…but…' Her voice trailed away as his hands moved over her, seeking out all the contours of her body. He lightly cupped her breast, his thumb brushing the hardening nub in slow, mesmerising circles. 'Tyler, I…'

He stopped her words with tender kisses over her mouth, her cheeks, gliding along the column of her throat in a sensual, exhilarating journey of exploration. 'I can't bear to think of him sweet-talking you into going back to him. I need you,' he said again, his voice rough with desire. 'I want you so much.'

She lifted her hands to his chest, feeling the warmth of his skin emanating from beneath his shirt. She let her fingers trail over the rigid six-pack of his stomach and upwards to explore the inviting, smooth silk of his pectorals. As her hands roamed a soft groan escaped him.

'It feels so good to have you touch me that way.'

She lifted her face for his kiss, lost herself in the wonder of being with him this way. But at the back of her mind she couldn't help wondering whether she was making a big mistake. Could she really be letting this happen?

She wanted him, loved being in his arms. She longed to have him tell her the things she wanted to hear, but how could that ever come about? He didn't love her, did he? He'd never said those words she desperately needed him to say. And through it all he was still her boss, the man who held power over her future. Hadn't she told herself she would never get into this situation ever again? What was wrong with her that she couldn't find the willpower to keep him at arm's length?

A piercing beep came from somewhere on the desk behind them, and for a moment she stayed perfectly still, unable to take it in. It wasn't the beep of a phone or any other sound that she recognised right away.

It came again, and Tyler stiffened. 'No...no...how could I have been so stupid?' He straightened and eased himself away from her.

'What is it?' She looked at him in confusion.

'The laptop—the battery's about to give up.' He grimaced. 'I need to sort this out; I've got to save my work before I lose what I've been doing for the last hour.'

He looked at her, his expression full of frustration, exasperation and apology.

'It's okay.' She stepped to one side so that he could sort out the problem. Perhaps it was just as well that they had been interrupted. She still wasn't clear in her head that she was doing the right thing. Hadn't Michael used soft words and easy charm to convince her that he was the right man for her? Wasn't she in danger of falling into that same old trap?

She left Tyler to work his magic with the computer, telling him briefly, 'If you need to go on working, you can use my laptop. You just need to save your work to a memory stick and transfer it over. I brought it with me.'

Distracted, he looked at her. 'Thanks. That would be great.'

She took her laptop to him then shut the study door and went to help the children get ready for bed.

She had to go next door to pick up what they needed, but she was back within a few minutes, glad of the light burning in Tyler's house and the warmth that emanated from the flickering flames of the gas fire in the lounge and the heat from the Aga in the kitchen.

Tyler was still working in the study when she decided to go to bed. It seemed that whatever he set out to do, he gave it everything he had. Wouldn't it be something if he decided he wanted her at all costs?

It wasn't long, though, before doubts began to creep back in. Hadn't he said that Imogen was the ideal woman for him? Perhaps not in so many words, but he'd said they were very much alike and asked why they wouldn't be a couple. So why was he kissing another woman? Had his kisses been born out of a momentary, compelling desire, or was there something more going on in his subconscious?

She didn't sleep well. The storm raged through the night and she tossed and turned as flashes of lightning lit up the room and thunder growled. In the early hours Charlie clambered into bed beside her, snuggling into the shelter of her arms.

He wasn't there when she woke in the morning. Sitting up in bed, she looked around, befuddled for a second or two until she had her bearings. The electric clock at the side of the bed still had a blank screen so obviously the power hadn't been restored overnight. That had been some storm.

Hurriedly, she washed and dressed, pulling on a pair of blue jeans and a button-through top that clung to her curves and outlined her slender waist.

'Can we make breakfast?' Becky asked, coming into the room as she finished dressing. 'We're all hungry.'

'Yes, I should think so. I'll see what there is.'

'We had cereals first thing, but Charlie's starving and Caitlin says we have to wait till you come down before we help ourselves to anything else.'

'Well, she's right. This isn't our house.' She mulled it

over. 'I'll have to do a grocery shop and stock up again
for Tyler. Is he up and about yet?'

'I haven't seen him.'

'Okay, well, we'll go and see what we can rustle up,
shall we? I expect he'll want something to eat before
he leaves.'

'All right.'

Saskia's jaw dropped when walked into the once pristine kitchen a couple of minutes later. It was a mess.
Whoever had set out the cereals for breakfast—Becky
and Charlie, she suspected—had left small puddles of
milk, sugar and wheat flakes all over the worktop. And
that wasn't all…

'I gave Boomer wheat flakes for his breakfast,' Charlie said. 'He liked them. And then he wanted to go out,
so I let him into the garden. I think it's a bit muddy out
there after all the rain.'

'Yes, I can see that.' A trail of muddy paw prints ran
higgledy-piggledy across the tiled floor.

'Good grief.' Tyler's voice sounded from behind her
and she half turned to look at him. His eyes were wide
with disbelief. His face was dark with overnight shadow,
lending him a roguish, sexy air, and his hair was glis-
tening as though he'd just come from the shower. 'How
long have the children been up?'

'Um…about an hour, I think. They're used to being
up and about early for school.'

He winced. 'Have you seen the state of the lounge?
It looks as if a bomb's gone off in there.'

'Uh…no, I haven't yet.' She frowned. 'We cleared
everything away last night. Are you saying it's less
than perfect?'

'Hah.' He made a choking sound. 'You're joking,

aren't you? You can't see the floor in there for plastic, among other things, and it looks as though the new cushions have been used for some kind of pillow fight. How can three young people cause so much devastation?'

She pulled in a calming breath. 'To be fair, I don't think Caitlin would have had much to do with it.'

'Just the two of them, then…that's even worse! How do you live with all this chaos?'

'I'm not sure I do.' She shrugged vaguely. 'This is all new to me, too, you know.'

'Yes, of course it is. I just don't think I could ever live like this.' He looked beyond her to the window and the garden outside and exhaled sharply.

She could see the reason. One part of the once perfect lawn was a quagmire, an unpleasant memento of last night's storm.

'That part of the garden is always getting waterlogged.' His mouth flattened and he looked down at his watch. 'I need to finish getting ready. I only came down for coffee—on second thoughts, I'll get it later.'

He obviously needed to get away for a while from the scenes of devastation all around him. 'I'll make it for you,' she said. 'Will you have it in here?'

'Uh…I don't think so. I need to sort some papers out for my briefcase. I'll be in the study. Thanks.'

She left the coffee on his desk a couple of minutes later and went to rummage through the cupboards to see what was available for breakfast. He wouldn't have time for anything much, she guessed, so she switched on the gas oven and started to heat up a batch of croissants. He hadn't meant what he'd said about not living like this, had he? Did he never want to have a family of his own?

She began to clear up the kitchen, wiping down the surfaces and mopping the floor, until it was restored to its former glory. The room was warm from the heat of the oven and her face was flushed from her exertions so after a while she undid a few buttons and ran a hand through her shoulder-length curls, pushing them back from her cheeks.

Leaving the children at the table, spooning jam on their croissants, she slid a couple more on to a plate and took them along to the study.

Tyler was in there, standing by the desk, sipping coffee while leafing through a stack of papers. His briefcase was open, next to his laptop bag, and it looked as though he had everything more or less in hand.

'I brought you these,' she said softly. 'You should eat something before you go.'

Perhaps she had taken him by surprise when she walked into the room. It may have been that he hadn't heard her knock or he was absorbed in what he was reading...whatever caused it, he suddenly seemed to swallow his coffee the wrong way and coughed, staring at her with a stunned expression. She had no idea what was wrong. All she knew was that his gaze never wavered from her and as he stood, as though mesmerised, the coffee started to spill from his cup in a slow, inevitable drip, drip onto his papers.

'Tyler, your coffee—'

He came to with a snap, putting his cup down and muttering something incomprehensible under his breath.

'Here, let me help.' She hurried forward, pulling

some clean tissues out of a box on the table, but he put up a hand and warded her off.

'No…don't help me…don't do anything…please.' He gritted the words through his teeth. 'Just stay away…I can manage. Thank you.'

She didn't understand his rejection, and seeing his irritability she backed away from him, feeling hurt and awkward. Why could she never get anything right? Or, rather, why was nothing ever right for him where she was concerned?

'You know, Tyler,' she said carefully, 'you should start to think about what's most important in life. You can work towards making an awesome presentation, and you can live your life in a beautiful show house, but none of those things are important in the grand scheme of things. People are what matter…people who care for you and make it so that you want to come home to them. Perhaps you need to take some time to work out what it is you really want.'

He stared at her, straightening up from mopping up his damp papers. 'Saskia—'

'No, please don't say anything. I think you've already said enough. I'm going to leave you to get ready for your trip to the mainland. I hope everything goes well for you.'

She went back to the kitchen and tidied up, doing anything she could to keep busy and avoid him. She made sure that the children gathered up their belongings and returned the house to the way it had been when they'd arrived.

The power came back on a few minutes later as they left the house.

CHAPTER NINE

'WILL MUMMY AND Daddy be coming home soon?' Becky sat patiently on the edge of the bed on Sunday morning while Saskia brushed her hair. Her golden curls gleamed in the sunlight that filtered through the curtains.

'I hope so,' Saskia answered cautiously. 'Your mummy is feeling a lot better, so that's good news, isn't it? Perhaps we should get her some flowers and magazines, and maybe take some books in for your daddy to read?' Though whether he'd be feeling up to reading was up for debate at the moment.

'Yes. He likes detective stories.'

'Okay, we'll sort some out for him.'

Becky went off to play and Saskia sat for a while, thinking about everything that had happened in these last few weeks. It was as though she'd been caught up in a whirlwind that had tossed her this way and that.

And through it all there had been Tyler. She sighed. Did he even know how much he was missing out? Was it so important that everything be organised and carefully structured?

He'd been under stress yesterday—it had been the culmination of a long tense previous day and he'd been up into the early hours, getting things just right. It was no wonder he'd lost his cool. When he was under that kind of constant tension something was bound to give way. Even so, it hurt that he couldn't seem to get his priorities right.

Pulling herself together, she made her regular call to the hospital. Perhaps Sam would be feeling a bit better today. She could really do with some good news.

'I'm afraid he's taken a turn for the worse and we're really quite worried about him,' the nurse told her, and her spirits sank. 'We're doing everything we can to make him comfortable, but he's finding it difficult to get his breath. The doctor's coming in to see him some time this morning—fairly soon, we hope.'

Saskia cut the call after a minute or so and tried to think what she should do. She needed to go and see Sam, but it wouldn't be right to take the children with her when he was so ill. It would worry them too much.

There was only one thing to do…she would have to ask Tyler for help. She didn't want to do it, but she really didn't see any other way out. Rosie wouldn't be able to look after the children today and there was no one else she could call on.

She went downstairs to prepare breakfast for everyone and then left Caitlin in charge while she hurried next door.

'Saskia—it's good to see you.' Tyler invited her into the house, obviously a little puzzled because she was on her own. 'Have you left the children to their own devices? Are you sure the house is going to be safe from them while you're out?'

She managed a rueful smile. 'I'm sure everything will be fine for a few minutes.' She walked with him to the kitchen but turned down his offer of a cup of coffee. 'No, thanks. I can't stay.' She looked around. The place was spotless as usual.

'How did the presentation go yesterday?' she asked. 'It must have been good—you put a lot of work into it.'

He smiled. 'Yes, it went well, thanks. I think some changes will be made regionally now, based on our model for cardiovascular services.'

'A success, then.' Her mouthed tilted a fraction. 'I expect Imogen is pleased.'

'Yes, she is. She put a lot of effort into getting things right.'

'With your help.'

'Well, yes…we're friends, after all, so when she asked me for advice I did what I could for her.'

'You're just friends?'

Perhaps something in her voice implied she thought otherwise, because he said quietly, 'Yes, that's all. There's nothing going on between us.' He gave her a probing glance. 'Saskia, about yesterday—'

'It's all right. You don't need to explain.' It was a huge relief to have her mind put at rest on that score, but things had moved on and now she doubted she and Tyler could ever get together in the way she wanted. They were way too different in their outlook. As much as she loved him, she doubted it would ever work between them.

She said carefully, 'You were under a lot of stress. It was difficult for you, having us all invade your space, and then it seemed as though your hard work might be ruined at the last minute. I do understand.'

He shook his head. 'I don't think you do. I try to do my best, but somehow when I'm with you things never go according to plan.' He frowned. 'The trouble is, I can't think straight when I'm around you. I get distracted and I'm not usually like that. I've always been clear-headed and on the ball and it's frustrating not being in control any more.'

Her mouth quirked. 'So I'm to blame for your mistakes? Sorry, but it won't hold up in court.'

He laughed. 'You know what I mean.'

'I think so, yes.' She gave a rueful smile. She was glad he couldn't think straight around her—but it still worried her that they were miles apart in the way they lived their lives, and there was nothing on earth she could do to change that.

She frowned. 'Tyler, the reason I'm here... I came to ask a favour. I'm worried about Sam—there's been bad news from the hospital and I need to go and see him. The only thing is, I don't think it's a good idea to take the children with me, so—'

'You want me to look after them for you?'

She nodded anxiously. 'I know it's a lot to ask.'

'That's all right. They can come round here and hang out.'

She breathed a sigh of relief. 'Thanks. I didn't know what else to do. They could watch DVDs if you want to make life easier on yourself...and Becky and Charlie can bring their colouring books. Those usually keep them quiet for half an hour or so. Caitlin's no trouble, of course. She'll sort herself out.'

'Don't worry about it.' He studied her face. 'Have you called the number I gave you to arrange a boat ride over there?'

'Not yet. I had to sort this out first.'

'Okay, I'll give Tim a ring for you. I'm sure he won't

mind taking you over there and picking you up again later. He's Nicole's husband—he owes me a few favours.'

'Thanks. That'll be a great help, if he really is okay with it. I'd better go and organise things.' She made to turn away but he stopped her, laying a hand gently on her arm. For a second or two her heart gave a staccato beat, but he didn't take her into his arms or try to kiss her, and despondency made her shoulders droop a little.

'Have you taken your seasickness tablets?'

She pulled in a quick breath. 'No…I didn't give it a thought.' She winced. 'They won't work in time, will they?'

'I'll give you an injection. It'll make you a bit sleepy for about an hour, but you can curl up in a chair until Tim arrives, and he won't mind if you doze off on the boat. I'll explain things to him.'

She frowned. 'How is it that you have the right medication to hand? You can't keep everything in your medical bag, can you?'

'This is an island community, and people use boats quite a lot to get around. We're used to islanders and tourists having problems, so now we're prepared.' He waved her to a chair. 'Make yourself comfortable while I go and get things sorted out. I'll organise the children so all you need to do is rest and let the injection do its work.'

Half an hour later, feeling very drowsy, she was on the boat, heading for Cornwall. She only hoped that Tyler wouldn't regret agreeing to watch over the children. For a man who craved peace and quiet and pleasant, tidy surroundings above all, it was a tall order.

'Give me a call when you want to go home,' the boatman said when he eventually helped her onto the tow-path on the mainland. 'My mate will see you the rest of the way. I hope everything works out all right for you with your brother.'

'Thanks, Tim.'

Tim's friend was waiting to drive her to the hospital, and she couldn't help thinking how smooth the process was once Tyler had taken a hand in the organisation.

Things were not so good when she arrived at the hospital and went to Sam's ward. She barely had time to say hello to him before a team came to wheel him away towards the lift. She looked at them in bewilderment. What was going on? Sam was in pain and too breathless to talk so she simply squeezed his hand and said softly, 'I'll wait. I'll be here when you come back.'

'He's going to Theatre for a catheter embolectomy,' a nurse explained. 'He's very poorly. He had a chest pain that came on suddenly, stopping him from getting his breath, and his heart rate is very fast. We had to send for the doctor urgently and he took him to have a CTPA scan. I'm afraid it showed a blood clot on the lung.'

'Oh, no…' All at once Saskia was very afraid for her brother. The symptoms were ominous, given that Sam had been hospitalised for some length of time. Being stuck in bed could mean that the blood coagulated to form a clot in the deep vein of the leg and in Sam's case it had broken away and travelled through the heart to the lung, where it had stopped the blood from flowing freely. It was a terrifying event. The patient could collapse suddenly or even die.

Saskia reached for a chair and sat down, feeling very weak. The fact that they were doing a catheter embolectomy meant that the doctors felt he was in real danger.

A fine tube would be passed through the blood vessels until it reached the clot and then the embolus would be carefully pulled out along the tube using specialist procedures.

'Can I get you anything?' the nurse asked. 'A cup of tea perhaps? That might help to make you feel a bit better.'

'Thanks.' Saskia was too worried to concentrate on anything properly. Her brother's life was at stake and she was helpless to do anything about it. Worse still, as a doctor she knew the risks involved.

Her mobile phone trilled and she went out into the corridor to answer it. It was a huge relief to hear Tyler's voice at the other end of the line.

'How's he doing?'

'It's not good.' She quickly told him what was happening. 'He's been really ill for the last couple of days and finally this morning the blood clot started to cause problems with his heart.'

'I'm so sorry, Saskia. I know you must be feeling awful right now…but at least they suspected what was happening and looked into it. Sometimes it's hard to know what's going on and these things can be missed. Sam's getting the treatment he needs.'

'I know. I just have to wait and hope and pray that he'll be all right.'

'He's in the best place for that kind of procedure. They have all the facilities they need and the surgeons are brilliant. He's in good hands.'

'Yes.' She tried to absorb all that and to allow his words to calm her. She said thoughtfully, 'How are things with you? Are you coping with the children?

They're very quiet—I can't hear a sound from them in the background.'

'Ah, well, gags can do that. They're a very effective measure when you're desperate.'

'Tyler!' In spite of all her worries she laughed.

He chuckled. 'No, seriously, they're fine. We're getting along okay. I think we'll cope until you get back.'

She gave a sigh of relief. 'Good. That's one less worry, anyway. Thanks for doing this for me, Tyler.'

'You're welcome.'

They talked for a few more minutes and then she cut the call. He'd managed to boost her spirits and he'd given her the strength to face up to what was happening with her brother.

She heard the rumble of a bed being wheeled back into the ward some time later, and straight away she stood up and went over to the bay where Sam was being treated.

He was drowsy and sedated, but he managed a smile. 'Hi, Sassie,' he said wearily. 'I'm glad you're still here. That was a bit scary, huh?'

'Too right,' she said, holding his hand in hers. 'How do you feel?'

'Tired…a bit sore…a whole lot better.'

'That's brilliant news.' She gave his hand a squeeze. 'You have to stop doing this to me, do you hear? You're to get better from now on and stop idling about in this bed. We want you back home.'

He smiled. 'I'll do my best.'

She gave him a hug and sat with him for some time until gradually his eyes closed and he fell into a deep, restful sleep.

'What happens now?' she asked the nurse. 'Has the doctor prescribed anticoagulants?'

'Yes, he has. He'll be on them for the next three months, I imagine.' She smiled. 'But I'm sure he'll be back home long before that. He should start to pick up from here on.'

Feeling much happier, and after a quick visit to Megan, Saskia set about making arrangements for her journey home. She was looking forward to seeing Tyler and the children, but her thoughts were tinged with apprehension. Would he really have been able to cope with the mess and noise and general disorder that three boisterous children could create? Why did she have to go and fall in love with someone who was the total opposite of herself?

Everything was quiet at first when she arrived back home later that afternoon. It was very odd. Boomer barked from somewhere in Tyler's house but no one came to answer her ring on the doorbell and she stood for a moment, wondering what she ought to do next. Then she heard childish laughter coming from the garden and she went in search of everyone, following the path around the side of the building.

Her eyes widened at the sight that met her. Dressed in jeans and T-shirts, Becky and Charlie were on their knees in mud where the garden had been flooded during the storm. They were wearing Wellington boots and gardening gloves and were busy putting plants into the ground under Tyler's supervision.

'Now, where did we say this one should go?' Tyler asked. He, too, was on his knees. 'Oh, I remember. Over there, where there's a space—it'll look good won't it, with those red flowers against the hosta in the background?'

Becky was studying the label. '"Late-flowering primula",' she read. 'It smells nice, doesn't it?'

Tyler sniffed the coppery-red blooms. 'You're right, it does.'

Charlie heaped soil over the roots and patted it into place. Then he laughed, wriggling about and waving his arms in the air as he sang, '"Another one bites the dust!"'

They all chuckled, and Caitlin, who was sitting at a table with a pad and pen, said, 'All right, here's the next one—Japanese water iris.' She consulted her pad. 'That one has to go next to the weigela.'

'Here we go, then.' Tyler handed the plant to Becky. 'Do you want to plant this one?'

'Yep, I do.'

Saskia stepped forward and Tyler glanced up. She was flabbergasted by the way Tyler and the little ones were happily ensconced knee deep in mud—Tyler, who preferred everything clean, neat and shipshape. She couldn't believe her eyes.

'Hi, you're back! That's great.' He stood up, brushing his hands along the length of his blue jeans to get rid of the worst of the dirt. He searched her face cautiously. 'How's Sam? How did the procedure go?'

'He's all right. Everything went really well, without a hitch. I think he's going to be okay.'

'That's fantastic.' He grinned as he moved towards her. 'I'd hug you if I wasn't so dirty.'

She looked him up and down, puzzlement in her green eyes. 'I can't believe what I'm seeing,' she said. 'You're grubby from head to toe, the children are filthy—how am I supposed to get their clothes clean after this?'

'They'll be fine. I told them to change into their oldest clothes. I'll shake the dirt off them and then we'll put them in the washing machine. No problem.'

She shook her head in disbelief. 'I would never have expected you to get involved in anything like this. I'm surprised Boomer isn't here with you, diving in among everybody.'

Tyler nodded. 'Oh, he tried. He kept wanting to help out with the digging, so in the end I had to put him back inside the house.' He waved a hand towards the area they were planting. 'What do you think of it?'

'I'm absolutely amazed,' she said. 'This is not like you at all. It's all curved edges and back to nature—there's nothing formal in it at all. You've actually dug up part of the lawn.'

'Well, it was always flooding, which made it difficult to maintain, and Caitlin caught me looking at it. She said, "Why don't you plant it with things that like a lot of moisture?" She's a clever girl, isn't she?'

Saskia nodded.

'So I took them all along to the garden centre and we picked out some plants that we thought might be good. And, hey, presto! It's done. Almost.'

'Good heavens.' She shook her head again. 'I can't get over it.'

His mouth curved briefly. 'Look, I need to go and take a quick shower. Why don't you stay here and see that they follow the plan Caitlin's drawn up, and I'll be back in two ticks?'

'Yes. I'll do that.'

He hurried away, leaving her to look around. She

was stunned by everything that she'd seen. Tyler didn't do this sort of thing. He'd never had much to do with children and mess and what bit he had seen he hadn't liked. So this was a whole new aspect, something she had trouble taking on board. And the children were mud-spattered! Good grief.

He came back into the garden as she was helping Caitlin identify a pretty plant with pink flowers and spiky foliage. He'd given her a sitting-down job because she was supposed to be convalescing. '"Hesperantha",' she said, reading the label. 'It's not one I'm familiar with.'

'I've made some tea,' Tyler announced. He was fresh and clean, wearing chinos and a shirt open at the neck, and he looked good, so different from the way he'd looked just a short time ago. Still, even grimy, he'd had an air of devil-may-care sexiness about him. 'Do you children want to finish off now, and then go and get cleaned up?' he said. 'You can leave your wellies in the utility room.'

'I'll see to it that they tidy up,' Caitlin said. 'We've about finished here, anyway.'

'That's good. Thanks. You've all done a brilliant job.'

He went with Saskia back to the kitchen and she stood by the table, simply staring at him. 'This is such an earth-shattering event,' she said, 'you throwing off your inhibitions and getting mixed up with we ordinary, untidy mortals. I can't get used to it.'

'Don't you like it?'

She smiled. 'I love it. I'm just wondering whether it will last. I mean, people don't change, do they?'

'Not usually, maybe.' He came over to her and put his arms around her. 'I'm glad your brother's all right—

your sister-in-law, too,' he said. 'Perhaps now you'll be able to relax and look forward to the future.'

'Yes. It's a good feeling.' It was heavenly having his arms around her. She wanted to rest her head against his chest and feel the beat of his heart beneath her cheek, but would things turn out the way she hoped? Dared she believe in a future where Tyler was there for her, come what may?

'I thought about what you said,' he told her. 'Ever since I was little I've longed for stability and security, but it was always elusive. The only way I could control what happened in my life was to make everything around me structured, methodical, neat and tidy. That was the only thing I felt I had any influence over.'

His hands stroked gently along her spine. 'And then, after you told me I should think about what was important, I realised that I was letting the most vital, essential part of my life slip away…you. I was pushing you away.' He lifted his hand to her cheek and lightly trailed his finger over the line of her jaw. 'I couldn't bear to have you leave me,' he said huskily. 'I want you above all else, Saskia. I love you. I'd do anything for you.'

A soft, shuddery sigh escaped her. 'That's all I ever wanted to hear, Tyler…that you love me. I fell in love with you against all my instincts, all my fears that everything would go wrong. But I know now that you're the only man I could ever truly love.'

A muffled groan of relief rumbled in his chest and he hugged her close to him, kissing her deeply, fervently, holding her as though he would never let her go.

'I can change,' he whispered against her cheek. 'For you, I'll do it…and it won't be a hardship. It'll be a new beginning.'

'You don't have to do anything,' she said. 'I'm sure we'll work things out—as long as we have each other, everything will come right.'

'It will if you say you'll marry me,' he said, his voice roughened. 'Will you marry me, Saskia? You'll make me the happiest man on earth if you say yes.'

'Yes,' she said, smiling up at him. 'I will.'

His breath caught in his throat. 'You've made my life full, brought me so much warmth and love and shown me what I've been missing. As long as I have you I could never ask for anything more. I'll never let you down.'

'I know you won't,' she said. 'I love you. From now on we'll be together and life is going to be good, so good.'

She lifted her face for his kiss, and for the next age they were lost in one another. It felt as though she'd come home.

* * * * *

A DOCTOR TO
HEAL HER HEART

BY
ANNIE CLAYDON

Published in Great Britain 2014
by Mills & Boon, an imprint of Harlequin (UK) Limited,
Eton House, 18-24 Paradise Road, Richmond, Surrey, TW9 1SR

© 2014 Annie Claydon

ISBN: 978-0-263-90785-8

Harlequin (UK) Limited's policy is to use papers that are natural,
renewable and recyclable products and made from wood grown in
sustainable forests. The logging and manufacturing processes conform
to the legal environmental regulations of the country of origin.

Printed and bound in Spain
by Blackprint CPI, Barcelona

Dear Reader

The work-life balance. Which of us gets it right all the time? I'll be the first to admit that sometimes I bite off more than I can chew, and work seems to overtake everything else, but still I aim to keep a balance.

Sam doesn't even try to get it right. She's always worked hard, but now she's working to forget the personal tragedy which shattered everything she'd built. And since the memories won't go away, that means she's working pretty much all the time. When she meets Dr Euan Scott work suddenly takes on a whole new meaning for her. But if he's going to help her face her past he'll have to persuade Sam to take some time off.

I hope you enjoy Euan and Sam's story. I'm always delighted to hear from readers and you can e-mail me via my website at www.annieclaydon.com

Annie x

Dedication

For George and Jenny

Recent titles by Annie Claydon:

**These books are also available in eBook format
from www.millsandboon.co.uk**

**Praise for
Annie Claydon:**

'Well-written brilliant characters—I have never been
disappointed by a book written by Annie Claydon.'
—*goodreads.com* on
THE REBEL AND MISS JONES

CHAPTER ONE

AT HALF PAST six in the morning the beach was deserted, apart from a few joggers and an early-morning dog-walker. After a hot, sticky night, the breeze from the sea was refreshing.

'You look like something the tide washed in...'

Euan Scott dropped into the faded deckchair that was set out, waiting for him. The temptation to close his eyes was almost irresistible. 'Yeah, I know. If it's any consolation, I feel...'

'Worse?' Canvas and wood creaked alarmingly as David Watson leaned across from his own deckchair, and swept Euan's face with an assessing gaze. 'What happened?'

'One of the kids from the clinic, Kirsty...' Euan blinked, trying to drive the picture of Kirsty's golden hair and blue lips from his mind. 'She took an overdose yesterday.'

David shook his head. 'How is she?'

'Hanging on. Her heart stopped three times and she's had intercranial bleeding. Her parents are with her.'

'Dammit. And she was doing so well...'

Euan didn't want to think about that. He didn't want

to think about how Kirsty might be, either, when she woke. If she woke.

'Yeah.' He scrubbed his hand across his face, trying to banish those thoughts. There were other kids who needed him, and he couldn't afford to fall apart over just one of them. 'So what's on the agenda for this week?'

'First thing is you go home and get some sleep.'

'What about the Monday morning meeting?' Euan nodded towards the sea in front of them. 'The board-room's all set up…'

The two directors of the Driftwood Drugs Initiative hardly saw each other during the week, David doing what he did best, raising funds and keeping everything running, and Euan working with their clients. The Monday morning meeting was the only uninterrupted time they got together and it was so sacrosanct that it didn't even take place in the office. When the weather was bad they were the first customers in the coffee shop by the pier, and when the sun shone they adjourned to the beach.

David shrugged. 'My side of things is fine. Your side needs some sleep.' He closed his laptop with an air of finality and slipped it into his bag. 'Any other business?'

There probably was, but it was dancing somewhere in the haze of fatigue that seemed to have suddenly blown in from the sea and Euan couldn't pin it down. 'Not that I can think of.'

'Right, then. Mel's on duty today, she'll deal with anything that comes in, and I'll see you in the office at lunchtime.'

'What's happening at lunchtime?'

'The software guy's coming down from London, re-member? To demonstrate his program.'

Euan could happily pass on that one in favour of another hour in bed and a very late breakfast. 'Do you need me? This is your baby.'

'That's why I need you there. I'm sold on the idea, it's you who needs convincing.'

This morning wasn't exactly the time. But he'd promised David he'd give the software a fair evaluation, and he wouldn't go back on that. 'Okay. I'll be there at twelve.'

'Half eleven. And wear something suitable.' David grinned at him.

'Suit and tie?'

'You possess such a thing?'

Euan shrugged. 'Maybe. Somewhere.'

David chuckled, rising from his deckchair and folding it. 'In that case, just don't wear shorts. I want to impress this guy that we're a bona fide organisation, and that we'll be a good place for him to launch his software.'

'I can type in shorts. I do it all the time...' Euan broke off, laughing, as David shot him a glare. 'Okay. Half past eleven. Showered, shaved and without the shorts.'

At ten to twelve Euan sat in the large, bright room that doubled up as David's office and the meeting room. The door had been firmly closed to indicate that they were unavailable, and the window was wide open in an attempt to dissipate some of the midsummer heat.

'Maya's going to bring the coffee...' They'd spent twenty minutes going over their requirements, and now David was fiddling with the chairs that stood around the conference table.

Euan batted a fly that had found its way into the room and it shot upwards, buzzing around the ceiling. 'We're a charity. We throw our money at our work, not our office accommodation.'

David eyed the fly as if it had the capacity to spoil all of his arrangements single-handedly. Footedly. Whatever. Euan reached for the newspaper on the desk beside him, waited for his chance and swatted it. 'Look, you know this isn't really my thing. But I've said I'll back you all the way on it, and I will. If this guy isn't right for us, we're not just going to forget about the computer project, we'll find someone else.'

The phone rang and Euan hooked it from its cradle. 'Yeah, Maya…'

'Sam Lockyear in Reception for you…'

'Thanks. Send him up. I don't suppose you could bring some coffee, could you?' He could do with something to dispel the lingering fuzz in his brain.

A stifled giggle sounded down the phone and Euan wondered what was so funny about coffee. 'I'll bring some with the sandwiches in half an hour.'

David sprang into action. This was what he did best, and Euan knew he'd have little to do in the next couple of hours other than to think of a couple of questions to ask and try to look interested in the answers. David would steer the meeting effortlessly from the moment he met their guest at the top of the stairs to the final handshake.

'Sam, meet Euan, my co-director here.' If David felt as wrong-footed as Euan suddenly did, he gave no sign of it.

'Pleased to meet you.' The woman smiled and held out her hand. A small, perfectly manicured hand, which, when he grasped it in a momentary handshake, turned out to feel as soft as it looked. A subtle waft of scent, which couldn't be anything other than expensive, assaulted his senses and the room began to spin.

Her suit was unmistakeably designer, although Euan wasn't really up on these things. She would have fitted in effortlessly in any business gathering, from a top-level meeting to corporate entertainment. But fitting in was clearly not what she wanted. No one wore that shade of red unless they wanted to stand out from the crowd.

She sat down quickly, as if she took it for granted that the men would wait for her to take a seat before they did and didn't want to keep them standing. Another practised smile, and then she slid a laptop from her bag, along with two small tablets.

'Thanks for coming.' David was about to go into the standard spiel about what Driftwood did, and Euan stared at the ceiling. It was that or look straight at her, and that was strangely unsettling.

'It's good to be here. I've been reading about your work with a lot of interest.'

'Yes?' David was well versed with this kind of interview, and he called her bluff.

'The Driftwood Drugs Initiative.' She paused. 'Any particular reason for the name?'

'When we started out pretty much everything we had was scavenged from somewhere. We all used to joke about it, and the name stuck.' Euan wondered whether she was really interested or just trying to change the subject.

She nodded, smiling. 'I see you've grown since then. You're operating from two locations now, this office deals with admin and public awareness, and there's a separate clinic, where you work directly with your clients. You're practical in your approach, providing both medical and social support for drug abusers and for their families. Your community-based approach has had a lot of praise from both drugs agencies and local healthcare providers—'

David cut her short with a chuckle. 'I doubt you got all of that from our website.'

'No, I didn't. Your website could do with an overhaul. You have good information on there but it's not organised to make it easy to find. I imagine that's not helping the public awareness side of your operation.'

She was well informed, astute and honest. And beautiful. Like a siren on the shore, calling to lost sailors… Euan put the thought out of his head, telling himself that he was neither lost nor was he a sailor.

'You have a point.' David glanced at Euan and he nodded dutifully. 'We're thinking of doing something with it, aren't we?'

'Yeah.' Euan hadn't been aware that he was thinking any such thing, but this was David's department. His was primarily medical care, and he was still to be convinced that a computer program had anything to offer in that context.

'Perhaps we should start by looking at the program.' Sam Lockyear had effortlessly taken control of the meeting now. 'I'm sure you'll have some questions for me.'

'Yes…' David reached for his notes.

'I hope that the software will answer some of those. I think it speaks for itself.' She leaned forward, proffering the tablets with a smile.

'That's what we're hoping.' It was impossible not to be drawn in by her smile and suddenly, almost against his will, Euan wanted her attention. When he got it, it jolted him into a new level of wakefulness. The kind where every nerve tingled at the slightest touch.

'Then we're off to a good start.' Her grey eyes held just the right amount of quiet humour, trapping his gaze for an endless moment, before she turned her attention to her laptop. He almost sighed with relief when she pressed a couple of keys and the tablet in front of him flashed into life.

Neat. David had dragged him along to a few of these software demos, and they usually involved a data projector and a lot of pointing at the wall. She had this down to a fine art. He ran his finger tentatively across the screen and tapped. Another screen flashed up in front of him.

She gifted him with a look of gentle reproach. Euan wondered how she would look with her hair spilling around her shoulders, instead of tied up in a dark gleaming knot at the back of her head.

'You can play with it in a moment. Let me take you through the basics first.'

'Right. Sorry.' He was grinning like an idiot and Euan composed his face into a look of stern assessment. He and David had a business decision to make, and however mesmerising Sam Lockyear was the software was the only thing that mattered.

The software was just as impressive as she was. She'd paid attention to the list of requirements that David had sent and had set the program up to demonstrate how it could meet their needs. By the time Maya brought in the sandwiches and a pot of coffee, David was clearly already sold.

'I'd like to see the reporting module.' David received a plate from Maya and left it undisturbed in front of him. 'It's essential for us to be able to report back to our funders on the various projects we have under way. Many of them have specific questions concerning targets and outcomes, and whether or not we receive ongoing funding depends on our answers.'

'Ah.' She leaned forward slightly, a look of unreserved happiness on her face, as if she had a real treat up her sleeve somewhere. Maya put a cup of coffee and a plate in front of her, and she flashed her a smile. 'Thanks…Maya.'

'You're welcome.' Maya pushed the plate of sandwiches towards her, clearly deciding that Sam deserved preferential treatment and that Euan and David could fend for themselves, then slid from the room.

'Mmm. These look nice.' Her hand hovered over the sandwiches and she selected a few, pushing the plate back towards David. The tricky balance between eating a sandwich, drinking coffee and typing was accomplished effortlessly, and she demonstrated how questions and keywords could be entered onto the system and individual reports generated for each funding body.

'Good. Very good.' David was obviously impressed. 'Euan, have you any questions?' He was already glancing at the agenda in front of him, clearly expecting the answer to be no.

'Yeah. I do have a couple…'

In meetings like this it was necessary to know what you were up against, and Sam had already made her decision about the directors of the Driftwood Drugs Initiative. David Watson was the organiser, the one who kept things running. Dr Euan Scott was the wildcard. Unpredictable, not yet convinced, and clearly capable of coming up with a few tricky questions and off-the-wall suggestions.

She focussed on his face, making herself look at him. 'Fire away, then.'

He leaned back in his seat, his brow furrowed in thought. Euan Scott was one of a kind. Handsome certainly. But even if she hadn't researched his career before coming here and been duly impressed by his qualifications and achievements, she would have known there was a lot more to him than surfer-blond hair and a tan. Behind his caramel-coloured eyes there was a cauldron of thought and emotion, none of which she could quite interpret.

Sam applied a mental slap to the back of her own head, trying to steady herself. *Don't let him draw you in. It's going well, don't blow it now.*

'The program's not being used by anyone else yet?'

His first stab, and he'd instantly found her Achilles' heel. 'No, not yet. I'm looking for someone who'll take that challenge on.' Sam paused, wondering whether that had been the right thing to say. Of course it was. The curl of his lips told her that this guy just loved a challenge.

'And you think that's us?'

She leant forward slightly, narrowing her eyes. Six years ago, when she and Sally had first ventured out together to sell their software, Sam had been awkward and terrified. Sal had taught her all the little tricks and techniques, when to hold back and when to be candid, and the two of them had been a great team. But even Sal's wisdom couldn't help her now. Imagining Euan Scott naked was *not* going to calm her down.

'This is the deal. New software, particularly third-sector software, isn't easy to get off the ground. Not many people want to stick their necks out and be the first to use a program that has no demonstrable track record, however good it is. I need an organisation that's forward looking enough to try something new, and in return I'm willing to work with you to make sure that the software meets your needs.'

'Bit of a catch-22 situation, really.' He ran his hand through his short-cropped hair, although whether it was to smooth it or create further disarray she wasn't sure.

'No more than the one you're already in. I've done some research and you fit the profile for the kind of organisation I want as clients. You're small, innovative and successful, and you're looking to expand. A good software system will help facilitate that, but I'm guessing you don't have a lot of spare cash to spend on it.' She took a breath. Her profile stipulated a drugs charity as well, but they didn't need to know that.

He nodded, a slow smile spreading across his face. 'I imagine there'll be some surprises along the way.'

'I'm hoping we'll be able to learn from each other. That always involves an element of surprise, doesn't it?' She gave a small shrug to indicate that the question was a rhetorical one, even though she wasn't very confident about the notion. Sam would bet good money that Euan Scott had plenty of surprises up his sleeve and generally, in software terms, surprise was not a good word.

'Why are you doing this?'

The question came straight out of the blue and

smacked her between the eyes. 'You mean why do I produce software?'

'No, it's clear that you're very good at that. I want to know why you're so committed to what's essentially a free piece of software. Why you're devoting so much time to something that's not going to bring you any financial rewards.'

She had a well-rehearsed answer for that. 'As you'll have seen from my personal CV, I was the director and co-owner of a very successful software company. Two years ago, when I sold up, I had the choice of going somewhere sunny and sipping cocktails or doing something that I love and giving a little back at the same time.'

'You don't like cocktails? Or sunshine?' He looked almost affronted at the thought.

'I like them both, actually. When I'm on holiday.'

His heavy-lidded eyes were probing, looking for the real answer. There was no judgement there, no expectation. He gave you the feeling that he could accept and understand pretty much anything, as long as it was the truth.

'I…' She took a breath. 'I'm doing what I do best in an effort to help a cause that I feel very strongly about. I have…personal reasons.'

His gaze held hers for a moment and then released her. A strange, almost dizzy feeling that she was about to slide from her chair onto the floor, and then he nodded. 'Yeah. I can understand that.'

David had seen her off the premises with a promise to call with their decision. When he walked back into his office he was shaking his head, smiling.

'Well, that was a turn-up for the books.'

'I thought you said that Sam Lockyear was a man.' She was all woman. From the crown of her immaculately coiffed head to… Euan decided he'd already given far too much head room to the thought of her perfectly manicured toes.

'I thought she was. Easy enough mistake to make, I suppose, with the name, but you've seen her emails. None of the women I know write emails like that.'

Euan saw David's point. Concise, almost to the point of being brusque, and devoid of anything that might be construed as a pleasantry, Sam's emails had given no hint of the delights that meeting her in person had brought. 'So what do you think?'

David snorted with laughter, flopping down into his chair. 'Don't pass the buck. What do *you* think? It's you she's going to be shadowing for two weeks, not me.'

'I don't think she's given us much choice. The program's great, and the offer she's made is too good to pass up. I'm not sure how she's going to fit in at the clinic, but we can deal with that one when we come to it.'

David nodded thoughtfully. 'What do you suppose the "personal reasons" are?'

'Does it matter?' Euan had been wondering about that too.

'You tell me.'

Euan's own personal reasons were a matter of record. In any other line of work his ex-wife's addiction, and the marriage that had been smashed by drugs, would have been no one's business but his own. But he demanded honesty from those around him, and could give no less himself.

'She's not directly involved with our work, she's just going to be observing. All we need to know is that the software's going to work for us.'

'You're beginning to sound convinced about this.'

'I'm open to changing my view. As always.' Euan rose from his chair, checked his wallet and found it empty. 'Will you call her? I've got to go to the bank and get some cash. And pick up something else to eat.'

'So your best advice is to go with the flow, eh? Feel our way...'

Perhaps not anything as tactile as that. 'If she's willing to spend two weeks with us to find out more about what we do, I'll do my best to...accommodate her.'

Euan batted at the ball of crumpled paper David had tossed at his head, smirking as it dropped neatly into the bin. He'd deal with the mysteries of jemmying the more intangible aspects of his work into computerised classifications when he came to it. Two small sandwiches for lunch wasn't enough and he was still hungry.

It appeared that Sam Lockyear wasn't going to be relegated to the bottom of his list of priorities without a struggle. Although the bank was in the other direction, a brisk walk along the promenade wasn't much of a detour, and it was Euan's preferred route, particularly when his head was still full of the dim echoes of last night.

If he hadn't stopped to lean against the thick stone wall between pavement and beach for a few moments and stare out to sea, he wouldn't have seen her. A hundred yards further along the seafront she would have been lost in the crowd if it hadn't been for the bright flash of her red jacket, draped over the back of her chair. She sat at a table at one of the open-air cafés that sprang up at the edge of the beach in summer, bare legs stretched out in the sun, her silky blouse open at the neck and shivering against her shoulders in the breeze.

Euan wondered whether she wanted some company, and decided that he didn't. Which didn't mean he couldn't watch her for a few more moments. Her head jerked suddenly and she reached for her bag, checking the display on her phone before answering it.

It was probably David. Euan wondered what his partner's reaction would have been if he could have seen the way she absently pulled the clips from her hair as she talked, shaking her head slightly to let the breeze style it around her shoulders in a mass of shining, dark strands.

She was looking at her phone now, as if she was checking back on the conversation she'd just had. Then, laying it on the table beside her, she punched the air in a motion that shouted of both joy and accomplishment.

Euan found himself smiling as he watched her jump to her feet, clearly apologising to a waiter, who she'd almost caught with her flailing arm. A laughing exchange and she accepted a coffee cup from him then pointed to the menu.

It was impossible not to wait and watch her sit down, hug herself and take a few sips from her cup. When the waiter returned, Euan smiled. An ice-cream sundae, which looked as if she'd ordered all the trimmings with it, and which she received with obvious joy and tucked into straight away.

Maybe she'd fit in at the clinic a little better than

he'd thought. He turned away from the sea, heading for the bank by the more direct route, turning that thought over gently in his mind.

CHAPTER TWO

HIS SECOND IMPRESSION of Sam was just as baffling as the first. Euan had hardly recognised her when she banged on the door of the Driftwood Initiative's offices at eight-thirty the following Saturday morning. The weak sunshine was diluted by clouds, but in what looked like overkill her eyes were shaded by both sunglasses and the peak of a cap. If she'd turned up at the clinic looking like that, he might have wondered what they concealed.

She nodded a hello, took the hat off and stuffed it into the pocket of her cargo pants. Without high heels, her face clean of make-up and her hair caught in a plait that snaked over her shoulder and tangled with the strap of her courier bag, she seemed younger, more fragile. Her green leather jacket wasn't too battered, but it wasn't too new either, and scuffed on one shoulder, as if she'd been in the habit of leaning in doorways.

'I hope I'm not too early.'

The remark might have been construed as condescending, given that she'd travelled down from London this morning and Euan lived ten minutes' walk away. There was nothing in her face that betrayed anything other than a straightforward question, but Euan still couldn't see her eyes.

'No.' He indicated the mug in his hand. 'Just in time for coffee.'

'Good.' She picked up the soft travelling bag at her feet and he stood back from the door, locking it shut behind her.

'Let me take that.' He gestured towards her bag and she hesitated, giving it to him with an air of slight suspicion, as if she thought he was about to run off with it.

'Would you like to see the bedsit upstairs? It's not very big…' Euan decided to concentrate on the practicalities first.

'That's fine. All I need is a bed and a bathroom.' She seemed different as well as looking different. The assured businesswoman had disappeared completely, as if she'd sloughed that identity off along with the red suit.

He motioned her up the stairs, careful not to touch her as he squeezed past her in the small space outside David's office and opened the door to the narrow, dark staircase that led to the loft apartment. The smell of disinfectant drifted down the stairs, and then the subtler scent of freshly washed linen.

'This is great.' She glanced into the cubbyhole that boasted two easy chairs and a small coffee table and made her way straight through to the slightly larger area, which contained a bed and the smallest wardrobe known to man. Euan dumped her bag onto the bed and she sat down next to it, bouncing up and down slightly. 'Good mattress. That's all I need.'

Her smile seemed genuine enough, but it had done the last time they'd met. 'Is this okay for the clinic?' She spread her arms, looking down at her costume. That was what it seemed like, a consummate actress wearing a costume for a part. 'David told me not to dress up, so I came as I am.'

'This is how you are?' The question seemed a bit forward, but it slipped out before Euan had a chance to stop it.

'Yes.' She grinned, finally taking off the sunglasses. Her grey eyes were the same, at any rate. Thoughtful and clear, almost luminous, the most beautiful eyes he'd ever seen on a woman. 'I'm a code-hacker at heart.'

Her smile was still infectious too, and before he knew what he was doing Euan had smiled back. 'And this is what a code-hacker looks like?'

She shrugged. 'Well, the stereotype has a couple of days' worth of stubble on his chin and wears T-shirts with nerdy computer jokes printed on the front. That's not a good look for me.'

Euan sighed. She was like a Russian doll. Every time you thought you'd got to the real Sam, there was another underneath, exquisitely painted and quite different. Bringing a woman that he couldn't fathom, who had admitted to nameless personal reasons, into the delicately balanced community of the clinic suddenly didn't seem like such a good idea.

'I'll…' He'd intended to take her with him this morning, but instinct had just changed his plans. He needed to think, and he didn't seem to be able to do that with any clarity when Sam was around. Perhaps because she smelled so nice. 'I've got to get going in half an hour, I've a surgery at the clinic this morning.'

'Saturday morning?'

'The weekends are often our busiest times. People who are working can only make evenings and weekends.'

If he was looking for surprise in her face, he was

disappointed. So many people reckoned that substance abusers automatically slept on other people's floors, wore dirty clothes and had no prospect of a job. There was that element, of course, but Euan numbered a stock-broker and a couple of company directors among his clients as well.

'Yes, I suppose so.' She slipped out of her jacket, revealing a purple printed top made from some kind of gauzy material, which begged to be touched. 'When can I join you?'

The little quirk of her mouth betrayed that she'd noticed that he'd sidelined her. He supposed he ought to feel guilty, after she'd got up early and come all the way here, but his clients came first. 'Why don't we meet up for lunch? David will be here in half an hour, and he'll take you through the clinic procedures and tell you about the new residential centre we're planning to open soon.'

She brightened, seeming to have put the rejection behind her, now that there was an alternative to occupy her. 'That's a good idea. Yes…it'll be good to have an overview before I see how it all works in practice.' A glimpse of the woman in the red suit. She looked at her watch. 'Say…twelve-thirty? Is that convenient?'

His footsteps sounded on the stairs, and Sam heard the street door slam. She flopped down onto the bed, looking around her. The apartment was small, scrupulously clean and already warm from the sun. Sam wondered whether the dormer window above her head would open to afford some ventilation, and decided that her first task was to find something to climb up on so she could find out.

Here she was, then. She'd promised Sal that she would do this, and here was the first real step towards making it a reality. Two years' work and a load of false leads from people who'd pretended to be interested in her software just so they could say they'd explored all the options.

'We'll be on top of the heap by Christmas…' The old joke made her smile and set a tear worrying at the side of her eye, all at the same time. Whatever the time of year, and however unlikely the prospect, Sally had always marked their triumphs with tubs of ice cream and that toast to the future. One Christmas they'd actually found themselves on the top of the heap. At least Sal had lived to see that.

Sam shook her head. It didn't matter how alone she felt in this empty building, or that the familiar pain of rejection seemed to twist deeper when it came from Euan Scott. He could be as handsome as he liked and as difficult as he pleased. She had a goal to achieve, and no one was going to get in her way.

The quiet, deliberate nature of the morning's work with David had settled her. He had offered to walk her down to the clinic, in much the same way as one offered to walk you into a lion's cage, and Sam had smilingly refused, zipping her purse and her keys into her jacket and pocketing her phone. If Euan thought she couldn't blend in, then she'd show him that melting into walls was her speciality.

The clinic was at the end of a row of small shops and offices in one of the streets that led from the shabbier end of the promenade. It didn't advertise itself, and once inside the main door there was another set of doors straight ahead, almost as if you needed to pass through an airlock to get into the place. Sam noticed the discreetly placed surveillance cameras, and wondered who was watching her.

Whoever it was, they buzzed her in and she found herself in a large, bright area that boasted comfortable chairs, a reception desk and a mural that appeared to have been made from the fruits of a beachcombing expedition. Euan was on the far side of the room, deep in conversation with a young man in overalls, and didn't look her way.

'You must be Sam. I'm Liz. Welcome.'

The woman who greeted her was of medium height, medium age and had an extraordinary smile. She wore jeans and a flowery apron, carried a mole wrench and seemed preoccupied with whatever was going on through the doorway behind the reception desk.

'Thank you. I've come to see Euan, but he looks pretty busy.'

'He usually is...' Sam followed Liz's gaze over to the two men. Euan's body language was relaxed but he was listening intently. 'That's my son he's talking to. Jamie's supposed to be mending the leak in the kitchen sink.'

'But you've been left holding the spanner...?'

Liz laughed. 'Exactly. Jamie's got a bee in his bonnet and he needs to talk to Euan about it. Meanwhile, I'm holding back the flood.'

Euan was talking now. Animated, concentrated, he had a long-limbed grace about him, the look of someone who was comfortable in his own skin. Just watching him made the tiny hairs at the back of Sam's neck shiver to attention.

'What do you normally do here? Apart from plumbing?' She dragged her wandering thoughts away from Euan.

'I'm a volunteer. I spend two days a week on the reception desk and doing odd jobs. Whatever it takes.'

'And Jamie…?'

'Jamie's the reason I'm here.' Liz waggled her finger in her son's direction. 'This place saved his life.'

Sam couldn't help but look back towards the two men. She'd read the statistics, pored over the reports, but this was different. Jamie was standing right there, and Euan had managed somehow to change the course of his life, where she had failed so conspicuously with Sally.

Questions flooded her mind, most of which she didn't dare put into words. Sam reminded herself that she wasn't here to get help, she was here to give it.

'Do you mind if I ask you something?'

'Isn't that what you're here for? David said you'd have plenty of questions.'

'This isn't really one of them. I was just wondering how Jamie is doing now.'

Liz laughed, her face lighting up. 'He's fine. Has his ups and downs, like everyone, but he's on the right track. He's working at his uncle's building firm, and he's gone back to college to get his qualifications.'

'Good. I'm really glad to hear it.'

'Thank you. It's good to be able to say it…' Liz broke off as the buzzer for the door sounded. She checked the screen behind the reception desk and released the lock. A small group of people entered, who Liz seemed to know, followed by a middle-aged couple who were looking around as if they were new here.

'I'm sorry, I won't be a moment. I think they're here to see Euan. Why don't you go and sit in the garden?'

'I'll sit here, if that's okay.' Sam gestured towards one of the chairs in the corner of the reception area.

'Yes, of course.' Liz walked over to the couple and started to talk to them, showing them to seats.

Euan was still talking, but he seemed to sense her gaze, as if it was something corporeal that had sauntered over to him and tapped him on the shoulder. He looked round and for a delicious moment it was as though he and she were the only two people in the room. Then reality broke in.

He acknowledged the couple who had just arrived with the smile that Sam felt should, by rights, have been for her. 'I'll only be five minutes…' Turning back to Jamie, he guided him through an open doorway to finish their conversation in private.

Euan had heard the door buzz, and knew that it must be Sam, but Jamie had caught him on the way to the door, and Liz had appeared from the kitchen to let her in. He caught a glimpse of her, just enough to want more, and then Jamie claimed his attention.

'So what's up?'

'I went to see Kirsty the other day.' Jamie was staring past him at a point somewhere behind his left shoulder. That was always a bad sign. 'Took Mum with me, so her parents wouldn't think I was a bad influence.'

'And did they?' Euan tried to catch Jamie's eye, but failed.

'Nope. Her mother cried and her dad shook my hand.' Jamie's shoulders squared a little.

'So how does it feel to be a good influence?'

Jamie dismissed the idea with a shrug, his mind obviously on something else. 'I just keep thinking. Kirsty's always been careful...'

'There's no safe way to take cocaine, Jamie.'

'Yeah, yeah. I know. All the same, there must be something different on the streets.'

There was. Euan had already heard some talk, and the results of the police tests on the remains of the white powder found on Kirsty had confirmed it. Cocaine that had a higher level of purity than usual was very bad news. Euan decided not to go into the details with Jamie.

'I still know some people. I could ask around, find out what's going on...'

'You think that's a good idea?' Euan asked with concern.

'I have to do something. Kirsty's not going to be the same again, is she?'

'Don't write her off. She's already made much better progress than I could have hoped, and she's still in recovery. If you really want to do something for her, she needs all the friends she can get at the moment.'

'And when it happens again I'll just go and make friends with that person, shall I? My social life's going to expand no end...' Anger was radiating from Jamie's tense frame.

'The drug agencies and the police are working on it, mate. What you need to do is to concentrate on helping Kirsty and on helping yourself. Let them do their jobs.'

'And if they don't...' Jamie's fists clenched. 'I can't just sit around, doing nothing.' A glimpse of the angry youth who had come so close to ruining his life.

'There are no answers, Jamie. Life's a problem. It's

supposed to hurt, and to make you angry and to keep you up nights, staring at the ceiling.'

Jamie puffed out a sigh. 'And the trick is to stay clean for today.'

'You said it.'

Something seemed to whisper across the back of his neck. The breeze as the entrance door opened, perhaps. When Euan looked round, he fell into the dizzying depths of Sam's luminous, thoughtful eyes.

Dragging his gaze away to steady himself, he saw the middle-aged couple talking to Liz. If they were who he thought they were, they were an hour late, but they'd come a long way to see him. Even if he doubted that he could be of any help in finding their daughter, he had to at least try. He acknowledged the couple and drew Jamie to one side, away from the people who were straggling through the door for this afternoon's group session.

'Call me, Jamie.'

'I don't need to. It's Kirsty we're talking about here, not me.'

'You sure about that?'

Jamie stared at him and then shrugged. 'Kirsty's a friend, and I didn't see this coming. What kind of a person does that make me?'

It was a question that Euan had struggled with for years. He'd been too blind, too busy to see his own wife's addiction. He knew all about the corrosive quality of that kind of guilt and Jamie deserved better than that.

'It makes you human. You've been a good friend to Kirsty, but you can't take responsibility for what she does. You're not to blame for what happened to her.'

Jamie's small, wordless nod was enough to tell Euan

that he was thinking about it and that he shouldn't press the point further. 'I'm going to the hospital later. I'll call you and let you know how she's doing.'

'Thanks. Are you going to be okay?' He searched Jamie's face for any sign that he was thinking of doing something stupid.

'Yeah. Go and sort someone else out. I'm fine.'

'We'll talk later, then.' He waited for Jamie's nod and then let him go.

He found Sam in the kitchen, making tea, while Liz watched the entrance door and chatted to Mr and Mrs Pearson. When she turned her face towards him, it was full of expectation.

'Want a cup of tea?' There was a clear, unspoken addendum to that, he realised. *Are you ready to give me some of the time you promised?*

'Sam, I'm sorry, but there are some people here to see me and it's important...'

She nodded gravely. 'Okay. I'll wait. Do you want the tea?'

It seemed churlish to take the tea and then desert her again. But on the other hand he could do with it. 'Um... if there's a spare cup in the pot.'

'There's enough to go around.' She opened the cupboard above her head and reached for another cup.

'Thanks, Sam. I'll be as quick as I can. Why don't you go and sit in the garden?' The clinic's garden was a place to relax. She shouldn't be having to help out, much less make the tea.

'That's okay. I may as well make myself useful.' She wouldn't meet his gaze, looking past him as Ian, the leader of this afternoon's group session, appeared in the doorway.

'Euan, can you see Pete? He's got some nasty cuts and bruises, looks as if he's been in a fight.'

'What, again? When was that, last night?'

'Yep. And he still doesn't trust the hospital enough to go there...'

'Okay, I'll be up in a minute.' Euan was uncomfortably aware that Sam was listening intently to the conversation.

'Does your group usually have tea?' She flashed a smile at Ian, leaving Euan out in the cold.

'Yes—that would be great, thanks.' Ian obviously thought that she was one of the new volunteers.

'Sam, there's no need—'

She cut him off in mid-sentence, concentrating on Ian. 'How many cups?'

'Six, thanks. Is there any ibuprofen in the medicine cabinet?' Ian turned to Euan.

'No, we're out.'

'That's okay. I'll pop to the chemist and get some.' Sam was obviously going out of her way to be helpful. Euan reckoned she was probably making a point as well. There was nothing for it at the moment but to let her get on with it and hope that Liz would rein her in if she started to do anything inappropriate.

'Bring the ibuprofen to me. All medicines have to be accounted for.'

Finally she looked at him. For all of two seconds. 'Okay. That's good to know.' Then she turned, opening the cupboards in search of more cups.

He'd done what he had to do then retreated back into the quiet of his empty surgery. Sometimes it was the looks on the faces of the families that were the most heart-rending. Mr and Mrs Pearson had given him their contact details, thanked him and left. They were probably sitting in their car right now, trying to find the words to comfort each other.

Euan picked up the phone, staring at the picture on the desk in front of him. He could at least make a few calls on their behalf, in the hope that someone had seen their daughter, Ellie. Maybe she'd even make it through the doors here, but somehow he doubted it.

He spent a fruitless fifteen minutes on the phone, and then made a note to circulate Ellie's details among the case workers and volunteers at the clinic. It was unlikely that any of them had seen her, but he'd promised the Pearsons that the Driftwood Clinic didn't give up on anyone.

His own words came back to smack him squarely on the jaw. Wasn't that exactly what he'd done with Sam this morning? A quiet knock interrupted his self-reproach, and Liz popped her head around the door.

'I'm on my way down now,' he said.

'It's okay. Sam's in the garden with Jamie. I gave them both lunch.'

At least someone had thought that she was probably hungry. 'Liz, you're a star. Thanks.'

'That's okay. You had to speak to those poor people.' Liz's face was strained with the knowledge that she could so easily have been in their shoes a few years ago. 'Can you give them twenty minutes before you come, though? Sam's just showing Jamie how to set up a blog for himself.'

Euan stood, craning his neck towards the window. They were sitting on a bench at the end of the garden in the shade of a massive tree, both focussed completely on their task. When she laughed, gesturing to make her point, he almost found himself envying Jamie. Which was stupid, because Jamie had only done what Euan had neglected to do, made her feel welcome and taken a bit of interest in what she did.

'So Jamie's decided to do it? That's good.' He smiled at Liz. 'Why don't you join them? I'll go downstairs and keep an eye on Reception.'

'No, that's okay. They don't need me to help. I don't even understand what a blog is.' Liz glanced in their direction with a hint of regret and then turned away resolutely.

Euan nodded, giving her a smile. Liz and Jamie had come a long way together, and Liz was only just learning to trust Jamie again. 'I'll bring you a cup of tea, then. Some of that ginger and honey stuff you like?'

Sam had seen Euan sitting on the steps that led out into the garden, and decided to stay put when Jamie left. If she didn't pester him, just showed that she could fit in and be of some use, perhaps that would begin to erode whatever objection he obviously had to her being here.

She purposely didn't watch as he strolled across the grass towards her. Didn't look up from the screen when she felt the bench she was sitting on take his weight. 'That was nice of you,' he commented.

At last. Something. 'It's easy to do when you know how. Didn't take long.'

'So it wasn't nice at all, then.'

She looked up and he was grinning. His smile sliced through all her resolutions to appear unconcerned about whether he noticed her or not.

'Do you have time to talk to me now?'

'That's what I wanted to say...' The flash of uncertainty in his light brown eyes only made him more difficult to resist.

'If you don't, that's okay. Just being here is telling me a lot about how the clinic operates...' She broke off as he held his right hand out. 'What?'

'Can we start again?' he asked.

She reached out tentatively.

'Don't look so suspicious. I'm trying to apologise.'

'So that's what this is. I generally find that "I'm sorry" works pretty well.' Sam's fingers were almost touching his. Not quite. Not yet.

'Fair enough. I'm sorry. You've made time for us, and I'll make more time for you from now on.'

Why did that sound like he was propositioning her? The tips of her fingers were trembling. 'You've got your doubts about this project, haven't you?'

'It's important to us. David needs some of the weight lifted from his shoulders...' He gave a rueful grin. 'Yeah, I do. But I'm listening now, and I'm open to being convinced.'

That was enough for now. She grasped his hand and gave it a little shake, trying not to notice the way his fingers almost caressed hers.

'Hi. I'm Euan.'

'Sam. Good to meet you, Euan.'

CHAPTER THREE

SHE COULDN'T ACCUSE Euan of doing anything by half-measures. Watching him give his undivided attention to others had been frustrating and Sam was unable to deny that she'd been a little jealous. Now that she finally had that attention, it was making her knees wobble.

His quiet enthusiasm, as he showed her around the clinic, seemed to seep through her skin, warming her. The comfortable counselling rooms and the tranquil garden. The community room, where a small group was talking over coffee. People were coming and going all the time, and he had a smile to spare for everyone.

He saved his surgery, which doubled up as his office, for last. Now that they were away from the community areas he seemed more animated, propping himself against the side of his desk to talk, while Sam scribbled notes. 'We're in transition at the moment. When the new residential centre is up and running it'll take some of the pressure off the clinics here, and allow us to extend our outreach services.'

'When's that going to be?'

'In the new year.'

'And you'll extend your services how...?'

'We're planning to set up clinics and groups especially for users of party drugs. Amyl nitrates, ket-amine hydrochloride, MDMA, methamphetamine... And we're getting an increasing number of people coming in with steroid abuse problems, so we're looking for someone who has experience of working with those kinds of body image issues.'

'Will you be doing different things here than at the residential centre?'

'Yeah. This place is ideal for clinics and groups, because it's central and easy to get to. The residential centre's out of town, so it's good for weekend conferences and long-stay patients.'

'And people will pay for the residential centre?'

'If they can afford it, they make a donation. We don't turn anyone away on the basis of money, and everyone's treated the same whether they pay or not.'

'It all seems so...' Sam couldn't really think of the right word. She'd expected the place to have more rawness about it. 'So calm here.'

Euan chuckled. 'Today's a good day. We try to keep the atmosphere here relaxed, but it's not always like this. Getting the better of an addiction is a long, tough process.'

'But you guide people through that. Bring them back.' She wanted to hear that Euan could single-handedly move mountains. Save the world. Someone needed to, because she couldn't.

He was suddenly sombre, sitting down opposite her in one of the chairs reserved for his patients.

'We can't bring them all back. The clinic has a great success rate, but we can't work miracles. Some of our clients will stop taking drugs altogether, some modify their habit and...some we lose.'

Her throat was suddenly dry. 'But surely... Once someone *wants* to give up drugs, and they get help...'

'That's a great start. But addiction's a powerful thing. Wanting to give up and getting the appropriate help is the first, all-important step on a very long road. Many of our clients have been through rehab more than once.'

'How do you deal with that?' Sam could hear an edge of desperation in her voice. For the last two years she'd thought that if only Sally had said something about her drug-taking, everything would have been okay. It hadn't been much of a comfort, but it had been something to hold onto in a world of ever-shifting pain, and now Euan was snatching it away.

He leaned forward, his gaze searching her face as if he was trying to fathom out what she was really asking of him. 'Sometimes I don't. There are times when not being able to deal with something might be the most appropriate reaction.'

Sam would have to think about the implications of that statement. Later. 'But you're still here.'

'Yep. So are you.'

Touché. Sam had her own reasons for that, and clearly Euan did too. She picked up her pencil and tried to think of a less demanding question.

'What time does the clinic stay open until?'

'Eleven o'clock. But my shift ends in ten minutes. I'm on call, but only for emergencies.' His lips twitched into a smile. 'Do you like Chinese?'

That sounded like a trick question. 'It depends...'

'In that case, you'll like the place I've booked for dinner.' He grinned at her discomfiture. 'A working dinner.'

'Oh, so you're going to make me sing for my supper, are you?' Almost against her will she smiled back at him.

'Were you thinking of clocking off yet?'

No, she wasn't. Working too many hours was a way to keep from thinking too much. And if she fell into bed exhausted every night, that just meant that she slept a bit better. She did have to eat, though.

'Am I okay to go as I am?' Sam looked at her cargo pants and sneakers.

'You want to show me up?' He placed a hand on his chest, laughing. 'Although you can if you want. This place doesn't have a dress code.'

It would be impossible to show Euan up. He could ruffle his hair all he liked, wear whatever leapt out of his wardrobe at him, and still look good. His broad shoulders and the show-me-more ripple of muscle under his casual shirt attested to the fact that he'd already put in all the work he needed to on his appearance.

'I left my tiara at home. I'll show you up next time.'

He grinned. 'I'll look forward to it.'

When he ushered her out of the building he seemed to take a deep breath, sloughing off the cares of the day. They strolled down to the seafront together, walking along the promenade for half a mile, until Euan turned inland towards the centre of town.

'Do you always go via the seafront?' Sam was still getting her bearings, but she had an inkling that they probably could have cut ten minutes from their walk by taking a more direct route.

'Usually.' He grinned. 'No point in living by the sea if you don't grab as much ozone as you can.'

Sam jerked her thumb back towards the sea. 'That's

the English Channel out there. I didn't know there was any ozone...'

He chuckled. 'Probably not. I like the beach, though.' He made a sharp left, and opened the door of a glass-fronted restaurant, motioning her through.

Inside, there was already a hum of activity. Euan was clearly a regular, and the waitress who came to their table greeted him by name and handed Sam a menu, chatting to Euan while she scrutinised it.

Perhaps he brought his girlfriends here. No one seemed much interested in her, and Sam imagined he probably turned up with a different woman on a fairly regular basis. If he had a regular partner, she would have attracted more attention, and Euan was the kind of man who was unlikely to go short of female company...

'Decided yet?'

Sam jumped and focussed her eyes back on the menu. 'Um... What's the Kung Po chicken like?'

'Good. Very good,' the waitress replied.

'I'll have that, then. With some rice and...' The waitress nodded, scribbling her order down in Chinese characters on her pad.

'Something to drink?'

'Water, please. Sparkling.' Sam never drank when she was working, and although tonight fell into a grey area somewhere between work and socialising, she needed to be careful around Euan. His job involved getting people to talk about how they felt, and he was obviously good at it. It would be horrifyingly easy to tell him her darkest secrets before she'd even realised it, and she wasn't here for that.

He didn't seem to make such distinctions, though. His work was intimately personal to him, bound up with feeling and hope and dreams. Even his discourse on health and safety procedures seemed more intimate than it should have been. Leaning across the table so that they could hear each other in the ever-increasing din of the restaurant, lost in the compelling magic of his eyes, it almost felt like a tryst.

'So tell me something about yourself.' They were waiting for their coffee now.

'Not much to tell, really.' She grinned at him. 'I was born. I went to school, then university…'

'Computer sciences?'

She nodded. 'When we were at university together, my best friend and I had an idea. After we graduated, we thought we'd lose nothing by seeing if we could make something of it. We started off working from Sally's parents' spare bedroom.'

Even *best friend* didn't cover it. The two girls had been seven years old when Sally had asked Sam back to her house one day, after Sam's mother had become unavoidably detained by a bottle and some bad company and it had slipped her mind that she even had a daughter. With the benefit of hindsight, Sam could see that Sal's mother had only needed to take one look at her to divine the situation, but she'd said nothing. Just laid an extra place at the table and made sure that Sam got home safely that night. After that, Sal's family had become hers. And the two girls had been inseparable, like the closest of sisters.

'And you made quite a go of it.' Euan was nodding her on, and Sam realised that she'd fallen silent.

'Yeah. Sal was the creative one, she had the ideas, and I did the programming. We made a good team.'

'But you sold up?' The look in his eyes told Sam

that he wasn't falling for the sugar and spice version of the story.

'Yeah. Things change.'

He didn't ask. Maybe he was thinking about it, and maybe he realised that she wouldn't answer if he did ask. He paused, as if to allow her to reconsider her decision, but she couldn't.

A tone sounded and he pulled his phone out of his pocket, giving her a mouthed apology before answering it. 'Yeah, Mel. What's up?' His face darkened as the relief doctor at the clinic spoke at the other end of the line.

'Okay. Yeah, that's all right. Leave it with me.' He cut the line, shoving his phone back into his pocket. 'I'm sorry, Sam.'

'That's okay. We have to go?'

'I have to go.' He stood, pulling some notes from his wallet and beckoning to the waitress. 'You have coffee. Call this number…' he put a card from a cab company in front of her '…and tell them to put the fare back to the flat on the Driftwood account.'

'I'm coming with you.' Where the hell had that come from?

'This is not part of your job…'

'It's what you're all about, though, isn't it? Give me a chance to at least see that.' Sam was overstepping the mark, and she knew it. But here, at last, was the whole point of the infrastructure, the policies and the software. She'd found her way down to the heart of what made Euan tick.

He paused, clearly grudging even the two seconds that it took to think about it.

'Give me a chance, Euan. I won't get in the way, and I'll do as you say. I promise.'

'Okay.' He pushed the notes into the waitress's hand and she took them, clearly used to Euan leaving abruptly. 'We need to hurry.'

CHAPTER FOUR

EUAN MUST LIVE close by, because his car was only two streets away in a quiet backwater of a road. Sam didn't have much chance to take in the neighbourhood, because her lungs were bursting from their dash to the car.

His one concession to her presence was to open the passenger door of the black SUV for her before he got behind the wheel and started the engine. They drove in silence while Sam caught her breath and Euan negotiated the traffic through the centre of the town.

'Where are we going?'

'It's only another couple of miles. Mel's heard about someone who might be in trouble…' He caught her questioning look and puffed out a sharp breath. 'The clinic's a community. People look after each other and they'll often come to us before they go to the authorities if they think there's a problem.'

There was obviously a great deal more to it than that, but Euan was keeping his own counsel. 'They come to you before they go to the police, you mean.'

'Yeah. Which doesn't mean that we won't refer things on to the authorities if we need to.'

'Must be a hard line to tread.'

He shrugged. 'Not really. We abide by the law. We

don't abandon those of our clients who fall foul of it to the system, though.' The car slowed as he turned off the ring road. 'Look, Sam, I want you to stay in the car...'

No. She'd got this far, she wasn't staying in the car. 'Perhaps I can help.'

'If everything's okay, I won't need you. If it's not, then...it may not be the place for you.'

It was the only place for her. Sally had died alone, as a result of drugs abuse. Sam would have given anything to be able to go back and be there for her friend, but that wasn't possible. Maybe being there for someone else would help her sleep at night.

'I want to go with you. I understand what that means.'

A quick, searching look as he slid the car against the kerb. Euan made his decision in the tick of a second. 'I'm not sure you do. But you can come if you do exactly as I say.'

'It's a deal.' Sam jumped out of the car before he could change his mind and followed him up the front path of a large, detached house.

When Euan rang the bell, there was silence, then a thumping sound from inside and the door was flung open. 'Hi.' A tall blonde smiled out into the night, her gaze roving across them and sticking on Euan. 'Can I help you?'

'My name's Euan Scott. I'm a doctor, and we've had a report that a Carrie Grayson is unwell. At this address.'

'Carrie? She's in her room, I think.' The girl looked behind her and shouted back into the house. 'Paul, have you seen Carrie?'

'Upstairs,' a bored, male voice said. 'She came in

about an hour ago, said she was going to bed. She looked like shit.'

'Please, will you check on her?' Euan's voice was gentle but firm. 'It's important.'

The blonde hesitated. 'Okay. Stay here.' She closed the door in their faces, and Sam could hear the sound of voices inside the house.

'Ohh!' Sam almost stamped her foot in frustration and Euan smiled grimly.

'Would you let two strangers into your house on a Saturday evening?' He felt in his pocket and handed her the car keys. 'Here, my medical bag's in the boot. Would you fetch it, please?'

Maybe it was a test to see if she really would do as he said. Maybe he just reckoned he was going to need the bag. Whatever. If bag-carrier was the role she was being offered, she'd be the best damn bag-carrier he'd ever seen. Sam hurried to the car, opened the boot and heaved the bulky bag out, staggering slightly as she slung it onto her shoulder.

Did he really need all this? She supposed so. There were so many different ways a person could die, and that meant a lot of different ways to save them. Sam slammed the boot shut and was halfway back up the front path when the front door was flung open.

'We need help…' The blonde's eyes were wide with panic, her hair flying around her shoulders.

'Okay.' Euan stepped inside without a backward glance in Sam's direction. 'Where is Carrie?'

Sam made the front door at a run, and followed Euan up the stairs and along a wide, well-decorated hallway. The blonde was motioning Euan into a doorway at the far end.

'I think she's dying…' The blonde caught Sam's arm as she went to follow Euan inside.

'We don't know anything yet. Let the doctor see her…' Sam prised the clenched fingers from her arm. 'Stay here and stop anyone else from coming into the room. Can you do that?'

'Yeah. Call me if you need me. My name's Helen.' The girl was younger than Sam, a student probably, and she was tearful but resolute.

'Will do.' Sam took a deep breath and stepped into the room.

A young woman was lying on the bed, fully clothed, her limbs jerking fitfully. The smell of vomit was sharp in the air and Sam ignored the bile that rose from her own stomach and hurried over to where Euan was examining Carrie, putting the medical bag down next to him.

'Thanks.' He hardly looked at her. 'Call an ambulance, please. Let me speak to the controller when you get through.'

The rapped-out instructions told Sam how grave the situation was. She dialled quickly, watching as Euan pulled a blood-pressure monitor from the bag, wrapping it around Carrie's arm. She waited until he'd finished and then held the phone to his ear so he still had both his hands free to stop Carrie from rolling off the bed. He spoke quickly, words that Sam half understood and couldn't comprehend through the sharp misery of having to stand by and watch, unable to help. 'Okay, thanks… Ten minutes. Good…'

He glanced up at Sam as she ended the call. 'Can you hold her still? As gently as you can, just try to stop her from lashing out and hurting herself. And be careful she doesn't hurt you.'

'Okay.' Sam was trembling but she crawled onto the bed next to Carrie and put her arms around her. Maybe she should talk to her. She wasn't sure whether Carrie could hear her or not, but it might be worth a try. 'It's all right, Carrie. You're going to be all right. Just let the doctor do his work.'

She caught what might have been a brief smile on Euan's lips as he took Carrie's arm and injected something into it. Perhaps he thought that she was being stupid, but all the same she kept talking in the hope that Carrie might hear her reassurances.

'Okay, shift over a bit, I need to listen to her heart again.' Sam moved, and pulled Carrie's rumpled blouse open so that Euan could press the end of the stethoscope to her chest. He nodded. 'Good. Just stay there.'

There was approbation in his eyes and Sam felt tears begin to well. She blinked them back, turning her attention to Carrie, dimly aware that Euan was taking something from his bag. 'Here, hold the oxygen mask over her face. Yes, that's right.'

Euan had Carrie's wrist between his fingers, checking her pulse, watching her intently for… Sam didn't know what. She couldn't think about what at the moment. Carrie was breathing, and that was all she knew.

The doorbell rang, and Helen's head poked around the door. 'What do I do?'

'Answer it, it's probably the ambulance.' Euan didn't look up.

'Yes. Right.' The girl disappeared, and then the clatter of heavy boots on the stairs heralded the ambulance crew's arrival. Euan took a moment to brief them, and then Sam moved away from Carrie to allow them to take over.

She almost staggered backwards, unable to help any more but unable to leave either, so she perched herself awkwardly against a dresser in the corner of the room. Euan and the two ambulancemen were busy, and she tried to keep her eyes on Carrie's face, silently willing her to get through this.

Finally they were finished. Euan repacked his medical bag while Carrie was strapped securely into a carry chair, and slowly, gently the ambulance crew manoeuvred her down the stairs. Sam followed, unsure what to do next.

Helen caught her arm. 'We didn't know she was ill. Is she going to be all right?'

'You'll have to ask the doctors.' Helen was chewing her lip, watching through the open front door as Carrie was lifted into the ambulance. 'Do you want to go with her to the hospital?'

'She's my friend.' Tears were rolling down the blonde's cheeks now. 'I didn't know... Really I didn't. We were all downstairs and Pete said that Carrie had just gone to get an early night...'

Sam recognised that kind of guilt. 'Look, it's all right.' She took Helen's hand and squeezed it to emphasise her point. 'You can't change the fact that you didn't know Carrie was ill. Don't let how you feel about that stop you from being there for her now.'

Helen still hesitated. Sam would have done anything to have had this opportunity with Sally. 'Carrie's got a second chance, and so do you. Are you going with her or not?' she asked firmly.

Helen pulled a coat from the rack and picked up a shoulder bag. 'Yeah. I'm going.'

Sam nodded and led her out to the ambulance, catching the attention of the driver and shepherding Helen into the back of the vehicle. When she looked around for Euan, he was leaning against the bonnet of his car, arms folded and watching her.

'What?' There was a half smile on his lips when she walked over to face him.

'You've got something on your trousers.' He caught her hand as she bent to brush whatever it was away. 'No, don't do that.'

For a moment her gaze met his. For just one second she thought she felt his grip loosen into a caress, and then he let go of her wrist. 'Here, let me.' He snapped a surgical glove onto one hand and bent to scrub at a large blob, just below the knee, which looked suspiciously like vomit.

'Eugh!' It seemed that Sam's usual sensibilities were returning. 'Is it all off?'

'Yeah.' Euan got to his feet, rolling the glove off his hand and over the wipe he'd been using in one swift movement. 'Would you like to go home?'

'Mmm, I think so.' The smell of the bedroom where Carrie might have died seemed to be clinging to her, and she wanted to have a shower and change her clothes. 'Is Carrie going to be all right?'

'I hope so. She wasn't in very good shape when we found her, but we got to her in time.'

'What would have happened if we hadn't?'

He looked at her, his eyes dark in the gathering gloom. 'Why don't I take you back to the flat so you can get a shower and change your clothes? We can have that coffee we missed out on after we ate.'

He seemed to know that she was just itching to get out of her clothes. Sam wondered whether he felt the same way. 'Don't you want to get home?'

'Nah, that's okay. The feeling that you want to scrub your skin raw wears off.' He grinned at her.

She couldn't let go of this as easily as Euan appeared to have done. She needed his help. 'In that case…yes, coffee would be good.'

Euan sat staring at the wall of David's office. He'd left Sam to go upstairs alone, and he could hear the shower running. Now that he was by himself he was shivering, almost as if he was in shock.

Something about Carrie must have reminded him of his ex-wife. That was all it was, he'd been thinking about Marie and the old guilt had just pushed its way to the surface and slapped him in the face. Asked him whether he thought that caring about Carrie really let him off the hook for not caring enough about his own wife.

Or maybe it was Sam's reaction. The way she'd been so determined to help, how she'd almost willed Carrie not to die. How she'd practically bundled Helen into that ambulance. The questions that he'd resolved not to ask just wouldn't go away.

Whatever. He'd deal with it. He'd dealt with all of this before, and he would do it this time too.

A noise at the doorway jerked him out of his reverie. Sam was dressed in comfort clothes, a pair of faded jeans and an oversized cardigan wrapped around her as if there was some need to keep warm. Her hair was sleek and still damp, spilling around her shoulders like a cascade of tears.

'Hey.' Somehow the grinding sadness, the guilt that was so old he could hardly name it any more, lifted. Sam needed him, and Euan knew how to respond to need. He felt himself smile at her, and before he knew it, he believed in the smile.

'Hi.' She sat down in the chair that he'd pushed towards her with his foot.

'Feeling better?'

'Yes, I'm fine. Things are going to be all right, aren't they?'

Euan had no idea whether things were going to be all right, but there were times when reassurance had to take precedence over the truth. 'Everyone's in one piece. And tomorrow's another day.'

The endless redemptive properties that tomorrow seemed to hold finally made her smile back at him. She hesitated and then her grey eyes met his gaze. 'Will you tell me what happened? With Carrie?'

'I can't tell you everything without breaking a confidence. Let's just say that a friend of a friend knew that she was in bad shape.'

She nodded. 'I meant what happened while I was there.'

She'd been so capable, so cool that Euan had almost forgotten that this was probably the first time she'd been in a situation like this. It was likely that she didn't even know what had been wrong with Carrie, although he'd recognised her symptoms straight away.

'Carrie had been taking cocaine. Her blood pressure was very high and her heartbeat was fast and irregular.'

'And you gave her something to counteract the drug?'

'No. There's no reliable antidote for cocaine, and by itself it's not fatal. It's the side effects of its use that are dangerous, and we treat them as and when they present themselves. I gave her a shot of diazepam, which is a sedative.'

'And that got her heart rate under control?'

'Yeah.' He smiled at her. 'And talking to her, reassuring her, didn't do any harm at all.'

She flushed pink, but shook her head as if it was nothing. 'And she'll be all right now?'

'She's not out of the woods yet. But she'll be closely monitored at the hospital, and they can keep her stable until the drug's worked its way out of her system.'

Sam nodded. 'What would have happened if we hadn't turned up?'

'It's difficult to say. Her body might have coped with the effects of the cocaine, and she'd have woken up tomorrow morning feeling pretty grim but otherwise none the worse for it. Or she could have died.'

She was looking at him intently, as if everything that he was saying was being fitted into a giant jigsaw puzzle in her head. 'How much do you think she took?'

'Impossible to say. Illegal drugs aren't regulated, and they vary enormously in purity and composition, so it's impossible to predict their effects. And with cocaine, even small amounts can produce the kind of effects we saw tonight.'

Her brow was creased, as if with some gargantuan effort. 'Is that what you wanted to know?' Euan asked the question as gently as he knew how.

She nodded, clearly not quite trusting herself to speak.

Euan had a question of his own. 'I'm glad Carrie's friend went with her to the hospital.'

She didn't take the bait, and he tried again.

'I saw you talking to her…'

'Yes. She was feeling pretty guilty that she'd been there in the house and hadn't realised that Carrie needed help.'

'It happens.' His observation prompted a downward twitch of her mouth. 'What did you say to her?'

'That she had another chance to be there for her friend and that she should grab it with both hands.' She lifted her face towards him and Euan almost choked. So much pain there.

'You did really well tonight, Sam. I was glad that you were there.' The words seemed pretty inadequate in the face of whatever it was that was going on behind those beautiful, agonised eyes, but she smiled anyway.

'Thanks.' She waved her hand in front of her face, as if to bat away the bad thoughts. 'Are we going to have some coffee, then?'

It was a clear invitation to drop the subject before they got too close to the mysterious *personal reasons*. He could do that. Euan could wait.

CHAPTER FIVE

THEY'D TALKED FOR a long time last night. As if something important had happened and neither wanted to let go of it, even though it remained unspoken.

Unspoken maybe, but it *was* important. Sally had died alone, from what had been described as a cocaine overdose, but at the time no one had bothered to explain to Sam what that actually meant. And now Carrie had lived. That had to mean something, although Sam had been too tired by the time Euan had left to work out what.

She'd slept deeply, and woken up late on Sunday morning. When she moved her head, pain splintered through her right temple.

Sam groaned, rolling onto her back, holding her head between her hands as if somehow that would lessen the pain. Fat chance. She wondered whether she was going to be sick or not, and whether it would be prudent to get herself to the bathroom first, before hunting down the migraine tablets in her handbag.

She managed to get to her feet and the world lurched sickeningly. Bathroom first.

Euan hadn't meant to go to the office on Sunday morning, but he was vaguely aware of unfinished business from last night. Perhaps if he bumped into Sam, he'd be able to work out the nature of the business, and quite why it was unfinished.

The place was quiet when he arrived, and he settled down in David's office to do some paperwork. She was probably asleep.

It was ten o' clock before he heard the sound of running water from upstairs. Euan forced his attention back to the report in front of him. She'd make an appearance in her own good time.

A moment later a crash and the sound of breaking glass brought him to his feet. He hurried to the closed door of the flat and knocked on it. 'Sam...? Are you okay?'

No answer.

'Sam!'

He wasn't sure whether she could hear him or not, or whether he would hear her if she called for help. Finding the spare key for the flat in David's desk drawer, he unlocked the door, stopping at the bottom of the stairs.

'Sam, I'm coming upstairs.' He heard her voice slurring something that might have been an answer, or might not, and he didn't wait to work it out.

She was leaning against the tiny kitchen sink, dressed in a white cotton nightdress, shards of broken glass and rivulets of water around her bare feet. He spoke her name and she hardly seemed to notice he was there.

For a moment everything that he was sloughed away like a discarded skin, leaving just a creature of instinct behind. All he could think about was a primitive urge to gather her up in his arms and make everything all right.

'Don't move…' He crunched across the fragments of glass on the floor, and she tried to bat him away.

'It's okay…' She was groggy, shading her eyes from the light. At the back of his mind the doctor was scrolling through all of the substances that could produce those particular symptoms, and Euan pushed those thoughts away.

'Here. Careful now.' He lifted her up gently, clear of the broken glass, and she moaned, clutching her head. Carrying her through to the tiny sitting room, he put her down in the chair.

'Migraine…' She seemed to be struggling to put a cogent sentence together. 'My tablets are in my handbag…'

Of course. Euan wondered wryly whether he'd been doing this job too long. Not everything was the result of illegal drugs. 'Okay. I'll get them for you.'

He covered her with a throw that lay folded over the back of the chair, and made for the kitchen. Euan found her bag, sitting on top of the refrigerator. He wondered briefly whether he should be looking inside it, and reminded himself that he usually had little compunction in turning a woman's handbag upside down in the name of effective treatment. Gingerly he nudged her purse and a bunch of keys to one side, and saw the top of a bottle of tablets. Pulling them out, he checked the label.

'Here.' He knelt down beside her chair, put two of the tablets into her hand and held the glass of water steady as she curled her shaking fingers around it. 'Careful…' A dribble of water ran down from the side of her mouth as she drank, and he caught it with one finger, brushing it away.

'Let me see your feet.' The request seemed somehow improper, although Sam had hardly reacted to it.

She ignored him, seeming ready to curl up in the chair and sleep right there. Euan bent down, examining her feet for any signs of glass or blood, and found nothing. Carefully he covered them up again with the throw, tucking it around her.

'Thanks.' She shaded her eyes with one hand, opening them a crack. 'I'll be okay in a minute.'

'You should lie down.'

'I'm all right. Don't fuss.'

'You'd be more comfortable.' Euan broke off, realising what the problem was. 'Stay here for a minute.'

'Yeah. I'll stay...' Her words tailed off into nothing as he stood and made his way to the bedroom.

The bed was rumpled, the morning sun shining through the skylight above it. A perfect way to wake up, bathed in warm sunlight. Unless, of course, every shard of light seared its way through your head. Euan moved the bed out of the way, got a stool from the kitchenette, and reached up to the window.

It took a shove to get it open, but once he had a breeze started to circulate in the room. That done, he pinned a couple of tea-towels across the frame, blocking the light.

'Okay.' He tapped her hand to rouse her. 'I've covered the skylight...'

'Uh?' She stared blearily at him.

'Come with me.' He gently tried to guide her to her feet, but she wasn't going anywhere. So he lifted her in his arms again, catching his breath as he felt her snuggle against him.

All he could think about as he carefully manoeuvred her through to the bedroom was her scent. The feel of her warm skin. The tumble of her hair, caressing his arm.

'Euan…' When she murmured his name he felt his legs tremble, and he held her closer. 'It's too hot…'

'I've opened the window.' She gave a little sigh as he laid her down carefully on the bed and covered her with a sheet. All he wanted was to lie down beside her, feel the curl of her body against his again. 'Sleep now.'

'Mmm. I'll be okay in a minute… When the tablets kick in.' She was half-asleep already.

'Sure. Is there anything you want?' Euan looked around the room. One of the chairs from downstairs would fit in the corner, and he could watch over her while she slept. Just in case she woke up and needed him.

'Will you go away, please?'

She was still pale, and she looked somehow small and frail in the light summer dress she wore, but at least she was back on her feet. Euan had cleared up the broken glass from the kitchen floor, checked that she was sleeping, and gone back downstairs, leaving the door to the flat open so that he could hear if she called for him. He was almost disappointed that she hadn't. Two hours later he'd heard the sound of the shower and then the pad of her bare feet on the stairs.

'Feeling better?'

'Yes. Thanks.' She sat down beside David's desk, the filmy printed material of her dress moulding itself to the shape of her legs. 'I'm…sorry, I was feeling pretty rough this morning. I didn't mean to be rude.'

If she had been, he hadn't noticed. Probably too busy

drinking in the pleasures of having her close. Which was wrong, on almost every level that he could think of. 'It never occurred to me you were.'

She seemed to be weighing the statement up. 'Thanks.'

'You get migraines often?'

'Once every couple of months maybe. I take the pills and sleep a bit and then I feel better.'

He nodded. 'Do you always use the tablets you had in your bag?'

'Yeah. For years.'

'They might not be the best thing…'

Stop. Right now. Euan's sense of self-preservation snapped into action. It was inadvisable to throw attraction into the mix with someone who could end up supplying one of the charity's most important organisational tools. It was wrong to want to hold onto someone when the two emotions that most readily sprang to mind when he imagined himself in a relationship were guilt and betrayal. And now he was thinking about getting involved with her medical treatment? That was professional suicide.

'Might be an idea to go back to your own doctor and get him to review your medication. There are new drugs coming out all the time. Migraine's one of those things that we're still in the process of understanding,' he said instead.

Her laugh was cut short, and she pressed her fingers to her temple. 'My doctor doesn't understand it at all. Most of what I know about managing it came from other sufferers on discussion boards on the web. He's just good for the drugs…' She flushed. 'Sorry, I didn't mean…'

Euan smiled. 'It's a fair point. A lot of people who suffer from chronic illness know more about their treatment than doctors do.'

This time she thought before she spoke. 'Yeah. I didn't mean to imply that all doctors are useless.'

As there was no one else in the room, Euan took that as a compliment. 'Never thought you did.'

A lazy smile spread across her face. A particularly beautiful smile, Euan thought.

Usually a migraine didn't stop her from working for more than a couple of hours—as soon as the drugs kicked in, she'd be back at her computer screen, wearing dark glasses if necessary. It appeared that Euan had other ideas.

'Do I have to confiscate that?' Sam had picked up her laptop when she'd gone upstairs to find something to eat and he looked at it pointedly.

'You could try...' She smiled, as if somehow that might be a joke, but no one touched her laptop. Ask any software developer and you'd get the same answer. 'I'm just going to do something while I eat...'

'No. And no.' He was smiling too, but this was rapidly turning into a battle of wills. 'You're not going to open that laptop today, and you're not going to work while you eat. Doctor's orders.' He frowned, as if the last bit was somehow a problem.

'I...' Sam decided that telling him she did that all the time was only going to get her into more trouble. 'It's no big thing.'

'Then don't do it.' He was purposely misunderstanding her. He opened one of the drawers of David's desk and Sam saw a pile of files inside, neatly stacked. 'Put it in there.'

Okay, if it was going to make him happy. She could always take it back out again. 'There. Okay now?'

'Yep.' He smiled and turned the key in a lock set into the frame. The click of levers told Sam that the whole desk was now probably secure, and Euan put the key into his pocket.

'You think that's going to stop me?' She picked up the paper knife on David's desk and Euan looked at it warily, as if she was about to stab him. 'I've opened enough locked drawers before.' She tapped the point of the knife on the top of the desk.

'Not with that, you won't. David keeps all the sensitive stuff in his desk drawers and that's a security lock.'

One look at the lock told her that he wasn't bluffing. Sam put the knife down with a clatter and plumped herself down on a chair, wincing when her head throbbed from the sudden movement.

'You're in no shape to work today. And I wouldn't eat that if I were you either.' He pointed towards the limp, pre-packaged salad that she'd fetched from upstairs. He might be right. On a second look it didn't look all that appetising.

'So what am I supposed to do? Sit around staring at the wall all day?' The images that formed in her mind when faced with blank walls frightened her. 'I'll get a headache just from being bored.'

'Is that a challenge?'

'Maybe.' Of course it was. Challenging Euan could turn into a regular pleasure if she wasn't careful.

'In that case, you'd better come with me.'

CHAPTER SIX

HE'D INSISTED THEY have lunch at his house, and she'd put on a panama hat and sunglasses for the ten-minute walk. A pair of plimsolls didn't seem the first choice of footwear to go with the pretty summer dress she was wearing, but they were practical and she carried it off. Sam made everything she wore look stylish, irrespective of whether it was a designer suit or a pair of jeans.

When he turned into the quiet street where he lived and led her up his own front path she seemed surprised. 'This is lovely, Euan!'

He stopped to look at the white rendered front of the house, which had pale blue-grey shutters and a shade darker for the door to match the roof slates. He hadn't done that in a while, but the sense of satisfaction at what was almost all his own handiwork was still there.

'Thanks.' Her approval cut deep. Right down to the places that he tried so hard to defend. 'The place was a bit of a wreck when I bought it.'

'You did it up?'

'Yep. A few years ago now. I moved here from London when I finished medical school.' He'd left the flat that he'd shared with his wife, breaking his last ties with that life. Brought nothing with him, just his clothes and

ANNIE CLAYDON

65

his medical books. If asked, Euan would have said that
he regretted cutting Marie off so completely now, but
since he didn't generally bring the subject up, no one
had ever asked.

He ushered her inside, leaving her in the hallway inspecting the tangle of metal, shells and pebbles fashioned into the shape of a mermaid that stood in the
corner. 'This is gorgeous. Did you do it?'

'No, someone I know made it. She works with glass,
but also uses bits and pieces that get washed up on the
beach.' Juno had been a client at the clinic, but her
addiction wasn't what defined her any more. Her art
spoke up for her much more eloquently. 'Would you
like some toast?'

'That would be great, thanks.' When Euan looked
back through the open door of the kitchen, he could see
her running her fingers lightly along the mermaid's tail.

'Juno's got a workshop in town.'

'I'd be interested to see what else she does.'

'We can walk down there this afternoon if you like.
I haven't seen her for a while and I've been meaning
to drop in.'

She walked into the kitchen, skimming one hand
along the shiny, sea-green cabinet doors and squinting into the light-filled conservatory beyond. 'Sounds
good.'

'We'll do that, then. After we've eaten.' Euan flipped
open the fridge and left her to wander into the conservatory and look around.

'What broadband speed do you get here?' The question seemed like an innocent enough one, if a little
geeky.

'I have no clue.'

'Hmm. I could check your speed for you. If I had my laptop with me.'

Euan chuckled. She wasn't getting her laptop back today, even if she begged. 'You mean you can't just sniff the air and tell me if my internet's working as it should?'

'Normally I could. But all I can smell is the toast at the moment.'

He made a lunge for the toaster, saved the two thick slices before they burned and dropped them onto a plate, gesturing to her to sit down at the kitchen table, where he'd put out butter, ham and a selection of salad vegetables from the fridge. She sat down, her hands folded in her lap.

'Don't wait for me.' Euan dropped two more slices of bread into the toaster and carried a couple of glasses to the table, along with cartons of milk and fruit juice. 'I'm afraid it's a bit makeshift.'

'It's great. I can just take whatever I want.' She grinned at him and started to butter her toast. 'So this is your sanctuary, is it?'

He supposed it was. 'Everyone's got to have somewhere. It's important to have your own space.'

She took a bit of toast, nodding as she chewed. 'Yeah. I have office premises, but I usually work at home. I'm rethinking that.'

The sudden slice of candour made the back of his neck tingle. 'It's good to have separate spaces for work and leisure.'

'Yes. Working at home seemed like a good idea at the time. No fighting my way to and from work on the Tube. For the first six months that was enough to keep me happy. Then the novelty wore off.'

'And you started to get stir-crazy?' Euan imagined

that there were plenty of days when Sam opened her laptop as soon as she was awake, and only closed it again to go back to sleep.

'Yes. I make sure I go out every day now.'

'Coffee shop?' He could just imagine her, sitting with a coffee, her laptop open in front of her.

'How did you know?'

'Just a lucky guess.' He sat down opposite her, and she handed him the knife she'd used to butter her toast. Taking it from her to butter his own felt like an act of intimacy. 'If you feel up to it, we can go for a drive after we've been to Juno's workshop. There's something I want to show you.'

'Yeah?'

'Yep.'

Sam had completely lost her bearings as Euan led her through a maze of streets, finally emerging at the back of a row of small shops. They walked along an uneven path and then he shepherded her into a long, low building.

It was shaded inside, and for a moment Sam's heavy sunglasses rendered her almost blind. When she propped them on top of her head, she gasped. The wall was framed and criss-crossed with shelves. Spun and fashioned glass was displayed there in a blaze of colour and texture, so vibrant that it almost hurt her eyes.

'Euan!' A woman's voice sounded, and Sam turned. She was tall, with short, bleached blonde hair and a pair of work-stained overalls. She stripped off her heavy-duty gloves and grabbed the front of Euan's shirt. 'Come here, stranger.'

'Whose fault is that?' Euan didn't resist when the

woman pulled him towards her and planted a kiss on his cheek.

'Yours. Where were you at my show?' Juno let go of him, and took a swipe at his shoulder.

'I'm sorry. I would have been there if I could. Bit of an emergency.'

'Yeah.' Juno turned to Sam looking her up and down with an unmistakeable air of scrutiny. 'I'd be cross with him if I didn't know that's not an excuse.'

'Juno had her first show three weeks ago. I hear there was quite a bit of interest in her stuff.'

'It's not *stuff*, Euan.' Juno protested with a laugh. 'It's an unique view of the world through the eyes of a talented young artist.'

'Right.' Euan and Juno were chuckling together. 'This is Sam. She saw one of your unique views of the world in my hallway…'

'The mermaid?' Juno swung towards Sam. 'That's one of my favourite pieces. I nearly didn't let him have it, but then…' She shrugged, as if the rest was already well understood. 'What do you think?'

'I love the glass. You made these?'

Juno became suddenly bashful. 'Yeah. Thanks.'

'Sam's working with us for a couple of weeks. Why don't you show her the pieces you've made for us?' Euan's quiet suggestion seemed to impel Juno into life again, and she grinned, leading the way to a small side room. Polished pebbles, twisted metal and glass all combined to make four sculptures. On a high shelf a blue and gold figurine, exquisitely crafted from glass, gleamed insistently.

'It's a phoenix. I think it's kind of appropriate.' Juno lifted the piece down, holding it for Sam to see.

'Breathtaking.' Sam murmured the word and Juno's face lit up.

'Isn't it?' Euan was smiling too. 'Now all we need is to get the residential centre up and running and we'll have somewhere to put it.'

Juno snorted with laughter. 'Since when did you worry about flying in the face of the odds?'

'I worry about it all the time.' This seemed to be a private joke between Euan and Juno, and Sam shifted her weight from one foot to the other, wondering if she really ought to be here.

Juno replaced the phoenix on its perch, and turned to face her. 'These are a thank-you. For what Driftwood did for me.'

'You did it for yourself.'

Juno cut Euan short with a wave of her hand. 'Yeah, yeah. That's what you always say. If you really believed it, you wouldn't spend every waking hour chasing around doing…stuff.'

'I do not do *stuff*.'

'Well, I don't make *stuff* either.'

Both of them were laughing now. Sam wondered how many bad times there had been before this easy intimacy had bloomed. How many times Juno had tripped and fallen and Euan had been there to pick her up again.

'It's beautiful, Juno.' She nodded up at the glass phoenix. 'More than that, it's hope, isn't it?'

'Yeah, exactly.' Juno grinned. 'So what are you doing for Driftwood? Apart from trying to get this mope under control.'

'I write software for charities. It helps with fundraising, day-to-day running, that kind of thing.'

'They certainly need something.' Juno shrugged in

response to Sam's enquiring look. 'David lets me use the computer in his office for a couple of hours a week, for my business. He's drowning in paperwork.'

'You don't have a computer?'

Juno shook her head. 'No, it was a choice between that and the van, and I needed the van to deliver the bigger pieces. David's taught me how to keep my accounts on a spreadsheet, and I'm learning how to make my own website.'

Her enthusiasm was so fresh, so shiny. Sam had been like that once.

'My colleague's coming down from London with half a dozen laptops that we're going to donate to Driftwood. They're secondhand, but they're in good condition. You should ask David for one of them.' She flashed a warning look at Euan, hoping that he wouldn't spoil her subterfuge.

Juno hesitated. 'I don't know…'

'That's a good idea. David and I were thinking that one of them should go to you,' Euan waded in, and Sam shot him a grateful smile.

'Really?' Juno turned to Euan for confirmation.

'You heard what Sam said. You need a computer to help you run your business. We've had some donated to us. Sounds like a no-brainer to me. When's, um…'

'Joe,' Sam said helpfully.

'When's Joe coming?'

'About lunchtime tomorrow. Give me an hour to put some software on there to help you with your website, and it'll be ready to go.'

'Pop in any time after three, then.' Euan's grin took in both Sam and Juno.

'Right.' Juno looked from Euan to Sam, and then the

uncertain look on her face cracked into a smile. 'I don't know what to say... Thanks...'

'My pleasure.' It really was Sam's pleasure. It had been a long time since she'd had anyone who could second-guess her the way that Euan just had. Or who would support her, in spite of not having a clue about what was going on.

'Would you be interested in seeing some of the things I've got in progress?' Juno clearly wanted to show her work off.

'Love to.'

'Well, that was bizarre.' Euan was still smiling broadly, but had refrained from any comment on the proceedings until they were back in the car.

'You think so?' Sam was nursing a taped-up bundle of newspaper in her lap. She hadn't been able to resist one of Juno's swirly paperweights, and this one was particularly beautiful.

'You don't? First I get to agree to distributing laptops... No, actually, I don't remember agreeing to that at all.'

'I'm sure you would have if I'd asked you. And, anyway, it just seemed better somehow if Juno got the laptop via you and David than from me.'

'You're probably right on that score. So where do these mystery laptops come from?' He shot her a suspicious look.

'I have a contact in a large company that buys its executives a new laptop every year. The old ones get given away or binned. He'd heard that I was writing software for charities and offered them to me.'

'For free?'

'Yep. They've all been wiped clean, so you have to know what you're doing to get them back up and running. Some of them are a bit bashed about, but there are a couple that are pretty much like new and I was hoping they'd come in useful. I'll get Joe to sort out a good one for Juno.'

He shook his head. 'Okay. Who's Joe? What's all this about website software?'

'Joe works for me. He's coming tomorrow to survey the office so he can write up the specs for the new computer installation there. It's all been agreed with David.'

'Right. And David knows he agreed this time? I'd hate to spring anything on him.'

'Of course he does. And the website software is an online program I've written. All Juno needs is an account, which I'll set up for her tomorrow, and she can use the system to make a starter website for herself.'

'And how much does this cost, usually?'

'I wrote it, I'm allowed to put any value I like on it. Any other concerns?'

He threw back his head and laughed. A rich, warm sound that seemed to fill the car with happiness. 'Since you ask, what's with the haggling you did with Juno over that paperweight?'

'You're supposed to haggle when you buy things, aren't you?'

'Down. You're supposed to haggle down. When someone says twenty-five pounds, you say twenty. Not forty.'

'There was another paperweight there, just the same only a different colour, and that had a sticker on it that said forty pounds. I love this, and it's well worth the money. A handmade item like this would be twice the price in London.' Sam tightened her grip on the well-wrapped bundle on her lap.

'Yeah. Well, that's Juno all over. She undervalues her work. I've told her about it enough times. She never used to put a price on anything, just let things go for a song.'

'Well, there you are, then. What's the problem?'

'Nothing. Nothing, it was a kind thing to do. I just think you may be the most contrary person I've ever met...'

'You know, you say the nicest things.'

He choked with laughter, opened his mouth to reply then closed it again. Sam smiled to herself. Good decision.

CHAPTER SEVEN

IT WAS HALF an hour's drive out to the site of the residential centre, and Euan spent most of it wrapped up in his own thoughts. Juno could be a bit prickly at times, particularly if she thought that someone was making a charity case out of her, but Sam had won her over completely. It felt as if he too was slowly, inexorably, becoming mesmerised by her.

'Here it is.' He drew up at the mouth of the drive, so they'd have to walk to the house. She'd get a better view of it that way.

'Wow! This is nice.' She got out of the car, leaning against the door to take a long look at the ten-bedroomed country house. 'It's really peaceful here.'

Euan nodded. It was the perfect place. 'This house and the land around it have been given to the charity.'

'Really? So this is your new residential centre? It's a fabulous gift...'

'Yeah. It belonged to a record producer—it was one of many homes.'

'Why did he give the house to the charity? Not that it's not a good idea, of course...'

'His daughter had problems with drugs. We tried to help her.'

'And she's okay now?' Sam smiled up at him.

'No. We did our best, but…'

'Oh.' The smile slid from her face like wet seaweed. 'I'm…'

'Yeah, I know.' Euan was becoming accustomed to the idea that Sam seemed to feel all of their losses almost personally. 'We have to do our best, and take what successes we can.'

'And the failures?'

'We never forget them. Every day they remind me that I have to do better.'

The heavy sunglasses stopped him from seeing her eyes, but her lip was quivering and Euan would have bet that there were tears behind the protective lenses. He was about to lay a hand on her arm, ask her what the matter was, when she turned away from him abruptly.

'So…this guy…?'

Clearly she didn't want to betray her emotions. 'A lot of people gave up on his daughter and we didn't. He says that the house is no good to him now as he can't come back here because it was the place he associated most with Kathryn.'

'That's her name?'

'Yeah. And this is Kathryn House. In memory of her.' Euan looked at the sun-warmed bricks, the low spreading eaves, cradled in a wide circle of trees. The place *was* perfect. And the gift entailed an enormous amount of work.

He couldn't see her face, but her hand trembled as she hefted the car door closed. 'Can we go inside?'

'Of course. I brought you here to show it to you. We need to redecorate, and make a few modifications, but we've raised enough to do that now and the work starts soon. We have enough in our reserves to get the place up and running, and…well, getting the ongoing funding for it is where you come in. I thought you might like to see what it is we're all working towards.'

She nodded, half turning towards him. 'And this is where Juno's sculptures will be.'

'Yeah. A lot of people have been very generous. Beyond what we could possibly have ever hoped for. We have offers to help with the renovations, volunteers to help with the work. It's humbling.'

'And terrifying, I imagine.'

'That too. Although less so than not doing it.'

'I can imagine. I think that's why I wrote this software. I was more afraid of not doing it than I was of doing it.'

The inevitable questions began again, throbbing once more in his brain. He started to walk along the gravel driveway towards the house, and felt her falling into step beside him. 'Come and see the house.'

Sally would have really benefitted from this place. Not just the house, or the grounds, but the calm, peaceful environment that Euan described as he showed her through the house. The muted colours, which were currently just tester blocks on the unprepared walls. The light, streaming through the large windows.

'And this is where the phoenix is going to go?' They were back in the wide hallway.

'Nope. We thought about it, but one of Juno's sculptures is specifically in memory of Kathryn—she knew her. When David and I saw it we knew that it belonged here, where it's the first thing that people see when they walk in. The phoenix goes through here.' He opened a door that led through to a long, light-filled room, which led in turn onto a veranda that ran along the back of the house. 'This is going to be a community room.'

Sam nodded. 'Yeah, this is the place for it.' The phoenix would shimmer and sparkle in here. A symbol of hope.

He walked over to one of the glazed doors leading to the veranda, twisting the key in the lock and opening it. 'So, your computer program. The work you're doing here with us. That's your phoenix?'

'What do you mean?'

He was gazing out at the broad expanse of lawn. 'I mean that you have a reason to do what you're doing, just as Juno does. Just as the donor of this house did.'

'Yes, I do. I made that clear at the interview.' She'd said personal reasons. *Personal.* 'Does that really matter?'

'I think so. Sometimes it's helpful to examine our motives for what we do.'

Right. So he was thinking she needed counselling or something? Sam felt the muscles across her back and shoulders stiffen. 'And...?'

'We rely on the generosity and good hearts of a lot of people. But it would be ungrateful of us to give the impression that those gifts will make things right for them. That's another process entirely.'

He was watching her now, his gaze seeming to probe the nastier corners of her soul. The anger, the grief, the night she'd gone into Sally's empty office, screaming and smashing until she'd been exhausted, then cried over a pink stapler that she'd hurled against the wall. Sam could almost feel herself pushing him away, closing the door and locking it, the way she'd done with Sally's office.

'That's clarified your position, then.' The words were brisk, businesslike, and they felt good. She'd been drawn in too far already, and needed to keep things on this less personal footing with Euan.

He waited, obviously wondering if she was going to say more. Cave in, and start baring her soul to him. Like hell she was.

'Okay.' His eyes told her that it wasn't okay at all. That this was just the start of something, not the end. 'Would you like to see the grounds?'

'I'm a bit tired. Can we do it another time?' Sam wanted out of this world. The one where you couldn't just put the clamour of voices to sleep by closing the lid of your laptop. Where real people did real things, and if you were going to push them away, some kind of physical effort was needed.

'Of course.' He closed the glazed doors and locked them. 'I'll take you back now.'

She'd asked him to leave the makeshift blind over the skylight in her bedroom, and then shooed him away. A good night's sleep, without the morning sun breaking in directly on her face, had obviously done her good and Sam had regained some of her colour and lost the air of trying to balance on shifting ground. And, being Monday morning, she was back in business mode.

She was sitting in David's office when they returned from their Monday morning meeting, dressed in a pair of dark, slim-legged trousers and a neat shirt, with a peacock-blue jacket slung across the back of her chair.

When she raised her gaze from her writing pad, her

eyes looked bigger and yet somehow soulless. Make-up, he supposed. Or, more accurately, war paint.

In front of her, were four A4 sheets filled with writing and diagrams. David craned over her shoulder to look at them, and shook his head, bemused. 'What's all this?'

'It's the schema for the Kathryn House information. Euan took me to see it yesterday and explained a bit about the services you plan to provide from there.'

'Ah. Yeah, I think I might have a list somewhere.' David flipped through a pile of papers on his desk and gave up, obviously unequal to the task of finding it. 'Actually, I think I'll make a new one. Things have changed a bit in the last couple of weeks.'

'Good. Thanks.'

'What are you planning to do today other than sort out that laptop for Juno?' Since he was standing directly in her line of sight, Euan reckoned it was impossible for either of them to pretend that the other was invisible any longer.

'I learned a lot at the weekend.' She focussed on him without a trace of hesitation. 'If it's all right with both of you, I'd like to do some work on the database set-up today.' She looked at her watch. 'I've got plenty of time, even after Joe delivers the laptops and I've sorted the website software on Juno's.' Now that she was looking at him, her gaze seemed to melt into his, forged together in a blistering heat.

'If that's what you want.' Euan almost staggered back when she broke eye contact with him.

'Well, I don't want to get under your feet too much.'

That was utter rubbish. She'd tried one approach, and it hadn't worked out the way she'd expected it to. In

anyone else Euan would have put that down to inflex-
ibility, and maybe she was inflexible in her determination to make this project work. But that wasn't all. He
had a strong feeling that the way he'd questioned her
last night had a lot to do with it as well.

'That's okay. Whatever works for you.' He shot a
glance at David, who nodded in agreement. 'If today's
enough time to do what you need to do, I was thinking of getting together a group of people who've been
through rehab with us. Dual purpose—it'll give me a
chance to hear a bit of feedback and you a chance to
get an idea of the process and what it means to our clients. Would tomorrow be too soon?' If she thought that
he was going to give up on her, she could think again.

She considered the prospect and then nodded.
'Sounds good. I'll compile a list of questions I want to
ask. Would you like me to email it through to you so
you can combine it with your list?'

She was assuming he had a list. Euan had reckoned
on taking a reactive approach, hearing first what everyone had to say. 'No, that's fine. I'll probably just go
with the flow.'

She gave him a little frown, and then obviously decided to agree to differ. 'Okay. What time shall I come?'

'About ten?' That should give her enough time to
plan whatever she wanted to plan.

She nodded. 'Ten's fine. Would you unlock the desk
for me, please?'

Euan silently cursed himself. He'd forgotten to give
her laptop back last night. 'Yeah. Sorry.' David raised a
questioning eyebrow, and Euan confessed his mistake.
'I locked Sam's laptop in your desk yesterday.'

'Ah. Good idea. You can't be too careful, can you?' David pulled a bunch of keys from his pocket.

She smiled. One of those composed little smiles of hers, which Euan couldn't even begin to fathom the meaning of. 'No. You can't be too careful.'

The fifteen-minute walk to the clinic took half an hour if you took a detour, stopped at the coffee shop and then went down to the beach to stare at the sea while you drank. Pebbles scrunched under him as Euan sat down on the shingle.

Sam didn't fool him. She was accomplished, driven and successful. Under all of that there was someone who was lost enough to believe that other people's expectations of her were what really mattered. He'd gone too far in trying to get her to open up about things she obviously preferred to keep private, and instead of just telling him to butt out Sam had reacted by transforming overnight into someone else.

He spun a pebble towards the sea, and it fell short by twenty feet. It was ridiculous to suppose that the images of Sam that had haunted him last night were anything other than dreams. He didn't have any space in his life for a relationship, let alone with someone as high maintenance as Sam, and he'd proved beyond all doubt that his talents lay elsewhere.

'Right.' He addressed a seagull, which was eying him cagily from the top of one of the wooden windbreaks. 'Calling her high maintenance isn't really fair, is it?' The high-maintenance part was only because he couldn't stop thinking about her.

The seagull didn't reply. Taking that as a prompt to

get his act together, Euan swirled the dregs of his coffee, draining them in one gulp, and got to his feet. He could do better than this. He would do better.

CHAPTER EIGHT

SAM WAS FULLY aware of how much she'd missed Euan. She'd had twenty-four hours to explore the extent and nature of the feeling, and she'd worked almost every waking moment in an attempt to give herself something else to think about.

She saw Liz walking in front of her and ran to catch her up, falling into step beside her. 'Are you going to the clinic today?'

'Just for the morning.' Liz was looking summery and relaxed. 'I've got my book club this afternoon.' She patted the cloth bag that hung from her shoulder. 'I'm only halfway through the book.'

'Well, I guess you'll get more out of the end once you've discussed the beginning.'

Liz laughed. 'S'pose so. I think I'll just keep quiet, the others don't like it much if you haven't read the book when they have.'

'You could always bluff it out…'

'I'm not very good at that kind of thing.' Liz reached inside her bag and displayed the cover of her book. 'It's a good read so far. Would you like to borrow it when I've finished it?'

'Yes, that would be great. Thanks.' It would be ungracious to refuse, but Sam didn't have much time for reading these days. She'd probably keep it for a week and then gave it back, untouched.

Liz used a key for the outer door of the clinic and then rang the buzzer, a succession of short, sharp rings to announce herself, and then waved up at the security camera. The door buzzed open, and Sam followed Liz inside.

Euan was leaning over the reception desk to reach the door release button, and he turned to greet them. Every time she saw him he seemed to impress Sam all over again, as if her imagination wasn't big enough to hold him and the reality was always better.

'Hey, Liz. Sam.'

'Morning.' Liz bustled past him. 'I'm going to make a cup of tea before the rush starts. Sam?'

'Oh. Yes, thanks.'

'Euan?'

'Thanks, but I've had one already.'

Liz disappeared into the kitchen, and Sam swallowed down the lump in her throat and reminded herself that she wasn't sixteen any more.

'I overstepped the mark on Sunday.' Euan's habit of getting straight to the point flustered her even more.

'No…no, you didn't. I just—'

'Don't want to talk about it. I should have respected that.'

'Thanks. I… We're not going to have to start all over again, are we?'

He laughed, and suddenly all the worries that had kept her sitting in front of her laptop far into the night dissolved in a puff of smoke. 'Not unless you want to.

But personally speaking, I think we've made some good progress. Be a shame to waste it.'

Her fingertips began to tingle. Either she was getting another migraine or Euan just had that effect on her. 'Yeah.' She was going to say 'Me too' but that was two words too much at the moment. 'So, did you manage to set up the group session?'

His gaze softened into a gorgeous heat, which threatened to melt every last one of her defences. 'I did.'

'I'm looking forward to it.'

He nodded, obviously pleased with her answer. 'Good. I might live to regret it, they're a pretty outspoken lot.'

'They won't... I mean they wouldn't give you a hard time, would they?'

'Don't see why they should stop now. The moment I stop having a hard time from our clients is the time I know I need to apply for another job.' He chuckled at her look of concern. 'It's okay. We're okay.'

His eyes questioned her again, as if he was wondering whether *they* were okay. Sam had been wondering that, and now she knew. As long as they stayed on their present path, working together, friendly but not too much personal intimacy, they'd be just fine. 'I appreciate it, Euan. This is really going to help me get a feel for things.'

'Good.' He grinned, looking at his watch. 'I've a couple of things to do first, so I'll leave you with Liz. The group get-together starts at ten-thirty, upstairs in the community room.'

The group that Euan had assembled couldn't have been more diverse. Jamie was there, along with a young woman who had left her toddler downstairs with Liz. A middle-aged man, who looked as if he'd be more comfortable in a suit and tie, a red-haired girl who was a student at the university, and a young man with tattoos all the way up his arms. Juno came in late, muttering something about an overnight curing process by way of an apology.

'So, there are no rules, then?' Sam was responding to Jamie's laughing description of some of the subjects that he'd raised for therapy group discussions, and she was met with a chorus of nos.

'First one's not to overturn the tea things.' Juno nodded towards the side table, stacked with cups and saucers and a couple of flasks that Liz had brought in before they'd started.

Jamie laughed. 'You were so mad that day....'

'Yeah. Mad's the word for it.' Juno gave him a rueful smile.

'Or punch the moderators.' Dianne, the young mother, broke in.

Euan nodded. 'That's a personal favourite of mine. We have a very strict set of rules. Break them and you're out.'

'For good?' Sam looked around at the circle of faces.

'No. We've all broken the rules at one time or another.' Tim, the man who should have been wearing a suit, and who looked as if he'd never broken a rule in his life, spoke up. 'But a condition of returning is to undertake not to do it again. You have to earn your place if you want it back, and if you transgress again...'

'Three strikes and you're out.' Dianne was nodding. 'Only it's not as easy as that.'

'Why not?' It sounded to Sam like the perfect way

out for anyone who didn't want to go through the rigours of therapy.

'Because when I was thrown out of the group Euan took me on for personal counselling.' She grinned at the assembled company. 'If you guys think that the group's tough, try doing it one to one. For the first three sessions I turned up five minutes before the hour was up.'

Sam wanted to ask, but she wasn't sure whether she should.

'If you have a session booked, that's your time,' John explained, flexing his tattooed arms. 'If you turn up late the counsellor will confront you about it and then finish the session on time.'

'But…' Sam frowned. 'I don't understand. What's the good of a counselling session if you don't turn up?'

'Exactly.' Jamie grinned at her. 'What John's saying is that you take responsibility for your own actions. We all get held up once in a while, but being late all the time is a deliberate act. Apart from when your glue won't stick, eh, Juno?'

'Hey! I was up until two this morning—'

'And this isn't a therapy group.' Euan cut in. 'The rules don't apply.'

'You mean I *can* punch you.' Dianne's eyes were alive with laughter.

Euan pulled a face, rubbing at his jaw. 'I'm getting myself into trouble now. Look, guys, I want to hear what you've got to say about the rehab process, things that worked for you and things that didn't. And Sam's here to get an idea of what that process is like from your point of view.' He leaned back in his chair, his body language clear about the fact that he was there to listen, not to talk. 'I think Sam's got some questions…'

Sam had her questions on a typed sheet, inside the portfolio on her knee, but it suddenly didn't seem right to draw it out. 'I'm here to listen. So...um...who wants to start?'

'Good session?' Euan asked her afterwards. Something about Sam had changed. When she'd demonstrated her software she'd been impressive, beautiful and quite definitely in control of the proceedings. Now she was beautiful, clearly happy not to be in control and all the more impressive for that.

'Yeah. I learned a lot.'

'Did any of it help?'

'All of it helped. I'm going to need to adjust a few things. There were some good points that I hadn't thought about.'

'We don't want to take advantage of you, you're already giving us a great deal of your time...'

'I'm not looking to just do the bare minimum. I'm here to learn and to make my product better. And to give you something that exceeds your expectations.' She shrugged. 'That's the way I work. You don't get a say in it.'

He thought about asking why Driftwood should be so important to her, and decided that would be a bad idea. He'd already crossed the line twice. Three strikes and, according to the rules that he'd made, he should be out. 'As long as you're okay with it.'

She nodded. 'I'm okay with it.' She turned, almost as if she sensed that Jamie was hovering behind her, staring at the back of her head. 'How are things, Jamie? Getting to grips with the blog?'

'Yeah, it's great. I've almost written my first post, it's called *Where do we go from here?*'

'Blimey.' She smiled at Jamie. 'And do you know the answer to that?'

'Nah. Maybe someone else does.' Jamie's gaze was darting between Euan and Sam. 'I've…um…got something…'

'Shall we go and get some tea?' That was Euan's usual way of getting someone who wanted to talk to sit down and open up.

'We could do. But I was thinking more of having tea with Sam.' Jamie grinned at him.

'Is this some kind of code?' The puzzled look on Sam's face made Euan want to smile.

'Yeah. It means I want to talk to you both.'

Sam shrugged, as if Jamie might have said that in the first place. 'Let's talk, then.'

Jamie waited until the room had cleared and closed the door. 'I've got Kirsty's computer.'

Sam looked at him blankly. 'Kirsty…?'

Euan sighed. He had a nasty suspicion he knew where this was leading, and he wished that Jamie would just let it go. 'Kirsty is one of our clients. She's been in hospital for a while.'

'Yeah. She took something…' Jamie pursed his lips. 'But a week before that she lent me her old laptop because mine was really struggling and I needed to get one of my college assignments in. I used her email to send a couple of questions to my tutor.'

'Right.' Euan had been hoping that he was wrong, but it didn't look too much like it.

'And when I picked up the emails again to get his

reply, there were some others for Kirsty. I wasn't snooping, they just appeared...'

Sam nodded. 'Yeah, they would. Until you change the settings on the old one, both laptops will pick up her emails—'

Jamie cut her short. 'That's not what I mean. I haven't given the laptop back yet because she's been in hospital. And last night I went back and looked at her mail.'

Sam was frowning, clearly lost as to the point of this conversation.

'There's an email that just gives a date, a place and a time. It's the Saturday evening before she took the overdose.'

Understanding crept across her face. Euan wished there was some way he could shut this conversation down, but he knew full well that if it didn't happen here and now, it would happen at some other place, some other time. Jamie was like a dog with a bone and he wasn't going to let go of this easily.

'And you think that the email's from the person who supplied her with the drugs.'

Jamie nodded triumphantly. 'I've seen on the television where they trace things back and find the computer they came from. There's a map and it zooms right in on the house...'

'Well, that's on the TV.' Sam seemed to understand the need to keep a sense of proportion here. 'You can't always do that in real life.'

'But you can sometimes?' Jamie wasn't letting this go.

'Yes.'

'I've got her laptop in the van.' Jamie turned and made for the door, as if everything else went without saying.

'Whoa, hold up there, Jamie.' It was time for Euan to step in. 'First of all, why would someone use their own email address to set up a drugs sale?'

'They might have spoofed the address. There's a way to get around that and see where an email originally came from.' Sam fell silent as Euan glared at her. She might be right technically, but the comment wasn't helpful.

'Okay, so it's possible. Jamie, the police and the drug agencies are handling it. You don't need to get involved with this.'

'Yes. I do.' Jamie gave him a truculent look.

'So what do you think you're going to do?' Euan asked.

'Sam can find out where the email's coming from, she said so just now. And then we find the people who gave the drugs to Kirsty and we do something about it, instead of just sitting around talking about *feedback*.' He spat the word out as if it was some kind of poison.

'Jamie, I know you're angry—'

'Damn right I'm angry! Just tell me what you're doing about it, Euan.' Jamie pushed his face up close to Euan's in ferocious defiance.

'Stop it, you two. Right now.' Sam's voice was suddenly so assertive that even Euan blinked, and Jamie jumped back suddenly. Euan bit back the temptation to defend himself and claim that it wasn't he who was being reckless, deciding that sounded a bit too much like a kid caught fighting in the street.

'Now, look here.' She turned the full force of her stare onto Jamie, and all Euan could think about was that he was glad it wasn't him. 'Sometimes you can trace the source of an email from the data that comes with it. Sometimes you can't, it depends on how the person's sent the email. If it's from a web client then all you'll get is the IP address of the host servers...'

'What?' Jamie's expression turned from defiance to grudging incomprehension.

'Okay. Take my word for it, there are loads of different ways to send an email and not all of them can be traced. If...' She gave Jamie a look of the utmost severity '*If* it's possible to trace the email, and *if* it's from who you think, then you might get some idea of where someone was two weeks ago. Is that enough?'

Jamie sighed. 'No. Not really.'

She nodded and the steel in her voice gave way to warmth. 'I'm sorry, Jamie. That's how it is.' Then she turned to Euan.

If he'd thought he was going to be the one who got off lightly in this, the expression on her face shut that possibility down straight away. 'The police and the drug agencies are handling this, right?'

'Right.' Under the intensity of her stare he felt like a child being brought to account for its actions. And also a man. He felt like a man who wanted to see what might happen if his own spirit clashed with hers. What kind of fireworks that might produce.

'And you think that's enough information? Enough for anyone who's lost a friend?'

She hadn't noticed her own slip of the tongue. Jamie hadn't lost a friend. Maybe Sam had. But he'd promised not to go there. 'Perhaps not.'

'There's no perhaps about it. It isn't.' Something like fire sparked in her grey eyes.

'You've made your point. I could have said more.'

He turned to Jamie. 'The police have already interviewed Kirsty—'

'What? She's still in hospital, for crying out loud. What the hell are they doing, upsetting her?' Jamie's passion flashed to the surface again and Euan held up his hand.

'They sent a policewoman in plain clothes, who treated her very gently. I was there for her the whole time. We talked about it with her parents first, and Kirsty decided she'd rather not have them present during the interview.'

Jamie sighed. 'She wouldn't have wanted to upset them.'

'She doesn't want to upset you either.'

'She doesn't need to worry about that. I've been there, remember.'

Euan took a moment to consider his reply. This was what Jamie needed to hear, but maybe Sam needed to hear it as well. 'Being close to a drug abuser isn't easy, and it's okay to have your own feelings about that.'

'But the email…' It looked as if Euan wasn't getting through to either of them. Sam was shaking her head slightly, and Jamie was still protesting.

'Kirsty's given permission for the police to look at her laptop, the new one that she uses now, and all her emails will be on there. They have forensic IT capabilities and if there's any information to be had, they'll get it. In the meantime, they've put out a warning.'

'Wait,' Sam broke in. 'A warning?'

'There's a particularly dangerous batch of cocaine on the streets. In this situation the police and drugs agencies issue warnings.'

Jamie snorted. 'Yeah. Don't take cocaine, but if you absolutely have to, don't take *that* cocaine.'

'It's the best we can do for now, Jamie. We're just trying to keep people alive. Give yourself a break and let me deal with the rest. I'll keep you informed.'

Euan held his hand out to Jamie, and they shook on the deal. Sam gave a satisfied nod, shot them both a look that promised deep trouble if either of them went back on the agreement and excused herself.

'She's scary when she wants to be.' Jamie was staring after her with undisguised admiration.

'Yeah. Tell me about it.'

CHAPTER NINE

SAM GOT THE key for the staff lavatory from Liz, and locked herself inside. Filling the small handbasin, she splashed her face with cold water.

She was shaking. She'd resolved to keep her own counsel, be an observer. Blend into the walls. But the atmosphere here, where everyone seemed to say whatever was on their mind, was infectious. She was going to have to be more circumspect in future.

She stared at herself in the mirror. This was a world of grey areas, of *if* and *maybe* and *we just have to do our best*. Not at all what she'd expected and it was getting to her. She just needed to take a step back. That's if Euan didn't invoke one of his mysterious rules and ban her from the place altogether.

Sam pulled a towel from the dispenser and scrubbed her face with it. She'd wanted this. She might have bitten off more than she could chew, but she'd make it work. A dash of lipstick, and she'd be able to face the world, Euan included.

'Sam! Euan's been looking for you.' Liz looked up as Sam put the key back onto the reception desk in front of her. 'If you hurry, you'll catch him.'

'What's the rush?' Sam had just been doing breathing exercises in front of the mirror to calm herself and it seemed a bit of a shame to ruin it all now.

'There's been a call from the police. They want Euan to check on someone…'

'He works for the police?' Was this yet another responsibility that Euan had forgotten to tell her about?

'Occasionally. Usually when there are drugs involved.' Liz flapped her hands at Sam. 'Don't just stand there…'

Euan was already behind the wheel of his car when the street door of the clinic slammed behind her, and he leaned across, opening the passenger door for her. 'Are you up for this?'

'Yes.' She climbed into the car. 'I'm sorry about earlier. I shouldn't have intervened between you and Jamie.'

He looked at her as if he didn't know what she was talking about. 'I thought it was a very helpful addition to the discussion.'

'Right. Well, it won't happen again.'

He shrugged. 'If you say so.'

She stuck close to Euan as he strode into the police station. 'She's with me.' He didn't stop to go into details with the officer at the desk, and the buzz of a door-release mechanism sounded.

A policewoman met them on the other side, smiling at Euan. 'Thanks for coming.'

'Glad to help. Sam…this is PC Lisa Burroughs.' He waved his hand in a hurried introduction as they walked. 'Sam's working with the charity.'

Lisa scrutinised her for a moment and then nodded briefly before turning her attention back to Euan. 'This guy's new on our patch, no one's seen him before, and he's pretty much non-responsive. He was arrested, but he's being released now. We can't tell what's up with him—drugs or some kind of mental problem. He's in quite a bad state and I'd like you to take a look at him. It would be good if we could get him the appropriate help.'

Lisa showed them into an interview room. A man was sitting, hunched over the table. He was dirty, and even though the day was warm, he seemed to be wearing many layers of clothes.

Euan dumped his bag by the door with a glance at Sam that told her to stay there. He approached the man and pulled a chair up to sit down opposite him.

'Hello, there, mate.'

No response.

'I'm a doctor, my name's Euan Scott. What can I call you?'

Nothing.

'Have they given you a cup of tea?'

The man raised his head slightly. Somewhere there was the flicker of acknowledgement that Euan was looking for. 'Lisa...'

Lisa nodded. 'And a bacon sandwich?'

'Thanks.' Euan gave her a broad grin and turned his attention back to the man in front of him. 'You're in luck. They do a pretty respectable bacon sandwich here.'

It took ten minutes of gentle cajoling before George gave up his name. Ten more before he would allow Euan to touch him so that he could examine him. Euan was patient, and respectful, talking to George as if he were a private patient paying hundreds of pounds for his time.

'You're a soldier, then?' When Euan had opened George's heavy overcoat, something had caught his eye and he gestured towards a dirty medal ribbon pinned onto his plaid shirt.

That seemed a touch too much like conversation for George and he glared at Euan.

'Regiment?' Euan tried again. 'Army number?'

George seemed to straighten and he muttered a reply. Euan wrote the numbers down on the pad that lay on the desk. 'Sam, can I have my stethoscope, please?'

Right. Stethoscope. Must be in the bag at her feet. Sam tugged at the zip and found what he needed, stepping forward to hand it to him.

For a moment George's eyes focussed on her, and Sam realised suddenly that he was probably only in his thirties. Perhaps she should say something or hold out her hand. Perhaps not. Euan was wearing surgical gloves and she probably shouldn't let George touch her. She felt the back of her neck redden.

'That's great. Thanks.' Euan met her gaze and nodded. 'Can you see if you can find some antiseptic wipes in there?'

'Right. Antiseptic wipes.' She stepped back again, feeling both relieved and guilty. George was one of the invisible men, the ones who were ignored by the world in general. Even when she'd been jolted out of her own little world, and had stopped to buy a magazine or give coffee or food to someone in need, she'd always been too afraid to make eye contact.

Euan wasn't afraid. She could see it in his body language, the way he dealt with George. He was a man, not just a bundle of dirty clothes. He finished his examination and ushered both Sam and Lisa out of the room.

'There's evidence of sustained alcohol abuse. I'll

call one of the ex-servicemen's charities, see if they can help.'

Lisa nodded. 'Right. Can I leave it with you?'

'Yes. Give me ten minutes.'

'So someone's going to come and pick him up?' Sam was sitting in the front seat of Euan's car, wondering whether it was her imagination or not that the smell of stale liquor seemed to have followed them out of the police station and down the road.

'Yes. They'll get him a bed for the night, and if they can hold onto him he'll get the treatment he needs. It looks as if he has some kind of psychiatric problem, maybe delayed PTSD. Maybe something else entirely.'

It didn't seem much of an answer, but Sam knew that it was the best that Euan could give. Both he and Lisa had done their best for George. She tried to comfort herself that at least he was in the hands of the right people now.

'What'll happen to him?' she asked.

'I honestly don't know.'

And so the day continued. People turned up at the clinic, wanting medical help or needing just to talk. Euan moved from one case to the next, seemingly tireless, but by the end of the day Sam was mentally and emotionally exhausted.

The next two days weren't much better. Euan had given her exactly what she'd asked for, allowing her to shadow him without prying into her own thoughts and feelings about what she saw. She was alone and rudderless, trying to make sense of things that couldn't be rationalised or explained. Sam was beginning to think that she should have been more careful about what she'd wished for.

'Are you finished for today?' He strode into his surgery on Thursday afternoon with as much energy and enthusiasm as he'd had that morning. How did he do that?

'No, I'm still making changes to the database.' It was going to be another late night, tonight.

'Can't you do that tomorrow? You've got the day free, remember, as it's my day off.'

Sam hesitated. The thought was tempting. Spend an evening with Euan and then fall into bed. She adjusted the thought. Spend an evening with him then go back to the flat and fall into *her* bed. 'I'd forgotten about that. I suppose...'

He grinned. 'You need a break. Put that away and come with me.' When Sam didn't move, he walked over and peered over her shoulder at the screen.

'I'm closing you down in three...' One finger hovered at the top of the screen, threatening to snap the laptop shut.

'Wait...wait...' Sam hit the button to save her work. He seemed ever so close all of a sudden.

'One...' She could smell his skin. Soap and something else that was making her tremble. Something she couldn't place, but it was his alone, and it made her think of sex.

'Two...'

'Wait...' Her bare arm brushed his, and the back of her neck started to tingle. She was sure she could feel his breath on her skin, and all of a sudden she'd forgotten how to close down her own database.

'And a half.'

'Don't rush me.' The 'Close' button came to her rescue, and then three keystrokes for sleep mode. Just as the screen went blank, Euan's finger made contact, closing her laptop.

'Three.' He gripped the arms of the chair she was sitting in, swivelling it around to face him.

'What would you have done if my machine had crashed?'

'I guess I'd be nursing a broken nose right now.' He grinned provocatively. 'Timing's everything.'

He was still gripping the arms of her chair, imprisoning her and leaning in impossibly close. She'd bet that his timing was absolutely perfect, and the thought made her shiver.

'I thought we were going somewhere.' She tapped the back of his hand with one finger. Even that degree of contact was one degree more than she could bear at the moment.

Euan chuckled, suddenly all movement and searing, heart-aching life. Propelling himself upright, he walked to the door. 'We are. How's your head for heights?'

'Okay. What did you have in mind?'

'Just a little tour… Call it sightseeing.'

They went back to the flat so Sam could fetch a warm jacket. Apparently this mysterious little tour was going to be chilly. Then they were on the road, driving out of town and into the countryside. Half an hour later they turned off a country lane and bumped across a field.

'Oh, wow!' There were parked cars, people and a barbeque. But all Sam could see were the six brightly coloured hot-air balloons at the far end of the field. 'We're going to watch?'

Euan chuckled. 'Watching's not as much fun as taking a ride.'

'But don't we have to book?'

He shrugged. 'I've booked. I know one of the guys who pilots the balloons, and I gave him a call this afternoon and asked if he'd had any late cancellations. It just so happened that he had. I reckoned we both needed a bit of a break.' He manoeuvred over the uneven ground into the makeshift car park.

Most people just went to the pub or chilled out in front of the television. Why did it not surprise her that Euan would come up with something a bit different? 'And this is what you do when you want to unwind?'

'Not usually. But it's a particular challenge to tempt you away from your work, and I defy anyone to think about database configuration when they're suspended in a wicker basket one thousand feet above the ground.'

She couldn't help smiling. And once she'd started, she didn't seem to be able to stop. 'Which one's ours?'

'That one.' He pointed to a vividly striped blue and yellow canopy that was spread across the grass, ready to be inflated.

'Oh. That's the best one, I think.'

Euan chuckled. Warm and rich, sending an extra tingle of excitement through her. 'Let's go and see it, then.'

CHAPTER TEN

EVERYONE WHO WAS booked in for the ride had helped to spread the balloon envelope across the grass and watched while it was inflated. Then it was time to climb into the basket. Euan helped her up the steps cut into the side, and then clambered in.

Finally, they were ready to go. Sam hung onto the side of the basket, feeling a small jolt as they left the ground. Slowly they climbed, the trees and cars receding as they glided through the air.

The pilot was explaining how the balloon flew and pointing out landmarks below them. Sam listened politely, nodding along with the other passengers, but the real delight was just to be flying through the air. In the intervals between the deafening noise of the hot-air burners, it was almost eerily quiet.

The broad sweep of the sky had no room for her cares or her inhibitions. By the time they'd reached their full altitude she had released her grip on the edge of the basket and was holding onto Euan instead.

'You've been up in a balloon before?' Sam felt almost as if they were alone together up here. Everyone else was either concentrating on the view or talking to the people they had come with and it was just her and Euan.

'When I was a kid. My parents took me and my sister. I thought it was the best thing I'd ever done.'

Sam nodded. She'd been thinking exactly the same herself, and been feeling just like an excited child. 'We weren't too big on family outings when I was young. Single-parent family.' She shrugged. 'Just the two of us.' In the main it hadn't even been two. Just her, on her own, making her way the best she could.

He nodded. Didn't ask. Euan had stuck by his promise and hadn't asked her about anything personal in the last couple of days. This evening Sam almost wished that he would.

'Look. Down there.'

She followed the line of his pointing finger. 'Oh! Are they sheep? It looks like a model farm.'

They watched as farmland gave way to woods and then back again to yellow fields.

'Where are we going to land?' Sam didn't want to land at all, but they were going to run out of hot air at some point.

'No idea.' He grinned down at her. 'That's one of the best things about it.'

They bumped back down into a field and when he helped her out of the basket it seemed natural to jump down into his arms. To stay there for a moment while she acclimatised herself to being back on the ground.

'Enjoy it?' The grin on his face told Sam that he was in no doubt about her answer.

'Wonderful. Thank you so much.'

'My pleasure.' He caught sight of her raised eyebrow and laughed. 'No, really. It was.'

'How do we get back?' In her excitement Sam had forgotten about the practical considerations. She'd pretty much forgotten about everything other than how much she'd been enjoying herself.

'They have pursuit vehicles. They'll be along soon to take us and the balloon back.'

'Does that mean we get to help pack it away?'

He chuckled. 'Yeah. We can do that.'

Back at the launch site they waited to see the last of the balloons take off, before driving back into town. Ending the evening there seemed almost criminal, and when Euan asked, Sam readily agreed to a stroll along the promenade.

They watched the sun set over the sea and wandered down onto the beach. Sam was getting to like the beach as much as Euan seemed to. The sound of the sea washing against the sand. A warm breeze, moonlight, and... It was impossible not to acknowledge that Euan deserved his place at the top of that list of pleasures. When she slipped her hand tentatively into the crook of his arm, he trapped it in place against his body.

'I was thinking...'

'Yeah?' I was rather hoping that you might have stopped that. Just for tonight,' he teased.

'It's not a big thing. I was wondering if...' She hesitated, and then took the plunge. 'If I might sit in on one of the groups for friends and relatives of drugs users.'

She felt his body stiffen against hers. 'Why?'

Good question. 'Just to get a full picture. I just thought it might help with the database.' When she said it out loud, it didn't sound particularly convincing.

Another couple of slow steps and then he stopped. 'Sam, I have a responsibility... I have to ask you this. Is that your only reason?'

'It's…' She could lie to him. She could go on lying to herself. But tonight had made her believe that somewhere there might be a possibility of a way back. The one area of Driftwood's work that she hadn't asked to see first-hand had suddenly seemed the most important to her and she'd spoken without thinking first.

'It's what?' She couldn't see his face, but his voice was gentle.

'I don't know. No. I don't think it's my only reason. I'm sorry, I shouldn't have asked. I'm not here to talk about myself…' She could feel a tear about to fall from her eye and she wiped it away with her fingers.

'Don't!' He said the word with such intensity that Sam started. 'Some things we have to listen to, not just brush away. Tears, laughter, joy…grief.'

'How…?'

'There's nothing to it. Here, sit down.' She sat down next to him on the still-warm shingle. 'Just listen.'

She head the crash of the waves, and somewhere in there was Sally's voice. The knock on the door when the police had come to tell her that Sal was dead. The stiff, broken grief of her father and brother, and the sound of Sal's mother weeping. Sam just wanted it all to go away.

'Nothing. I don't hear anything.'

'Then listen harder.'

It was no use. She so wanted someone to understand. Euan most of all.

'My partner in the old company, Sally…'

He nodded her on.

'She died. From an overdose of cocaine.' Sam remembered Euan's words when they'd been to see Carrie. 'Not an overdose as such… I mean…that's not right, is it?'

'Just say it. However you want to.'

'She had a heart attack. She was alone. She died alone.'

There was no sign of reproof in his eyes. He probably didn't understand.

'She was my best friend. From when we were children I practically grew up in her house. When we went into business together we both worked long hours, trying to get the company off the ground. I didn't see that it was too much for her. I didn't realise that she was taking cocaine just to keep up.' Sam choked on the words, squeezing her eyes shut.

'Sally never told you that there was anything wrong?'

'No. But I should have known. I was her friend. We worked together.'

'And that made you responsible for everything she did?'

He still didn't get it. She was going to have to tell him everything, and then maybe it would be in his power to forgive her. If Euan could forgive her, perhaps she could forgive herself.

'My mother was a drunk. When Sal's parents found out that my home life wasn't up to much they pretty much opened their house to me, and I used to spend most of my time there. When my mother got a new boyfriend and threw me out, they took me in.'

'How old were you?'

'Fourteen. That doesn't matter…'

She felt his hand, light on her shoulder. Not quite comforting. More steadying, as if he was making sure she didn't chicken out on him. It was too late for that, now.

'What matters is that they took me in. And that in return I let everyone down—Sally's parents, her brother.

I let Sally down, because I just didn't see what was going on.'

'Did you have anyone to support you? Friends? A partner?'

'Sally was my friend. Her family was my family. My partner was…well, we weren't all that serious, we both worked pretty long hours. It wasn't the kind of relationship that stood any real test.'

That was it. The words were finally out, and they brought more tears with them. Sam hardly registered that his arms were around her, pulling her against his chest, cradling her while she wept.

'This isn't…' Finally she managed to gulp some words out. 'This isn't any good, Euan. It doesn't change anything.'

'No. Not for Sally it doesn't. Maybe for you, though?'

He might be right. She did feel different. She wasn't sure yet whether different was going to turn out to be better. 'I'm not the one that matters.' Sam was becoming acutely aware that she was practically sitting on his lap. That her fingers were clutching at his shirt. She let go, smoothing the bunched fabric, and suddenly all she could feel was the skin beneath. Hard and warm.

'You matter.' His tenderness was becoming a little too much to bear. 'I was wrong when I said that this, all that you're doing here, is your phoenix.'

The beautiful glass phoenix, which shone in the light and which suddenly seemed just a poor counterfeit of his eyes. 'What do you mean?'

'It's your penance, isn't it?'

How could she defend herself from something that was true? 'I don't know about that.' Sam got to her feet and walked away from him.

His footsteps crunched on the shingle behind her. 'Do you think you should talk about this? Give yourself permission to cry about it a little?'

She twisted round to face him again. 'I've already done that, haven't I?'

'I meant with other people. In the kind of group that we run.'

'I don't know.' Maybe she should. Not talking about it clearly hadn't worked as well as she had intended.

'Perhaps you should think about it.' He let the silence work on her. The sound of the waves crashing on the shore.

'Would you...? I mean, could I join one of the groups here? One of your groups?'

He shook his head. 'No. I can give you the name of someone else who runs a group, up in London.'

The rejection cut her to the bone. It hadn't seemed as if he was judging her, but he had, and he'd found her wanting. Of course he had. She'd done the very same herself.

'Okay. I'll think about it.' She heard her own voice, brisk, as if this was some kind of business agreement. Covering the hurt.

Euan caught her arm. 'It's not what you think.'

'What isn't?' How the hell did Euan know what she was thinking when she wasn't even sure herself?

'Our groups have rules. I can't let you join one of them.'

'Why?' Somewhere, deep in his eyes, Sam thought she saw the answer, sparking and fizzling. No. Surely not.

'Because of this.' He brushed his thumb across her

lips. She could pull away at any time. She didn't need to go any further. Who was she trying to kid?

She was mesmerised by his eyes. His mouth curled into a smile and hers followed suit. He drew closer, an unspoken question on his lips, and in response to Sam's unspoken answer his fingers slid along her jaw, burying themselves in her hair.

Reaching for him, she curled her arm around his neck, pulling him closer. When his lips brushed against her cheek Sam forgot all the reasons why this wasn't such a good idea.

He stopped, his mouth barely an inch from hers. 'This is the best part.'

Waiting. Her whole body felt as if it might melt in his arms. 'Wondering whether you'll kiss me?'

'Wondering what it'll be like when I do.' She felt his lips curl against hers.

'We could do this for hours…' Sam could stare into his honest eyes, feel his body against hers, warm and protective, for as long as she liked.

'Nah. I don't have the self-control.'

He kissed her. He'd lied. The waiting wasn't the best bit at all.

She was soft, and warm and yielding. The yielding bit she did the best of all. Just when she'd let him in, her eyes soft and promising more than he had a right to expect, she pushed back. A delicious last stand that made him fight for her and sent the blood rushing to his head.

It was like nothing he'd ever done before. Every nerve aware of her every movement. The way her hands slid down his back, coming to rest on the leather belt at his hips. The way her thumbs hooked into the belt loops, gaining traction to pull him closer, although in truth he was already about as close as he could get without throwing off his clothes and making love to her.

Was that what he was about to do? For a moment, lost in the taste of her lips, the smell of her hair, it seemed inevitable. Every move he made seemed to please her, and left him wanting only to please her more.

Not tonight. She was too vulnerable. Not ever. If he let her down, it would crush him.

Tenderly, slowly, he ended the kiss, his heart pounding with longing and grief for what wasn't going to be. He held her close, stroking her hair, wondering whether the internal battle between what he wanted to do and what he knew he should do was going to subside any time soon.

'I think—'

He finished the sentence for her. 'That it's time to go back now. It's beginning to get chilly.'

Relief showed in her eyes. 'Yes. I'm sorry, Euan, but this is a lot to process all at once.'

'I know. I shouldn't have…'

She gave him a wicked smile and longing flared in him, kicking in hard and strong. 'Did I slap you?'

'No.' Right now she could do anything she damn well pleased with him.

'Then I guess it's okay.'

'In that case…' Relief seemed to quell his more visceral urges and Euan found himself able to think rationally once more. 'Would you do me a favour?'

'Depends…' That smile again. Euan drew back a little before it got the better of him.

'Would you leave the work alone? Just for tonight?'

She thought for a moment. 'I'm not really tired… And there's nothing much else to do.'

That was the problem. Take her work away and she was lost, drifting aimlessly with the rejection and grief that she struggled so hard to forget. Euan had likened her to a Russian doll, and this last, beautifully detailed version of Sam explained all the rest. This was the one he was in imminent danger of falling in love with.

'Okay. If I find you something else to do…?'

The look on her face told him that she thought she was on sure ground here. 'All right, then. It's a deal.'

He held her hand as they walked, guiding her through the still-busy streets to a little shop that he knew. The souvenir shop was open late in the summer and he wound his way past the tea-towels and little glass domes full of coloured sand to the back, where there was a large stack of second-hand books and DVDs.

'Choose something.' She couldn't fail to find something she liked in this lot.

She nodded, running her finger along the backs of the DVDs. 'I can play these on my laptop.'

Maybe not such a good idea. Euan reached for a book, pulling it out of the pile. 'What about this?'

'Oh, Jane Austen…' She opened the front cover and her eyes began to jump back and forth as the page reached out and drew her in. 'You know they say that this is one of the best opening lines in the whole of English literature…'

'I guess it'll do, then.' He took the book from her, grinning, and before she could protest he was at the cash desk.

They strolled back to the office together, stopping on the doorstep as if by mutual consent. 'Thanks for the book. I promise I'll read it.' She turned her face up towards his, and all Euan wanted to do was to kiss her again. Not just her lips this time.

'You're welcome. I'm…um…I've got to go out of town tomorrow.'

She nodded as if it was of no consequence. But, then, she didn't know where he was going and he couldn't quite find the words to tell her. 'I'll see you on Saturday. At Kathryn House,' she said.

'You're coming to help?' A group of volunteers was going to start on the decorating there this weekend.

'Try and keep me away.' She grinned up at him. This was what Euan loved about her. Despite everything, you couldn't keep Sam down. She'd been rejected and wounded all her life, but when she got knocked down she just picked herself up and tried again.

'I'll take you down there. About nine?'

She nodded. 'Yeah, that would be fine.'

'In the meantime…' he shrugged, as if it were nothing '…you've got my mobile number. Call me if you want to talk. About anything. If my phone's switched off, leave a message.'

For a moment time seemed to stand still, silence hanging in the air between them, like an awkward guest at a party. Then she stood on her toes to brush a brief, almost formal kiss on his cheek. 'Yeah. And I'll see you on Saturday morning.'

CHAPTER ELEVEN

EUAN HAD BEEN up since six. Yesterday had been difficult, and this morning all he could think about was the
night before last. The way that Sam had kissed him.
The way he'd wanted her.

When he turned up at the office, at half past eight,
he could already hear her moving around upstairs. Five
minutes later she appeared in the doorway to David's
office, looking more beautiful than he remembered,
and more tired than she should be.

'Hey, there. Are you ready?' He stepped forward, his
fingers brushing her elbow in a gesture that hovered
somewhere between friendship and something else.
Then all hell broke loose.

'Don't you dare touch me!' She snatched her arm
away, turning with such abruptness that she jabbed him
in the ribs.

'Ow! Sam…?' Clearly she'd also had time to think,
and it appeared that whatever conclusion she'd come to
wasn't particularly favourable.

'How could you, Euan?' Tears glistened in her pretty
eyes, held in check by the anger on her face.

'What? Sam, what is it?'

'You know perfectly well what. I'm here for another

week, and we're going to have to work together, but if you lay one finger on me...' she thrust one of her fingers in front of his face, in case he was unclear what she meant '...you'll be walking with a limp for the next month.'

Euan took a step back, just in case she changed her mind and decided to take another swipe at him again anyway. 'Sam, just calm down.'

'Calm down!' His words only served to make her even more angry. 'You...you sleaze merchant. I know where you were yesterday.'

Yesterday. Okay, so he hadn't told her where he was going. He had his reasons for that. But even if she had found out, surely that wasn't enough to provoke this kind of reaction.

'I trusted you, Euan.' She was crying now, wiping the tears away as if they were badges of shame.

'You can trust me now. Just talk to me, Sam.'

'There's nothing to say. Just go downstairs and get into your car. I'll get a taxi out to Kathryn House.'

This was ridiculous. 'No, you won't. We're going to sort this out, here and now.'

'There's nothing to sort out, Euan. Nothing you can say is going to make any of this any better, so you might as well save your breath.' She turned abruptly, flinging the door open and slamming it behind her.

'Oh, no, you don't.' He muttered the words under his breath and followed her, catching her in the hallway, blindly trying to open the door to the flat upstairs. 'Sam, will you just stop it, and start from the beginning? What's going on?'

She turned around, icy cold this time. 'Maya asked

me whether I was going down to the clinic yesterday. I said no, because it was your day off.'

'Right. Then what?'

'And then she told me.'

'Told you what?' If she didn't get to the point soon, he was going to shake it out of her, even if that did involve touching her.

'She said, "Ah, yes, that's right. He's gone to see his wife." I suppose that slipped your mind on Thursday night, did it? That you had a wife…' She turned away from him in disgust.

'Sam, wait. Maya didn't tell you—'

'Enough, Euan. There's nothing more to say.' She got the door open, and would probably have slammed it in his face if he hadn't caught it and pulled it closed before she had a chance to get through it. Imprisoning her between his arms, one on either side of her, planted against the door, he took a chance on the belief that she wouldn't try to lash out at him and do any permanent damage.

'She's my *ex*-wife, Sam. We haven't lived together for fourteen years. We divorced ten years ago.'

'So why did Maya tell me she was your wife?' She faced him defiantly. 'Not a particularly easy mistake to make, I would have thought.'

'No, it's not. She was probably trying to be tactful. Said one thing instead of another and didn't correct herself, because she didn't want to elaborate too much.'

'And why wouldn't Maya want to elaborate?'

'Because my ex-wife's in prison. That's where I went yesterday.'

She stared at him, her face starting to redden. 'But Maya said…'

'I know. You already told me what Maya said. You want to listen to the facts now?'

The expression on her face made it very clear that she thought there was some kind of catch to this. All the same, she nodded.

'Okay. I married Marie when I was twenty-one. I was still in medical school and she was studying for her PhD in fine arts. It didn't last a year.'

The tearing, nagging guilt took hold of him. Then he looked into Sam's eyes. If she could face her demons, then he could face this. 'She was an addict. She hid it from me, but I found out that she'd cleaned our bank account out to buy drugs. She'd been getting them in other ways, too.'

'Wh—?' Understanding dawned in her eyes and she lay her hand on his arm. 'You mean…'

'Yeah. When she didn't have money for drugs, she traded favours. I was humiliated and hurt, and I confronted her about it. We argued, and she left. Just walked away.' Suddenly he felt as if the life had been drained out of him and he took a step back, leaning against the wall.

'And then?' Sam was done trying to run away from him, and now compassion showed in her face. Perhaps she was about to tell him the same thing that he'd told her, that he was beating himself up over other people's actions. She couldn't be more wrong.

'I let her go. Didn't try to look for her. You've heard me say that we don't give up on anyone at Driftwood.'

'Yes.'

'Well, I was the one who suggested that rule, because I know just how easy it is to give up on drug abusers. I finished my studies and got a divorce. I tried to put it behind me, but I couldn't, and I ended up at a meeting.' He gave a short, grim laugh. 'When I suggested to you that talking about it would help, that came from first-hand experience.'

'But you're back in contact now.' She laid her hand on his arm, her fingers trembling.

'Yeah. A couple of years back she got in touch with her parents. I'd kept in touch with them, and they called me and said she'd been picked up by the police on charges of fraud and theft.'

'Did she do it?'

'She did it. A habit like hers isn't cheap to maintain. She was sent to prison, and yesterday she was released.'

Sam looked around, as if Marie had followed him home and was going to suddenly appear somewhere. 'Her parents have organised a flat for her, close to where they live, in Northumberland. I picked her up, took her there, and we all had tea and cake. Then I drove back home.'

'Will she be okay?'

'I hope so. She had counselling in prison and she's clean now. We've organised for her to have ongoing support and she's got some part-time voluntary work at a local community farm.' Euan shook his head. It was all too little and too late. He'd let Marie down, been too blind to see what must surely have been obvious to any husband. He was bad news when it came to relationships, and he should have remembered that before he'd kissed Sam.

The weight of that knowledge seemed to bear down on him, and his back slid down against the wall. He hit the floor with a bump, and it was a few moments before he realised that Sam was still there, sitting next to him in the hallway.

'Do you...still love her?' She was looking straight ahead, as if afraid of what his face might tell her.

'No.' The answer came without any hesitation. 'Not for a long time. I care about her, and I'll do what I can to help her be healthy and happy. I don't love her, though.' It wasn't Marie that stood between them. It was his own shortcomings.

She nodded, her body relaxing as she leaned against him. It was as if they were shoulder to shoulder against the world.

'I'm sorry. I shouldn't have called you a sleaze merchant.'

He shrugged. 'It's exactly what I would have described myself as in the circumstances. It was just a misunderstanding.'

'I probably didn't give Maya much of a chance to explain. When she said *wife*, I freaked out a bit. Couldn't get away fast enough.' She reached over, her fingers brushing his sleeve. 'I didn't mean to elbow you in the ribs.'

'I know. Everyone gets clumsy when they're tired.'

'Hey! I'm not clumsy. You just didn't get out of the way fast enough.'

Euan chuckled. 'What time were you up till last night.'

'Two-ish. Three, maybe.'

'Working?'

'That's what I do.'

Euan had thought as much. Sam worked to shut everything else out and this time he'd been responsible for the hurt. 'Why don't you give today a miss? Take a rest?'

'But I was looking forward to it.' She bumped her shoulder against his. 'Shouldn't we get going?'

'I'm taking you for breakfast first.'

'But we'll be late…'

'It's Saturday, we're allowed to be late. And I want to celebrate still being in one piece.'

She laughed. 'Yeah. I think I do, too.'

'Still friends, then?' He hadn't dared ask until he was sure of the answer.

'Yes. Surprisingly enough.'

He got to his feet, holding out his hand to help her up. 'Let's go, then.'

They had eaten breakfast under a red and white striped parasol at a café on the seafront. It was a bright, clear morning, and the breeze from the sea seemed to whip away the last of the cobwebs fogging Sam's brain. Euan was talking to her, she was talking to him, and that seemed like a minor miracle right now.

The number of cars parked outside Kathryn House indicated that plenty of people had turned up today. Euan parked next to a battered van and waved to Juno, who was opening the doors at the back.

'Want a hand?'

'Ah! Yeah, just the person I needed.' Juno grinned at them both. 'I had a hell of a job getting this lot into the van on my own.'

'Why didn't you call?'

'I did, yesterday afternoon. Your mobile was switched off.'

'Ah. Sorry about that. My day off.'

'Do something nice?'

It was just an idle question, and Sam guessed from the lines that appeared on Euan's forehead that he'd brush it off with an equally vague answer.

'Actually, I was springing a friend of mine from prison.'

Juno didn't flinch. 'Nice one. Go well?'

'Yeah.' Euan was smiling, now. 'I think it did.'

And that was it. The thing that he'd kept so tightly to his chest had turned into something that could be talked about and left alone. Maybe he'd done this on purpose, just to show Sam that. Or maybe he'd just done it for himself.

Whatever. The moment had passed, and Euan had jostled Juno to one side and was lifting one of the heavy sculptures, swathed in plastic, carefully from the van.

'Watch the bit at the top. Don't knock it off when you go through the door.' Juno was shouting instructions, and Euan was cordially ignoring them.

'I've got it.' The muscles of his arms and shoulders had swelled to take the strain of the load, and Sam watched greedily as he manoeuvred himself and the parcel through the entranceway.

'Right.' Now he was out of sight, Juno had consigned her precious piece to fate and Euan's care. 'Can you take this box? I think I can manage the smaller piece...' She gestured to one of the smaller statues, wrapped up in the back of the van.

'Leave those for the men.' Sam carefully slid the box out of the van and gave it to Juno. 'That's the phoenix, isn't it? You should carry that in.'

Juno laughed, but took the box anyway. 'Okay. Perhaps you could get the doors for me.'

Inside the house was a hive of activity, the sound of a radio echoing from the back rooms and David in charge, holding a clipboard. 'Through there…' He pointed to a door at the end of the hallway. 'We'll lock them in the office so they're not damaged.' Euan was on his way back to the van, and stopped when he saw the women.

'Ah. So the phoenix is home now.'

'Yep.' Juno's tone was as if this was just another phoenix, in just another place, but her face was wreathed in a smile. 'Watch out! Coming through!' She bellowed at a young man in overalls, who was a good fifteen feet away, and followed Sam into the bright office, stacked with flat-packed furniture and boxes of computer equipment.

'Where do you want this?' Euan appeared, with a second statue.

'Over there, by the first one.' Juno gave a nod of approbation and produced a roll of tape with the word 'FRAGILE' emblazoned on it in red letters. 'Better put some of this on them.' She tore off a long strip, and handed the roll to Sam.

'Juno…do you do commissions?' The idea had been rolling around in the back of Sam's head for the last week, one of those things that get thought about but never done. Suddenly, she wanted it done.

Juno stood and faced her. 'Kind of. People come in sometimes with drawings or photographs of something they want to have reproduced, and I generally say no to that. But if someone wants to pick a colour, or an emotion, something like that, then I'll do some sketches and make the piece.'

'Yes. That's what I meant. Would you make something for me?'

'Really?'

'Don't look so surprised.' Sam rolled her eyes and ventured a little business advice. 'The thing to do when someone asks you that is to say that you can, and then pull out your diary. Look busy. People value something that everyone else wants.'

'I haven't got a diary.'

'Then get a notebook. And when you do, I'd be very grateful if you'd put my name in it.'

'You'll be first on my list,' Juno chuckled. 'Friend's dis—'

'Don't you dare. No friend's discount. Can I come by and talk to you about it next week?' There was the familiar lurch of her heart, the lump at the back of her throat, but this time Sam ignored it and kept talking. 'It's for the family of a good friend of mine who died. I want something bright…nothing gloomy because she loved colour. Something to celebrate her.'

Juno nodded. 'Sorry to hear about your friend. Yes, come to the workshop and we'll figure out something that does her justice.'

'Good. That's great.' Sam took a deep breath. Somewhere, down in the depths of her heart, Sal was smiling in approval.

CHAPTER TWELVE

THERE WERE ALMOST fifty volunteers. Anyone who could wield a scraper was in one of the teams that David had organised, preparing the walls of the rooms for papering later on today. The younger children were being looked after in a roped-off play area on the lawn, and there was a team of mostly older women in the kitchen, preparing food and washing up.

'This is fabulous!' Sam caught David as he hurried through the hallway.

'Isn't it? I didn't think everyone would turn up. Euan!' David had just caught sight of Euan and he beckoned him over.

'What have you got me down for?' Euan peered over his shoulder at the clipboard.

'You're not on the schedule. You're just generally making yourself useful. Rabble-rousing and so on.' David winked at Sam. 'I believe in getting everyone to do what they're best at.'

'Thanks for that. Do I get anyone to help me? Sam's not doing anything…'

'Sam's on photography.'

'Yes, I've an idea for your website,' she explained. 'An area where we can have photos and stream video…'

Euan was wearing the bemused look that always accompanied anything vaguely technical. He should stick with rabble-rousing, he was much better at that. 'I'll show it to you when it's finished. You'll like it.'

'I'm sure I will.' There was the hint of a quirk to his lips, a shadow in his eyes of the look he'd given her when he'd kissed her. Then it was gone.

David was consulting yet another list. 'Sam, when you need them, the cameras are in the blue bag in the office. I'm just off to help Sandra with the tea, it's about time everyone had something to drink.' David was on the move again, making for the kitchen in search of his wife.

'Do you think he wants a hand?' Tea for this many people sounded like a mammoth task.

'He'll have it under control. This is the kind of thing that David does best. I keep out of his way, and try not to throw too many spanners in the works when he's in this kind of mood.'

'Probably best.' Euan's free spirit, his approach to any given problem couldn't be contained on a clipboard. 'Have you got the key to the office? I took the lock off the latch when Juno and I were finished in there.'

Euan's gaze had already wandered to the front door, where Jamie was trying to shepherd through a couple of men with bulky boxes. 'Hey, Jamie. There's a trolley right there. We can wheel those around the side of the house…' He pulled a bunch of keys from his pocket, dropped them into her hand and strode towards Jamie, leaving Sam to guess which key fitted the door to the office.

Two days. Sam had captured it all on camera, the volunteers at work, the regular supplies of food that came from the kitchen, the smiles and the catastrophes. At the end of each day a group photo, and on Sunday afternoon the finished rooms. Finally, she videoed as everyone crowded into the community room and Juno placed her glass phoenix in the alcove that had been reserved for it, to a roar of cheering and applause.

'Did you get a chance to look around the summer house?' Euan joined her on the veranda as the last of the cars scrunched out of the drive.

'Not yet. I got pictures of the frame going up and everyone working on it, but I haven't seen the inside yet.' She turned to Euan. The light in his eyes seemed to reflect her own feeling of exhilaration. 'Thank you. I can't remember when I've had such fun.'

'We should be thanking you.' Sam had noticed that David and Euan had made sure to thank each volunteer personally. She supposed it was her turn now.

His arm snaked around her waist, and he bent to kiss her cheek. Not so different from the kisses that he'd exchanged with Juno and some of the other volunteers, only with them he hadn't lingered quite so long.

'You want to stroll down there? Take some photos of what it looks like now it's complete? I need to go round and make sure everything's locked up, there's been a spate of burglaries in the area.'

'That would be nice.'

His hand brushed against hers as they walked. Talking about the day, laughing together. 'It looks bigger now it's finished.' She nodded towards the summer house.

'Yeah. It's insulated, so we can use it during the spring and autumn, even in winter if we can get some heating in there. It was donated to us.'

'Really? That was generous of someone.'

'It was a local manufacturer. It's an old design and the wood's not been properly treated. They were going to scrap it, but David said that we'd give it a good home here. Apparently a few of tins of wood preservative and a brush are all we need.'

'How does he do it?'

Euan chuckled. 'Goodness only knows. Without him the charity would grind to a halt.'

'Without either of you. You two make a great team.'

He led her round to the far side of the summer house, where timber steps led up to a small deck with sliding glass doors leading inside the structure. 'Wow, this is smart. I must have some pictures of this…'

Euan sat down on the steps, turning his face to the late afternoon sun. Immediately at ease with the world. He was like a large cat, stretched out and purring in front of the fire. Somehow it was impossible not to relax when he was like this.

'Is this David's?' She'd moved a cool bag to get a better shot of the glass doors and the view beyond them.

'Uh? Yeah, I think it is. We'll take it back to the office for him.' Euan took the bag and feeling its weight unzipped it. 'Ah! Look what I found.' He pulled out two bottles of beer. 'Want one?'

'Seems churlish to let them go to waste.' Sam sat down on the steps next to him, watching as he gave the top of each of the bottles a sharp, expert tap on the stair rail then pulled the caps off.

'How do you do that?'

'Just hit it in the right place. Not too hard, but quite firmly… Then, if you twist the cap just right, you don't cut yourself.' He glanced at his hand, where a droplet of blood was forming. 'On the other hand, sometimes you do…'

'Want a hanky?'

'Nah. It's okay…' Euan looked as if he was about to put his finger into his mouth to stem the flow of blood, and then thought better of it. 'I think I'd rather bleed than poison myself.'

'Come here.' Sam pulled her handkerchief from her pocket and folded it, winding it around his finger and tying it tightly. 'You can put some antiseptic on it when we get back to the house.'

His lips quirked into a smile. 'Yes, ma'am.' He held the bandaged finger up. 'Are you the very last person in the world who carries a cloth hanky?'

'Probably. Just as well I was here, eh?'

'Who knows what might have happened?' Euan grinned and picked up one of the bottles, laying it against her cheek before he put it into her hand.

Sam gasped. 'Still pretty cold.'

'Mmm-hmm.' His smile was making her tremble. Heat and cold. Who knew what he could do with those two elements if there was nothing to separate his imagination from her naked skin?

He picked up the other bottle, dangling it thoughtfully between his fingers. 'We made some pretty good progress this weekend.'

'Fabulous progress. I never thought that so much could be done in such a short time.'

'You get enough people working together and you can do almost anything. Move mountains, jump tall buildings…' Euan was chuckling now.

'Jumping tall buildings is child's play. Remaking a human life is real super-hero stuff.' Euan was always so appreciative of what others did. Sometimes he forgot his own contribution to all of this.

He looked at her, nothing but questions in his eyes. 'Super-heroes save everyone. That's part of their remit.'

Marie. The phantom of the woman that he hadn't saved squeezed in between them, her broken life pushing them apart. 'Just because…' Sam sighed. Marie was like a blurred photograph, ephemeral and unknown. It was difficult to get to grips with something you couldn't even see properly.

She took a sip from her bottle to moisten her dry throat. Loosened the messy plait that snaked over her shoulder, combing her hair out with her fingers and shaking her head.

He caught his breath, and when Sam looked up at him his face held all the promise of a kiss. For a moment she was drawn back towards him, and then doubts seemed to crowd in again and he shook his head.

'I'm no miracle-worker. I've failed in the past, and while I'll try not to do it again, I can't be sure that I won't.'

'Marie?'

A flash of defiance, and then he nodded. 'Yeah. Maybe I could have helped her, but I didn't. I was too…' He shrugged. 'I don't know what it was that stopped me.'

'You were too close to her, perhaps.'

He took a long swig from his bottle. 'Didn't that make me the one person who should have helped?'

'You've been telling me for the last week that families and friends give one kind of support. That successful rehab requires a commitment from the individual, and structured, professional support.'

'And you think that lets me off the hook?'

'I think…' Sam wasn't sure that she was equal to this, but she had to try. 'I don't know how to reason you out of this, Euan. But it doesn't seem fair to me that someone who's done such a lot, who's made such a difference to so many lives, should feel so guilty.'

'But…' He was shaking his head, as if she didn't understand.

Enough of this. 'There's no *but* about it. I might not have your training and experience in these things, but that doesn't give you a monopoly on being right. Relationships take two people. None of us is solely responsible for what happens, and you don't have to carry that weight alone.'

Sam stopped for breath, holding up one finger to forestall any interruption. Hadn't he said that to her about Sally? It sounded vaguely familiar. Whatever. She was on a roll now and he could say whatever he wanted later.

'You're the most honourable man I know. You're dedicated, loyal to the people you work with, and you've been a good friend to me. So just…just give yourself a break.'

She'd expected him to come back at her with some smart answer, but there was silence. He was staring at the ground, almost as if he hadn't heard.

'Well, what have you got to say to that?'

He looked up at her. 'Thank you.'

That was the last thing she'd expected. 'Is that all?'

'I think so.' He put his arm around her. The kind of gesture that any friend, sitting on any steps, might make, but it made her shiver. 'That means a lot, Sam. Thank you.'

'Nothing else?'

'I could make some comment about being glad you're on my side, because you can be too scary for words at times.' He was grinning now.

He said the nicest things. 'Well, just hold that thought.'

'Yes, ma'am.'

'And while you're doing it, what do you say to a takeaway for tonight? My treat, I could eat a horse...'

Euan chuckled softly, helping her to her feet and pulling out his keys to lock the summer house. As they strolled across the lawn together, the low sun at their backs, a trick of the light made their shadows appear to touch...

The alarms up at the house started to sound.

'Someone must have come back...' He was suddenly watchful, his eyes scanning the windows at the back of the house, looking for any clue as to who it might be. 'Stay here while I go and see.'

He strode on ahead of her and Sam followed, running to keep up with him. 'Sam, will you stay here? Please.'

'If someone's there, I'd rather be with you.'

'If someone's there, *I'd* rather you were safely out of the way.'

'Safest place I can think of is with you.'

He rolled his eyes, but there was nothing he could do to stop her, save carrying her screaming to the car and locking her in, and he seemed to know it. 'All right, then. But stay with me.'

He was checking the windows as he walked along the veranda and unlocked the doors that led into the community room. He punched a combination into the console on the wall, and the din of the alarm stopped.

Silence. 'It's probably someone who's forgotten something and come back to get it.' Sam walked over to an empty bookcase and retrieved her laptop from where she'd stowed it out of the way.

'Yeah. Probably.' Euan was still on the alert, listening for any sign of someone else in the house. He moved over to the door that led to the hall and opened it, then threw his hand out behind him in a signal to Sam to stay where she was.

'All right, lads. There's the door.' He spoke to someone in the hallway, the words unhurried and calm, then walked through the door, closing it behind him.

Why did he have to be so bloody protective? Sam crept over to the door, pressing her ear to it in an effort to hear what was going on. Euan's voice sounded again, but she couldn't hear what he was saying. There was a scuffling sound and a thump, and then the sound of the front door slamming.

The alarms went off again. Inside the house the shrill tone was almost unbearable, and Sam turned to the console, wondering if just glaring at it would do any good.

Someone stood inside the open door to the veranda. Probably just a teenager, from his build, with the hood of his jacket tied tightly to obscure most of his face. Maybe he was just as frightened as she was but if so why didn't he turn and run? The alarm cut out again and he took a step forward.

'Give me the laptop.' Sam realised she had her laptop clutched to her chest, like a shield.

'Okay.' Her voice sounded peculiar, high and trembling. 'Take it and go.'

The youth beckoned her with one hand, the other reaching behind his back. When it reappeared he was holding an ugly-looking knife. Sam put the laptop on the floor and started to back away. 'Take it.'

'Come *here!*'

He was getting angry now. This wasn't how it was supposed to go.

'Pick it up. Bring it here. And what's that you've got around your neck?'

Sam's hand instinctively moved to the gold locket hanging inside her blouse, below the neckline. The laptop was backed up, insured, and if you tried to get in without a password, the hard drive would be wiped. The locket was irreplaceable.

'Nothing. It's nothing.'

'Give it to me!' the youth shouted at her, clearly unaware of Euan's presence in the house. She heard two running steps behind her, and she threw herself against the wall in terror. Then, with a flood of relief, she realised it was Euan.

'Knife… He's got a knife…' She screamed the words, but she was too late. Euan had charged the lad, and the two of them clashed for a moment, then the youth was running.

'That's all of them.' He turned, grinning. 'I checked out front and there were three motorcycles.'

'Euan…'

'It's okay, Sam, they've gone.'

'Euan!' This time he followed her gaze, down to the rip in his shirt and the blood pluming across it.

CHAPTER THIRTEEN

'OH.' FOR A moment he stared at her, and then he cursed softly and suddenly fell to his knees.

'Okay. You're going to be okay.' He was grasping at his shirt, trying to pull it away from the wound on his side, and she batted his hands away, ripping the side of his shirt to see. 'Stay still. Just sit down and let me look.'

'I don't think it's hit anything vital.'

'How do you know that?' Suddenly Sam felt very alone. The only person here who knew anything about medicine was Euan, and he was the one who'd just been stabbed.

'It's not bleeding enough for it to have hit a major artery. My kidney's lower down and my liver's further round.'

'Okay.' Sam looked at the gash on his side. It seemed to be wide rather than deep, and, despite Euan's assertion that it wasn't bleeding very much, there seemed to be an awful lot of blood. 'Lungs?'

He took a deep laboured breath, wincing with pain. The shock of the blow must be wearing off and he was clearly feeling it now. 'No, I don't think it's punctured a lung.'

'Good. That's good.' Sam wondered whether it was

even slightly reliable to allow a patient to diagnose himself, but it was all she had at the moment. 'Right, we'll stop the bleeding and call an ambulance.'

'There's a hospital with an A and E department ten minutes down the road. It'll be quicker if we drive.'

'Okay. Hang on for a moment while I get your medical bag from the car.' She slid two fingers into the pocket of his jeans and hooked out his car keys. 'Just stay with me, Euan.'

He forced a grin. 'I generally keep that one for when someone's in immediate danger. If you don't want to unnerve me, just say you'll be back soon.'

'Right. I'll be back soon.'

Sam ran to the car, dragging the heavy medical bag out. When she returned, she found Euan trying to get to his feet.

'Sit down!' She skidded to a halt next to him. 'You're a bloody terrible patient, Euan.'

'And you can nurse me any time you like…'

'Shut up.' She rummaged in the bag and pulled out a thick wad of gauze. 'This?'

'That'll do. Put a pair of gloves on first, and then apply the gauze. Press as hard as you can.'

He winced when she pressed the gauze against his side. 'Now tape it.' Sam reached into the medical bag with her free hand, and pulled out a roll of tape.

'Not with that. There's a roll of wider tape in there.'

'This one?'

'Yeah.'

She taped the gauze firmly over the wound, noting with some satisfaction that the bleeding seemed to be stopping. 'Right. I'll help you up, and we'll be on our way.'

'Aren't you going to give me pain relief?'

'No, because I don't know what to give you. And I'm not going to rely on you to tell me, you're probably in shock. You'll just have to put up with it.' Sam leaned in, wondering whether she could lift his bulk if he couldn't get to his feet, and he pulled her close.

'Just a smile, then…'

'Stop messing around or I'll stab you myself.' She couldn't help but give him what he asked.

'That'll do. Feeling better already.'

'Can you stand up?'

'Yeah.' Sam steadied him as he got to his feet, but he didn't falter.

'Now we're going to walk to the car. Take your time.'

He walked slowly but steadily, only wincing when Sam helped him into the passenger seat. 'Your laptop. And you'll need to reset the alarm. We need to report the break-in to the police, as well.'

'Forget it. The doors are locked and David's only fifteen minutes away, I'll call him and ask him to deal with it.' Sam leaned over him to clip his seat belt into place then got into the driver's seat, pulling it forward, and started the engine.

He was beginning to feel sick and more than a little dizzy. Shock, he supposed. Euan knew that the wound he'd received wasn't life-threatening, and he hadn't lost enough blood for that to be the cause of the light-head-edness that he was experiencing.

Sam had pulled his phone from his back pocket and slid it into the hands-free cradle, so she could call David while she drove. She navigated the SUV smoothly into the hospital car park, which stood opposite the entrance to the A and E department. When she flashed the head-lights an ambulance crew, who were standing outside, came over to help.

'Let's take a look.' A paramedic squatted down by the open door of the car and carefully inspected the damage. 'I won't remove the dressing here, we'll get a chair over and take you inside straight away.' He looked up at Sam. 'Nice job.'

Euan shot him a smile. Sam had done well, and she deserved a bit of praise. She was smiling as she got out of the car, walking beside the wheelchair into the A and E reception area.

It was still early, and the Saturday night rush hadn't set in yet. He was wheeled straight through to a treatment bay, and a nurse helped him up onto a gurney.

'How are you doing?' Sam was still by his side, look-ing down anxiously at him.

'Fine. I'm fine.' He found her hand and held onto it, although he wasn't sure whether it was to give or receive comfort. Or whether he just happened to like holding her hand. 'We'll be out of here in no time…'

'Euan?'

A familiar voice. Euan struggled to sit up, and Dr Rob Ames's hand on his shoulder pushed him back down again. Euan was a regular at various A and E de-partments, and had got to know many of the staff here, but he wasn't usually the one on the receiving end of their ministrations.

'What's this?'

Euan opened his mouth to tell Rob that he just needed a couple of stitches, but he didn't get a chance. Sam cut in, the story tumbling from her lips.

She was an A and E doctor's dream. Clear, concise,

sticking to the facts, and while she left nothing out, she didn't embroider her account with unnecessary details either. Rob was nodding, listening to her carefully.

'Right. Let's have a look at you.' Rob helped Euan to roll onto his side, and he saw the sharp stab of pain reflected in Sam's face.

'Can't you give him something for the pain?' She shot an imploring look at Rob.

'It's okay. Let him take a look… He knows what he's doing,' Euan said.

A short, sharp laugh from Rob. 'Glad to hear you think so. I'm going to take the dressing off now.' Rob paid him the professional courtesy of skipping the bit about keeping still and that it might hurt a bit.

It hurt a lot, but not as much as the tears in her eyes when she saw the wound. Not as much as the helplessness he felt.

'It doesn't look too deep.' Rob seemed to be taking his time over probing the gash on his side. 'Any loss of feeling in your leg?'

'No, my leg's fine.' Euan tried to keep impatience from his voice. Everyone seemed to be forgetting that Sam had just been through a traumatic experience too. She'd come face to face with an intruder, had had a knife waved at her. Then she'd had to deal with dressing his wound and bringing him here. He hadn't expected her to fall to pieces, Sam kept far too tight a grip on her emotions for that, but he almost wished that she would.

Rob seemed finally to have come to a conclusion. 'Good. We'll irrigate the wound first, and if there's no sign of any other damage, I'll stitch it.' He snapped off his surgical gloves, throwing them into the waste bin. 'I won't be a minute.'

'Yeah. Thanks, Rob. I appreciate it.'

'All part of the service.' Rob grinned at him and walked out of the cubicle.

'Where's he going?' Sam leaned in close, whispering to him.

'He'll ask a nurse to clean the wound.' Euan still couldn't quite get his head around it being his own wound. He felt he should be doing something, not just lying there. 'They'll make sure there's nothing in there, and then stitch it up.'

'Hmm.' She gave the cubicle an assessing sweep of her gaze. 'They seem pretty good here.'

'They're very good.' Euan frowned.

'What's the matter? Do you want me to call someone?'

'No, it's okay.' Nothing was okay. He'd let Sam down, leaving her alone to face a kid with a knife, and now he couldn't even comfort her properly. Adrenaline was still flooding his system, urging him to either fight or fly and he was expected to lie still. 'It's you I'm worried about.'

It seemed like a perfectly reasonable thing to say, but she rolled her eyes. 'Is it really so hard to let someone take care of you, Euan? You never know, you might be good at it.'

'I might not.'

'There's always beginner's luck.'

She made him laugh, with that dry humour of hers. When he wasn't laughing, she made him smile, in about a hundred different ways. He took her hand and swore a silent oath that as soon as he got out of here, he'd take much better care of her.

They seemed to have been at the hospital for about a week, but when Euan looked at his watch it had been a little more than a couple of hours. A policeman had turned up to take statements from them both and then Rob had declared him fit to go home, releasing him into Sam's care. Euan had made no objection, largely because he knew that Rob wouldn't let him go home alone.

He needed her help to get out of the car, but he could walk well enough. He'd be okay as long as he didn't need to break into a sprint.

'I'm going to call David. You should stay with him and Sandra tonight,' he announced.

She'd followed him through to the kitchen and now she took the phone out of his hand and put it back into its cradle. 'You're supposed to be taking things easy. And the doctor said that you shouldn't be on your own tonight.'

'Don't fuss.' He'd almost snapped at her and regretted it immediately.

'I'm not fussing.' She flushed red.

'Sam, I really appreciate everything you've done…' Euan was usually too proud to beg, but these were special circumstances. 'Please, do as I ask. I can manage for myself.'

'No, you can't manage for yourself. You've just been stabbed. So you can drop the macho act, stop being so pig-headed, and bloody well sit down.'

'There's no need to shout.'

'What the hell do you expect me to do? You're walking about, you won't sit and take things easy. Any minute now you could start bleeding, or something could rupture.' She flailed one hand in the air, to cover a multitude of unknown medical conditions. 'Don't you dare make me lose you, because I won't do it.' She was shaking now, tears running down her cheeks.

This wasn't going the way he'd planned. Euan took a step towards her and she moved to steady him. Suddenly she was in his arms. He held her tight, and it seemed that they supported each other through to the sitting room, where Euan lowered himself onto the sofa. He reached for her and she sat down next to him.

'What's going on, Euan? Don't you want me here?' She was calmer now.

'Of course I do. But you've been through enough already. I should never have put you in a position where you had to face someone with a knife.'

She stared at him in disbelief. 'It wasn't your fault. And, anyway, you came back for me.'

'I was too late, Sam.' He'd been too late to help Marie, and now somehow he'd managed to make the same mistake again. History was starting to repeat itself and he had to stop it right now. 'You'll be much better off at David and Sandra's tonight.'

'You don't get it, do you?' She took his hand, holding it between hers. 'I don't need to be anywhere but here. You came back for me. Do you know how many people have done that? How much it means?'

He hadn't thought about it that way. 'No, I… Sam, I'm so sorry.'

'Don't be. I'm not asking for your pity.'

'Good. You're not getting it.' Pity wasn't the word that sprang to mind in connection with Sam. Respect, yes.

She smiled. It was luminous in the gathering dark-

ness of the evening. 'I won't pretend that I didn't get a
scare when I saw the blood.'

'Yeah. Me too.'

'So it was just bravado. All of the it's-just-a-scratch
stuff.'

'I don't think I actually said that, did I?'

She wrinkled her nose at him. 'No. That would have
been a stupid thing to say.'

He chuckled. 'Okay. You want to give me a break?'

'I'll think about it. If you behave.' She pulled away
from him, levering herself to her feet. 'I'll call David,
let him know that you've been discharged, and that I'm
staying here tonight.'

'Thanks, Sam.' With a sigh he leaned back on the
cushions she'd arranged for him and closed his eyes.

He'd asked for water and had drunk two glassfuls, obviously thirsty, either from the heat of the hospital or the
painkillers that Rob had given him. Or maybe from the
loss of blood, but Sam didn't like to think about that.

Blood and grime still streaked his forearms, and he
was awkwardly trying to keep his injured side away
from the sofa cushions. He needed to wash, get comfortable and get some food inside him. She could send him
upstairs to the bathroom while she prepared something
to eat, but suppose he became dizzy and fell? Surely, in
the circumstances, it would be all right to go with him?

*If [a condition holds true] Then [take one course of
action] Else [don't even go there]*

If...Then...Else. It was a simple, logical sequence,
part of the programming language that Sam used every
day, and it had become second nature to approach almost any decision on those terms. But logic didn't help

much when it came to dealing with Euan. She was going to have to take a leaf from his book and just go with the flow.

'Come upstairs.'

He raised one eyebrow and she ignored him. 'You need to wash and I'm not having you fall and crack your head open in the bathroom. I've had enough of hospitals for tonight.'

'I can manage.'

'I dare say you can. I'll just make sure that you live up to that promise.'

He hesitated then got painfully to his feet and made for the stairs. Maybe now he was willing to admit that even though he could do it alone, it was better with someone there. Or maybe he was just humouring her.

By the time he'd climbed the stairs, exhaustion was showing on his face. He allowed her to take his arm and support him into the bathroom then fetch a stool so that he could sit down by the basin.

He said nothing when she carefully stripped his shirt off, taping some plastic film from the kitchen over the dressing on his side. Watched as she filled the basin with warm water.

'Give me your hand.' She'd soaped hers, and she took his hand, massaging it gently. His palm, in between each finger. Then the other, slowly and carefully. It seemed as if he'd needed care for a very long time.

Then his arms. Sam was doing a reasonable job of not thinking too hard about his skin, golden from the sun and slightly cool to the touch, but she couldn't help noticing. Feeling the way that the tight muscles across his shoulders relaxed under her fingers. She worked calmly and methodically, across his back and chest with a flannel, the warm silence curling around them both protective and healing.

'How's that?' She handed him the towel and he dried his face.

'Better.' He reached for her, pulling her between his outstretched legs, wrapping his arms around her waist, and she cradled his head against her chest. Just for comfort. If she kept telling herself that, she might begin to believe it.

'All done.' She gently disentangled herself from him and led him through to the bedroom.

'You should go and take a shower.' He sat on the bed, watching her, as she pulled the curtains and searched in the dresser for some clean clothes, his gaze edged with hunger. This was an undisguised invitation to go before things got out of hand.

'Yes, I could do with one. You'll be all right for a few minutes?'

'I'll be fine.' His eyes were telling her to stay, but he waved her away. 'Go and get cleaned up. I can manage to dress on my own.'

She was a long time in the bathroom, and Euan began to wonder vaguely if Sam had fallen asleep in there. He'd stretched as far as he dared, testing his body's remaining strength and flexibility, and then changed into the sweatpants and T-shirt she'd left for him, before lying down against the pillows that she'd piled up at the head of the bed.

He could still feel her fingers on his skin. The brush of her hair as she'd leaned over to towel his back dry. It had been a sensation that he hadn't been able to define. It had warmed him after the chill of cold steel against his ribs. Steadied him against the sudden realisation that he wasn't invulnerable.

Who was he trying to kid? It had been like sex. The kind of sex where you gave up something of yourself and received more than you'd ever bargained for in return. The kind that he'd managed to avoid since Marie had left.

Hold it! Right there. Sam wasn't like the women who had drifted in and out of his life over the years, leaving nothing behind other than the vague feeling that something inside him was irretrievably broken. She was vulnerable, scarred and yet strong in ways that took Euan's breath away. He'd made his decision, and he needed to stick to it. It was friendship or nothing.

A movement, right on the periphery of his vision, caught his attention. She was standing…no, hovering…in the doorway, the borrowed sweatshirt and pants rolled up at the ankles and wrists but still swamping her frame. Her cheeks were pink from the shower and somehow she managed to look like a barefoot angel.

'I'm going to get a warm drink. What would you like?'

A rather awkward, undeniably gorgeous, barefoot angel. The least he could do was make her feel at ease, without crossing the firm lines he'd just drawn regarding his own behaviour. 'Tea would be nice.'

She shook her head. 'No, you should have something more substantial. I was thinking soup or hot milk. Do you have any hot chocolate?'

Euan grinned at her. An assertive barefoot angel, then. 'I think so. Anything you want.'

'Right.' She gave him a nod and disappeared.

* * *

Sam did her best to breeze back into the room as if it was a matter of no importance that this was his bedroom, and they were alone. She put the two mugs of hot chocolate on the nightstand, and he pulled himself upright on the pillows.

'Are you going to sit down?'

There was no chair, so Sam sat on the edge of the bed, one foot firmly planted on the floor.

'I like what you've done in here.'

Stupid. She sounded like someone who'd dropped in for a spot of afternoon tea. The room was nice, though. A warm oak floor, pale walls and crisp, cream-coloured sheets. A bright throw folded at the end of the bed and striped in many shades of blue gave a dash of the seaside, along with an old ship's timepiece on the wall.

'Thanks.' He was looking at her as if she posed an unanswerable problem. 'Are we being filmed?'

'What?' Sam glanced over instinctively towards the window, looking for a chink in the curtains, and then realised he was joking. 'What do you mean?'

'Well, this is what they used to do in all the old films, isn't it? When the censors allowed two people in a bedroom, as long as one had a foot on the floor at all times. Any time you want to get a bit more comfortable, I can always take over for a while.'

The ice cracked and then shattered in the face of his humour. 'I think it's probably all right. We could pretend that I'm a doctor.'

'I *am* a doctor. Doesn't that work for you?'

'No, not really. One of us has to be the doctor, and the other one the patient. And I think we've already established who's the patient around here.'

Euan laughed. 'Good point. Well, in that case, I think there are a couple of pillows in the blanket box.'

The jolt of adrenaline in his system had taken a while to wear off, but he was asleep now. They'd squabbled over ownership of the TV remote, and he'd finally handed it over to her. They'd watched a programme about an archaeological dig that had taken place in the area, and had decided they both wanted to visit the site. Talked. And talked some more. They'd both lost track of the old film that Sam had tuned into, and now exhaustion had overtaken him and he lay on the bed, eyes closed, one hand lying protectively over his side.

Sam flipped the TV off and arranged the throw from the end of the bed across him. She'd stay here for a few minutes, just to make sure he was sleeping soundly, before she went next door to the spare room. She lay down next to him, listening to the sound of his breathing.

CHAPTER FOURTEEN

'BREAKFAST?'

Sam's eyes snapped open. Had she…? Had *they*…?

Of course not. Euan had been in no state last night for anything other than sleep. Unsure whether to be relieved or disappointed, Sam concentrated on the rich aroma that had accompanied him into the room.

'Coffee? You made coffee?'

'I did.' He was smiling and dressed, as if last night had never happened, but he winced when he bent to put the coffee down beside the bed.

'Mmm. Wonderful.' Even though she was still wearing the sweatshirt and pants he'd lent her, she took the sheet with her when she sat up, wrapping it across her chest. 'Thanks.'

'You slept well.'

It wasn't a question but an observation. He already knew, of course, he'd been lying right next to her. 'Yeah, I…' She hadn't woken once in the night. And try as she might, Sam couldn't remember any of her dreams. 'I didn't…um…disturb you, did I?'

'Nope. You slept like a baby.'

How did he know that? Perhaps he'd been watching her. 'And you were awake?'

He grinned cheerfully. 'I woke up a couple of times.' His hand floated to his side, hovering over the wound. 'Went back to sleep again. You were curled up and dead to the world.'

Right. No thrashing about, punching the pillows, and no waking up, crying. No bad dreams. She hadn't had a night like that since Sally had died. Sam said a private thank-you to the unknown source of that particular miracle, and decided to enquire no further into exactly how long Euan had been awake while she had slept.

'So, how are you feeling?'

'Fine. A bit stiff, but the dressing's still clean.'

'Which is good I assume.' She reached for her coffee and took a sip.

He laughed. 'Yeah. Means the wound hasn't been bleeding during the night.'

'I suppose I didn't need to stay after all.'

'I was glad you were there.' For a moment his gaze caught hers, and he seemed about to say more. Then the moment passed.

'I hope you're not going to use this as an excuse to go to work today...'

The look on his face confirmed her suspicions. 'I thought—'

'Well, you can think again. We'll have breakfast—'

'Thought you didn't eat breakfast.' He grinned at her.

'Well, it's not an inflexible rule,' she replied. 'I can have breakfast if I want it. We'll have breakfast and then we'll see. David said last night that he was getting Mel in to cover for you at the clinic, so you're not needed.'

He pursed his lips. 'Harsh. Very harsh.'

'But true. You're only irreplaceable when you're in one piece.' She slid towards the edge of the bed and flapped her hand to shoo him away. 'Now, go and do nothing for ten minutes while I get a shower...'

Monday morning with no work to do wasn't as daunting as she'd thought it might be. A leisurely breakfast and then they divided the Sunday paper between them. Argued over the crossword, Sam filling in the answers while Euan reclined on the sofa.

'What are you doing there?'

She hardly knew. It had been years since she'd made one of these. 'You fold the paper like this, and it makes one petal.' She held the results of her labours up for him to see. 'Then you put the petals together to make a flower, and the flowers together to make a ball. It doesn't work so well with newspaper.'

'Better with the supplement.' He slid the magazine out from the cushions beside him, and handed it to her.

'Oh, yes, it will be. Got any glue?'

'In the kitchen drawer.'

He watched lazily while she cut and folded the paper, gluing it to make the first of her paper flowers. 'See...' She held the flower up.

'That's nice. How many do you need to make for a ball?'

'Twelve.' She laid the flower down on the carpet beside her, staring at it. 'We used to make these all the time when we were kids. Sally and I.'

He didn't ask, but he was waiting. Somewhere, in the warmth of the silence between them, there were still so many questions waiting to be answered.

'We used to hang them up on the ceiling. Sal's father brought us some fluorescent paper and they used to glow in the dark, like weird planets.'

He chuckled quietly. 'Sounds like fun. That's a good memory to have.'

It was. Sam hadn't brought it out and enjoyed it for a long time now. Suddenly it was too much to bear, and she brought her palm down on the flower, flattening it.

He flinched, as if she had driven her fist into his wound. 'Right now, the good memories can't break through the bad. That won't always be the case.'

'You mean time heals everything?' She knew that wasn't true, and she was daring him to say it was.

'No. It brings a sense of balance.'

'If there was any balance to any of it, then I would have been the one who died.' She could hear the resignation in her own voice.

He shook his head. 'You don't really believe that?'

'No. I can't wish away my life. But Sal had a lot more people to mourn for her than I do. I don't know that my mother would ever have known or cared, I haven't seen her for so long.'

'I think that I would have cared.'

'You wouldn't have known me. I wouldn't even be here now if…' Maybe in some strange twist of fate it would have been Sally, sitting here on his lounge floor, making paper flowers.

'You would be. I'd get a glimpse of you from time to time out of the corner of my eye.'

'That doesn't make any sense.' She twisted round to look at him, suddenly glad that she was here. If Sally couldn't be, then she would take the moment for herself. 'You can't see all the million things that might have happened if things had been a bit different in the past.' She stopped to think for a moment, trying to compute the odds. 'Trillions, probably. In fact, it's almost certainly an infinite number...'

'Stop being so literal. Can't you take a compliment when it's offered?'

So that's what it was. 'Well, in that case...' Sam tried to pretend that the world wasn't suddenly warm, full of promise. 'Thank you for thinking that you might have known me if I hadn't existed.'

He chuckled. 'Missed. Not known.'

Suddenly something slotted into place. The great gap in her heart that had always been there always made her feel that she had something more to prove. Someone would have missed her. The thought almost made her choke.

'We should call David.' She couldn't think about this any more. Not until she'd had some time to process it. 'He said he'd come round at lunchtime.'

He nodded, easing himself up to a sitting position. 'Yeah. I was thinking we could go to the office. Just to show willing...'

'I don't think that's a very good idea. You'll get there, and find something that you need to do, and then decide to just pop down to the clinic. Before I know it, I'll be sitting in A and E with you again, trying to explain to the doctor why I didn't make you do as he said.'

He gave her a look that was half-defiance, all humour. 'Okay. Suppose I promise to take it easy. We'll walk down there, and I'll find a comfortable chair in David's office and watch you both getting on with your work.'

'And you won't move.' There wasn't a lot of point in trying to be firm with him, he must know that he could get away with almost anything he liked when he gave her that look. She wasn't going to let him think she was that much of a walkover, though. 'Not a muscle.'

'I might drink a cup of tea, if someone's good enough to offer it. Tender the odd helpful comment here and there. If that's allowed.'

She grinned at him. 'Tea's okay. I think I can do without the helpful comments.' Right now, almost everything about Euan seemed indispensable.

'Nah.' He got slowly to his feet. 'You have no idea how helpful I can be when I try.'

David growled threateningly at Euan when they arrived at the office, and then gave in to the inevitable. Sam went upstairs to change out of the borrowed T-shirt and put her own bloodstained blouse into the washing machine.

'I've got something for you.' David was grinning, like a magician who had just whipped a rabbit out of a hat, when she entered his office. 'I was talking at an online conference the other day about some of the work you'd done here with us. One of the other delegates, from a small drugs charity up in London, asked for your details and I gave her your number.'

'Thank you. That's kind of you.' Maybe this was where it started. One client made it easier to get a second. A second almost guaranteed a third. Excitement began to trickle down Sam's spine. She wondered if it would be in order to ask the name of the charity, but decided not to sound too eager.

'The CEO called me this morning. Said he'd tried to get in touch with you but he couldn't get through, and he wanted to check he had the right number.'

'My phone!' The last time she'd had her phone had

been last night, when she'd checked her emails. 'It must be…' The words dried in her throat. She'd checked her emails and then laid her phone down on the bed beside her. Her phone must still be there, in Euan's bed.

'I think I saw it in the kitchen.' His slow, amused drawl came to her rescue.

'Ah. Yes. By the toaster.' Did he even have a toaster? He must have as she'd made toast that morning.

'That's right.'

Sam turned and shot him a grateful smile, aware that her ears were beginning to burn. 'I'll…um…phone them back from here, if that's okay.'

'Of course. He left a message. I don't know if you've heard of the charity, it's called The Centre.' David looked around on his desk and located a slip of paper. 'They're talking to some other software providers on Thursday, and they'd like to see you as well if you can make it.'

'This week?' Disappointment began to claw at her, but Sam knew what she had to do. She couldn't break a promise to one client in order to try and land another. 'That's much too short notice. I'm afraid I'll have to give that one a miss.'

'Sam…' Euan's voice again, behind her back. She ignored him.

'I have plenty to do here. One thing at a time.'

'Sam, don't be an idiot.' Euan wasn't going to let this drop. 'You need to go and see them this week.'

'I've committed myself here for the whole of this week. If they can see me next week, that'll be wonderful. But I won't go back on the commitments I've made here. It's not the way I work.'

Euan's gaze was making her tremble. Warm, sexy and currently uncompromising. 'Tell her, David.'

'What? Tell me what?' There was obviously a silent understanding between the two men.

'I'm busy on Thursday. I won't have any time to spend with you.' David was grinning.

'And I'll be resting. I'm under doctor's orders, you know.'

'Quite. And if you're driving up to see them on Thursday, perhaps Euan can go with you if he's up to it.' David was brooking no arguments now. 'This charity has a programme dedicated to steroid abuse. When I said that we were looking at setting something up ourselves, they offered to share their experience.'

'Looks as if it's all sorted, then.' Euan was leaning back in his chair, chuckling. Sam turned to David, who nodded, clearly enormously pleased with himself.

'I…suppose I don't have much choice, then.'

Euan nodded. 'Looks like it. And, of course, if we're using the same database as they are, I imagine it would be so much easier to share information.' He gave her an innocent look, and the three of them burst into spontaneous laughter.

The afternoon was as relaxed and easygoing as the morning had been. Euan and David disappeared for a belated Monday morning meeting, and Sam tackled their website. At five on the dot David shooed them both downstairs and into his car, and the evening was spent at his house. Then back to the tiny flat above the charity's offices, dropping Euan at home on the way.

It was still early, but Sam had hit a brick wall of exhaustion. All she wanted to do was sleep, and at first she hardly noticed the bright package propped up on the stairs, tied with raffia and bearing a label from one of the shops on the trendier side of town. There was no note, but she knew who it was from. Japanese paper, brightly coloured and beautifully patterned. The kind you used for origami flowers.

CHAPTER FIFTEEN

EUAN WAS CONTENT to sit and watch her. In fact, there was nothing else in this world that he'd rather do.

They'd driven up to London early that morning, Sam insisting that she take the wheel of his car and Euan giving in gracefully, even though he was feeling much better. Her flat was comfortable, unprepossessing and, considering the amount of cash that the sale of her company must have netted, understated. Sam had disappeared for half an hour to get ready for her interview, leaving him with coffee and the paper.

Considering the transformation that she'd wrought, half an hour was miraculously fast. Her hair was in a shining knot at the back of her head. Her make-up perfect. Designer suit, this time in a shade of blue that made her eyes look like mother-of-pearl.

'You look great.' He decided to go for understatement.

'Thank you.' Even the smile was different. Cool, professional, but with a flash of the woman that he now knew beneath it. The effect was intoxicating.

He watched as she carefully slid her laptop into her leather bag. Everything in order. Pausing to check she hadn't forgotten anything. Euan had seen the results of this careful preparation, and he didn't need to wonder whether she'd wrap today's interview up with the same efficiency as the one at Driftwood.

'I'm a bit nervous.'

You wouldn't have thought it to look at her, but there was a slight tremor in her voice. 'This means a lot to you, doesn't it?'

She nodded. 'Yeah.'

'And it's tough going in there on your own.' Euan hadn't realised how alone she must have felt at their interview. She'd seemed so assured, so in charge.

She pressed her lips together. 'Does it show?'

'No. You impressed the life out of David and me when you interviewed with us. These guys...' he snapped his fingers. 'No problem.'

'My secret's safe with you, then?'

Safe, and treasured. 'Yeah. Always.'

'Just until this afternoon will be fine.' She looked around, as if checking that she had everything, and hesitated. Euan wondered if there was a final pre-interview ritual that she'd rather do alone.

'I'll wait for you in the car, shall I?'

She shook her head slowly. 'No need. I already have my good luck charm.' She reached inside the neck of her silky blouse, pulling out a little gold locket. 'Sally's parents bought us one each when we started out together. We used to wear them for luck at interviews.'

'Well, you look great. And you've got a great product. You've everything to be confident about.'

'Yeah, you can't feel bad in silk knickers.' She bit her lip. 'Sorry. Something Sally and I used to say to each other.'

'It's a good thought.' It was a great thought. One that

he couldn't stop framing in his head into a beautiful, sensual image. One that was going to shatter all their plans for the day if he didn't move. Now. He looked at his watch, blind to the time, and still gripped by the idea that Sam would feel just great in silk knickers. 'I guess we'd better be on our way.'

He picked up the car keys, handing them to her without daring to even look at her face.

She was shining. Sitting behind the steering-wheel of his car, happiness radiating from her, as Euan emerged from The Centre's day clinic. He hurried across the pavement and slid into the passenger seat.

'Sorry to keep you waiting.'

'No problem. How did it go?' All he could see was her mouth, a red, sensual curve of pleasure. His pleasure, and hers, filled his head.

'Really interesting. They gave me plenty to think about when we implement the new groups at Driftwood.'

She nodded. Waited for him to ask, but he didn't need to. Euan snapped his seat belt closed and leaned across to look into the rear-view mirror. She wrinkled her nose at him, muttering something about back-seat drivers, and navigated out into the stream of traffic.

They drove in silence.

'Okay, ask!' The car swung around a corner and she accelerated from the crawl of the main road.

'I already know how it went. It was a foregone conclusion,' he protested.

'I want you to ask!' The car came to an abrupt halt in the middle of the road.

'We're blocking the road.'

She leaned around to face him. 'We're not going anywhere until you ask.'

This was beyond all endurance. Her skirt had ridden up as she drove, just by an inch but it was an inch of sheer delight. The seat belt crushed the almost translucent fabric of her blouse against her breasts.

'Okay. In the interests of traffic control, how did you do?'

A smile spread across her face and desire clenched its delicious fingers around his heart. 'It was great. Really good. I answered all the questions they asked me, they loved the look of the program. They're not concerned that I don't have much of a track record, they say that David gave me a glowing reference...'

'That was never going to be a problem.'

'Yes, but it made all the difference.' Her hands fluttered tremulously in her lap. 'I think they're going to take it.'

He couldn't hold out much longer. He had to kiss her. They both jumped as the insistent sound of a horn blared behind them.

'Drive.' All that Euan could think about was getting her alone. Out of the car. Into her flat. After that... Goodness only knew.

She laughed, signalled an apology to the driver behind her, and drove.

The first two items on Euan's list had been accomplished with almost no effort on his part at all. She almost danced out of the car and up the stairs to her front door, and swept into the neat, pale blue and white kitchen.

'Perhaps we should have ice cream.' She was grinning from ear to ear.

'Ice cream? Is that some kind of after-interview tradition?'

She raised one eyebrow in a query and Euan laughed. 'When I went out for lunch, after you interviewed with David and me, I saw you eating ice cream.'

Her eyes opened wide, as if she'd been caught in a guilty secret. Then she smiled. 'Yes, I suppose it is. Sal and I used to celebrate with ice cream and all the trimmings when things went well. I've got chocolate sauce, and wafers. Or caramel sauce if you prefer. Or both…'

She opened one of the drawers, pulling out a pair of long-handled spoons and a stainless-steel implement. 'And I have a proper scoop. That's essential.'

She was holding the scoop up in front of her, and he took it out of her hand and put it on the counter. Moved closer, until his aching body almost touched hers. 'Don't think I'm not mindful of the honour of being asked to share the ice-cream tradition but there's something I want to talk to you about…'

The fragile, unspoken agreement that had held between them while Euan was recovering from his wound had finally broken. Small intimacies, delicious fantasies, had been okay when anything else had been out of the question, but now he was strong again. If going forward was hazardous, then going back was just as unthinkable.

'Talk?' She closed the gap between them, wrapping her arms around his waist. 'You want to talk?'

'Actually, no.' Talking was about the last thing on his mind at the moment. 'But I think we should.'

'There are some things that you can't work out in advance.'

The sheer audacity of it made him chuckle. 'Who are you? And what have you done with Sam?'

She turned her beautiful eyes up to meet his gaze. 'She's okay. Busy working out her next move. She's wasting her time...'

'You think so?'

'Yes, I do. Sometimes you just have to take a step in the dark.'

In respect of pretty much everything else, he'd be the first to agree. 'I'm not much good as a lover, Sam.'

'Really?' She laid a finger on his chest, her touch seeming to burn through the fabric of his shirt. 'Would that be in the emotional sense or the physical?'

She was taunting him now, and a man's ego could only take so much. Euan kissed her, giving it everything that he had, until his body screamed and hers melted. 'You can push a guy too far...' His voice didn't sound like his own. It was gruff, demanding. The kind of voice that took what it wanted, whatever the consequences.

Fire sparked in her grey eyes. 'Yes, I know. You think I can't handle this?'

That was exactly what he'd been thinking. 'You're a strong woman, Sam. But—'

'Then don't second-guess me. I know who you are, and I know who I am. And I know what I want.' Her hips rolled against his, and for a moment Euan lost the ability to focus. 'Seems like you want it too.'

He twisted her round, imprisoning her against the fridge. 'No rules, Sam. No promises. We take it slow and easy.'

'Yeah. Slow and easy sounds good to me.' She took

his hand and laid it over her breast. A perfect fit. Euan took his time, exploring the various ways he could make her gasp, indulging his senses with how much she wanted him.

'Will you...?'

She kissed him and in that moment he knew the answer to all his unspoken questions. It was a big, beautiful yes.

He wanted to undress her. Which was just fine with Sam, because that was exactly what she wanted too. Carefully, he undid each button of her blouse and slipped it from her shoulders. Slid his hands across the silk and lace of her bra, and then turned his attention to her skirt.

She batted his hands away. 'Hey. Hey, you too.'

He grinned, pulling his shirt open with considerably less care than he'd taken over her. She tugged at the belt of his trousers, and they joined his shirt on the bedroom floor.

'Now you.' He slid his hand past the hem of her skirt, and upwards until he found the top of her stockings. 'Mmm. I've been wondering all morning...'

His eyes were shockingly tender. Dark with desire and wicked and exquisitely teasing. His free hand adroitly unhooked the waistband of her skirt, drawing the zip down, steadying her as she stepped out of it.

Sam put her hand up to the back of her head, but his was already there. Carefully removing the pins, twisting the long coil of hair around his hand, as if measuring its strength and thickness, then finally disentangling the elastic loop and smoothing her hair around her shoulders. She shook her head and an inarticulate growl of approval escaped his throat.

There was no need to ask whether he liked what he saw. His lips moved against the skin of her neck, his hands following the silk route that led from her hips to between her legs. Laying her down on the bed, he slowly began to peel her stockings off, caressing her legs, kissing her toes.

'Be careful.' She murmured the words, her hand drifting to his side. The dark red line that sliced across his ribs, seemed so much better than it had on Sunday evening but she couldn't really tell.

'I'm okay.' He stood up, slipping his boxer shorts down. 'I'd far rather you concentrated on the task in hand.'

He was beautiful, strong and muscular, and if his words had left her in any doubt about how badly he wanted her, his body was unequivocal. He lay down beside her, measuring the length of his body against hers. And then, as the heat built between them, there was no more *me* or *I* or *him*. Just *we* and *us*. *Together*.

She could feel sweat at the small of her back, soaking into the sheet beneath her. Skin against skin. The soft erotic slide, as a film of perspiration covered her limbs. His gentle, insistent hands, and the heat of his body.

He slowed a little when her body jerked convulsively in response to his caress.

'Hold me…' Her words were instinctive, as unexpected as the movement of her limbs had been. Something seemed to have taken hold of her, dictating her responses before she had a chance to think them through.

'I've got you.' She was in his arms, warm and safe.

He smoothed her hair back, making way for his lips to brush her forehead. 'I can't let you go now.'

'Are you sure?'

He kissed her, letting the slow, gentle rhythm send the temperature up close to boiling point.

'It's about the only thing I am sure of.'

He was as lost as she was. Both making it up as they went along, and in the bright fire of his embrace that seemed blissfully right. Each movement a reply to the last. Each sigh a promise for the next.

The woman who planned everything, always calculated her next move, melted away. There was only Euan, and he was making love to someone who was a stranger to Sam. Someone who gave herself up to the moment, made each one last, in case the next should be too much to bear. But somehow it wasn't. He took her to the very edge of a scream, and then flung her past that, into a world where only sensation mattered, making it last until they were both trembling with the force of the climax that had fused them together in long moments of fiery release.

CHAPTER SIXTEEN

THEY MIGHT HAVE been twisted together on the bed like this for some time. Maybe it was just minutes, but if it was, they were minutes when every second felt like something new minted, softly ticking away in the silence. Euan shifted slightly, and she heard him catch his breath.

'You okay?' Sam gently disentangled her limbs from his and sat up, leaning over to inspect the wound on his side.

'A lot better than okay.' He wound his fingers around the back of her neck in a sign that he wanted a kiss instead of her concern, and she resisted him.

'Stop it. Let me see.'

A resigned breath, and he rolled over slightly, letting her inspect the gash on his side. 'There. Does it look okay.'

'Yes, I think so.'

'Is it bleeding?'

'No.'

'Then it's okay.' This time he didn't take no for an answer, and pulled her back for a kiss. 'It just catches me sometimes. There's nothing to worry about.'

'You think I shouldn't worry about you?'

He chuckled. 'Just a little maybe. You can plump a few pillows if it makes you feel better.'

Sam rolled her eyes, pulling him upright and arranging the pillows behind his back. 'There. Is that more comfortable?'

'Much. And you could kiss me. Just here.' He laid a finger on his jaw.

'There?' Sam bent to kiss him, right on the spot he'd indicated.

'Up a bit.'

She kissed him again.

'To the left perhaps.'

Sam brushed her lips against his cheek then ran her tongue around the edge of his ear.

'Yeah. Nice touch. Come here.' He made a spot for her, curled in the warmth of his arms.

'Anything else?'

'I'm making a mental list. Just working on relative priorities. Dependencies.' His lips curled with still-hungry humour.

'Oh, so you were listening? When we ran through the timetabling the other day.' She trailed one finger across his chest and then downwards to the flat sheet of muscle over his stomach.

'I always listen…'

'And then you go ahead and do whatever you were going to do in the first place.' She nudged him gently.

'That's not quite true.' He ran his hand across her breast, drawing a gasp. 'I listen…' The next caress came from his lips, and Sam squirmed with pleasure. 'And I modify my approach…'

'Like this?' She returned the gesture and he caught his breath.

'Yeah. Just like that.'

It was a delicious novelty to feel that he loved every minute of it when she made free with his body. All of the urgency was gone now, but none of the desire. Talking, kissing. Letting the afternoon slide gently away.

'Your skin is so soft...' His touch had worked its way lazily down her spine, and he spread his fingers, as if measuring the curve of her hips. Soft and gentle began to give way to possessive, and he rolled onto his back, pulling her on top of him, guiding her body so that she was straddling him.

'I thought you liked being in control.'

'I *love* being in control.' His eyes teased her. 'So do you.'

She dipped for a kiss. His lips were cool against hers. 'Then this is all for you.' She wanted to please him. Wanted more than anything to feel him inside her again, and to make him roar with pleasure.

'But I was looking forward to watching you...' There was no one else in the room, but he whispered the words into her ear. 'I want to see you move.'

It seemed unbearably intimate. Having him watch while she took her own pleasure. If he hadn't been so tender, it would have been impossible. Sam reached for the open box of condoms on the bedside table and he grinned, holding out his hand to take the foil packet from her.

'I'm supposed to be in control here, remember?' She batted him away and unwrapped the foil package.

'Whatever you say.' He was grinning, his eyes darker suddenly when she touched him. 'Did you know that you put your tongue out when you're concentrating? Oh...' He groaned when she sank down onto him.

'And you have a crease…' she ran her finger across his forehead '…just there.'

'I'm concentrating on taking in the view.' His hands rested lightly on her waist. Waiting for her to make the next move.

Her courage deserted her. What if…? There were so many unknown ways in which she might fail him.

'You're frowning.' One finger tapped lightly on her skin, as if to draw her attention to the fact that he was there. 'Stop thinking…'

Easier said than done. And then she looked into his eyes. Warm and loving, accepting her for what she was. Asking for nothing else. As she slowly started to move he encouraged her with words and caresses. His body grew harder, hotter, and she knew now that she could satisfy him.

Everything that she wanted was what he wanted, too. When her orgasm finally started to bloom, pulsating in ever stronger waves of pleasure, it was Euan who groaned, gripping her waist tight. She held onto him, fingers digging into the muscle of his shoulders. Here and now. This was all there was.

It was late in the evening by the time they had eaten and got back on the road again. The sea was like a moving expanse of glittering flint as Sam drove along the promenade. 'I don't want you to take this the wrong way.' She'd been wondering how to ask him for the last five miles, and had got no closer to a resolution.

'I'll take it any way you want me to. What is it?'

'Do you mind if I go back to the flat tonight?'

She could feel him watching her and she kept her eye

on the road in front of her. 'Yeah, I mind. But I'd mind
a lot more if you didn't let me know what you wanted.'

'I just…' She couldn't explain it. Sam felt almost raw
after that afternoon. As if he'd peeled off her protective
layer and the world could hurt her now.

'Need some space? That's okay.'

'Yeah. Thanks.'

When she drew up outside the office he got out,
opening the driver's door of the car for her. Walked her
to the door and kissed her.

'I'm sorry…'

He laid his finger over her lips. 'Never be sorry. Not
for anything we did today.'

'No. I'm not. Would it be okay if I dreamt of you?'

Euan chuckled. 'I think I'm going to insist that you
do. I want a full report in the morning.'

He waited until she was inside, and Sam watched
through the window as he walked to his car and got into
it. He was everything that she wanted. All the love and
acceptance that she could ever handle. She just had to
get over the nagging feeling that she didn't deserve this.

She'd really thought that she might dream of Euan tonight, but she didn't. It appeared that whatever had happened during the day, there was still no such thing as
forgiveness during the hours of darkness.

Sam woke with an overwhelming feeling of guilt.
How had Sally turned to drugs for help in coping when
Sam had been there all along? The answer was the same
as it had always been. She *had* been there, but she'd
been absorbed in her work. And now she was neglect-
ing that work, as if it were nothing, in favour of doing
the things that she and Sal had talked about but that Sal

had never got around to doing. Finding the right man. Falling in love.

Maybe this was survivor guilt. Maybe it didn't matter what it was called. Experience told Sam that by the time she'd showered and dressed, the claws of the night would have released her, and she'd be ready to face the day.

Euan's side felt a little stiff, but nothing that the walk to work wouldn't take care of. His body had still been humming with remembered pleasure when he'd woken up that morning, but he'd woken up alone. He checked his phone, wondering vaguely if she might have called, picked up his keys and wallet, and headed for the front door, a trickle of dread grasping at his heart. He'd given Sam her space, but what if she thought that gave her the right to leave without a word, the way that Marie had done?

They met on the doorstep. She was dressed all in white in a lacy top and white linen trousers. He could see the curve of her body, the soft skin that only yesterday he'd felt he had a right to touch. Now he wasn't so sure.

She smiled. 'I was just on my way to the office. Thought I'd call in and collect you.'

'It's a bit of a detour.'

She nodded, and took a step closer. He waited. When she stood on her toes, he bent to meet her, taking her into his arms as she pressed her lips against his. 'Worth it, though. Good morning, sweetheart.'

Euan could almost hear the drip-drip of all his fears melting away in the sunshine. 'Mmm. That's a good way to start the day.'

He pulled the door to behind him, and she fell into step beside him as Euan shortened his stride. It seemed natural to put his arm around her shoulders as they walked, and she looped her thumb around his belt at the small of his back.

'What's the plan for today?'

'I still have some work to do on your website. I thought I'd do that today, and stay over until next week to finish off the database configuration.'

He grinned. London was only ninety minutes' drive away, but this was still very new. He wanted her here, for another few days at least, so they could find out where it was going. But from the tone of the email that had pinged into his inbox this morning…

'Have you checked your emails yet?'

The blank look on her face told him that she hadn't. He should let her do that before he extracted any promises from her with regard to the weekend. He'd only skimmed The Centre's email, but the paragraph that talked about sharing information and comparing notes on implementation had left him in no doubt about their decision concerning Sam's software.

'You haven't, have you? You're going to tell me that you came to see me, without stopping to check your emails first…' He twisted to face her, walking backwards along the pavement in front of her.

'I…' She was trying to avoid his gaze.

He stopped walking, suddenly enough that she almost bumped into him. 'Go on. Say it.'

'Okay, so I wanted to see you. I haven't checked my emails. What's the big deal?'

They both knew it was a huge deal. Sam didn't go anywhere without checking her emails first, and this morning Euan had knocked that task from the top of her list of priorities.

He resisted the impulse to punch the air and decided he should be magnanimous in victory. 'You'll see. Perhaps we should talk about our plans for the weekend after you've got around to that.'

She slid one finger behind the buckle of his belt. Just one finger, and every nerve in his body quivered. She had that power. 'What do you know that I don't?'

'Nothing… Nothing. Not that I can say, anyway. We take confidentiality very seriously in this business.'

'Give me your phone.'

Euan chuckled. 'You mean you've come out without your phone as well?'

'It's in the office. I didn't think I was going to be long…' She stepped closer, stretching up as if to kiss him. 'Give it to me…'

'What for?' He'd stretch this delicious torture out as long as he could. Euan reckoned he had a good thirty seconds more before he reached the limits of his endurance.

'So I can get onto the internet and see my mail.' She reached around behind him, pulling his phone out of his back pocket. 'You should password your phone, you know. Anyone could get hold of the information on it.'

He chuckled. Her body was pressed against his still, and she was thumbing the screen of his phone. He was enjoying this a little too much… 'It wouldn't matter if they did. It may be a smartphone, but I'm not smart enough to use it for anything other than calls.'

She rolled her eyes, and resumed her scrutiny of the small screen of his phone. Then she caught her breath. 'Yes!'

'Got it?'

She turned her shining eyes up towards him. 'The Centre wants my software... You knew that, didn't you?'

Euan shrugged. 'The email they sent me rather indicated that, without actually saying it.'

Sam punched his shoulder. 'Why didn't you say?'

'I just wanted you to hear it from them. I suppose you'll have to be back in London for Monday now...'

She raised one eyebrow. 'No. I told them that I wasn't free until the week after next. Unless you want me to go?' She looked up at him, and all the things that one weekend could hold washed over him in a never-ending stream of possibilities.

'No.' He felt his fingers tighten possessively around her waist. 'I want you to stay.'

'Then I'll stay. You want to get some ice cream? We need to do something to celebrate.'

The vision of Sam, a bowl of ice cream and a bed drifted into his head. Stayed there, refusing to move. Euan turned, grabbed her hand, striding back towards his house.

'Where are we going? The café's that way...' She was laughing and almost running to keep up with him.

'It's seven-thirty in the morning. I have ice cream in my freezer. And if we try doing what I've got in mind at a pavement café, we're going to get arrested.'

CHAPTER SEVENTEEN

ON SATURDAY MORNING Sam was up early again. She knew that Euan would be waiting for her.

Yesterday they'd worked together, eaten together and made love together, not necessarily in that order. He'd seemed to accept her going back to the flat to sleep, just as he had the night before. That slow smile of his, the quirk of his mouth that signalled he regretted her going, and the assertion that there were 'no rules' other than the ones they made for themselves. This morning she knew that he'd be waiting for her.

She picked up the key he'd left on the small chest of drawers in the flat and tucked it into her pocket. Almost ran to his house and let herself in. He was still asleep, and she quietly got undressed and slid into the bed beside him.

'Mmmph. Your hands are cold.' His sleepy growl greeted her.

'Want me to take them away?'

'Don't you dare.' He rolled over, his body hard and strong against hers. 'We agreed last night.'

'We did.' Just when she'd begun to think that this might well break them apart, Euan's honest pragmatism had come to the rescue.

'You take your space. No need for excuses, no having to pretend you have work to do, or a headache, or an early start in the morning.'

'Yes.' She kissed him, feeling the scratch of his morning stubble. 'And I let you know that I'm coming back.'

That was what he'd asked in return. He'd said he needed that, and it was the least she could give. Even if it did make her wonder whether he'd put his ex-wife's behaviour behind him quite as much as he'd said he had.

'And now you're here...' He kissed her neck. Brushed his lips against the soft, sensitive skin of her breasts, and Sam whimpered with longing. It was that easy for him. A few short moments and all she could think about was how much she wanted Euan.

'What have you got in mind?'

'Want me to spell it out for you?'

'Yes, I think I do.'

He chuckled, settling himself on top of her, pinning her down. She stretched her arms above her head, and he reached to grasp her wrists. 'Listen carefully.'

He stripped away yet another layer. Breached one more set of defences, with just his free hand and his imagination. Euan's words, murmured against her ear, caressed her senses as he caressed her body, held captive under his. By the time he was ready to make love to her, she wanted him so much she could have begged. Probably had done.

She'd never let anyone else in like this before. Never admitted her need, let alone demand that another human soul should understand and give her what she craved. Sam felt as if she was supposed to be here, with Euan. As if she'd finally found a home.

Home. Sam had wanted a home for as long as she could remember. Sally's parents had given her the closest she'd ever had to somewhere she could call home, but Sam had always felt that it was just lent to her for a while. When she and Sal had built a company together, that had felt like home, but it hadn't lasted.

'I'm meeting Ann and Paul this afternoon. Sally's parents.'

'Yeah? What time?' He craned his neck to see the clock by the side of the bed.

'About two. Just for a couple of hours. They're driving down to see Sal's brother Josh and his wife. They want to stop by and see where I've been staying.' Dared she ask him to meet them? Perhaps he'd think it was too early, or that she was being clingy. Or pushy. Pushy *and* clingy. She shivered. Sounded like something out of a horror movie.

'Is that a problem?' He'd felt the tremor of her limbs against his.

'No, not at all.'

He nodded, accepting her answer the way he always accepted whatever she had to say. 'If they'd be interested in seeing Kathryn House, I could drive you out there.' He left the offer hanging in the air. No pressure. 'Or perhaps another time.'

Ann and Paul would want to see Kathryn House as much as Sam wanted to show it to them, but she wasn't sure quite what Euan was offering. 'What's best for you?'

'What would be best for me...' he trapped her against him, face to face '...is if you tell me what you want. If you want to see Ann and Paul on your own, that's fine.

I'll find something else to do this afternoon. If you'd like to take them to Kathryn House then we'll do that.'

'Kathryn House. If it's not too much trouble, I'd love it if you would show them around.'

He laid a finger over her lips. 'I'd be honoured. In the meantime, what takes your fancy for this morning? There's the Saturday market, or we could take the cross-word down to the beach. It's a nice day.'

'Both. We'll do both.'

He chuckled, rolling back to his side of the bed to let her up. 'All right, then. And since you're so eager for action, you get first turn in the shower.'

She was wearing another of a seemingly inexhaustible selection of pretty summer dresses. There was a sense of unexpected pride at having Sam on his arm. Euan never let what anyone else thought of him weigh on his mind too much, least of all passers-by in the street, but the idea that they might be looking at him and thinking he was a lucky man seemed oddly attractive.

He'd reckoned she might like the hat stall in the market, and he was right. They picked out hats for each other to try on, and then she selected one for herself, a straw hat with a purple band, which matched the flowers on her dress. He offered to buy it for her, but she refused, saying she didn't really need it. Then capitulated when two other women browsing at the stall said she really must have it.

She'd texted the directions to Kathryn House, so that Ann and Paul could meet them there. Euan went to speak to the plumbers, who were sorting out the pipework in the kitchen, leaving Sam to wait in the hall. When he heard the sound of a car scrunching on the gravel outside he wandered to the door, to see Sam flying into the arms of the woman who got out of the passenger seat.

Ann couldn't have been more different from Sam if she'd tried, blonde and half a head shorter than her adopted daughter. There was no mistake about the warmth with which the two embraced, though. Euan had reckoned on hanging back for a moment, but Sam practically ran towards him, dragging Ann behind her into the house.

'This is Euan…'

Ann took a moment to catch her breath and then turned the full force of her attention on him, holding out her hand with all the well-mannered ferocity of a suburban mother bear with a cub to protect.

'Euan. Nice to meet you. I want to hear all the things that Sam hasn't told me about you.' Three-quarters joke, but just enough of a threat about the words to make Euan smile. Sam had good people. Good people who were on her side, and would stop at nothing to protect her.

Sam was flushing bright red. 'What's with the third degree?'

She didn't need to worry. Euan would gladly submit to whatever vetting procedure Ann cared to put him through, the more exhaustive the better. He was just glad that someone cared enough about her to do it.

For a moment, though, that was forgotten. A slight, fair man appeared in the hallway and Sam flung herself into his arms. 'I have something for you.'

'Yes? What is it this time?' Paul was teasing her, chuckling with pleasure.

Sam retrieved the box she'd brought with her from

the hall table, suddenly uncertain. 'I…hope you like it. It's just something that I made…'

Paul's face creased into a smile as he drew the ball of folded paper flowers from the box. 'Will you look at that, Ann?' He held it up, twirling it in the light to show off the brightly coloured glass beads threaded at the base, which Euan recognised as Juno's creations.

Ann was looking at the folded paper, her hands over her mouth. 'That's beautiful, Sam. Just like the ones you and Sally used to make when you were children.' She ran her fingers lightly over the paper flowers, as if to test that they weren't just a faded memory. 'Such pretty paper. Where did you get it?'

'Euan bought it for me.'

Paul's pale blue eyes focussed on Euan for a moment. The smallest of nods, which said that maybe, just maybe, he was going to turn out to be good enough for Sam. Then back to the paper ball. 'Where can I hang this, then?'

'I made it for your home office. Something to brighten it up a bit.' Sam was all smiles now.

'That's the place. By the window, eh?'

The matter was settled. Paul put the paper ball back into its box and took it out to the car. When he returned, he approached Euan. 'Ann and I are very interested in your work here.' Ann nodded hesitantly, and Euan saw Sam slip her hand into hers. 'We appreciate you offering to show us around.'

'It's a pleasure. Sam's one of the people who is making it possible.' He saw her flush with pleasure and Paul nodded. Euan turned, leading them through to the newly decorated community room.

* * *

'Do you like him?' Euan and Paul were inspecting the summer house, staring up at the eaves and kicking at the wooden supports, as if the structure was about to fall down any minute if they didn't check it thoroughly. Sam and Ann were sitting on the veranda.

'It's not a matter of whether *I* like him. I think you're the one those rather splendid smiles are intended for.'

Sam squirmed with embarrassment. 'I didn't say…'

'Oh, please.' Ann rolled her eyes. 'All right, if you want it that way, he seems like a fine doctor and he's obviously doing some very good work here. I think he'll make an excellent first client for you.'

Sam laughed. 'I didn't say that either.'

'No, you didn't say anything. Which is generally a sign that you're waiting for my approval before you tell me about something. Of him…?'

'No.' Sam dismissed the idea out of hand. No one with any sense could disapprove of Euan.

'Then maybe you want that stamp of approval for yourself. You've found yourself a handsome doctor, and you want me to tell you that it's okay.'

'You think he's handsome?'

Ann snorted with laughter. 'I may have been married for thirty-five years, but I'm not blind. Don't you think he's handsome?'

'I think he's gorgeous.' Why did this feel so hard?

'And he makes you feel good?'

'Yes.' Another tough admission.

'So what's the problem? You don't need my permission to get on with your life.'

Sam could feel tears beginning to swell in her eyes. 'What did I do to deserve you and Paul?'

Ann heaved a sigh, as if this was simple and she wasn't sure why Sam hadn't realised it long ago. 'When you were little, you were the best-behaved child I'd ever seen. You used to tidy Josh's and Sally's toys away, never shouted in the house, never knocked anything over. As soon as you were tall enough to reach the sink, you'd always be the first out of your seat at mealtimes so you could do the washing-up.'

'I was…trying to be helpful. I reckoned that if I made myself useful around the house then you and Paul would let me stay.' It had worked, hadn't it?

'We cared about you, Sam. And then we came to love you. That's why we wanted you to stay.'

A tear rolled down her cheek, and Sam took Ann's hand and squeezed it. 'You mean I did all that washing-up for nothing?'

'Well, I wouldn't say that. I appreciated it.' Ann patted her hand. 'Is he special?'

'Maybe. I don't know yet.' But that wasn't exactly true, was it? Euan was special all right. Perhaps a bit too special for her.

'Give it time.' Ann settled into her chair, squinting across the lawn to where Euan and Paul were fiddling with one of the windows of the summer house, which seemed to need a shove to close properly. 'Men and sheds, eh?'

'It's a summer house, not a shed.'

Ann grinned. 'It's made of wood, and not joined to the house, isn't it? It's all just a matter of scale.'

Euan had liked Ann and Paul. Paul's quiet, easygoing sense of humour had thinly disguised what was obviously a keen interest in Euan's work, and the part that Sam's software would play in the charity's operation. Euan had answered his questions as candidly as he could, brushing away Paul's apology for being direct. The man had lost one daughter and was obviously keen to protect the other. Euan could only offer compassion for the former and agree with him with regard to the latter.

'So what's the matter with the window of the summer house?' Sam was stretched out on the sofa in his house with him, doing nothing now that Ann and Paul had gone home. Doing nothing with Sam was better than doing pretty much anything else with anyone else.

'It's swollen a bit. Just needs a rub down and another coat of wood preservative.'

She nodded. Yawned, and shifted in his arms. 'Thanks for today. I enjoyed it.'

'Good. Would you like me to walk you back to the flat?' He'd learned that if he suggested it as if it was a part of the natural state of things Sam was less embarrassed about going.

'Um… No. Not yet.' She snuggled in closer and Euan suppressed a grin. Maybe tonight she'd lie down with him to sleep. It would make him feel a lot happier about having sex with her, as if he wasn't just taking what he wanted and then letting her go.

'Do you think…?' She tapped his chest with her finger, just in case she didn't have his full attention.

'All the time. What am I thinking in particular?'

'Do you think I'm too…well behaved?'

'Much too well behaved. Considering you do bad behaviour so well…'

She giggled and applied an elbow to his ribs. 'I don't

mean that. Ann was saying this afternoon that I was too well behaved when I was little.'

An astute lady. 'And...?'

'I don't know. I wondered what you thought.'

'Well, at a rough guess...' Euan dropped a kiss onto her forehead '...we all seek approval from the people around us. Some kids react to rejection by trying too hard. Being too well behaved.'

'Mmm.' She snuggled sleepily into his arms. 'I'll think about it.'

He chuckled. 'Do that. And talking about bad behaviour, I personally don't have any objection to you snoring.'

'I don't snore.'

'Or if you fart in bed, or thrash around in your sleep. Or if you become a creature of the night and try to bite me. Actually, that might prove interesting...'

She was laughing now. Just the way he wanted her to. 'Will you stay tonight, Sam?'

Sam had thought that perhaps tonight, of all nights, she would sleep peacefully. But still she woke up, cold sweat pricking at her back and the tendrils of a dream clutching at her chest.

Euan was asleep, one arm stretched out towards her, as if he was reaching for her. If only she could just curl up in his arms and go back to sleep. The panic was still too real, though. She was afraid that if she even touched him the poison would somehow migrate from her veins to his.

She got out of bed and pulled on his dressing-gown, padding downstairs and pouring a glass of cold water from the refrigerator. The conservatory was in darkness, criss-crossed by moonlight, and Sam walked through, sitting down in one of the deep, squashy chairs.

'Can't sleep?' She wasn't sure how long she'd stared up through the glass ceiling at the stars before Euan's voice made her jump.

'I got up for some water.'

'Mind if I join you?'

'Of course not.'

He sat down opposite her. He'd thrown on a pair of shorts and a T-shirt, and his brow was as creased as the crumpled fabric.

'Penny for them?'

'Not worth it.'

'They're all worth it.'

Sam smiled at him wearily. 'No one wants to pay for the same thing over and over.' Whatever she did, she seemed to spiral back to the same thing. It was like trying to find your way through a maze and coming back to the place where Sal had died every time.

He gave a small nod. 'Do you want to go back to the flat?'

'It's three o'clock in the morning…' Things like that didn't bother Euan. She knew he'd get dressed and take her back if that was what she wanted, without any further questions. 'I want to be here. With you.'

'Go back to bed, then.' His voice brooked no argument, and what she could see of his face was unreadable. 'I'll be up in a minute.'

She should probably try to get some sleep. 'Okay. Don't be too long.'

As she rose, he caught her hand, leaning forward to press his lips to her fingers. 'It'll mend, Sam.'

She wasn't so sure about that. But sharing her fears

on that score wasn't going to help. 'Yeah. Everything mends.' She gave him a hug and padded back upstairs.

Euan stared up at the stars, asking silent questions that they were not qualified to answer. One thing he knew. He'd asked too much of Sam, right from the beginning. He'd shared all the most difficult aspects of his work with her, practically forced her to confront her most painful memories, and now he was getting far too involved and greedy for her time.

Euan had promised her nothing, and she'd given him everything. He'd asked her to stay, and she'd stayed. What had he been thinking? That somehow just loving her would chase the nightmares away?

He needed to take a bit more responsibility. Give her a bit more space. He had a feeling that those were just the first two entries on a very long list, but they were a start. Picking up the rug that was draped over the back of his chair, he wandered into the sitting room, arranging the cushions on the sofa and lying down. Tomorrow he would do better.

CHAPTER EIGHTEEN

SAM HAD MEANT to stay awake for him, curl up in his arms and kiss him before they both slept, but she was too tired. She woke in the morning alone.

She found him in the living room, sprawled on the sofa and fast asleep. When she laid her hand on his he didn't wake, but his fingers curled around hers in an automatic, sleeping reaction.

She made coffee and warmed the croissants they'd bought yesterday. Put it all onto a tray and carried it into the living room. Then put on a smile and woke him.

'What are you doing here?' A touch of gentle reproof.

'Hmm? Fell asleep…'

'Right.' And the throw from the conservatory had just happened to find its way through here and arranged itself and the sofa cushions into a makeshift bed. 'You didn't think that you might do that upstairs? With me?'

He didn't seem to want to discuss it. Rubbing his eyes, he focussed on the tray. 'Breakfast. That's nice, thank you.'

She plumped herself down into an armchair. Suddenly the sofa was off limits. 'Are you working today?'

'Yes. I'm on duty at the clinic until four. Why don't you stay here?'

Something was up. But if he wasn't going to tell her what it was, she wasn't going to stay here, staring at the walls and wondering. 'No, I'll come with you. I'll bring my laptop and find a quiet corner, there's plenty to be getting on with.'

'I'll be pretty busy.'

'I won't distract you.'

'You distract me wherever you are.' He relented suddenly, a warm, lazy smile crawling across his face. 'I'll clear out of my surgery and you can sit in there.'

Working seemed to steady him. A morning spent with other people's hopes and fears instead of his own, and Sam's bright smile whenever he entered his surgery to fetch something, almost made Euan believe that his doubts were just night shadows, burned off by the heat of the sun. He'd managed to keep two minor emergencies and an embryonic crisis away from her notice already, and was feeling reasonably pleased with himself.

'I'm going to fetch some lunch.' She caught him as he hurried through the reception area. 'What would you like?'

She was holding a list, obviously intent on making herself useful. Sam never quite seemed to get the message that people might want her for herself. Perhaps he should have been a little clearer when he'd told her all the things he loved about her. Not done it before, during or after their lovemaking, when there might be other things to think about. Made a list, so that she could study it later.

'I'm fine, thanks. I'll have something later.'

'Okay.' She grinned at him, planting a kiss on his cheek, and then she was gone.

When his phone vibrated in his pocket fifteen minutes later, Euan was already deep in conversation with Ian about the next counselling session, and almost didn't answer it. But when he saw that it was Sam, he signalled an apology and accepted the call.

'Sam...?'

'Come out here quickly. I need help.'

Her tone said it all. Forget about everything else, this was important.

When he flung open the entrance door, she almost toppled inside at his feet, along with the limp body of a man. 'They dumped him. I saw them...'

'Okay. Let me see.' The man had flopped over onto the floor inside the doorway, and Sam scrambled out of the way to allow Euan to get to him.

'Look at his lips, they're blue. I don't think he's breathing.' Her voice was steady, calm. Saving the emotions for later.

'Right...' Close up the man was little more than a boy, and Euan recognised him as Damien. Dumped by his so-called friends when it had looked as if he was in trouble. Euan had seen it before, but this never failed to shock him.

Ian was dealing with the hubbub inside, clearing everyone back from the reception area. Damien was making gurgling noises as his body tried to breathe despite the drugs in his system and Euan rolled him onto his side, clearing his airways.

'You know him?'

'Yep. Heroin user.'

'What do you need?'

Euan pulled his keys from his pocket. 'My medical bag. It's locked in the surgery.'

'I know.' She grabbed the keys from his hand and was gone.

He'd barely started resuscitation procedures before Sam was back, pushing his medical bag towards him, pulling the zip open. When he reached for his stethoscope she was already holding it out towards him.

'Thanks.' It was little enough recognition of her presence of mind, but that would have to wait until Damien was more responsive. Quickly, Euan examined him, found the supply of nalaxone he always carried with him and prepared the syringe. When he repeated the dose aloud, more out of habit than anything, he was vaguely aware that Sam had pulled a pen from her pocket and written it on her hand.

He heard her gasp when he plunged the needle through Damien's clothes into his deltoid muscle. Seconds ticked by. Nothing.

He was going to have to try again. Euan repeated the procedure, and waited. Thirty seconds to find out whether some mother was going to lose her son. To stop a young man dying in front of Sam's eyes.

The effect was almost immediate, and he felt Sam jump back in surprise behind him. A great gasp of air, and Damien jolted into a sitting position, staring wildly around him.

'You're okay. You're at the Driftwood Clinic. You overdosed.' Orientate him as quickly as possible. Euan left out the bit about having been dumped on the doorstep.

'What…?' Damien lashed out, and Euan instinctively threw out a hand to shield Sam, forgetting to duck himself and getting a blow to the jaw for his pains.

'You're at the Driftwood Clinic. You overdosed.'

Sam had caught hold of his flailing arm and was struggling to stop Damien from doing any more damage. 'You're okay. Let's get you inside.'

Ian was there to help now and together they got Damien to his feet. Behind him, he could hear Sam asking the passers-by who had gathered outside the open doorway to stay back. Moving them away from the little scene of life and death that had just been played out. She was too late. Damien caught sight of them and shouted a couple of curses in their direction.

'Damien. Enough!' Ian's firm voice cut through the rumble of outrage.

'Should just let him die…' A low voice came from somewhere and Euan ignored it. Damien started to struggle, and Ian propelled him inside, while Euan picked up his medical bag.

He heard Sam's voice behind him, cold with anger. 'Next time you're hurt, be thankful that there are people who don't care who you are and what you've done and who'll help you anyway.'

Euan couldn't help a grin. She was fire, and commitment, and compassion. Sam had his back, and he couldn't deny that it was a good feeling.

She followed them inside, closing the door quietly behind them. Damien was on his feet, restless and aggressive, and Ian was shepherding him through to one of the counselling rooms. At last Euan had a moment for Sam.

'Is he going to be all right now?'

'We'll need to keep a close eye on him. The nalaxone I gave him has counteracted the effects of the opiate drugs he's taken, and put him straight into withdrawal. He's hurting pretty bad…'

'And you?' She brushed his jaw with her fingers.

He'd almost forgotten about that. 'I'm fine. One of the hazards of the job.'

She nodded. 'What will you do now?'

'We'll keep him here as long as we can. The nalaxone has a half life of an hour or so, and he may start getting symptoms of an overdose again when it wears off. And we need to stop him from taking anything more...'

The sound of Damien's voice, raised in outrage, came from upstairs. 'I'd better see if Ian needs some help.'

'Sure. Go. Will you need anything else from your bag, or shall I lock it up again?'

Euan grinned at her. 'No. I think a dose of sense is what Damien needs most at the moment.'

She laughed, maybe a little too loudly and a little too long. The stress was beginning to show, and Euan wanted to get her out of here, take her somewhere where she could wind down. He couldn't. They were already stretched, and Damien was going to need watching for a while.

'Okay. I'll let you get on.'

'Make some tea. Go for a walk...' The suggestions were painfully inadequate but he was going to have to leave Sam to deal with this herself. 'Where's Liz?'

'She went home at lunchtime.' She shot him one of her no-nonsense looks, waving him away. 'I'm going out to find the sandwiches. I dropped them in the street when I saw what was happening. And I might pop in to see Juno this afternoon.'

'Juno?' If he had to pick someone to keep Sam company this afternoon, Juno's sometimes abrasive approach to the world wouldn't have been his first choice. 'Are you sure—?'

She silenced him with a flip of her fingers. Euan had got it wrong again. She didn't want sympathy, or to cry on someone's shoulder. She wanted... Sometimes he didn't know what she wanted.

'Juno's making a piece for me, remember? She wants to get a feel for what I want, and I could do with waving my arms about a bit at the moment. I'll be back here by four.'

Fair enough. Euan capitulated to the inevitable and dropped a kiss on her lips. That, at least, he *could* do.

Thinking about this didn't get him anywhere. But not thinking about it, while he engaged in the difficult task of calming Damien down and making arrangements for him to be supervised overnight, had made everything much clearer. Euan was silent as he strolled next to Sam back to his house, because he knew what he had to do.

She put her laptop down on the kitchen table, and picked up the kettle to fill it. 'Something to drink?'

'No. Sam, come here, will you?' He sat down, pulling a chair out for her. Not too close. He couldn't do this if she got too close.

She sat down. 'What's up?'

Maybe she knew. Maybe it would be a relief to her. 'I want you to go back to London. Tonight.'

Shock registered on her face. Then she reddened and looked away from him, fixing her gaze on the floor. 'Why?'

Her voice was so small, so defeated that he almost wavered. Almost. Euan tried to keep his voice steady.

'Because you have things to do there. You'll be busy with the installation for The Centre...' That wasn't what he meant at all. 'I just think that it would be better if we gave each other a bit of space.'

'You mean…you're sending me away.' There was a thread of anger there, but her voice was mostly just dull resignation.

How could he explain to her that this was different? That it wasn't like the rejection she'd suffered at the hands of her mother, or even the one that Sally's death had wrought. It was for her benefit. She couldn't carry on like this, so fragile behind her surface confidence, without confronting her demons.

'Sam, the last two weeks have been…' They'd been the best of his life. 'They've been great. But you have a chance to make a real difference. You need to give it all that you've got.'

She rubbed her hand across her eyes and met his gaze. She was composed now, her face a vacant mask. He wondered what the real Sam was thinking, and decided he probably didn't have a right to know any more.

'You're telling me that I should be getting on with my work. A bit of an about-face, don't you think?'

He deserved that barb. Deserved a lot more. 'I'm saying that coming here has raised a lot of issues for you and without sorting them out they will eventually tear us apart.'

Anger flashed in her eyes. 'Oh, so that's what this is, is it? I'm just another one of your projects, am I? The girl with the hang-ups…'

Never. She was so wrong it was almost laughable. But he knew Sam's pride wouldn't let her stay if he let her think it, and if she blamed him then all the better. At least she wouldn't be blaming herself.

'I know it was wrong, Sam. I'm sorry.'

She pressed her lips together, standing slowly. Reached for her laptop. For a moment Euan thought she was going to hit him with it, and rather wished that she would, but she clasped it to her chest, as if she needed to shield herself from him.

'Yeah. I'm sorry too.' She turned, and walked away, slamming the front door behind her.

Anger carried her back to the tiny flat over the office, where she threw all her things into her travelling bag, and impelled her up the hill to the railway station. An hour on the train, glaring through the window as a blood-red sunset began to form on the horizon, and then half an hour on the Tube and she was back home, kicking her front door open and throwing her bags onto the bed.

How dared he? *How dared he?* One of his projects, was she? He was a fine one to talk. Euan had a few hang-ups of his own. What about the one with that ex-wife of his, the one that made him so damn protective all the time? And what had happened to 'Whatever works for us is okay'?

She stopped, stood stock still. Euan wasn't the kind of man who manipulated his way into a woman's bed. He was honest to a fault, in touch with his feelings. Euan…

'Damn you, Euan.' It was she who'd said it, not him. He hadn't contradicted her, but when she thought about it he hadn't really confirmed it either. He'd let her think the worst of him.

Maybe he did love her? Sam tipped her handbag upside down, the contents falling onto the bed, and snatched her phone up. Found his number and then stopped. It didn't make any difference why he'd wanted her to go. He'd wanted her to go and that was that.

She flung the phone down onto the bed. She knew Euan well enough to know that once he'd made his mind up, decided that something was right, there was no going back on it. She sank down onto the bed, tears streaming down her face.

If he'd been less honourable, less aware of her issues, he wouldn't have done this. But, then, they were just two of the reasons that she'd fallen in love with him…

Euan couldn't keep away. He walked to the office in the gathering dusk, looking up at the darkened windows of the flat. Letting himself in, he picked up the keys that Sam had posted back through the letterbox.

Upstairs, her scent still lingered, like a cruel reminder. The flat was quite different from the home he'd returned to when Marie had left, but the silence was the same.

He stood for a moment, staring at the bed, resisting the temptation to bury his face in one of the pillows and pretend for a moment that she was still here. What next?

Nothing. Euan turned, walked down the stairs and out into the night. Nothing came next.

CHAPTER NINETEEN

SAM'S CAR WAS parked in the small car park outside the church hall. She'd been gripping the steering-wheel, unable to coax herself into movement, for the last five minutes.

Come on. Either go inside or go home.

That was easier said than done. She'd thought that turning up for the first session of the group she'd joined had been difficult, but going back for a second time had been harder. And now the third seemed impossible.

Juno did it. Jamie did it.

They'd had Euan, though. She had a rather vague middle-aged man, who seemed to do nothing but listen to what everyone said, and nod.

But his was the name that Euan had given her, the one she'd entered into her phone and then forgotten about until sadness had turned to resolve, and then hardened into determination. She'd made it through two sessions. If she lasted another two without smashing something, she'd be surprised, but she had to try.

A knock on the car window made her jump. Will, the group leader, was there. 'You're early. Would you like to come in and help make the tea?'

Not particularly. Sam didn't want to drink tea, or

make tea, and she definitely didn't want to be here, or to talk to Will or anyone else. She wanted to go home.

But she'd promised Euan once that she'd try this, and now she'd promised herself. She gave Will a smile, got out of the car and locked it, and walked with him across the car park and into the hall.

In the three months since Sam had first set foot in the Driftwood Drugs Initiative's offices, things had been moving fast. Joe had taken over the installation at Driftwood, and David had reported back that it was already a success. The Centre was also using the program, along with six other drugs charities. There were seven more charities that had expressed an interest, and one of the sector newspapers had contacted Sam, asking for an interview.

She looked around her London office one last time. Everything was just so. Her desk was tidy, the finger-marks had been polished off the glass coffee table, and the four brightly upholstered easy chairs were arranged around it. Through the glass partition, which looked out into the main office, Joe's workspace was unusually clutter-free, and hopefully the two empty desks that stood alongside it would be filled by the end of the day. Before she started on job interviews, though, she had a visit from a client.

The intercom buzzed, and the security guard's voice crackled through the small loudspeaker. 'Visitor. Some charity or the other. He's comin' up, anyway.'

'Thanks, Frank.'

Sam took a deep breath, smoothed down her dress, and waited for David to climb the stairs.

* * *

She was wearing a shade of dark red that Euan couldn't quite give a name to but which suited her colouring perfectly. The dress was businesslike, but however discreetly it followed her curves it still couldn't disguise them.

Sam was different. Her hair in a loose chignon, rather than clipped tightly to the back of her head. Her make-up a shade more natural. The overall effect was less like an attempt at a disguise, and a lot more like a beautiful woman, dressing to please herself.

'Euan.' She looked as if she'd just seen a ghost. If she was going to faint, he'd have to move quickly to reach her in time to catch her.

She didn't faint. He should have known that Sam was made of sterner stuff than that. Instead, she drew herself up to her full height. 'You're not David.'

'No, I'm not.'

She looked around wildly, as if she was trying to think who else he might not be. He noticed that one of her hands was trembling, her fingers clutching at empty air.

'Sam, I…' He took a step forward and she backed away. 'Sam, I'm sorry if I've given you a shock, but I want to talk to you. Please.'

She gave him a small nod. 'Come into my office.'

He followed her, keeping his distance. At least she hadn't thrown something at him, or refused to speak to him, or called the security guard from downstairs to eject him from the building. Just as well. The guy had to be past retirement age, and Euan might have had to help him up the stairs.

He wasn't sure where to sit down, thinking that perhaps she'd retreat behind her desk, but she waved him towards one of easy chairs. Perhaps that was a good sign.

'I've something to say.' She was still trembling.

'Me too.'

His gaze connected with hers, and he almost choked. He'd promised himself that he would say his piece and then go, but Euan wasn't sure whether he could do that. Wasn't sure if he could ever let her go again.

She swallowed. 'You first.'

That was fine. Whatever she wanted to say to him, it couldn't change how he felt. Wouldn't change what he was about to tell her.

'I lied when I sent you away.'

She gave a little huff of impatience. 'I know. That occurred to me as soon as I was done with wanting to strangle you. You were right about one thing, though. We were tearing each other apart.'

Poisonous disappointment crawled through his veins, heading inexorably towards his heart. 'Is there anything I can say to convince you that things could be different between us now?'

She thought for a moment. 'Words don't count for much. Actions…'

'I'm here. I wondered whether I should come or send a note first, but sending a note is the kind of thing a man does when he needs an answer before he risks everything. I'm not that man any more.'

She nodded, looking at him gravely.

The long, detailed speech he'd prepared and memorised seemed beside the point now. Really, it all boiled down to one thing. 'I love you, Sam.'

'But...?'

'No buts. No doubts or reservations. I love you.'

She stared at him, as if this was the last thing she'd expected. 'You do?'

'Yes. I've come to tell you that I won't let you down, and I'll never stop loving you. If that's not what you want to hear right now, I'll go, but I will never stop waiting for you, because I know I can be the man you deserve.'

'I was never in any doubt of that.' Slowly, she seemed to be getting the gist of what he was saying. Blooming in front of his eyes.

'It was your confidence in me that made me see that.'

She slid forward on her chair, seeming to stumble as she rose. Euan reached out to steady her and then she was in his arms. Sitting on his lap, crushed against his chest. One long breath. It seemed as if he had been holding his breath for the last two months, without fully realising how much he needed to breathe again.

'May I kiss you?' He still couldn't quite believe that this was happening.

Her eyes were bright, almost like quicksilver. 'Do you really need to ask?'

It was more. More in every way. That was the only way that Sam could describe it. Everything that she wanted and needed fell into place around his kiss. She clung to him, in case the lurch of the world turning should somehow throw them apart again.

'Am I dreaming?'

He chuckled. 'I don't think so. You can pinch me if you like.'

'You're supposed to pinch me...'

'Nah. I'm not going to pinch you.' He settled his arms around her, cocooning her in his warmth. 'You had something you wanted to say to me?'

He'd been listening. One of the things she loved about Euan was that he always listened. 'I phoned the number you gave me. The one for the guy who runs a group.'

'Yeah? Did you go?'

'I went. Listened to everyone else's stories. Told my own. I cried quite a bit.'

'And did it make a difference?'

'Yes. I didn't think it would at first, and I hated every moment of it. And then I started to feel the way that I did when Sal and I started out. When I couldn't wait to get out of bed in the morning to get to grips with the day.'

He smiled. That melting grin that she loved so much. 'That's the way it often goes. It takes a lot of courage to confront your past.'

'It was more like desperation. I loved you, and I just had to find my way back to you. So I talked it all out. Sally dying. My mother. Stuff about having to earn love, not feeling I had a place in the world…' He was nodding, and she broke off, laughing. 'You know.'

'Yeah. I know.' He brushed another kiss against her cheek. 'I never stopped loving you, Sam. You made me trust that I could finally come to terms with the past, and I realised that I trusted you to do the same. We just needed a little time by ourselves to achieve it.'

'I would have come for you. If you hadn't pipped me to the post and come here first.'

'Yeah? When?'

'I was thinking Christmas. Or New Year…'

'Christmas! That's two months away!'

'Or next weekend possibly. I was wearing down much quicker than I thought I would. I had this fantasy about you on the beach, sitting in one of those dreadful old deckchairs...'

'Hey! They're our Monday morning deckchairs. They're a Driftwood tradition.'

'All right. Sitting in one of your traditional deckchairs, with your eyes closed.'

'And then...'

The fantasy was so much better now that she knew how it ended. 'And I'd come and sit down. You'd say something grumpy and then you'd open your eyes and see that it was me, and not David.'

He laughed. 'It's a good plan. I'm glad you didn't, though.'

Sam couldn't believe that. 'You mean it wouldn't have been good for your ego?'

'Wonderful for my ego. But I'm the one who never goes back, remember? And you're the one that people don't come back to. I prefer it this way round, we can start as we mean to go on. Turning the tables on the past.'

She was only starting to explore the true beauty of that thought when a noise at the door of the outer office made her jump. By the time Joe had rounded the corner and was able to see through the glass partition, she was standing three feet away from Euan.

'Joe, what are you doing here? Has the Manchester trip been called off?'

'No, I forgot something.' Joe opened his desk drawer and drew out a box of DVDs. 'Hi, Euan. How's everything going?'

'Good. I was just telling Sam how pleased we are with everything you did for us.'

'Yes. He was,' she agreed.

'Great.' Joe didn't seem to notice that Sam only had one shoe on. 'Gotta go, or I'll miss my train.'

The door slammed shut behind him and Sam kicked off the other shoe. 'What now?' There was still no plan for anything past this moment.

'You could lock the door and keep going...'

His grin made her want that more than anything. 'If only. But I've got the first of six job candidates coming in half an hour. We've got two vacancies to fill.'

'Then I'll wait.' The grin broadened. 'I can make myself useful. Make tea. Answer the phone. Be nice to your candidates to put them at their ease.'

'Please tell me there's nowhere else you need to be tonight.'

'I've got the whole of this week off.'

She hugged him tight. Kissed him, and then kissed him again. 'You were that confident, were you?'

'No. I reckoned that you'd send me packing and that the rest of the week would give me a bit of time to plan my next move. Send flowers. That kind of thing.'

'So I've missed out on the flowers?' As if she cared. She had Euan.

'Not necessarily. I rather like the idea of wooing you back. I think I should do it anyway.' He curled his arms around her waist. 'We still need to plan, though. You're just getting established here—'

She laid her finger over his lips. 'It'll work. We'll make it work.'

He kissed her. Languid and lingering, and the only thing that she needed. 'Yeah. We will.'

CHAPTER TWENTY

THE WEDDING HAD been organised in six weeks flat, and was more joyful than Sam could have ever imagined. Ann had helped her into her silk and lace dress, producing a blue garter that she claimed to have worn at her own wedding, and Paul had given her away. She'd recited the vows that she and Euan had written together, and he had never once taken his eyes off her. When she'd seen him waiting for her at the end of the aisle, she'd almost knocked a flower girl over in her haste to reach him, and David had jabbed Euan in the ribs when he'd started to shake with suppressed laughter.

Kathryn House was due to open in the new year, and a huge marquee erected in the empty grounds took the overflow of people. Ann and Paul, Sal's brother Josh and his wife, Euan's parents, friends from London and everyone they knew from the Driftwood Drugs Initiative. Jamie was there with Kirsty on his arm, and Juno turned up, her hair dyed purple for the occasion, presenting Sam with a piece of swirled, shaped glass that gleamed in the light of the lanterns that hung along the veranda.

'It's beautiful!' Sam hugged Juno, who glowed with pleasure.

'There's a message for you both in there.' Juno tilted

the piece to exactly the right angle, and Sam stared at the coloured glass and metal strands.

'Oh!' Her hand flew to her mouth. 'Thank you. We'll make sure to do that.'

'Yeah. Often.' Juno snorted with laughter, grinning at Euan, who had decided that two minutes away from Sam was too long and had come to collect another kiss.

'What's so funny?'

'I'll show you later.' Sam smiled up at him.

'Where's the honeymoon, then?' Liz had squeezed through the throng of people to dispense hugs and kisses.

'We've got a beach house. Somewhere sunny.' Euan had made those two stipulations, but was still keeping the exact location a surprise.

'Yes. No internet. No phones.' Sam had specified those two details. Six months ago it would have been unthinkable. Now it sounded like paradise.

'Sounds wonderful.' Liz caught sight of Juno's present. 'Juno, that's lovely. May I see it?'

For a moment they were alone in the centre of a crowded room. Holding onto each other tightly.

'Happy?' He smiled down at her.

'Yes. You?'

'I could be better.'

'Oh, yes? And how could you be better?'

'Another kiss and then I get to dance with my beautiful wife. Then it'll all be just perfect…'

* * * * *

MILLS & BOON®

Fancy some more Mills & Boon books?

Well, good news!

We're giving you

15% OFF

your next eBook or paperback book purchase
on the Mills & Boon website.

So hurry, visit the website today and type **GIFT15**
in at the checkout for your exclusive 15% discount.

www.millsandboon.co.uk/gift15

MILLS & BOON®

Why not subscribe?

Never miss a title and save money too!

Here's what's available to you if you join the exclusive **Mills & Boon Book Club** today:

✦ *Titles up to a month ahead of the shops*
✦ *Amazing discounts*
✦ *Free P&P*
✦ *Earn Bonus Book points that can be redeemed against other titles and gifts*
✦ *Choose from monthly or pre-paid plans*

Still want more?

Well, if you join today we'll even give you
50% OFF your first parcel!

So visit **www.millsandboon.co.uk/subs**
or call **Customer Relations on 020 8288 2888**
to be a part of this exclusive Book Club!

MILLS & BOON®

Why shop at millsandboon.co.uk?

Each year, thousands of romance readers find their perfect read at millsandboon.co.uk. That's because we're passionate about bringing you the very best romantic fiction. Here are some of the advantages of shopping at www.millsandboon.co.uk:

* **Get new books first**—you'll be able to buy your favourite books one month before they hit the shops

* **Get exclusive discounts**—you'll also be able to buy our specially created monthly collections, with up to 50% off the RRP

* **Find your favourite authors**—latest news, interviews and new releases for all your favourite authors and series on our website, plus ideas for what to try next

* **Join in**—once you've bought your favourite books, don't forget to register with us to rate, review and join in the discussions

Visit **www.millsandboon.co.uk**
for all this and more today!